ACCLAIM FOR PETER CLEMENT

LETHAL PRACTICE

"Chilling . . . A fast-paced, engrossing medical thriller."

–JOHN SAUL

"ER meets Agatha Christie as Buffalo doctor Earl Garnet is suspected of murder via a cardiac needle. Heart-pounding suspense, indeed!"
–*Entertainment Weekly*

DEATH ROUNDS

"A classic medical thriller . . . The reader is immediately caught up in the tension of the hospital as a killer stalks its corridors."
–*The Mystery Reader*

"Clement's own background as a physician comes across in his use of technical terminology and ability to capture hospital politics, which adds up to terror."
–*Publishers Weekly*

By Peter Clement
Published by The Ballantine Publishing Group:

LETHAL PRACTICE
DEATH ROUNDS

THE PROCEDURE

Peter Clement

FAWCETT BOOKS • NEW YORK
The Ballantine Publishing Group

Published by The Ballantine Publishing Group

www.randomhouse.co/BB/

Library of Congress Catalog Card Number: 00-193360

ISBN 0-449-00622-0

Manufactured in the United States of America

First Edition: June 2001

10   9   8   7   6   5   4   3   2   1

ACKNOWLEDGMENTS

My heartfelt thanks to Denise Marcil for her support from start to finish, to Joe Blades for taking me under his wings at Ballantine, to my longtime friends Dr. Brian Connolly and Dr. Jennifer Frank for their encouragement and advice on medical matters, and to my eagle-eyed proofreaders Betty, Connie, Doug, James, Joan, Johanna, and, last but definitely not least, Tamara—you are all truly amazing.

This book is dedicated to James, Sean, and Vyta—and all their loving intrusions while I write—for teaching me every day what really matters.

THE PROCEDURE

Prologue

I had to watch the one with the needle.

No matter that I heard the psychiatrist step up to the side of my stretcher and coolly begin to explain what they were about to do with me, nor that I felt the tug of the nurse's hands as she secured the IV in my left arm with adhesive tape. I kept my eye on the silent anesthetist who was standing behind my head. His syringe lay capped on a nearby table.

". . . thirty seconds after the succinylcholine is injected, you will feel your muscles twitching, and then the paralysis will occur. The transmission of neuroelectrical impulses through the nerve ends to striated muscle will be blocked, and all movement, including respiration, will be stopped. It is the extreme unpleasantness of mounting air-hunger that will, in the end, condition your response, and so you will be allowed to endure it for eighty seconds. At that point the anesthetist will start to ventilate you and will carry on making you breathe until the drug wears off, in about four minutes. Your heart will continue to beat, and the drug won't affect your sphincters, so you won't soil . . ."

I knew that the psychiatrist's matter-of-fact tone was a lie—others who'd gone before had warned, "It feels like death." I ignored the droning words and strained my eyes farther back to keep the anesthetist in view. All I managed to see now were his hands as he deftly snapped the blade of a laryngoscope open to make sure the light worked. Then he glided his gloved fingers over an assortment of rubber tubes and black curved airways arranged on a tray like an array of hors d'oeuvres. He adjusted a few of these items so they'd be easier to reach. Close by, also near enough to him that he could pull them into position when he needed them, were portable oxygen tanks connected by green tubing to a black bag and thick rubber mask.

". . . you will pour a small amount of your usual drink into a glass. First, smell it, then take a sip and hold the . . ."

The nurse moved up beside the anesthetist, bringing with her a small steel table on wheels. It held a clear bottle the size of a large pickle jar and a vacuum pump to provide suction. She verified the motor was plugged into a wall outlet, then uncoiled a beige-colored catheter with a metal tip and connected it to a tube dangling from a stopper which sealed the bottle. The anesthetist flicked a switch on the table and adjusted the force of suction until it was adequate to clear vomit from an airway. A nod to the nurse, and they were ready.

I felt myself start to sweat as I sat up and watched the psychiatrist reach down into a briefcase and pull out the small green bottle—flat, contoured to fit in a hip pocket, and with a familiar yellow label. Some of his subjects, I knew, even at this point, gulped the contents greedily. Another had told me of being too overwhelmed by fright to drink anything. If I didn't play this part just right, and anybody saw through me, I could end up dead.

I saw the anesthetist pick up the syringe. The nurse swabbed a little rubber side port on the IV line with an alcohol wipe, readying it for the injection. At least my fear should pass muster, I tried to reassure myself. It was absolutely genuine and mounting by the second.

I took the container of whiskey from the psychiatrist when he held it out to me, but my hands started to tremble and I fumbled with the cap. Once I got it open, the nurse pressed a glass into my right hand, then steadied it for me while I poured myself a mouthful of the amber liquid. The familiar bouquet mingled with the medicinal smell given off by her fingers. I felt the anesthetist move up to my left arm and turned in time to see him jab the syringe into the rubber portal. His thumb was poised on the plunger.

"Now take a sip," the psychiatrist commanded, "then swirl it around in your mouth."

I needn't have worried about my giving a convincing performance. My hands began to shake so badly for real that I was afraid I'd slosh the contents over the side of the glass. The nurse again steadied them and helped me raise the drink to my lips. As the fluid entered my mouth I barely sensed the warmth on my tongue. Instead I kept straining to see the syringe, watching the plunger. My whole body was trembling now. *It feels like death!* I tried to swallow but gagged, and the whiskey dribbled down my chin.

I couldn't continue. I had to stop this. I heard myself start to moan.

"Swallow it!" the psychiatrist snapped, startling me with the sudden harshness of his voice.

"Noooooo!" I wailed. "I changed my mind!" I tried to twist my left arm away from the anesthetist's grip.

But it was too late. He'd shoved in the plunger before my move could pull the IV away from the syringe.

I sat frozen staring at my arm. The nurse quickly took the glass and bottle out of my hands, but I was so transfixed on the IV site that I barely noticed. The anesthetist moved to the head of the stretcher, ready for what came next.

I felt a tingling sensation pass through my elbow and rise toward my shoulder. I started to panic. "No! No!" I pleaded, looking first at the psychiatrist, then at the nurse. "Stop it, please stop it!" But their returning gaze was cold. I tried to yank the IV out, then clutched frantically at the upper part of my left arm in a futile attempt to prevent the injection from reaching the rest of my body. I was sobbing when the twitching started. The muscles in my arms, my trunk, and finally in my legs gave a few feeble jerks, then failed me, going completely flaccid. I flopped back on the stretcher, not breathing, still as death, yet fully conscious.

I caught my reflection in the large circle of stainless steel that encased the overhead light. My eyes—open, unmoving, the pupils dilated by terror—appeared unseeing and lifeless. But I saw all too well, and the expressions on the faces of the three who'd done this to me were chillingly indifferent as they leaned over to check my pulse, to document my loss of reflexes, or to simply stare down at the effects of their work.

Eighty seconds. It had sounded not so terribly long, like nothing much more than holding my breath. But I had no breath to hold because I hadn't timed my breathing properly, and when the succinylcholine blocked my respiratory muscles, what little air I had taken in was lost as my lungs deflated. The smothering pressure in my chest, unbearable at the outset, increased steadily. In my mind I bucked and strained against the grip of the paralysis, but my muscles remained slack, useless. I felt entombed, buried alive while locked inside my body.

"Ten seconds," the anesthetist said dryly.

It was beyond enduring. To be suffocating, and yet be so brutally clearheaded. There was no welcome slip into unconsciousness, not yet. I couldn't even close my eyes and escape the cruel scrutiny of the three onlookers. What's more, my senses seemed unmercifully heightened. I had to listen to the sounds of their breathing as I felt the pain of no air encase my chest and crush in on me like hardening cement.

Yet as horrible as it was, the ordeal was what the others had led me to expect. What came next wasn't. Suddenly I felt burning at the back of my neck and throat as vomit flowed up my esophagus from my stomach then poured unopposed down my windpipe. Oh, my God! I thought in alarm. I'd known without being told that I shouldn't eat or drink before the session, but during the evening, nervous and unable to sleep, I'd made myself some toast and tea before midnight. Normally it should have been digested by dawn, but obviously not by my stomach, churning as it had been on the levels of adrenaline I'd been pumping out all night.

"Thirty seconds," the anesthetist said, oblivious to the forming disaster.

The food particles in my windpipe filled me with the horrific urge to cough and gag, but the impulse went nowhere, the lifesaving reflex that might have cleared my airway fully blocked by the effects of succinylcholine. Instead I lay there, enduring the convulsive sensation of choking to death while being unable to move.

"Fifty seconds," the anesthetist intoned, methodically opening the valve on the oxygen cylinders and readying the bag and mask.

My eyes, though unblinking, could still cry. I felt the tears forming, welling up behind immobile lids and flowing down my cheeks. But my vision was dimming, the lack of oxygen finally, and mercifully, clouding my conscious state. Slowly I was freed from the sight of my tormentors; slowly I lost feeling; slowly the extreme pain of anoxia in my chest and limbs subsided somewhat. But the sensation of choking remained intact. It kept coming in waves. And I could still hear.

"Seventy," a distant voice said.

I sensed I was finished. Even if I survived this, if they discovered I was an impostor, they'd kill me anyway. The plan I'd made before coming here had gone so wrong—I'd stumbled into so much more than I'd prepared for. I felt the anesthetist roughly extend my head and flex my neck, as though forcing me to sniff a flower. I still could feel enough to know he'd plopped the mask onto my face, covering my nose and mouth.

Then, from even farther away, I heard him mutter what I feared would be my epitaph.

"Shit! The son of a bitch aspirated!"

Chapter 1

Five weeks earlier:
Tuesday, October 12, 7:00 A.M.

The sight of those tiny human remains spread out before us on the dissecting tray staggered me despite my knowing what to expect. The pink unspoiled lungs, a maroon heart, the small ocher-colored liver, and a spleen the size of a beet—all gleaming under the overhead light—looked new enough to hold the promise of a lifetime's use. But the brain, no bigger than my fist, was covered by a thick mesh of crimson streaks. These fanned out over its surface and obscured the tightly coiled ridges and grooves underneath to the point that I couldn't see their normal beige, gray, and yellow-white coloration. And the kidneys were so speckled with angry red blotches that a layperson would have thought someone had spattered them with paint.

From the silence of the other physicians and residents in the room, I'd deduced that everyone was struggling as much as I was to remain clinically detached. Not even the voice of the presenting pathologist, normally our guide to at least make scientific sense out of a death, could ever begin to explain why this child had died. Instead the words simply floated over me, like a Muzak of medical terminology, and consigned themselves to the back of my mind.

". . . the inflamed meninges, the characteristic pattern of

6

hemorrhagic petechiae on the surface of the kidneys, and the rapidity of the catastrophic process . . ."

When I examined the brain, holding it in the palm of my hand I could barely feel its weight through the latex gloves that I'd pulled on in order to inspect the specimens.

". . . the mother noticed symptoms attributable to an upper respiratory infection the day before. The baby was irritable, off his food, crying, and had a mild temperature. She gave him an appropriate dose of acetaminophen, attempted to keep him hydrated with juice . . ."

His name had been Robert Delany, and it was a week ago that his life had ended at eighteen months of age in our emergency department.

". . . she telephoned the after-hours number of her health maintenance organization, as it was late in the evening, but the HMO's triage nurse told her that the child probably only had a cold and could safely wait until morning to be seen. Yet the boy continued to cry, his fever remained elevated at a hundred and three despite the acetaminophen, and after a few hours the mother once more contacted her clinic. Again she was told that the baby most likely had the flu and that she should bring him over only in the morning. When the mother suggested taking the baby to Emergency that night, she was told she could if she wished, but since the illness seemed minor, payment wouldn't be preauthorized at any more than the rate of an office visit. . . ."

The balance of the cost, potentially a thousand dollars if a zealous resident did a battery of tests, they had told her, would not necessarily be covered. As a result she delayed several more hours, until the child had started to seize. The images of what had happened then, after he arrived in ER, haunted me still.

We'd been like giants gathered around his tiny form while his limbs jerked with the repetitive rhythm of a grand mal convulsion. He'd had no respirations, his pressure had been unobtainable, and his heart rate was slowing into single digits.

"Bag him!"

"His jaw's clamped shut."

"Anybody got a line?"

His eyes had kept flicking to one side, keeping time with the grotesque dance gripping the rest of him. His skin color, already blue from lack of oxygen, had quickly darkened to purple.

". . . get an IV in his neck . . ."

". . . do a cut-down in his foot . . ."

". . . diazepam up the rectum . . ."

Everyone had been shouting orders, residents had stuck him with needles, nurses probed him with catheters, but he continued to seize. In the end I'd had to grab his pumping right leg, encircle it with my thumb and forefinger to hold it steady, and drive a needle the size of a two-inch nail into the front of his tibia to access his circulation through the marrow within. The steel point had given a lurch as it penetrated the outer layer of bone with a little crunch, but finally I'd gotten a route through which I'd been able to infuse enough medication to make the convulsions stop. But victory had been short-lived. After he'd been intubated, ventilated, and pinked up a bit, what caught my attention was a red rash breaking out below his eyes and spreading over his trunk as I watched.

"Oh, my God!" a resident had muttered, peering over my shoulder. "Meningococcemia!" What he was seeing was also called Waterhouse-Friderichsen syndrome, but by whatever name we gave it, we'd both known immediately what it meant. Meningococcal bacteria were cascading through the bloodstream from infected meninges at the surface of the brain and arriving at the skin. Once there, these microbes produced toxins that attacked the lining of the blood vessels, and it was the subsequent hemorrhagic leaks that led to the red spots. The same process was going on in the vasculature of every vital organ in the boy's body, especially in the kidneys. He could be dead within the hour.

I'd turned him on his side, curled his tiny form into a ball, and held him as a resident pushed yet another two-inch long needle into him, this one between the spines of his third and fourth lumbar vertebrae. Through my hands, which I'd placed on his little back to keep him from moving, I felt the give of the needle tip when it punctured the membrane containing the spinal cord and its surrounding fluid. As the young doctor drew minute samples of this clear liquid into several tubes for testing, it flashed through me how the feel of the child against my arms was so much like that of Brendan, my own infant son. By the time we'd finished the procedure, one of the surgical residents had dissected open a vein in his foot and another had inserted an IV line into his jugular at the neck. We'd then infused a loading dose of ceftriaxone, the indicated antibiotic. With nothing left to be done, I'd stood away from the stretcher and viewed our work. The sight of that poor struggling infant, stuck with tubes, needles, and catheters, had brought me to tears.

Later, once all our efforts had come to nothing and I'd pronounced him dead, I cut each one of these lines off at the skin. My leaving their tips inserted had been in order to verify their position later at autopsy, but I hadn't wanted them protruding from the boy's body, in case the mother asked to see him. I'd then cleaned away the blood, covered the puncture sites with small Band-Aids, and placed a blanket over him. I'd had to concentrate especially hard doing that last simple act. Thoughts of tucking Brendan in kept rushing to mind, and once more I nearly lost the fragile hold I'd had on my own emotions. I'd then gone to tell the mother that her child had died.

Even now, a week after the boy's death, I could still visualize the horrible expression I'd seen on her face during the instant she looked up when I entered the room where she was waiting. In that second of exchange, before I'd spoken a word, the light flowed out of her eyes and her face collapsed from a rigid mask of hope into a fluid swirl of agony and grief.

Later, as I'd supported her, she stood over the already

whitening corpse of her child. "Can I hold him?" she asked. The nurses looked appalled. I'd swallowed my own alarm, lifted the tiny bundle off the stretcher, and handed it to her.

". . . Dr. Garnet, is there anything you wish to add to the presentation of this case, before pronouncing whether the death was expected or unexpected, avoidable or unavoidable?" The pathologist's question pulled my thoughts back to the present.

It took a few seconds longer before I could collect myself enough to speak. There were specific lessons I wanted the residents to take from this, but I wasn't sure how much of what I was thinking I should reveal. "I think we have to talk about what happened prior to the infant's admission to Emergency," I began. "In particular, if the mother hadn't been put off by her HMO, her instincts about the child being sick enough to warrant a visit to ER might have gotten him here sufficiently early that we could have saved him."

"What did the HMO representatives say when they learned of the child's death?" asked a young woman across the table from me. She was planning a career in ER and was doing a rotation in my department. "I presume you told them."

"Oh, I told them all right, but they'd covered themselves legally. Notice what their triage nurse said to the child's mother. She could take him into ER if she thought he was seriously ill, but if the visit wasn't justified, they probably wouldn't cover the cost of any tests. It's a variant of what HMOs always claim—'We don't withhold care; we withhold payment'—and by so doing they make the choice of whether to come into ER rest with the patient, or as was the case here, with the parent. According to this usual spiel of theirs, the delay was then her doing. Reminding her of company policy regarding trivial visits, and their refusing to preauthorize payment of costly tests, was simply standard procedure, not a violation of any law. The fact that she second-guessed her initial impulse to get the child help after hearing the reminder made it her responsibility, not theirs. And legally, they're right. Of course they are very sorry the baby died, and his visit will be covered, they were quick to tell me, since he was obviously quite ill."

Only the first-year rookies let out exclamations of disgust and surprise. Everyone else in the room was well used to how the deadly game for profit was played. "But that's wrong," one of the newcomers said. "They gave her medical advice not to come in. They have to be legally accountable."

"A lot of lawmakers agree with you, but not the law as it stands," I replied, watching the incredulity grow in his eyes. "In 1998 the so-called patients' rights bill that would have redressed that very issue was defeated. And watch out, all of you, while you're in ER, that you don't get caught by another dodge that these companies use, or you yourself will be left paying for the consequences of their decisions to withhold payment."

The resident looked alarmed. "How could that be?"

"If they refuse to cover an admission or a treatment of someone in ER, and you go along with that decision, despite your better judgment, you *are* liable for damages, even though they aren't."

"But that's crazy," another innocent exclaimed.

"That's reality," I snapped, "and in particular watch out for the HMO this poor woman belonged to. They're a new outfit in town called Brama Health Care, but they've been operating on the West Coast for decades and know every trick in the book about how to discourage people from going to the hospital yet still remain within the law. In fact, they're the ones who first pleaded the 'We withhold payment, not care' defense, thereby rendering it the industry's battle cry whenever a case goes wrong. Now they're bringing all that expertise to the East, and according to the junk mail they keep bombarding us with, they intend to be the first HMO to have a presence in all fifty states plus the District of Columbia. So wherever you plan to practice, you'll be crossing swords with them, and since the lawyers for Brama are the best in the business, I think every resident here with a desire to make ER a career should listen to them argue a case in court, because then you'll know what you're up against. Remember, their standard line means that it's up to you or me as doctors to know what to do medically, regardless of what any triage officer says they will or will not pay for. 'Those statements are simply policy guidelines, not medical decisions,' I've heard them claim, and the judges agree with them."

In previous years my sole duties as a teacher were to arm the residents against the wily ways of a disease like meningococcemia. These days the curriculum included instruction against the perils of managed care.

"You mean what Brama Health Care did to this baby will go unpunished?" someone else asked.

He was answered with silence.

The pathologist cleared his throat and tried to wrap up the meeting. "Dr. Garnet, would you care to give us your pronouncement on the case?"

Death Rounds always ended with a judgment on whether we could have prevented the patient in question from dying. It was the ultimate point of the exercise—to identify what we did right, and to temper our skills by learning from our failures.

I hesitated before answering, glancing over the young faces of the residents turned toward me.

"Dr. Garnet?"

I looked back at the organs on the table. "Okay, here's what I think. If we look at the case simply from the time the child arrived in ER, the death, tragically, was expected and unavoidable."

Immediately there was a murmur of agreement, followed by a rustle of movement and a scraping of chairs as everyone began preparing to leave. "However," I added, raising my voice above the noise, "we can't in all conscience ignore what happened in the prehospital phase of this child's illness." I waited a few seconds until the room grew quiet again, then continued. "Had the mother not been intimidated by Brama

Health Care and brought her son in earlier, the death might have been prevented."

"So that's your ruling? You're calling this a preventable death?" the pathologist asked, his forehead creasing. "That's really not the domain of these rounds, to comment on prehospital events—"

"Then let's make it our domain," I shot back, staring at the remains of little Robert Delany. I felt a surge of fury against the likes of Brama and the new world of medicine that they and their kind had created. A world where a decision to withhold care to maximize profit could cause injury and death, and yet by law no one was accountable. "In fact, I know exactly what we should label this death, and every death like it. No-fault murder!"

Chapter 2

Treating Dr. David Pearson for yet another drinking binge was about the last thing I was in the mood for when I got back to ER from Death Rounds.

"Don't turn your back on him," warned Susanne Roberts, our head nurse. "According to his wife, he's making threats against you again."

"Christ! Is he as far gone as usual?"

"Shaking like a leaf, seeing spiders all over the walls, and primed to seize. I put a resuscitation cart by his bed."

"Have his bloods been drawn?" I asked, flipping through the resident's admission note.

Susanne gave me her what-do-you-think stare and rushed off to meet two ambulance cases that had been wheeled into triage one after the other.

I started toward the room where they'd put David and tried to prepare my mind for the ordeal I knew awaited me there. But on my way I passed a row of patients who were all in some form of extremis. One man had just vomited frank blood into an already overflowing kidney basin. The alarm in his eyes grew as he watched the stain on his bedclothes keep spreading and spreading. Two residents, one at each arm, were starting IVs while a nurse was quickly snapping electrodes to his chest and connecting him to a monitor.

"You okay here?" I asked.

"Yeah, Surgery's on the way," answered the more senior of the two young physicians.

In the next bed a man was leaning forward and gasping for breath. "Doctor! Help! Can't breathe."

A nurse pushed by me and applied a clear plastic oxygen mask to his face, then attached a cylinder of albuterol to its tubing. She twisted open the wall oxygen outlet, a hissing sound filled the air, and within seconds a plume of vapor surrounded the patient's head. She glanced to where I was still hovering at the foot of the bed. "Everything's under control, Dr. Garnet. ICU's already waiting for him."

I tried to tune out all the other sights and sounds that beckoned to me from all corners of the emergency department and walked the rest of the way to David's room, resenting him for pulling me away from where I was obviously needed, despite the reassurances to the contrary. When ER was busy like this, even if the residents, nurses, and other staff had the individual cases covered, it was important I be around—visible at the helm and available to help out.

No sooner was I through the door than the sour aroma of exhaled alcohol, sweat, and stale vomit cut into my nostrils, pushing its way to the back of my throat, making it hard not to gag. David was splayed out on the bed, his wrists and ankles bound to the side rails with leather cuffs. Orange and green stains covered his hospital gown. Pale yellow fluid—a mixture of vitamins, glucose, and normal saline—ran into his arm through an IV. His vital signs beeped and flashed on an overhead monitor.

At first I thought he was unconscious, but his head jerked up as soon as I got near him. He stared at me, his black pupils glinting from the bottom of his puffy eye sockets. His face was crimson beneath what was left of his dyed black hair. "You!" he screamed. "You dare look at me, you fuck? You're the reason I'm like this!"

"David, stop it!" I ordered, and quickly closed the door behind me so he wouldn't disturb the other patients. "You know why you're here."

"Because you fired me, you bastard! Fired me—" His

roaring abruptly broke off and his eyes fixed on the wall behind me. The red color in his enraged face paled and his pupils grew even wider. His mouth moved noiselessly then he issued a low moan. He started to yank and strain against his straps.

"David, what are you seeing?" I asked, changing to as gentle a tone of voice as I could muster.

His groaning sounds made a crescendo into a scream.

"David, they're not real," I told him firmly while reaching for the medication tray Susanne had laid out. On it I found syringes and a selection of vials filled with injectable benzodiazepines—chlordiazepoxide for agitation; diazepam, or Valium, in case he seized.

"It's spiders!" he sobbed, his expression growing more terrified by the second. His eyes seemed to be tracking something coming toward him across the ceiling.

I grabbed the order sheet and quickly determined how much chlordiazepoxide the resident had given him. My calculation told me he could take more.

"Oh, God! They're going to drop on me. They're going to drop! Help! Help me!" His screams became a shriek, and he began thrashing his head from side to side. "They're covering me. I feel their legs. They're swarming all over. Oh, God, no!" He broke into a wailing sob, writhing in his restraints. Then he let out a bellow, his body arched backward, and his muscles locked in the quivering rigidity that marks the start of a seizure.

"Nurse!" I screamed, throwing open the door. By the time she arrived I'd grabbed a vial of Valium, injected the works into his IV, and managed to slide a nasopharyngeal airway down his nose to shove his tongue off the opening to his trachea. The seizure broke, he began to breathe, and I arranged to transfer him to ICU.

"He was once a doctor?" the resident who received him upstairs commented. The young man's face had registered disgust the instant he spotted David's bloated body covered with the spindly network of broken veins that are peculiar to alcoholism. His smug choice of tone further set me to gritting my teeth. Despite my own frustration with David, I'd be damned if I was going to let some kid barely out of his teens sit in judgment of him. "Yes, he was once a doctor," I said tersely, "and a good one. I only hope you're near as skilled as he was while you care for him now."

The resident's face flushed. "I'm . . . I'm . . . I'm sorry, Dr. Garnet. I didn't mean any disrespect—"

"Good. Now here's something else you should know. Help me turn him on his side." The startled resident moved smartly to assist me as I rolled David toward us until I could undo the ties on the gown to expose his back.

"My God!" my helper gasped.

We were looking at scars the width of a one-inch rope coiling up and down the length of his spinal column. Pointing to the gnarled red and white tissue, I explained, "On his chest X ray you'll see a half-dozen metal fragments embedded near the thoracic vertebrae. He got them in Vietnam, before you were even born." I turned and walked away, not wanting to explain any more of David's tragedy, but reasonably certain that I'd put an end to the resident making any more snide remarks.

I took the stairs leading down to ER and paused at one of the landings to cool down. David inevitably robbed me of my objectivity whenever he came in. The reason was pathetically simple. As much as I told myself over and over that I'd done the right thing with him all those years ago, I was never entirely sure that I couldn't have handled him better. It didn't help any that each time he turned up in ER at the end of a binge, he seemed to have a cunning ability to resurrect every one of those doubts. "Damn you, David," I muttered, and continued to descend the stairs.

Some judgment calls we are sentenced to second-guess for the rest of our lives. My decision to fire David when I'd first taken over as chief of the department ten years ago was one of those burdens.

Up until that time he'd been doing the ER shifts nobody else wanted—nights, weekends, holidays—in hospitals all over Buffalo, ours included. But useful as he was in his role as a permanent fill-in, it was also evident even then that he drank too much. As far as I knew, the man had never come to work drunk, but everyone in the department could routinely smell stale alcohol on his breath from the drinking he'd done when he was off duty. In addition, the telltale skin markings that I'd pointed out to the resident had already started to appear, and sometimes his hands shook, albeit ever so slightly, when he was doing an invasive procedure. Taken together, it was easily enough to make him the butt of departmental jokes.

"Is the red-nosed reindeer on tonight?"

"Need to swab a needle site with alcohol? Just have Pearson breathe on it."

"There'll be a whole lot of shakin' goin' on."

My predecessor as chief, rather than risk losing an easy way to fill gaps in the schedule, had turned a blind eye to the problem. By the time I took over, it was rumored that David regularly "topped himself up" midshift, claiming he was going to the bathroom, but returning red-faced and smelling of mouthwash.

"Get help," I'd told him when we met in the privacy of my office and I confronted him. "I'll set it up for you. It's been a miracle nothing's happened with a patient up to now. For God's sake, David, straighten out, and then we'll see."

"You're firing me?" he'd demanded.

"I can't let you work like this. You know I can't."

He'd suddenly stepped forward, bringing himself to within a foot of me, and yelled, "You're a fucking asshole, Garnet! I've made myself available to this ER for years, and this is how you pay me back?"

I'd been terrified by the rage I saw in his eyes, and his powerful-looking arms and shoulders always appeared formidable. He'd then brought his hands up between us, and I watched his fingers curl and uncurl inches from my neck as he threatened, "You'll be sorry! You hear me? Goddamned sorry!" But instead of attacking me, he stormed out of the room.

Soon afterward, I heard all the other hospitals had stopped using him as well. Subsequently, his drinking had gotten worse, and it wasn't long before he required his first admission to ER—mine—to be dried out. Each admission after that, he was in progressively worse shape, and every time he'd arrive blaming me for pushing him into the spiral that his life was hurtling down.

But out of the blue a small miracle had happened. In one of his sober periods, he started to write medical articles for a local paper. In them he'd shown a skill for explaining illnesses and their treatment in terms that laypeople could understand. There was a good public response, people began sending him questions about health matters, and soon he was doing a regular feature. In no time he was invited onto talk shows, answering questions about medical problems the listeners phoned in. So popular had the format been that the radio station offered him a regular half-hour slot. Almost overnight the man had a new career.

I'd occasionally catch his program and sometimes glance at his column. He had a nice blend of being easy to read or to listen to while remaining clinically accurate. But one night while driving home I heard him describe his own struggles with alcoholism, and on that occasion he'd verged on being great.

"I drink to escape the wrongs in my life—those of my own doing; those which were done to me; those which I witnessed being done to others. Not that these events were any worse than what's befallen the next person—others have endured greater calamity and not taken to drink—but I suspect my tolerance to the pain is less. What's harder to grasp is why I also drink when life goes well, yet that's often when I'm most afraid—those times when hope is as great an agony as despair; when success makes my fear of failure unendurable, or when love leaves me terrified of insurmountable loss. Then I end up drinking to obliterate the waiting for it all to go bad. Whatever the occasion that starts me off, however, the finish remains the same—drinking to obliterate the drinking itself, holding off the shakes, heaves, DTs, and, worst of all, the deep loathing which congeals like ice in the soul each time withdrawal threatens."

It was as good a description of what drives addiction as I'd ever known to have come out of a medical text.

During this period, his own frequent admissions to ER had stopped, and I held my breath, for a while.

Within a year the inevitable had happened. Intermittently his articles would not appear and his radio spots would be preempted, replaced without explanation with previously recorded broadcasts of his show. Sooner or later he'd show up in ER, once more raging at me while seeing bugs that weren't there, and we'd start again. For me, it added up to ten years of watching the man squander more chances than anyone had a right to expect in a lifetime. For him, it had been a slow stroll toward his own destruction, a stroll that not he nor anybody else seemed able to stop, a life rapidly running out of possibilities.

Back in ER, I rushed over to triage and took charge of the latest patient brought in by ambulance. Yet as I grabbed her chart and listened to her complain about being short of breath, David's bleak prospects continued to weigh heavily on my thoughts. "Damn you again," I muttered, and by sheer willpower forced him enough out of my mind that I could do my job.

By six A.M. our bed was usually a pretty crowded place. My wife, Dr. Janet Graceton, while as slender as a dancer, was tall and liked a lot of room. Muffy, our pet poodle, had a penchant for crawling between us in the early morning hours, placing her paws against my back and pushing until she made herself a big enough spot to stretch out in. She'd usurped this "right" ever since she was a puppy five years ago, except now she weighed fifty pounds and had enough strength in her legs to shove me half off the bed. Finally came the newest inter-loper, Brendan, our two-and-a-half-year-old son. Since he'd been able to climb out of his crib, he quickly learned what he had to do if he wanted a cuddle from his parents before they left for work. And so the predawn gathering had become a routine, one that served as an oasis from which Janet and I could greedily drink up a store of love and sanity before embarking on our increasingly long and brutal days at the hospital.

That morning it felt especially cozy to linger in bed, as out-side a gray mist was pasting itself against the windows and periodic gusts of rain peppered the glass panes like handfuls of sand.

Janet and I had been talking about the previous day while I lay on my back and held Brendan up in the air, swaying him from side to side while he, squealing with laughter, pretended to be a plane.

"No-fault murder?" Janet was saying. "That's quite a shot, Earl. The residents must have loved it, but I wouldn't advise repeating the charge outside of Death Rounds, in case some lawyers over at Brama start taking exception to it."

Brendan shrieked happily in agreement.

"I don't know. Going public with a case like Robert De-lany's might smarten up the members of their board. The way I read how people are feeling about HMOs these days, it wouldn't take much to ignite the kind of pressure even Brama couldn't ignore. And in some towns it's been the doctors who have brought local offices to heel."

Janet snorted. She was lying on her side, her head cupped in her hand, watching Brendan and me. "Don't count on it here," she said, stretching up with her free arm and tickling his side.

"Don't Mommy!" he screeched, then promptly demanded, "Do it some more!"

"Haven't your patients had enough?" I continued, waving Brendan through the air. "Christ, the other day I couldn't get preauthorization to admit a pregnant woman who was already in labor."

Janet giggled. "I heard about that one from the residents. Did you really threaten to deliver her on TV and invite expectant mothers to pay Brama a visit?"

"Of course not. I simply suggested that if that was their new obstetrical policy, I'd be glad to announce it to the media for them."

Janet flashed me a wicked grin. "You dog."

Brendan gave another shriek and invited more tickling. I swooped him into his mother's arms, where he squirmed around as Janet and I quickly obliged. His gales of laughter were now enough to make Muffy insert her snout under one of my hands and toss it in the air, her way of signaling that she too wanted some attention. I was scratching her ears and tickling Brendan behind his neck when Janet leaned forward and let her hair shower around his face like a gold curtain. "Do you know Daddy's best tickle spot?" she whispered, not too softly. Soon they were both attacking the soles of my feet, I was begging for mercy, and Muffy was barking excitedly.

In all the noise, I barely heard the phone ring. But Janet did. Like all obstetricians, she was so sensitized to being called that even in a deep sleep she would manage to pick up the receiver before it rang twice. "Dr. Graceton here."

I got both Brendan and Muffy quieted down.

"How many centimeters?" she asked coolly, all trace of her laughter vanished. She listened to the answer, then replied, "I'm on my way."

As she quickly dressed and gave me a string of instructions about Brendan, I marveled at the youthful forty-year-old woman who was such a force in my life. I couldn't count the times I'd watched her rise from our bed, pull on her clothes in the darkness, and rush off to a delivery. Since we first became lovers twelve years ago, then man and wife a year later, and now parents, her beauty and energy seemed undiminished. I couldn't imagine a job more fitting for her than bringing life into this world.

In an instant she was out the door, leaving the three of us to somehow muddle through breakfast without her.

A few days later I got a message from the nurses on the floor that David Pearson wanted to see me—to apologize. I kept putting off going, but by early evening when I finished in ER, I'd resigned myself to facing him yet again. If I didn't, I figured, I'd be even more haunted by the man than I was now.

He was standing by the window of his room looking out at the stumpy skyline of downtown Buffalo, watching it glow in the final minutes of the setting sun. But the golden light did nothing for him. His color was pale, his appearance wan, and his hand trembled as he reached to shake mine. Yet he greeted me with a steady gaze, and his eyes had the beginning of a spark in them, enough to suggest that he was coming back to life.

"I'm sorry, Earl. I can't say how sorry I am for what I did."

"It's nothing, David," I insisted with as much enthusiasm as I could muster. "Just get well. Are you going home soon?" I didn't dare ask about work. For all I knew, they'd already sacked him.

He grimaced. "No, I can't simply dry out and go back to my old routine this time. It's my last chance. The paper and the radio station both say if I screw up once more, I'm gone." He looked frightened, as he always did after a binge when he assured me of his determination to stay dry. The reality was that he had less than a forty percent chance of breaking off from his addiction, and each time he fell out of remission, the odds against him grew, while the risk of death drew closer.

I found myself looking away, hoping he wouldn't read in

my expression how little hope I had for him. "At least you've still got a chance, David. That's something," I said lamely.

He grabbed my arm. "I've got more than that, Earl. They've offered me a new addiction treatment. It's experimental, but they say the results are good."

The declaration took me by surprise. "What treatment? I haven't heard of any new program—"

"It's not here," he continued in a rush. His eyes had all at once become too bright. "It's in Mexico!"

"Mexico!" For an instant I thought he must be confabulating, having some sort of delayed alcohol-induced psychosis. "Look, David, maybe you'd better lie down—"

"No, Earl, it's true. I'm being sent to an addiction research center that's run by my HMO—in Mexico, somewhere near Tijuana. Apparently it's cheaper to fly me there than to keep me here and pay the daily room rate at St. Paul's. Believe me, I'm grateful, and my family's ecstatic. Obviously they're pretty fed up with me too."

"Still, it sounds pretty exotic, Mexico and all. I find it strange that any HMO would bother—"

"It's simple, Earl. If this program works like they say and I stay out of trouble, it'll save the company a bundle by avoiding an endless string of readmissions. Besides, I've got to quit. If they can just get good results with me . . ."

His speech became increasingly rapid, the blacks of his eyes widened, and he exuded a desperation that I found chilling. Whatever treatment he was going on about, he looked and sounded like a man who didn't think he'd succeed with it any more than I did. Then he added, "The Brama program's my last chance."

At first I thought I couldn't have understood him properly. "Brama? Brama's offering you a program? You're sure?"

He nodded. "Yep."

"But they hardly even cover basic care. Why would they be offering you a special program?"

"Like I said, they were very clear that it was a matter of

keeping both current and future costs down. They also made no bones about the fact that even if I didn't want to go, I had no choice but to accept. Their agent read it to me from the fine print of my policy. 'Noncompliance with any prescribed treatment which leads to further medical expenses is grounds to deinsure the patient.' So as far as Brama's concerned, I'm in, like it or not, or I'm out altogether, because either way it'll help their profit margin."

"But what's the treatment?"

"Probably it's one of the new anticraving drugs, but I won't know until I get there. I'm part of a study. Besides, I couldn't even tell you if I did know. I had to sign a confidentiality agreement which forbids me to talk about the method until they publish their results."

Largely because of David, I'd kept my reading on the long-term treatment of alcoholism up-to-date. Anticraving drugs were the latest hope to crack problem drinking. The first on the market, naltrexone, hadn't helped him. "How long will you be there?" I asked, still making an effort to sound hopeful.

"Again, no idea, though I gather it'll be at least a month. No other detox joint I've ever been in has kept me less than thirty days."

"Jesus, David, it sounds pretty strange. Are you sure—"

He grabbed me by the shoulders and looked at me with eyes that were as black as an abyss. "Earl, I told you, I'm beyond any more tries. One way or another, I won't be back in your ER stinking up the place and screaming about spiders. I have to make this attempt work—have to—or I won't have anything left—not my family, not my job, and before long, probably not my life!"

There wasn't much to say after that. We made a few minutes' worth of small talk, I managed to find some more hollow-sounding words of encouragement, then we shook hands. Before stepping into the elevator I glanced back to where I'd left him standing at the door to his room, and winced. He

appeared so pale and lost in the folds of his robe that he
resembled a corpse draped in a red shroud.

I rode down to the ground floor trying to digest the absur-
dity of Brama offering treatment to David while having withheld it from little Robert Delany.

Chapter 3

Exactly as Janet had foreseen, it hadn't been such a good idea to accuse Brama of practicing no-fault murder. Official minutes of the Death Rounds proceedings had quoted my comment, and although this document is normally considered so sensitive that it's limited to a few copies held in the hospital vault, somehow someone had leaked a photostat to the local Brama office. A few days later the media picked up the story. My accusation appeared on the front page of Buffalo's sole daily newspaper, filled the talk shows, and was the lead story for local TV newscasts. Although I refused to speak to the flurry of reporters that dogged me for follow-up quotes, the public debate over nonaccountability in HMOs had raged for days during hastily organized radio phone-in specials dedicated to that topic alone.

I'd since had about three weeks' worth of hindsight to show me the error of my ways for having caused such a stir, and most of that hindsight had been provided by some of the men and women in the room I just entered. They were the hospital leadership—chiefs, directors, administrators—gathered for a reception being held to honor a departing anesthetist. But for the moment they seemed more intent in displaying their displeasure with me. A few stopped talking as I walked by. Others whispered together while glancing in my direction, then glumly shook their heads and turned their backs on me. The most direct barb came when I drew near a group of internists. Their chief, Arnold Pinter, a mousy little man

27

dressed in an oversized lab coat, was complaining loudly. "They're sending all their patients to at least a dozen other hospitals, ever since that ER loose-lips mouthed off about their triage policy. I don't know about you, but my income's down ten percent." The rest murmured in agreement and a few slid their eyes toward me as I passed.

Shunning, St. Paul's style. At least they hadn't clucked their tongues and wagged their fingers at me.

I tried to ignore the silly display and looked around for the guest of honor, Dr. Hector Saswald, Chief of Anesthesia. He'd abruptly announced last week that he was leaving to work in a chain of freestanding day surgeries, run by Brama no less. I wasn't exactly surprised, or sorry to see him go. He'd spent a lot of weekends freelancing at these same facilities over the last year, and frankly, I felt his department functioned better without him around. He always seemed too taken by the business and politics of medicine for my liking, and I had no problem wishing him on Brama. Nevertheless, he was a fellow chief, had survived for longer than I'd served so far in the role, and occasionally had been on the same side of an issue as I was. Whatever I thought of him personally, I felt duty-bound to take the high road and wish him well.

Yet I had no idea how he would respond, given the trouble I'd stirred up with his new bosses, and I was relieved when I saw him talking with one of the few friends I still had among the ruling elites of St. Paul's. Where the anesthetist was short, balding, and terminally sullen, the man beside him, surgeon and chief Dr. Sean Carrington, was over six feet in height, had a mop of frizzy red hair, and a laugh that carried the width of any room. I quickly strode over to where the two of them were standing and heard the tail end of Sean telling a zany OR story that had coaxed a smile out of the usually humorless Saswald.

". . . after his friends put Krazy Glue on the toilet seat, they had to unbolt it so he could wear it to the hospital. The residents in ER sat him in acetone for an hour, but in the end I had to cut the thing away from the skin— Hey, Earl," he broke off, giving me a welcome grin when he saw me approaching. "I was just reminiscing about the toilet seat man. Weren't you on that night?"

The thought of it made me chuckle. "I was not only there the night he came in, but also the following morning when those so-called friends of his had the nerve to turn up demanding we give the seat back."

Sean's grin widened. "Remember what happened in triage?"

Now he had me laughing outright. "You mean when he waddled up to the receptionist with a toilet seat visibly stuck to his ass, and she still told him to 'take a seat'?"

Sean had said the punch line with me, like a duet, setting us to laughing even more. Yet I knew there was more than his love of fun behind our fooling around. There was no doctor more influential in St. Paul's. Over the last few weeks, as patient numbers fell along with doctors' incomes, and animosity toward me had grown, he'd made a show of our friendship whenever he could. Everyone went on blaming me for invoking Brama's wrath, but Sean's support seemed to put a ceiling on how far their hostility could go. Whenever I tried to thank him for being such a good friend, he pretended not to know what I was talking about, insisted that the only reason he kept on speaking to me was because no one else would laugh at his jokes, and proceeded to tell me yet another of his funny tales.

But when I turned to Saswald intending to wish him luck, I saw by the scowl on his face that he didn't care *whose* friend I was. I held out my hand anyway and said simply, "All the best, Hector," figuring I would get my well-wishes over with and slip out immediately, before my presence became any more of an embarrassment.

He shook it without any enthusiasm, and in a cool voice stiffly expressed his admiration for Janet as a wonderful surgeon. "Please say goodbye to her for me," he added, apparently prepared to act in a minimally civil manner despite his disapproval of me.

I just as stiffly assured him, "Why, I'd be pleased to pass on your compliment to her, Hector. I'm sure Janet will be delighted." Then, encouraged by the fact that we were at least talking, I decided it might be as good a time as any to ask him about something I'd figured only he would be able to help me with. "Hector, in your travels for Brama, did you by any chance ever run across an addiction research unit they run in Mexico?"

He pulled his hand out of mine, ending our shake and his civility. "Of course not," he replied, sounding annoyed. "Why would you think they'd need an anesthetist in an addiction center?" He then gave my hand, still suspended between us, such a look of disgust that I thought for an instant he might spit on it. I needn't have worried. He looked up and spat at me with words instead. "How can you laugh and joke, after what you've involved this hospital in? And I certainly don't see why I should tell you anything at all about Brama."

His harsh tone made people standing nearby fall silent. I felt my face burn as it grew flushed. "Look, I'm sorry. I didn't intend those comments to go public. I certainly never wanted to cause damage to St. Paul's. If I could fix this—"

"You could resign!" Saswald blurted. "Make a public retraction, and resign."

The burning spread down my neck, through my chest, and into my gut. "Your new bosses tell you to say that?" I asked, letting my anger sound.

He started, and I got to watch his face turn red. He took a step toward me. "You smart-assed cocksucker, I resent you, I resent what you did, and I resent what you said. How dare you insult me or libel where I work—"

"Easy, Hector," Sean warned. He'd swiftly moved up to lay a restraining hand on the man's shoulder.

Saswald shook it off. "Butt out, Carrington. Garnet can't slander a company like Brama and get away with it. Hell, it's one thing to get himself in hot water for spreading lies, but he's jeopardizing the hospital's relationship with an important provider of patients, and that's an unforgivable—"

"I think Dr. Garnet's absolutely right about Brama," said a voice from behind me. I turned to see our new CEO, Reginald Fosse, regarding Saswald and me with a bemused smile. He was a balding man in his mid-sixties with a few strands of white hair pulled across his bare pate. Though his portly tummy, full beard, and wire-rimmed glasses gave him a grandfatherly air, his flinty gaze could wither a man half his age. "In fact," he continued, "I think Dr. Garnet deserves our support for standing up to Brama for what they did to that poor little boy." Despite his being a head shorter than I, he stepped up and put his arm around my shoulder. "Now, Saswald, you have a lot of people to say goodbye to, so I suggest you get started. Earl, I'd like to see you over here for a moment."

Saswald's jaw dropped and he stood transfixed while Fosse led me away toward a quiet corner of the room. Sean gave me a wink as we passed, then turned to join a group of his own departmental members who were gulping down a plate of pineapple pieces the way surgeons always eat—as if they'd be called to the OR any second. The other onlookers went back to sipping a variety of colored juices and munching cheese cubes off toothpicks.

Fosse didn't say anything until we were well out of earshot. I'd only known him for little over a year. He'd been CEO at Janet's former hospital, and when our two institutions were forced to merge at the St. Paul's site early last winter he was named overall CEO. His degrees were in business, not medicine, but he seemed a good administrator, had a reputation of being absolutely ruthless with anyone who stood in the way of his running a well-managed hospital, and was extraordinary at raising endowments. But that he'd go as far as standing up for me and speaking out against Brama was a complete, yet comforting surprise.

"It's been rough on you these last few weeks, hasn't it?" he stated in a hushed voice.

I grinned at him. "Any other events on the calendar you'd like me to torpedo with my presence?"

He gave me a gracious smile. "I spoke out because I wanted you and the rest of the hospital to know that I support you, that I meant it when I said you're absolutely right about Brama and others like them. You've no idea how much it sickens me what they're doing to health care. But I also have to warn you that you've obviously struck a nerve with them. They wouldn't be coming after you and this hospital the way they are if you hadn't."

"Would it help if I issued a retraction? I never in my wildest dreams thought they'd punish a whole hospital—"

"They don't want a retraction, they want you fired. A lot of the board members have already been quietly approached and told that that's what it would take for Brama to lift their boycott of St. Paul's."

"What?"

"I know, it seems completely over the top, but managed care is terrified a case like Robert Delany's could be a rallying point for a public outcry that they couldn't contain. They've never forgotten how they nearly got their wings clipped by the patients' rights bill which almost passed in 'ninety-eight, and they know full well they only escaped that legislation because the country at the time was more focused on the President's zipper than on health care."

"Still, their response seems a bit excessive. It's not like I deliberately set out to accuse them in the media."

"As far as they're concerned, you might as well have, Earl. And never forget it's a trillion-dollar-a-year industry. Nothing's excessive when that kind of money sets out to protect its interest. I repeat, I'll hold off the board members for as long as I can, but be very careful, and be ready for a full-fledged attack on your continuing as Chief of Emergency at next week's meeting."

I groaned. The second Wednesday of every month was the fixed date when the directors of St. Paul's regularly got together, and I was the lone physicians' representative. I'd been appointed to the position last year, when I'd been a lot more popular with both doctors and management than I was now.

"You must show up," Fosse warned, his eyes flashing darkly. "Our best chance to get you out of this mess is to confront them head-on, and I'm willing to do that with you."

Shaken as I was from hearing the extent of the backlash that I'd unleashed, I took heart from the zeal of his support and thanked him, then headed for the door. After causing such a stir when I arrived, I don't think my leaving attracted anybody's notice. The surgeons, having cleaned out the pineapple tray, had moved on to a table laden with wedges of brown-looking pears. Saswald was working the more genteel parts of the crowd, where the internists circled around each other while continuing to nibble their tidbits. I could tell by the expression on his face that he was still furious, and when he greeted Arnold Pinter with a hearty slap on the back, the blow was forceful enough that it seemed more like a Heimlich maneuver than a friendly pat. The rest of Arnold's department got a less vigorous glad hand, as was appropriate to their lower rank.

The call came over the P.A. a few hours later that evening. I was still in Emergency seeing cases.

"Trauma! Code Blue! Doctor's parking. Trauma! Code Blue! Doctor's parking."

"Shit!" I muttered as I sprinted for the door, pulling on a pair of gloves as I went. Trauma, Code Blue, meant that someone was injured on the grounds outside. The call could be for anything ranging from a person having tripped and sprained an ankle to having jumped off the top of the building. Whatever the problem, it was ER's duty to respond with a trauma team. I could hear Susanne and some of her nurses following behind with a resuscitation cart.

I ran through the ambulance bay and, once outside, headed to the area designated for physicians' cars. I felt a cool drizzle against my face, and it was dark except where the overhead sodium lamps threw down cones of light that illuminated plumes of mist.

There was nothing in the parking lot except cars, but over near the wall of the building I saw a small group of people. It's a jumper, was my first thought while running toward the site. Instinctively I glanced up the side of the building to see if I could spot a broken window and estimate the height of the fall. In the poor light there was nothing obvious. Had they leaped from the roof? That meant an eight-story drop onto concrete.

Up ahead one of the onlookers spun away from what he was looking at, doubled over, and started to retch.

I slowed my pace as I approached the scene, braced myself, then ordered, "Let me through, please."

The dozen or so people standing in a half circle parted, and I could see the victim. At first I didn't recognize him. I saw only that it was a man dressed in a raincoat lying facedown in what seemed like a very large, dark pool of water. His legs were spread out behind him, his arms raised along each side of his head. It wasn't the pile of broken remains—usual for a jumper—that I'd expected. Tiptoeing through the black puddle to get to him, I quickly grew aware that the liquid wasn't water, but something dark and sticky, like oil. Yet when I kneeled down beside the body and was closer to the fluid, even in the dim light I could see its color wasn't black but dark red. With the slow motion of a nightmare, I realized I was kneeling in blood, more blood than I'd ever seen at a trauma site. I felt my stomach rise toward my throat but managed to keep the burning vomit down enough that I could warn Susanne and her crew as they came up behind me. "Watch it! This is all blood."

"My God!"

"Jesus!"

"What happened to him?"

Their horror, evident in their voices, matched my own. "Get ready to turn him, Susanne!" I quietly ordered, determined to keep us all on track. As I spoke I slid my fingers around the side of his neck from behind and felt for a carotid pulse. Instead my whole hand slid into a laceration the size of a jack-o'-lantern's grin. "Shit!" I screamed, jerking my fingers back out. The nurses jumped. Susanne's face filled with alarm. "His throat's cut!" I exclaimed, fighting as hard as I could to keep my composure. "Let's roll him!"

I slid sideways until I was at the top of his head and, swallowing until I had no more spit, took it between my gloved hands. It moved like a half-detached soccer ball. "Oh, God," I moaned, and swallowed a few more times, getting ready. "All together now, slowly."

As we rotated him around onto his side, his head seemed to have a floppy movement all its own. It kept wanting to fall backward, opening up the slash across the front of his neck. No blood spurted from the gaping ends of arteries or flowed from the dark openings of severed veins. He'd already exsanguinated.

But the biggest shock came as I brought his white staring features into view. Awash in blood and underlined by the jagged gash, it was the face of Hector Saswald.

Chapter 4

The first cop car arrived in minutes. It wasn't much longer before the parking lot looked like a pinball game of blue and red flashing lights. A few dozen police officers all tried to take charge at once.

"Stand back!"

"Nobody touch anything!"

"Who found him?"

I was still kneeling beside Saswald, though he was clearly beyond any resuscitation attempt. I felt I should stay there until somebody took charge of the body. But the young man who came up to speak with me saw the half-severed head, exclaimed, "Jesus Christ!" and threw up before he could get bent over. The orange and yellow contents of his stomach arced toward the nearby onlookers and hit the pavement at their feet with a splat.

"That'll move them back," muttered a policewoman who was standing over me. The crowd proved her right by shuffling away from the rookie who continued to gag.

An unmarked car pulled up behind the official vehicles, and four nonuniformed detectives piled out wearing look-alike beige raincoats. As they strode toward us their plain dress was an obvious statement of rank. The swarm of blue-clad figures milling around immediately made way for them, then stood by respectfully while the newcomers got a firsthand look at the carnage on the ground. The policewoman leaned down to my ear and said, "You'll have to step away from the victim, but we'll need you to give a statement, Doctor . . . ?"

"Garnet," I answered, and went to where she'd indicated I should wait.

She then knelt near Saswald's outstretched arms and shone a flashlight down on the pavement beside the dead man's left hand. "Sirs, look at this," she said, glancing up at her superiors. "There's something written . . ." The rest of what she said was lost as the detectives huddled around her and inspected whatever she'd found. More vehicles and police personnel were arriving. A dozen people in civilian dress climbed out the back of a large black van and proceeded to unload carrying cases much like the oversized tackle boxes used by medics. "Shit! Look at the blood!" exclaimed the first of the group to reach Saswald. His colleagues were already wearing latex gloves, and one of them immediately started passing more out among the uniformed police. The others set their equipment down in a circle beyond the perimeter of the congealing pool, where they proceeded to take out clear packets of zipper bags, labels, and specimen bottles. A few donned headlamps—the kind miners wear—and started scouring the area outside this ring. They all seemed to know exactly what needed doing and worked with a minimum of conversation. Much like an ER team, I mused.

A photographer with easily visible police ID pinned to his coat stepped forward and started snapping pictures. With a wet drizzle coating everything, the spectacle already had the veneer of a glossy tabloid photo. One of the detectives hunched over Saswald's right hand signaled that he wanted a few shots of the ground in that area. The white flash from the camera continued to cut the night like a strobe.

Station wagons emblazoned with the logos of local TV stations began pulling into the lot. Soon the area was flooded in the glare of camera lights as reporters, confined with the rest of the public behind a hastily erected line of yellow tape, resorted to standing on the roofs of their vehicles as they got video shots for the eleven o'clock news.

But as I stood watching, I periodically heard the sound of an ambulance pulling into the ER garage behind me. Despite the horror on our own doorstep, there was obviously no respite from the usual injury and illness going on in the rest of the city. After hearing three such arrivals, I walked over to the detective who'd been ordering the photographer around. "Excuse me, I'm Dr. Earl Garnet, Chief of ER. My team was called out when the body was discovered. I was told you might need to interview me, but I've got to get back inside." As if to underline my point, yet another vehicle roared into the unloading bay, having cut its siren at the entrance to the hospital.

The man studied me from under a pair of eyelids that drooped with what looked like years of fatigue, then nodded. "How long will you be there?" he asked, his voice impeccably neutral. I suspected it was a practiced tone, one learned at a police academy and designed to put innocent people on the defensive. To go with his eyes and manner of speaking, he had a hatchet-shaped face pocked with old acne scars. In all he resembled one of the bad guys out of a Dick Tracy comic.

"A few hours," I told him, and turned to leave.

"Hold it, Doctor. I need you to look at something now."

"Hey, I've been standing waiting while four cases have rolled in. There's only one other staff doctor on duty, and residents don't—"

"We think the victim was trying to write something in his own blood as he was dying. I'd like you to look at it please."

That stopped me.

"I want to know if you can make something of it," the detective continued. "I understand you told the responding officer that the deceased was head of anesthesia here."

"Yes," I answered, then added, "I didn't see any writing."

"Take another look." The detective stood aside and gestured toward Saswald's head and outstretched arms. "Shine a light on the letters," he ordered an officer who seemed to be guarding the area in question.

The spot he illuminated was about two feet away from where Saswald was still positioned on his back. At first I couldn't see anything except some dried streaks trailing away from the leading edge of the pooled blood.

"Before you rolled him over, that's about where his right hand would have been," the detective behind me said.

I bent closer, but again couldn't make anything of the marks. For all I knew, I might have been stepping on them while supporting Saswald's half-severed head.

"You can see the letters better if you get farther down and look at the pavement sideways from a forty-five-degree angle," said the officer holding the lamp.

I did as he suggested, and was about to repeat that I saw nothing when I made out what could have been a *P*. Then an *e* and an *r* came into view. Farther along in a line, I could swear I saw a pair of *o*'s. "My God, you're right!" I exclaimed. "Except I can't make out enough to read it."

"Oh, we'll manage that part, all right. We've got a chemical—luminol—that'll light up traces of blood until whatever's there will read like a neon sign, in spite of this rain. What I want to know from you is this: Could a man with his head half cut off remain conscious enough to even think of scrawling a message, let alone actually write one? Or is this a greeting from the killer?"

His question forced me to think about Saswald's last moments in terms I'd rather have avoided. I glanced over at the gaping trench across the front of his neck, swallowed a few times, and began reasoning through the answer. The first thing that struck me was that the killing stroke was probably a single slice with some sort of large smooth-edged blade, judging from the even demarcation of the cut. Since it had completely severed his windpipe as well as his carotids and jugular veins, he'd have been unable to make a noise or cry for help. If he'd tried, his exhaled air would simply have escaped with a quiet hiss out the wound instead of passing up through his larynx to the waiting vocal cords. And each inhaled breath would have filled his lungs with blood, leaving him choking, drowning bit by bit, again with little sound. He might have staggered a short distance at first, but with the massive amounts of blood that would have been jetting out from his wound he'd have quickly collapsed before getting too far.

I looked around and saw no trail leading up to the pool surrounding where he'd died. Perhaps after the attack the killer had held him down until he was too weak to walk or crawl. But he'd still be conscious. His spinal tract had been left intact, and the posterior cerebral blood supply would have continued to perfuse his brain from behind. I recalled a neuro-anatomy professor horrifying us with anecdotal writings that described victims of the guillotine during the French Revolution. Even completely severed heads held up to the crowd continued to look around and move their mouths as if making an attempt to speak.

"Yes, he'd have remained conscious, for about a minute or so," I replied at last, trying not to think of what terror Saswald felt during those seconds when he, like the heads held on high so long ago, knew he was already dead.

For the next two hours I saw patients in the emergency department, but working was difficult. Images of the near-decapitation kept crowding in on my thoughts and robbed me of my focus.

". . . and it was the worst headache of my life, Doctor. What really scared me was the double vision . . ."

". . . the pain went down the inside of my left arm and to my neck, like the last heart attack, so I knew . . ."

". . . my entire leg went cold and blue. But it's the pain. For God's sake help me with the pain . . ."

Somehow I kept them all straight in my mind, sorted who could go home from those needing admission, and made the treatment decisions that got them safely through the emergency room portion of their ordeal. But it wasn't the art of medicine at its best.

I was signing out to my replacement staff at eleven o'clock when the triage nurse told me that a big detective was in the waiting room requesting to see me. Inwardly I groaned, yet continued to walk from stretcher to stretcher, giving a brief synopsis for each patient that had been in my care.

Changeover is a time when most errors occur in ER, even under normal circumstances. But tonight, with the relieving staff abuzz over what had happened to Saswald, I knew the risk of someone getting distracted and forgetting what still needed doing was higher than usual. As if to underline my concern, I kept having to repeat key clinical points two and three times while the residents scribbled themselves reminders on index cards or pieces of scrap paper.

When our tour was finally finished—the whole process had taken twice as long as usual—I watched them stuff these notes into the depths of their lab coats, the pockets already bulging with manuals, crib sheets, reflex hammers, and otoscopes. As a rule, the more inexperienced a trainee, the more junk he or she carted around, as if it would compensate for what they hadn't learned yet. By this measure, I judged tonight's crew to be pretty junior, and warned the overnight physician who'd be supervising them to be particularly vigilant, especially with those few patients who were still unstable. Then, hoping for the best, I bid everyone good night.

Once I got out to triage, I was greeted by a familiar face.

"Hi, Doc," said Detective George Riley. He held out his hand and stepped forward from where he'd been slouching against an empty stretcher. He didn't smile, but his shake was firm. "It's a hell of a thing, what's happened." He was about an inch shy of my own six-foot-one frame, but more than made up for the discrepancy by the way his huge shoulders strained at the stitches of anything I'd ever seen him wear. Tonight it was his own version of the standard-issue beige raincoat that he was giving the stretch test to, and from its sodden look I figured the rain was still coming down outside.

"I'm glad to see you're here," I said. "In fact, if your superiors have any sense, they'll put you in charge." Probably no other cop in Buffalo knew the dirty secrets of St. Paul's better than Riley. We'd initially met about three years earlier, when I'd become a suspect in a murder case he was investigating. Since then we'd had an occasion to work on the same side of the law, and in the process, despite our inauspicious first encounter, I'd actually grown to like the man.

Now he grinned. "Looks like at least someone down at headquarters thinks the way you do. Yeah, for what it's worth, I'm heading this investigation."

"What can I do to help?" I asked.

He breathed out a deep sigh that must have emptied the innermost recesses of his lungs. "Lord knows. At this point anything you might think of would be more than what we've got. Even with so many people seeing him just before he was killed—your CEO told us about the reception and gave us the list of who was there—nobody noticed much that was useful. I was hoping maybe you had. Anything strike you in retrospect that was odd with the man?"

I shook my head. "No, not at all."

Riley shrugged. "That's been the story all night."

"Who else have you talked to?"

"We sent uniformed officers to just about all the medical units to ask whoever was on duty this evening if they saw or knew anything, but again, no luck. The scene of the killing hasn't yielded up much either. The murderer used gloves—there's not a fingerprint other than the victim's at the scene—and while there are a few bloody footprints, they don't lead anywhere. Probably whoever it was wore some kind of boots over his shoes during the attack, then carried them off with him. We can't even tell at this point whether the killing's connected to the hospital. Who's to say some creep from the neighborhood didn't go berserk on angel dust and decide to use your parking lot as a hunting ground. Dr. Saswald simply could have been in the wrong place at the wrong time."

"What did the letters scrawled in blood say?"

Riley's eyebrows shot up an inch closer to his hairline. "You know about that? Christ, you haven't told anyone else, have you?"

"No, of course not."

He exhaled again, this time a brief, quick breath, the kind that spells relief. "Thank God. It's all we have, and for the moment we're holding it back." He paused, then added, "But since you're already savvy to it, I'd like to know what you think. Come take a look."

He moved a few steps ahead of me once we were out in the parking lot and striding toward where Saswald had been killed. The air was much cooler now, and a brisk wind drove the thin rain into my eyes with enough force that I found myself squinting as we went. There was nobody about, my own sign-out having taken me well past the usual time of shift change when there's always a rush of people coming and going. I shivered and pulled my lab coat around me, hurrying to stay close behind the detective. Up ahead I could see a large plastic sheet lift off the ground as the wind got under it, and about a dozen police struggling to weight it down by placing sections of metal barricades along its edges. The opaque covering, obviously intended to protect the murder site from the rain, snapped and made loud crinkling noises as it pulled against the restraints, its center rising and falling like some giant shroud. I felt my stomach tighten at the thought of Saswald's body possibly still being under it. Surely he'd already been taken to the city morgue.

After retrieving what looked like a regular flashlight from

one of his men, Riley strode up to one of the barricades and lifted it off a corner section of plastic. He then quickly folded this part of the sheet back about six feet and invited me to look at the pavement underneath.

There was no sign of Saswald, but I recognized the spot as the place where I'd seen the traces of letters written in blood. Except when Riley held his lamp over the area, what I saw now was as clear as a specimen of graffiti written in green luminous paint.

Behind me I heard Riley start to explain.

"Luminol is a liquid that binds with even the slightest traces of old blood, and can then be made to fluoresce with so-called black light . . ."

But as intent as he was on making me understand the chemistry involved, the details drifted over my head as I stared down at the words scrawled across the asphalt.

They read: *Pearson . . . too young . . .*

"Does it ring any bells in connection to Saswald?" Riley asked as I stood over the strange-looking writing.

"Not at all," I told him without hesitation. But I kept to myself the uneasiness I felt stir in the pit of my stomach at seeing the name.

While driving home I kept insisting that it had to be a bizarre coincidence, that the name beside Saswald's body couldn't refer to David. For one thing, there were too many Pearsons in the world for me to jump to that conclusion—417 of them had a telephone listing in the greater Buffalo area alone. I know because as soon as I got to my house that night I took out our directory and counted them. For another, as far as I was aware, the only thing the two men had in common, besides knowing me, was one being a patient at a Brama clinic and the other working for the company itself. And whatever contempt I felt for Brama, I couldn't make that connection between the two men into anything other than a matter of chance, and one not all that remarkable either, given the size of the corporation and the huge number of patients and doctors in the area already doing business with the place. Besides, David was in Mexico, so why would I even think he had anything to do with the killing? Yet it was eerie that my last conversation, and quarrel, with Saswald was in effect on account of David Pearson.

While I'd been busy with the phone book, Muffy made it pretty evident she wanted to go out, dancing and twirling at my feet. Listening to the quiet upstairs, I knew the rest of the household was asleep. My own brain was far too jangled to even consider going to bed yet, so I decided I might as well take her for a walk. I found her leash, attached it to her, then stepped outside. It had stopped raining, and after taking a few lungfuls of the fresh night air while she tugged me along our back lane—one of the few in Buffalo—I got clear-headed enough to realize how lucky it had been that I hadn't used David's name when asking Saswald about the addiction clinic. Otherwise someone might have reported overhearing it and the police would have been all over me with questions about the man, trying to connect him to the name beside the body.

The lane I was following with Muffy had once been a side road used to access a country golf course, before urban sprawl brought houses to the edge of the fairways. It led between the back of houses and was lined by fences, hedges, and gardens. As she found her points of interest, I would have normally enjoyed the places where I could see into my neighbors' gardens. Instead I found myself thinking about what the rest of the writing beside Saswald's body could mean. *Too young* . . . Too young for what? The common completion of that phrase—*to die*—popped into my head. Had Saswald or the killer been trying to write *Pearson* . . . *too young to die* . . . ?

If it was written by the killer, why didn't he finish? Lack of time? Maybe, though two or three seconds more would be all he'd have needed. But if Saswald wrote it, why would he be so desperate to say someone named Pearson was too young to die? Guilt perhaps? Over a case he'd botched? Had he been killed for that, and tried to write a form of confession as he went? The image of him struggling to confess some fatal error as the life poured out of him sent a shiver through me.

Up ahead lay the tenth green, far from the clubhouse and security guards. It was where I sometimes ignored the NO DOGS sign and let Muffy run free if it was late enough that we were unlikely to be reported by other walkers or busybodies peeking out of nearby windows. As we got nearer she grew increasingly excited, tugging on the leash until I could barely hold her. We crossed onto the grass and, as was our ritual, came to a standstill in the shadows of the tall pines lining the course. Muffy quivered and made little whining entreaties while we scanned the area. The grassy expanse was full of nothing more than moonlight and a few white trailing wisps of fog. Overhead the breeze made soft hushing sounds through the bows. Somewhere in the distance an owl hooted.

"We're in luck, girl. The place is deserted," I whispered, reaching down and releasing her.

She raced away, a streak of black on silver tracing ever-widening circles through the dew-covered grass. While I watched, envious of her happy abandon, I tried to quell all thoughts of cryptic messages and to shove coincidences that gave me the creeps out of my mind.

Half an hour later I was back home and slipping into bed beside Janet, trying not to waken her. I thought I'd cooled my mind enough that I'd be able to fall asleep.

But then the bad dreams came.

I was walking toward where the killing had occurred, and the area was covered with the large opaque sheet undulating in the wind that I'd seen earlier. Except this time I knew Saswald's body was still under there—its dark shape visible through the plastic shroud which continued to rise and float downward. I tried to stop from going any nearer, but was propelled forward against my will. When the corpse was at my feet, the wind suddenly gusted and whipped the covering from off the ground and wrapped it around my legs. Tangled in its folds, I couldn't budge, couldn't get away from Saswald's uncovered face staring up at me, his slashed neck gaping open.

Then his lips began to move, mouthing, *Pearson . . . too young . . .*

I woke up in a sweat, my scream only half out of my throat and Janet shaking me. "It's okay, Earl, it's okay," she was saying in a soothing voice.

But Muffy thought otherwise. In the semidarkness I could see she was on her feet straddling my legs. She must have sensed my very real fear, because she threw back her head and howled.

Janet had already learned about the murder when she'd called the case room earlier in the evening about one of her patients. Whatever gory detail the nurses there had left out, she'd seen later on the TV news. "I know it's hideous, but there's no point talking further about it at two in the morning," she declared after we'd gotten Brendan back to sleep, and I'd reassured the nanny, who slept in the attic room, that I rarely had nightmares so she'd probably make it through the rest of the night without me setting Muffy off again.

By five, after sleeping only fitfully, I was awake for good and thinking of only one thing: I wanted to get back to the hospital and dig out the charts of every patient named Pearson, living or dead, who'd been admitted to St. Paul's since Saswald first came on staff. Deciding I might as well put my sleeplessness to use, I stole out of bed. Muffy immediately hopped up to fully occupy my vacant place with a languorous stretch.

It was still dark when I walked outside to get my car, and my breath showed white in the early morning frost. Overhead in the fog I heard the leaves of fall rustle in the breeze, and the moist coolness of the air felt like a shot of aftershave against my face. But I was much too uneasy about what we might be up against to pause and savor these sensations.

Once I was on the road, my driving along the familiar route was completely automatic. The glare from my headlights made a spotlight that sped over the asphalt while I chased behind it, lost in thought. Attacks against physicians were becoming all too common these days. As a chief of emergency I'd always had fears that my staff were especially vulnerable. The sickest people—the ones most likely to die—usually came through ER, and to an insane mind I figured we could be regarded as the starting point of someone coming to grief in a hospital, no matter what specialty they were ultimately admitted to. So if some mad avenging angel had set up shop in the neighborhood, I wanted to know about it.

The physicians' parking lot had only a few vehicles in it when I arrived at St. Paul's. I pulled up between the lines of a painted slot, shut off my motor, and sat there looking at the spot where Saswald had had his throat slashed.

Nothing remained around the the plastic sheet but the ring of metal barriers and strips of police tape warning a passerby not to cross over. Except here the wind, roaring in off Lake Erie, then accelerating through the concrete canyons of the downtown core, was much gustier than it had been in the suburbs, and the strength of it had ripped apart the yellow strands, turning them into streamers. Sitting there in the driver's seat, I watched these trail up into the night, where they coiled and snapped above the killing site, guarding it like some tentacled creature made of giant ribbons. Around it swirled the flotsam of a crime scene, discarded Styrofoam cups and bits of crumpled paper—sweeping this way and that in the eddying currents.

Feeling my own car shudder under the buffeting it was

taking, I braced myself to cross the deserted terrain between me and the nearest entrance to the hospital, took a breath, and opened my door. A particularly strong blast caught it and wrenched it out of my hand after half dragging me out of my seat. "Shit!" I exclaimed, grabbing the steering wheel so I wouldn't fall, then pulling myself upright. When I did step out of the car, the hem of my unbuttoned overcoat whipped and flapped around my legs so much that I had to turn my back to the onslaught and do up the remaining buttons before I could walk. As I turned to go, a solitary sheet of newspaper flopped and writhed its way past me, then pasted itself against one of the tires.

The distance to the hospital was a stroll of about a hundred yards, a trek I made on a daily basis without ever giving it a thought. At this early hour, huddled against the bursts of icy air that hit with the force of a wave, I found myself watching in every direction as I scuttled over the open space, feeling much like an animal on the lookout for some beast of prey. I wasn't quite running, but was close enough to it that my breathing started to quicken. I also kept looking back at the murder site, illogically afraid to take my eyes off it, as if anything there could hurt me. Except this time I saw the large plastic sheet slowly well up in the middle, fill with air, then deflate, just like in my dream. With a shiver I focused my eyes straight in front of me as I walked toward a well-lit entrance that now lay forty yards ahead. It was darker in this stretch, in the shadow of the hospital looming above me on my right and well beyond the range of the sodium lamps behind.

My lone footsteps were louder here, the slap of leather sole against wet pavement echoing up the brick sides of the building, the hollowness of the sound giving measure to its height. Along the base of that wall, between a series of Dumpsters parked in a row, were many shaded recesses, and I found it hard not to imagine the killer lurking in one of them before he'd come up on Saswald from behind.

I broke into a trot.

The door was about thirty yards away and I was adjacent to a particularly dark alcove when I saw a glint of metal about chest high wink at me from its inner depths. An instant later I made out the figure behind it, but even then it was more a movement than a form—black sliding through black—as whoever it was came toward me.

Chapter 5

My panic rocketed.

"Back off!" I screamed at the shape approaching from the side, and broke into a sprint for the hospital entrance. Before I knew it another silhouette had stepped out of the shadows in front of me, blocking my way, while the man behind bellowed for me to stop. Desperately I cast around for a place where I could run. Twenty yards to my left the hospital property abutted a large empty lot. It was full of weeds, litter, and low scrubby bushes, but it was the only option I had. I pivoted and headed toward it. Now both men were bellowing that I stand still, and out of the corner of my eye I saw the one who'd cut me off reach inside his raincoat. Jesus, I thought, he's got a gun! If I made a racket, maybe there were still some cops around. "Police! Help! There's a man with a gun!" I hollered, and found speed I never knew I possessed.

I was already at the curb and into the abandoned terrain when the beam of a flashlight caught me and a voice roared, "Wait! We're the Buffalo P.D.! We're not going to hurt you!"

Sure! I kept running.

"Is that you, Dr. Garnet?" the same voice demanded.

I pulled up and turned around to face the source of light. From behind its point of origin a man said, "I thought I recognized your voice, even with all your yelling. I talked to you last night, remember? I'm the detective who asked you whether the victim would have been able to do the writing we

51

found beside his body. I'm sorry for scaring you." As he approached he spoke in the same matter-of-fact tone he'd used at our first meeting and swung the light around to illuminate his own distinctively lean face. The severe angle of the beam exaggerated his acne into a moonscape of shadowy craters. His partner—a much younger man, from what I could see of him—followed behind but said nothing. Enough light spilled his way that I could make out that he was a uniformed officer, and I saw that the glint of metal that earlier caught my eye had been his badge.

My terror quickly changed to anger. "Scaring me!" I yelled at him. "You practically gave me a heart attack." Pointing to the younger man, I demanded, "What the hell were you hiding like that for? I took you for the killer. And as for you," I exclaimed, focusing my fury on the detective, "when I saw you reach for what could have been a gun—"

"Whoa, Doctor, now you listen to me!" he cut in, his tone now hostile. "Detective Riley ordered us to watch the area from where we wouldn't be seen. A couple of cops sitting in an unmarked car stick out like a sore thumb, so we stood around in those shadowy areas instead, to stay out of sight and be away from the wind. Frankly, we'd been figuring it was a total waste of time, until you showed up." He pointed a finger at me. "You were acting pretty strange, you know, spending all that time sitting in your car, staring at the scene of the killing, then running over here and surreptitiously looking around. I couldn't see your face, and, well, what do you expect us to think?" He shrugged, holding his palms to the heavens, as if someone up there would get his meaning and pass it on.

"Suppose you tell me," I snapped.

"Your behavior was suspicious as hell," he fired back. "I thought you were the murderer returning for more."

My resentment against the man shot up another notch, and I made no effort to conceal it. "Detective, surely it's possible for a competent policeman to interrogate someone who raises suspicion without scaring the innocent out of their skin. If you thought I was the killer, why didn't you cry out 'Police!' right away, and then question me?"

The two men looked uneasily at one another but said nothing.

"Well?" I pushed.

"Why don't *you* explain?" the uniformed officer said. There was a hint of anger in his voice, but whether it was directed at me or his partner, I couldn't tell.

The detective's eyes shot a warning at the younger man. Then he heaved a sigh and turned to me. "Because, Doctor," he began, his impatience obvious, "everyone who wandered through here tonight claimed they had something wrong with them medically—the runs, a headache, bronchitis—and that they were coming to Emergency for treatment. Now all these people sounded legit once we talked with them, and none of them got my sensors going, but I began to realize that if we ever did roust the killer for being around here, it would be too easy for him to make the same claim. Much better, I thought, would be to see how he reacted to someone coming out of the dark. If he went into battle mode and pulled a knife, for instance, we might have both a suspect and a murder weapon. So I figured, why not delay saying we were the police for a few seconds, in the hope of panicking him into revealing his true colors? Now, of course I wouldn't have pulled that move unless I already had cause to think the worst, and unfortunately, you fit the bill. But as soon as I saw how freaked out you were, I realized you weren't—"

"Wait a minute. You mean your scaring me like that was deliberate?" I could feel a new flush of anger spreading across my face. Up until that moment I'd figured they'd just been stupidly thoughtless.

He gave me a sullen stare, and then with a shrug replied, "Like I said, you behaved strangely, and I couldn't see your face."

His partner grimaced and averted his eyes. Of the two, he looked the more miserable.

Maybe I should have made allowances. Perhaps if the detective had been less obnoxious I might have been more understanding, seen his point of view, even reassured him that I understood his obligation to suspect any oddity that came across his path, or to adopt any means he considered necessary, including cutting corners, if it meant capturing Saswald's killer. But I said none of those things. "Listen, hotshot!" I growled instead, jabbing my finger at him, "before you resort to 'freaking out' anyone else tonight, let me advise you to get used to the fact that this is a hospital. Then you can get used to the fact that there will always be patients coming and going, no matter how inconvenient that may be for your so-called police work. Let me further warn you that the next person through here could be on their way to ER for what they think is indigestion but is really a heart attack, and you could literally frighten a person in that condition to death. If you try any more stunts like this one, I'll have Detective Riley ban you from the premises!"

He bristled at the rebuke, and in the ambient light from his flashlight I could see his pupils widen in anger. But he must have seen something in my face—I thought I'd snap a crown, my teeth were so tightly clenched—that convinced him he'd be better off to say nothing. After we'd breathed at one another a few more times, he wheeled around and strode back toward the parking lot, signaling his partner to follow.

Lord help us, I thought, watching the two men walk away. I knew from experience that whenever the police became involved in investigating a crime in a hospital, even when they were on their best behavior, there were inevitable clashes between their priorities and those of the patients and doctors. It would be rough enough around here until the killer was caught without the cowboy antics of an overzealous detective.

* * *

Five minutes later I was in Medical Records, determined to follow through with my plan despite the nasty encounter. There I discovered that another of Riley's men had kept one of our clerks up all night gathering the very information I wanted to see. At the officer's request, the clerk had pulled the files—eighty-two in all, including eight that were marked DECEASED—of every patient with the name Pearson who had been to St. Paul's at least once since Saswald came on staff ten years ago. Except the clerk hadn't let the officer look at them. Instead she rightly insisted that he must have proper authorization first—"Medical confidentiality takes precedence even over a homicide investigation," she told him sternly, much to his annoyance—and had placed them in the hospital vault for safekeeping. Yet she didn't have a problem with showing them to me. As a member of staff and Chief of Emergency, I was used to getting any record I asked for. She only requested that I speak with the detective in charge first, for her own protection.

Riley readily agreed with what I had in mind. "Frankly, your going through those records right now would be a big help. We filed for a warrant to look at them, but with so many—and our sole criteria being that they belong to people named Pearson—the judge delayed a decision until he's sure he won't get patients' rights groups on his back. You know, cops leading a fishing expedition through medical records— that sort of thing. Not that I'm surprised. Hell, it's always tough bringing medical files into a police investigation."

As it should be, I thought. Every now and then Riley unwittingly reminded me that he and I sometimes worked opposite sides of the street. I thought now was a good time to remind him of that. "You understand, if I do find anything incriminating on a patient, medical confidentiality dictates that I won't be able to tell you about it either. You're still going to have to wait for official approval from your judge."

I heard him sigh.

"Come on, you know the rules," I continued. "What I can

tell you, however, are negative findings. If none of them ever saw Saswald as a patient, I don't feel bound to keep that from you. But should I simply report 'no comment,' then you better move your tail and go after whatever warrants you'll need to get a look at those records yourself." It was awfully close to crossing over the line of what was ethical, but given what might be at stake—stopping a killer, especially one who might have an agenda against hospital staff—I knew it would hurry things along, and I was comfortable doing that.

"Fair enough," he answered. "But since we're setting terms, I remind you of mine. While we're asking if Saswald knew anyone named Pearson, we still aren't making it public that the name was written in blood by his body. Make sure you continue to keep our little secret."

"Got you," I assured him.

Seated at a rickety table set up in the vault itself, it took me an hour and a half to look through all the files. They ranged from the very thin—documents of a onetime visit to Emergency or a clinic where the patient had contact with only one physician—to massive multivolumed charts, each section an inch thick, each showing a patient's many admissions where he or she was under the jurisdiction of numerous doctors. Riley's man, slouched in a chair he'd propped against the massive steel door, looked on from the entrance as I worked.

When I came across David's files, besides confirming what I already knew—that he'd never been treated by Saswald—I used the opportunity to note his physician of record at the time he'd been transferred to the clinic in Mexico. I saw from the progress notes that when he left ICU, he was declared physically stable by Dr. Arnold Pinter, but that he spent his final few days at St. Paul's under the care of psychiatrist Dr. Peter Forbes. I knew Forbes was in charge of psychiatric admissions through Emergency this month, and having signed off on the transfer to the Brama clinic, he was the one most likely to receive an update of his former patient's progress. I'd call him later in the day, I promised myself, and ask if he'd heard how David was doing.

At 6:55 I flipped through the last chart, tossed it on one of the piles I had spread out in front of me, and leaned back in my chair for a stretch. The good news was that Saswald had never maimed or killed anyone named Pearson in all his years at St. Paul's, because he'd never had anybody with that name as a patient. The bad news was that all the alternative scenarios would now have to be considered.

I started ticking some of them off on my fingers. First, an avenger named Pearson was righting wrongs that he believed had been done to a patient of another name. Second, that the basis of why Saswald was killed might lie in some personal relationship he'd had with a man or woman named Pearson who was completely outside medicine. In that case, nothing in any medical file would reveal their identity, nor would the endless interviews with St. Paul's personnel that lay ahead. The police would have to track down God knows how many leads outside the hospital, presuming the name Pearson even applied to someone from Buffalo.

As I mulled over the magnitude of what might be involved in finding the killer, an even worse-case secenario popped into my head. What if the speculation that the killer himself left the message was correct, as a false lead to throw the police off track? All he'd have to do was dip Saswald's hand into the blood and then use it to scrawl the name of someone else who could be blamed. Hell, he might even have made the name up, and the authorities would be pursuing a person who didn't exist.

I stopped counting the problems. They seemed so vast and insurmountable that I shuddered at the job that lay ahead for Riley. If his work was always this daunting, it was little wonder he looked so worn-out.

A glance at my watch told me it was nearly time to get downstairs and meet the residents for teaching rounds. I pushed away from the table, groaning with stiffness as I got up. The sound startled the officer awake—he'd nodded off about an hour after I started—and though he was still pretty groggy, he made sure I hadn't taken anything I shouldn't have, while I watched to see that he didn't sneak a peek at anything he wasn't supposed to. Together we then shoved the huge door shut, double-checking that the locks had clicked home after we'd each given the dual combination dials a twirl. Heading for the stairs, I called over my shoulder, "Tell Detective Riley to reach me in ER."

As I descended a question floated to mind the way a small mound in the middle of a flat expanse becomes significant, or a speck on a white sheet is at once noticeable. Could the coincidences that I'd been trying to dismiss last night—David Pearson, the Brama clinic, my question to Saswald, even the testiness of the anesthetist's response—be more important than I'd previously thought? Possibly. But what to do about it?

By the next landing I was wrestling that one around a bit. On one side was my personal reluctance to say anything and my obligation not to reveal a medical history. On the other was my dawning realization that even though David was in Mexico, he might have had some connection to Saswald that I had no idea about. But again I was faced with how to find a way to say anything about the coincidences without somehow treading on my obligations to David under a doctor-patient relationship.

Midway to the second floor I passed a window where beads of water were starting to run down the outer panes of glass, obscuring my view of the asphalt expanse below. All I could get a glimpse of were the blurred figures of people emerging from vehicles in the parking lot and racing to the nearest entrances. A line from an old song by The Doors shot through me like a chill. Except the words became "Killer in the rain."

I taught for an hour, then saw patients for an hour, but during that time the presence of the police became more and more visible. We'd learned from the overnight nurses that investigators had continued questioning people—unit by unit—until about four A.M. By now it was well-known that the police kept bringing up the name Pearson during their interviews, but so far, according to the gossip I heard, nobody knew why.

I assumed from the influx of blue uniforms that Riley had summoned them to help interrogate the much larger day shift. Soon they were leading our own nurses away by twos and threes, and the sergeant in charge told me orderlies and residents would follow. He made a compromise with the staff doctors, agreeing to take them only after their shifts ended. Although each interview barely took more than ten minutes, the ceaseless comings and goings of different staff groups to be questioned was both disruptive and a constant reminder of what had happened just outside our door.

It was all too distracting.

As a result, everyone seemed to be taking longer than usual to process patients through ER. Even with the lighter load resulting from Brama's boycott, the waiting room was soon so backed up that people were spilling over into the ambulance bay. Then we had a ruckus when an orderly accidentally switched two charts and a woman trying to sleep off the effects of an alcohol binge suddenly found herself being prepped and shaved for an appendectomy. While I was trying to calm down the indignant lady, her husband—a bearded giant of a man—kept screaming, "She got no pussy now!"

Next, shortly after nine-thirty, we had a major medication error.

"Hold it!" I heard Susanne shriek in the curtained cubicle next to where I was working. I stuck my head in to see her yank a still filled syringe from the rubber side portal of the patient's IV. From the startled expression on the face of a second nurse, who was still holding the intravenous tubing, I assumed she'd been about to inject whatever Susanne had snatched from her.

The patient, a very pale, frightened-looking man of middle years who had blood running out of his mouth, cried out, "What's the matter?"

"You're going to be fine, sir," Susanne assured him, patting his chest with her free hand while his eyes darted to each of us. She then picked up the empty vial of whatever medication was in the syringe and turned to her protégé. "Outside!" she ordered, stepping between two curtained panels. Her flushed colleague followed, and I heard Susanne start in even before the two woman were in private, which wasn't her usual way of reprimanding one of her staff. "That was potassium, not vitamin K—"

A door slammed, cutting off the rest of it, but I'd heard enough to make my blood run cold. Oh, God, no, I thought, continuing to try and calm the man in front of me. Already pretty certain that I knew what had happened, I grabbed his chart from the head of the bed and found the order sheet. Sure enough, he was on anticoagulants and had begun hemorrhaging from a stomach ulcer. Instead of preparing a bolus of vitamin K for injection into his veins—the treatment to normalize clotting in the presence of warfarin—the nurse had drawn up a syringeful of potassium, an agent also symbolized by K+, but one that would have stopped his heart cold. Since the needle was already in the patient's IV tubing, I assumed that Susanne had recognized the empty vial on the counter nearby and caught the mistake just as her colleague was about to push down on the plunger. "We'll be stopping that bleeding in minutes, sir," I managed to say, barely able to maintain my usual it-will-be-all-right tone, which I kept for situations hurtling out of control. But get it stopped we did, after vitamin K restored his coagulation and a nasogastric tube decompressed his stomach.

"I hope you catch this nut fast, but you also better rein in the cowboys on your team," I warned Riley after explaining to him what had happened to me in the parking lot. It was mid-morning and we were having coffee together in my office. "If you don't, everyone at St. Paul's will either be too jumpy to function or at war with your investigators. I just spent an hour getting my own staff settled down, but I tell you, it wouldn't take much to screw up their concentration again."

He was seated across my desk, sprawled in the only chair I had for visitors. His coat was more rumpled than usual, and the stubble on his face gave testimony to his having worked all night. He'd made no comment while listening to what had happened to me in the parking lot, but by the way his jaw muscles bulged with tension, I knew he'd soon be giving the detective in question an attitude transplant.

"As far as how my search through the charts went," I continued, "unofficially I can tell you that there's nothing overt in those records to connect any patients named Pearson to Saswald." I then told him some of the alternate scenarios that had occurred to me.

After hearing me out, he leaned forward with a bemused look on his face. "Believe it or not, Doc, I actually came up with most of those same possibilities all by myself." But the hint of a smile was short-lived as his face creased into a frown. "You're right about one thing. Tracking down that name is going to take an army of cops, wild goose chase or not." Discouragement seeped from his voice. "By the way, did you know Saswald's family?"

I shook my head. "I've said hello to his wife at a few social functions, but I have to admit I'm not even aware if he had any children." It was often that way with doctors working together in a large hospital. We were acquainted through our work and often had intimate knowledge of one another's professional skills, for better or worse, but with a few exceptions, the minute we walked outside these walls we were strangers.

"I spoke with her last night," Riley said, after downing the remains of his coffee with a single swallow. He sat motionless for a few seconds, staring into the bottom of his empty plastic cup. "I don't know how it is for you, but talking to a family member after a loved one's been killed . . . well, I find there's nothing harder."

I knew what he meant, but said nothing.

"A very stoic woman," he continued, looking up from the dregs of his drink. I was struck by the sadness of his gaze, and recognized in it a darkness that was common to the eyes of older cops. I'd watched the same expression become etched in the faces of veteran ER doctors who'd borne too many of the inevitable losses that went with practicing medicine on the near and already dead. Lately, especially since the time of Brama and an increasing number of cases like little Robert Delany's, I'd started seeing a similar look staring back at me from my mirror whenever I'd spent more time than I should in the pit. What we shared in our two very different jobs, I suspected, was the burden of memory—from a lifetime of witnessing how people lived and died in a major city.

"She insisted on speaking to me as soon as possible," he went on, "despite the shock of her husband's death. But she hasn't any idea who Pearson is either. We ran into the same blank wall with his staff members. We're still checking with that outfit named Brama that he was going to work for, but so far no one over there has been very helpful. Saswald's children, a son and daughter, both married, are flying in from out of state, but I doubt they'll add much or will know who Pearson is. Mrs. Saswald intimated that her late husband had let work get in the way of his having time for them when they were kids. Now that they're grown with children of their own, they've had little time for him." He stood up with a groan and arched his back, his large form making my cramped work space seem even smaller. "Man, I'm getting too long in the tooth for these all-nighters. It'll take a week's sleep to set me right."

I knew he was about ten years my junior, yet the heaviness

in the way he moved made him appear much older. As he reached across my desk to shake my hand before he left, I could sense the depth of his weariness and doubted it could ever be entirely erased by sleep.

I don't know if it was the sudden flash of empathy I had for the detective or the overwhelming odds he'd just painted against us ever finding the killer that spurred me to think of it, but all at once I saw a way to narrow down the investigation for Riley that wouldn't violate any medical confidences. Why not simply suggest he look into Saswald's connection with the clinic—because of the anesthetist's odd reaction to my question about it—and not mention David at all. The idea struck me as so straightforward that I blurted out, "Wait a minute. There was something strange that happened at the reception which maybe you should know about."

Already halfway out the door, he turned, his eyebrows curling into question marks.

"When you interview people at Brama, inquire about Saswald's connection to an addiction clinic they run in Mexico. When I asked him about it last night, namely if he'd worked there, he became quite defensive and we got into an argument."

He stood looking at me expectantly. After a few seconds he said, "And?"

"That's all. I think you should look into what was behind him getting so upset about that clinic."

His expression grew even more curious. "What makes you think that might have anything to do with his being killed?"

"No specific reason, other than it seemed strange—such a hostile response to an innocent question."

"What exactly was your 'innocent question' about this clinic?"

"Nothing more than asking had he come across it in his work? Did he know anything about it? That kind of thing."

"And why did you want to know?"

Whoops! "Uh, well, I had heard about the place and wanted to know what it was like—"

"Why?"

I was beginning to feel uncomfortable. "Look, that's not the point. It's the man's reaction—"

"Look, Doc. I know you're trying to be helpful, but the fact that you asked the deceased about some addiction clinic and he got pissed off at you for it doesn't exactly sound relevant to the man's murder."

I felt my stomach start to tighten. "Well, maybe you're right. But I thought since you asked me about noticing anything odd—"

"Doc, you're not a good liar, and I've been around you enough to know you don't make suggestions that aren't well thought-out. There's got to have been some other reason that made you think Saswald's reaction to your question about a clinic was worth mentioning in the first place."

"Why, that's not so—"

"Level with me," he ordered, sounding almost gentle while the lines in his forehead deepened. "Why won't you tell me why you asked Saswald about that clinic?"

"I swear, there's nothing I'm keeping from you—"

"Cut it out!" he barked. His sudden change of tone made me jump.

All at once I felt a nearly irresistible urge to come clean as he stared at me, his brow gathered further into a frown. Shit! I thought. I should have just kept my mouth shut. Well, there was nothing to do now but claim doctor-patient confidentiality, but I felt as uneasy as if I were about to plead the Fifth. "I'm sorry, Detective. I can't tell you why I asked about that clinic except to say the reason involved a patient of mine—"

"Patient? Wait a minute." He came a step closer, the fatigue in his eyes instantly vanished. "Is this the 'no comment' we agreed upon?" His gaze now bore into me with the glare of floodlights.

"Not exactly," I cautioned, holding up my hand—palm

out—to slow him down. I was determined to keep control of this conversation and not inadvertently let something I shouldn't say slip out.

But Riley wasn't about to be slowed. "Then what is it *exactly*, Doc? If I can't see what's so important about you and Saswald having a quarrel over a clinic, what am I missing here? Or as I put it before, what are you holding back that made you think the incident was important?"

I started to squirm under his thousand-watt gaze. This wasn't at all what I'd intended. "As I told you," I countered, sounding unbelievably stiff, "I can't say anything more because my question about the clinic concerned a patient. But the patient had nothing to do with him getting upset. I never mentioned the patient. It was the clinic—"

"Shit! That patient of yours wouldn't be among the charts you just checked, would it?"

I felt myself flush. Desperate now to enforce the rules of medical privacy, I declared, "Detective Riley, I cannot reveal—"

"A patient of yours, not Saswald's, named Pearson? Now Saswald having a quarrel about someone called Pearson just before he died, that's pretty interesting."

I jumped to my feet. "Damn it, man, will you listen?" I demanded, jabbing at him with my finger. "I didn't say we had a quarrel over a patient named Pearson. I never told him the patient's name, period. That's my point. His hostility arose when I questioned him about the clinic. It occurred without him knowing I even had a patient connected to the place, so focus on *it*!" My voice had risen to the point of yelling. "Find out what the hell made him defensive about the facility!"

But Riley had become unstoppable. "Oh no, Doc, it's the name Pearson that's got to be the link here, and now I think I can see what you've been trying to tell me."

"But—"

"You inquired about the clinic on behalf of a patient named Pearson, didn't you, Doc? And Saswald reacted angrily to those questions. Then you saw the last name of that patient scrawled by Saswald's body. Did I put it together correctly?"

"Damn it, Riley, get it through your head. I didn't say Pearson was my patient's name—"

"Hey, it's okay, Doc," Riley interrupted, his voice chillingly quiet all of a sudden. "You don't *have* to say anything more. I know what to do now, and thanks."

Before I could sputter out more protests, he was gone.

I sat there a long time, feeling disgusted with myself. Why hadn't I just kept my mouth shut? Then if the police had eventually gone through David's file, the fact that he was at the Brama clinic wouldn't have meant anything to them. They probably would simply have thought, as I initially had, that since he was in Mexico at the time, it was unlikely he'd had anything to do with the murder.

But now? I didn't even want to think about what I might have set in motion. "Shit!" I muttered, burying my head in my hands. "Shit! Shit! Shit!"

Thirty minutes later, having been unable to think of anything else but David and what I'd probably done to him, I left my office, knowing I had to get a warning to the man.

After all, Riley would now move mountains to get into the files upstairs, and single out David in no time, what with my having primed him to consider that the clinic might be connected to the killing. Now, David having been a patient there would not provide him with an alibi, but instead would deem him in the eyes of the police as a man to be viewed with suspicion. Questions would be raised. Was David connected to Saswald? Had he any reason to want Saswald dead? Could he have organized the slaying? I shuddered and wondered how the police coming to him so early in the investigation, especially since they had nothing else to go on, might change their treatment of him or their diligence in pursuing other leads. Not that I thought they'd deliberately railroad David into anything. But after seeing how Riley had seized on the information I'd given him, it was pretty clear he'd make the most of it, and that meant trying to establish a link between David and the murder. The worst of it was, I could have predicted exactly all this if I'd only thought things through before making my brilliant disclosure.

Dr. Peter Forbes, the psychiatrist who'd taken care of him, was referring to a sheaf of papers while speaking into a Dictaphone when I knocked on his open door. "Why, Earl, this is a surprise," he declared, looking up from his work. "Come in. You don't visit this neck of the woods very often." He was a middle-sized man of middle age, balding, round-bellied, and in need of an orthodontist, but he dressed in suits that I only ever saw in fashion magazines. It was hard to believe, but the rumor around the hospital was that the ladies found him sexy. As for me, I always found it strange that a man specializing in addiction looked like a mini version of Bacchus.

"Thanks, Peter. I'm not disturbing you, am I?" Forty-five minutes had lapsed since Riley had raced off, probably already revving up the process that would eventually put David in his sights. I had no idea how long that would take—hours, days, more perhaps—but I had to hurry.

"Of course not. Here, have a seat." He gestured across his desk to a pair of overstuffed sofa chairs upholstered with maroon-colored silk and embroidered in gold braid.

A doctor's office, especially one provided by the hospital in which he or she works, can reveal a lot about the person and their status in the institution. Forbes's was no exception. His domain was twice the size of mine, and his furniture, made of laminated rosewood, was clearly superior to the metal issue I'd been provided with. His carpet was soft blue in color and, though half an inch shorter than the stuff in our CEO's suite, was a far cry above the gray linoleum that paved my work space. From what I'd learned after twenty-two years of observing such matters, I'd rank Forbes's place as being of middle importance—not a figure of national or world-academic stature, but someone who was nevertheless of use to the hospital—at least in the minds of whoever decreed these things at St. Paul's. The reasons for the psychiatrist's claim to this modest title—several hundred articles he'd written over the years—were on display in the bookcase lining the wall behind him. He'd arranged them in rows with the covers facing out so they'd all be in full view of anyone seated in his visitors' chairs, one of which I'd just settled into. The collage effect was overwhelming, but none of the journals in which they appeared were mainstream publications. Rather, they bore such titles as *Pharmacology Weekly* or *Psychotropic Drug Bulletin* and were the literature of what I called "me too" research—attempts of pharmaceutical companies to make small changes to a competitor's product in order to market it themselves.

When he saw me regarding these stacks that contained his life's work, he tapped the notes in front of him on his desk. "Number ten in twelve months." He beamed, laying aside the microphone into which he'd been dictating his latest epistle. "You know, I could throw some contracts toward your department. Drug reps are drooling to claim efficacy for a medication specifically tried in ER these days—TV has made your turf very sexy—and the extra money could keep you in defibrillators for a good while."

Even new medication that's only intended to increase market share needs clinical trials, and that's what he was suggesting I participate in. Through them, Forbes and his kind would sometimes catch unexpected side effects in a redesigned chemical that would have cost the company involved a bundle in lawsuits. The drug industry showed its appreciation for these "saves" by lavishing grants on the participating hospital, to cover such expenses as Forbes's office and the chair I was in. Up until a few years ago the man also had profited handily in a personal way—what with expensive junkets and lavish accommodations provided to him and his family for attending so-called scientific meetings—but then the Food and Drug Administration had regulated against such perks.

"I'm afraid my plate's pretty full as it is," I politely declined, not wanting to insult him with what I really thought of his "studies." After a few more pleasantries, I went after what I needed to know. "I wondered if you'd heard any feedback about how our patient in Mexico was doing?" I hoped I sounded appropriately offhanded.

Forbes immediately frowned. "You mean David Pearson? To tell you the truth, I haven't heard anything at all." He leaned forward, the lines of his face pushing into a scowl. "He's not the Pearson the police are asking about, is he?"

I made my face into what I hoped he'd interpret as astonishment. "The police aren't asking about David. Why would they? He's in Mexico." But they soon could be, I thought.

Forbes said nothing, his expression neither skeptical nor believing. "Yeah, you're right," he finally replied. "It must be another Pearson."

"Is there anyone in particular at the clinic who could tell me—"

"I understand you found Saswald," he interrupted, "after he was . . . well, you know."

"No, I was called to the scene with the resus team, but obviously it was too late. Now about David—"

"Is it true what I heard, that he'd nearly been decapitated?"

His persistence about the murder started to annoy me. I'd come to learn about David, hoping to hear that he was doing fabulously. I had the notion that if he was in any shape to handle the news, I'd phone him immediately, at the clinic, and tell him about what was coming his way. I owed him that, and more. Even if he had nothing to do with any of this, which was likely, Riley homing in on him would still be an ordeal. I figured the least I could do, having launched the detective at him, would be to give David time to prepare for the onslaught. But first I needed to find out the man's state of mind.

If he was pretty shaky psychologically, I'd have to think of another way to protect him, such as going down there if I had to. "Look, Peter, the police told me not to discuss what I saw. Now can you please tell me when you expect to know something about David?" I hadn't intended to speak as sharply as I had, but I wanted him off the topic of Saswald.

For a second I thought I saw the slightest of frowns emboss Forbes's brow, but I couldn't be sure—ever since I'd known him, he'd been a hard read. Finally he shrugged and answered, "Matter of fact, I wouldn't expect to hear anything about how David's doing. That clinic he went to is involved with an experimental protocol, and they aren't going to be too free with information about what they're doing until they actually publish their results. I must say," he added, "Pearson's prognosis isn't good, not at this stage. You no doubt are aware of how addiction goes through a succession of plateaus. . . ."

Oh, Christ, I thought, the last thing I wanted was to sit through one of his usual long-winded dissertations, even if it was a description of the latest line on alcoholism. Still, I figured that I better feign interest in the old goat, in case I needed his help later. It sounded as if the clinic was extraordinarily secretive, and as the referring doctor, he might be the only one who could convince the place to make an exception and release a report on David's progress.

". . . been no advance in treatment of alcoholic addiction in over thirty years . . ."

As he droned on I found myself musing about whether David had sat in this chair during therapeutic sessions, and what he'd thought of Forbes as his treating physician. I'd seen enough of the psychiatrist's clinical work in ER over the years to consider it reasonably competent. The fact that he was so unassuming physically, as long as he had a white coat over his four-thousand-dollar suits, made him nonthreatening to his patients, and he had the least judgmental manner of anyone I'd ever met.

". . . still just a forty percent chance of staying dry . . ."

As a result he could make people feel completely comfortable about who they were and what they'd done, sometimes even when they should have been damned upset with themselves. In fact, outside his performance in ER, I was always uncertain if in the long run Forbes might be failing to adequately motivate his patients to change for the better, simply teaching them to be comfortable with their same screwed-up selves instead.

". . . there may hopefully be better therapeutic options in the future. So is there anything else that brings you to my den?" Peter asked, whisking me back to the present.

The end of his soliloquy caught me by surprise. "Have you heard anything in general about this clinic?" I asked, scrambling to put together an intelligent question. "I must say, I found it odd, an HMO like Brama sending a patient to a special program, let alone all the way to Mexico."

"Ah, yes, I heard about your feud with Brama," he commented, without revealing the slightest hint of how he felt about it, for or against. "As I said before, I've been told nothing."

"Come on, Peter, even if they are doing a confidential study, doctors blab about their work to other doctors. What's the gossip about the place? Have you sent any other patients there?"

He stared at me a few seconds, again inscrutable, and I had no inkling whether he minded me pressing him. He finally replied, "I've only had one other patient go there, and he did very well—is still dry as far as I know. Now if you'll excuse me—"

"But what's the buzz on the place, from your colleagues in other hospitals around here, or in other cities? You must have had some feedback—"

"Yes, I've heard favorable comments from a few other psychiatrists around town who've sent patients there," he cut in, his tone still completely matter-of-fact. "Now you really must excuse—"

"You've no idea what their treatment program is? Did your other patient mention at least if they were using new drugs as part of their—"

"I repeat, I've no idea, and to find out you'll have to wait like the rest of us until Brama publishes what they're doing." As he talked he reached over to retrieve the microphone on his dictating machine and made a show of rustling his notes in front of him. "Sorry I couldn't help you more," he said, and smiled.

"Do you have their phone number?"

"No, I don't. Perhaps you could obtain it from the Brama offices here in town."

Yeah, sure. I was such a popular guy there right now.

Funny, I thought, once I'd thanked him for his time and was out in the hallway walking away from his office. A raft of questions like the ones I'd just asked would normally have been enough to set the usually loquacious Forbes spouting off for about an hour. Yet now, despite the man's impeccably even-handed manner, I was left with the distinct impression that he was no more interested in talking about the clinic than I'd been in dwelling on Saswald's murder. In fact, I felt as if the psychiatrist had just given me the bum's rush.

Chapter 6

It was just before seven the next morning and I was stuck in traffic under a knot of overpasses when I heard from Riley again.

"Morning, Doc. Guess what?" His excitement was audible even over the raspy connection of my cellular.

I braced myself, thinking he'd already found out about David.

"I think you were right about there being something fishy with Saswald's connection to that Brama addiction clinic. I went over to their offices late yesterday and had a talk with the president of the company himself."

"The president of Brama? You mean the local CEO, don't you?"

"Nope, I mean the president, a Mr. William Baines, all the way from their head office in San Francisco. He arrived from there yesterday morning for what he claimed was a pre-planned visit."

"Really?"

"Yeah, really. Of course, he said he was shocked to learn of Dr. Saswald's death when he arrived."

I was rapidly becoming intrigued. "You sound as if you don't believe him."

"You ought to meet the man. He's a real power dresser—not the kind to get his suit all wrinkled by a night in an airplane seat, albeit a first-class one, unless he really had to."

"You think he flew out here because of Saswald's murder?"

"If he didn't, it's another coincidence, isn't it, on top of the ones you told me about."

I felt a stab of apprehension. "Look, I won't talk about that anymore—"

"Doc, listen, there's more. On the surface everything at Brama appeared as smooth as the sides of that big glass building they're in, but a lot of little things bothered me."

"Such as?"

"For starters, this guy Baines insisted he take my interview himself. Up until then my officers had been dealing with a personnel manager and a few other middle people who'd handled Saswald's previous freelance work with the place. The highest they got was to the medical director who'd recently hired Saswald full-time. Now this Baines guy arrives off the red-eye, obviously tired, and insists on dealing with me personally. Then there's another thing I found strange . . ."

Static took away his voice as I reached the ramp leading up to the expressway overhead. Within seconds he faded back in.

". . . asked if anyone named Pearson had anything to do with Saswald at Brama. At that point Baines called in the CEO, and the two men made a show of scratching their heads and promising to have secretaries check their personnel records for anyone of that name and that they'd get back to me. Now, other officers had already brought up the name during earlier interviews, so I'm sure these two were prepared . . ."

Creeping through the shadow of yet another overpass treated my ear to more fuzz.

". . . questions about the addiction clinic and Saswald put a little wariness in their eyes, but Baines claimed an anesthetist would never be required at a research facility for alcoholism."

"That's essentially what Saswald told me, and frankly, it's a reasonable statement."

"Yeah, but then they wanted to know why I was asking about the addiction clinic. I didn't mention your name— didn't have to; I'd already checked and found a few others who'd been at the reception and overheard your argument with him. So I simply stated we had witnesses who'd seen Saswald get pretty exercised at being asked about the place. Baines and his CEO seemed to have a little trouble digesting that surprise—they both looked as if they'd just seen a turd on the rug—and when I demanded, 'Do you have any idea why he'd be upset like that?' they of course protested that they didn't. But I sensed that I'd really put them off balance. And when I asked if they knew of a patient named Pearson having anything to do with Saswald's freelance work at any of their other clinics, Baines, instantly becoming ice, told me very politely that any and all information involving patients was confidential. His CEO clammed up as well."

As he should have, I thought, still furious at my own laxity yesterday. "So what's your problem with that?" I snapped, but immediately regretted sounding so testy. I took a swallow and attempted a more civil tone. "In that regard, they acted appropriately."

Riley continued. "The CEO's not as tough as his boss. By now that man's smile was as frozen as a TV dinner, his eyes shifting anywhere but toward mine, and his leg dancing a nervous little jig. So I put my best question of all to him—if he knew specifically of an alcoholic patient at St. Paul's named Pearson who'd had something to do with the addiction clinic in Mexico."

Shit! "Goddamn it, Riley. You may have thought you were clever yesterday, but going public with what you inferred out of that inexcusable session we had—"

"They hit the roof too, Doc. Demanded to know who I'd been talking to at St. Paul's, who'd been giving out confidential information, who at Brama had breached security—the whole works. Then I set them straight." His voice was suddenly hard. "I informed them that nobody had told me anything inappropriately. I advised them that we had a lead from the crime scene suggesting someone named Pearson may be connected to the murder, and that in every phase of this investigation we would be looking for a connection between Dr. Saswald, his places of work—both at St. Paul's and Brama—and someone—staff, patient, or private individual—named Pearson. So get used to it."

In the silence of another truck cutting us off, I felt he was trying to set me straight as well.

"They also mentioned that I should take a closer look at you," I heard him saying when the static cleared.

"Pardon?"

"Just as I was about to leave, the two of them put on another dog and pony show, this time wringing their hands and professing their profound reluctance to bring it up, but they wanted me to know that there was an individual at St. Paul's who was extremely hostile to their company."

"What?"

"I frankly think they'd rehearsed how they would make the revelation. It was pretty slick. They didn't do anything as outlandish as suggest you were the killer. They simply intimated that since I obviously intended to leave no stone unturned, and since Saswald was connected to Brama, I should be aware of someone who had an axe to grind, blah blah blah—that kind of thing."

"But why do that? To what purpose?"

The silence on the line made me think I'd lost contact again, but a few seconds later I heard him sigh, loudly and clearly. "Why?" he repeated, after a few more seconds. "Probably because you're making them nervous about something and they want to discredit you. Didn't I read a few weeks back that you accused them of committing no-fault murder?"

"Saswald's death has nothing to do with that."

"Well, maybe they see a murder investigation as an opportunity to throw a little mud your way and undercut your effectiveness on other fronts. I have to tell you, your comments back then hit a real sympathetic nerve with everyone I know. Brama's got to be a bit afraid of you . . ."

At that point the static welled up and persisted for half a minute. When it subsided, the line was dead.

I finally reached the expressway and sped toward downtown Buffalo. In my rearview mirror I could see the sun peeking over a line of clouds, and in front of me the entire city became bathed in light for the first time that week.

Mulling over Riley's conversation, I was struck by what he hadn't mentioned. I didn't know if it was because he hadn't yet gotten his warrants, or if he had and was keeping the result from me, but he hadn't breathed a word about looking through the eighty-two charts in the hospital vault and finding David's.

The uncertainty was doubly frustrating because at the moment I had no idea how I was going to get a warning to David. After leaving Forbes's office yesterday, I'd actually tried to inveigle the clinic's number from Brama—several times.

"That's unlisted," I'd been told by a receptionist on my first try.

"Could I have your name, please?" another one had asked when I called back later with the same question. "I'm sorry, but you're not on our list of physicians with access to that information."

I'd then even called their headquarters in San Francisco, and got the same routine for my trouble. My last resort—an attempt in my high school Spanish to reach the place through information in Tijuana—got me connected to a liquor store.

Maybe his family had the clinic's number, I thought, despite the ban on incoming calls. But if I came out of the blue at them, saying that I had to contact David all of a sudden, I might get them worried and precipitate questions that I couldn't answer.

Finally breaking free of traffic, I was able to get up enough speed to do the expressway justice and shot along a stretch of road bounded on both sides by the veterans' cemetery. Farther to the left was the crumbling East Side, source of most penetrating injuries and drug overdoses at St. Paul's. Away off to the right were the upscale neighborhoods where the diseases of affluence abounded—heart attacks, diabetes, colon cancer—but poverty and poor food produced their share of these disorders on the opposite side of town as well. Other maladies were nondiscriminatory—lung cancer, AIDS, alcoholism—and frequented all parts of the urban landscape that sprawled in every direction as I drove into its center.

By the time I reached the exit ramp for St. Paul's, I still had no idea how to reach David, and my frustration was mounting. "Get used to it," I muttered, taking the turn far faster than I should have.

Her name was Maggie, and she'd arrived by ambulance late that afternoon. I could have told her age by counting her wrinkles, ripples of them forming pouches under her eyes extending into her cheeks. Larger folds of skin dangled from under her chin, and great slabs of veined flesh drooped down from her belly. She was having trouble breathing as she leaned forward in the bed so I could listen to her lungs. They mewed like a basket of kittens each time she exhaled, and I thought I also heard the extra sound a failing heart makes as it gallops to try and keep up with its workload. I gave her oxygen and checked her medications—a mixture of pills, pumps, and patches. Some were meant to open her stiffening lungs, others to drive her withered heart to provide even more heroics, such as sustaining the effort it took for her to walk across the room. But all were appropriate, and there wasn't anything I could add to what was already prescribed.

"Can . . . you fix me up, Doc . . . so I can go home." Her rapid breathing broke up her speech, and the sides of her cheeks flapped with the laborious effort of moving air in and out.

"Oh, I think we can make you comfortable," I dissembled, then gave orders to Susanne to give her pretty well the same drugs that she was already on, but by mask and through IVs. They'd be delivered at a slightly higher dose, which would help her for now, as long as she stayed quiet. But as soon as she tried to carry out the activities of daily living again, she'd once more be unable to breathe. She needed care in a nursing home.

"It's home . . . I want. You've got to . . . get me home."

"But you live alone, Maggie," I countered, reading the nurse's admission note.

She gave a toothless grin. "That's 'cause . . . I can't . . . get a nice . . . young man. . . . Wanna . . . apply?"

"Sorry, I'm married."

"Nice ones . . . always are."

"Do you have any family?"

"Not here . . . Son's in California . . . out of work."

"Maybe you shouldn't live alone anymore," I suggested gently.

"Rather die . . . than go . . . in a nursing home. House is . . . all . . . I got."

"But you'd be better off—"

"I've seen . . . the dumps I . . . would be able . . . to afford. . . . Rather die."

Leave it for now, I decided. "Well, you'll have to stay with us for a little while anyway, to get you back in shape."

"Don't . . . want . . . that."

"But—"

"My neighbor . . . two houses away . . . had to pay . . . her own hospital bill. . . . Thirty thousand . . . Lost her house."

"But you've got insurance."

"They don't . . . always pay."

I took her papers and faxed in the request for an admission. Fifteen minutes later I had a response. Provisional approval, subject to final authorization.

"Not . . . good enough . . . Doc," said my wary octogenarian.

I got their triage officer on the phone. "What will you look at to approve final authorization?"

"A documented acute deterioration," he said matter-of-factly. "Significant changes in blood gases, pulmonary function tests, and her echocardiogram results since last admission." It sounded like he was reading from a list.

I already knew that her readings weren't radically different. "She's so fragile, even minor changes could tip her into severe respiratory and cardiac failure," I protested, trying to introduce at least a modicum of medical reality into the conversation. But with these nondoctors who prattled out their rulings, the effort was invariably futile and always drove me to distraction.

"I remind you, Doctor," he said preachily, "that you have an obligation to do what is right medically. Admit her if you feel it's justified. I'm simply stating what our company will cover, and what it will not."

"But she lives alone. She'll probably relapse if she returns there."

"Well, according to our records, she's refused to enter a suitable geriatric facility. It would seem that's the problem, and as you know, we don't authorize social admissions."

I felt my teeth start to clench. "And what *do* you provide? For starters, could we get her into your extended care program?"

"Admission to an extended care facility is only for approved patients following their discharge from an acute care hospital," he intoned, "and meant solely for those who will ultimately be capable of living on their own."

"Any home care?"

"Sure, but again, exclusively to help resolve acute medical problems following an approved admission."

I knew all this. Maybe it once even made sense, when admitting patients in the first place wasn't such an ordeal. "Tell me something: Are all these tough guidelines for admission that you're imposing here something adopted recently?"

The line was silent a few seconds. "I have nothing to say about that," he then told me, his voice suddenly cold.

When I got off the phone, I explained, "We'll get you breathing better in ER, maybe even keep you overnight, Maggie." What I'd do with her after that I had no idea.

She grinned at me despite her distress. "Told you . . . they wouldn't . . . pay," she wheezed.

Worse, the company wasn't Brama, but a competing outfit that hadn't usually given me this much difficulty. I was left with the suspicion that they'd decided to see how much of the Brama-type tactics they could get away with.

A few hours later I'd finished my shift and was headed toward my office. It was located in a back corridor, ten seconds from ER if I ran, but far enough away in people's minds that unless there was a major crisis, they'd learned to leave me alone when I retreated there to do paperwork.

Since there was no one around in this part of the hospital at night, the cleaning staff practiced a strict lights-out policy—part of our new austerity measures—and the only illumination came from the red exit signs over the doors. But the glow was more than sufficient for me to find my way since I knew the area like the back of my hand, and I never bothered switching on the overhead lights for the thirty-foot walk to my door.

I was fitting my key into the lock when I heard a man's voice speak my name from the near blackness at the end of the corridor. "Dr. Garnet?"

I whirled and saw his shape rise up from a bench where he'd been sitting in the shadows. But the pleasant tone of his voice left me more startled than afraid. "Yes?" I said, watching him come toward me. "What do you want?"

He emerged from the dark into an area of ambient red under one of the exit signs, and at once I could see he was a patient, dressed in our standard-issue white robe over a green "Johnny-shirt." "You shouldn't be here," I told him sternly, assuming he'd come from ER.

"It's okay, Doctor. I'm going home in a few days and I'm allowed out of my room." He pulled his left hand out of his robe pocket and held it out to me. The sleeve rose above his wrist, and I could see the identification bracelet. He was from one of the floors upstairs.

"Well, you still shouldn't be in this area," I admonished, less harshly. I figured he must have wandered through Emergency, and no one had noticed him slip in here. "Now if you'll simply go back out that door—"

"But Doctor, I've been sitting here an hour to see you. You looked so busy out there, I decided to wait until you were finished rather than disturb you. This will just take a moment."

Even in the thin light I could see enough of his features to think he looked vaguely familiar. He was young—late twenties or early thirties—had close-cropped dark hair, a slightly pudgy face, and an intense wide-eyed look that made him seem almost childlike despite his large shoulders and stocky build. I must have taken care of him at one time, I thought, presuming he'd probably been admitted by my department. Despite his being where he shouldn't, I decided to be gracious. I figured he was there either to complain about how we'd treated him or to thank us for it, and whichever it was, giving him a stiff reprimand wouldn't help our public relations any. I finished unlocking my door, clicked the lights on inside, and turned to invite him into my office, intending to hear him out in as short a time as possible.

He removed his right hand from the robe pocket, his fist wrapped around something as he held it out to me. At first I thought it was a pen—a few inches long and dark—until its end caught the light streaming out from behind me. Even as the steel flashed in front of my eyes I couldn't believe what I was looking at. He had a scalpel.

"Oh, my God!" I heard myself say, backing away from him. It took me a heartbeat before I thought of slamming the door between us and locking myself in, but when I tried, he'd already entered the room enough to block the move with his body.

"Help!" I screamed, continuing to back away. "Help me!

Susanne! Someone! Help!" He stepped the rest of the way in and closed the door behind him, cutting off any chance I'd be heard as far away as our busy and noisy ER.

Reflexively I held up my hands, palms out in front of me. Even as I did so I knew it was a futile gesture, the times I'd seen defensive knife wounds on the hands of stabbing victims racing unbidden to mind. And what he was holding could shred flesh better than any knife. "Who are you?" I demanded, backing up the few feet that remained before I pressed against the front of my desk. My voice had easily betrayed my rising panic.

He said nothing, but stayed where he was, moving his free hand behind him and snapping the lock shut. He gazed steadily at me with his wide innocent stare. "I am the power; you are the Satan!" he suddenly roared.

I tried to steady myself while the rules I'd used in twenty years of encountering violent patients flipped wildly through my thoughts. *Assert control, be firm, but don't challenge.* "Tell me why you're doing this." To my own ear I sounded as if I was begging.

He remained at the door, the scalpel held out toward me. Was he about to charge, slashing as he came? I slowly flexed my legs, preparing to spring backward and roll across the top of my desk. If I got it between us, hopefully I'd have the nick of time I needed to dodge his first rush at me. But what then?

He stood motionless, simply continuing to look at me. I kept watching the scalpel blade and his expression, trying to anticipate his next move. Managing violent psychotics over the years had taught me another rule, one that wasn't in any of the textbooks: watch their eyes. Some had pupils that were wide, black, and alight with rage or terror—the result of massive adrenaline overload unique to some forms of psychoses. They were often the ones possessed by superhuman strength; only a dozen orderlies plus a syringeful of haloperidol could fell them. But the man in front of me had flat staring eyes, as lifeless as a shark's and as empty as the voids of space. His was probably a more methodical madness, the kind that could make him shove an unsuspecting stranger off a subway platform in front of an oncoming train, then let him calmly explain that voices told him to do it.

"I am the power; you are the Satan!" he repeated loudly, taking a step toward me.

I rolled back over my desktop, came up on my feet and grabbed for my phone. I had the receiver in my left hand and was reaching with my right to punch *O* when he sliced the back of my index finger with a swing of his scalpel.

"You fuck!" I screamed, more with horror than pain. I jerked away from him, dropping the phone and quickly squeezing the cut digit tightly in my good hand. Blood welled out between the encircling fingers and ran down both my forearms. But my attention was on him as he stepped around behind the desk to where I was standing and raised his scalpel for another swipe. This time he was holding it at the level of my eyes, his expression all the while remaining as indifferent as if he were about to offer me a haircut.

He had to be schizophrenic, I thought, desperately scrambling for some idea of how I could stop him. Most likely I'd treated him previously for relapses in ER. And his madness involved some sort of religious delusion.

He started to arc the scalpel toward my face. I ducked and rolled to my right. His arm swung over me, but when I came up on my knees, I saw him rotate his wrist and bring the blade at my head with a backhand stroke. I was now partly around one end of the desk, crouched between him and the door. All I could do was scurry away from him in a reverse crab walk while he kept up his advance, continuing to make downward swipes back and forth at my face and trunk, turning his scalpel into a pendulum.

"Get away! Get back!" I bellowed.

The tip sliced through the left lapel of my lab coat, missing my underlying skin. But coming back, he got me lower down on the same side, at my abdomen. I didn't feel any pain and thought he'd missed me again when a thin red line half a foot long appeared through the rip on the white cloth, then started to widen. "Christ!" I screamed, frantically trying to scuttle backward even faster, reflexively slapping my good hand over the spreading blood while teetering on my right.

My thoughts raced. I knew once I reached the door he'd be all over me and I'd be dead. I'd never have time to get to my feet, turn the lock, and escape. I had to try something, anything that would break off his steady attempt to further slash me to ribbons. The red stain was growing beneath my fingers.

I thudded into wood at my back. Out of chances, I grabbed a deep breath and opted for something that was very definitely against the rules of psychiatry. "I am of the son of God, and the power over your voices is mine!" I roared, making the sign of the cross at him. If I couldn't stop this madman, perhaps I could turn his demons against him. "They are the Satan!"

He didn't even flinch as he stepped up to straddle my legs and raised the scalpel over his head.

Oh, Christ! I thought, and yelled even louder. "Stop! You know I command the voices. You know I take them away. You know I've done it before! You're here now so I can take them away again. Obey me, in the name of God!"

He simply looked down at me.

"The voices of Satan are telling you to kill me, because they know I can destroy them with the medicine I give you. You must fight their evil with me. It's my voice which must command you now!"

For an instant he seemed to waver. His expression didn't change—it remained indifferent as ever—but he stood with his head cocked to one side, his weapon in the air, as if he was listening for something. His voices? Were they going to counter my bid for control of his mind?

I lay at his feet, not daring to move, not even to breathe. Seconds went by—I knew because I could feel my own heartbeat keeping time. Despite pressure from my hand, the blood kept seeping through my lab coat until the line was wider than my outstretched palm. I could also feel it trickling around my sides and into the small of my back. I still didn't notice any pain. All I focused on was the tip of the scalpel poised above me, watching for the slightest hint that it was starting down.

He began to mumble.

At first I couldn't make it out. The sounds weren't words, but gibberish, accompanied by nodding and pauses. He was talking to his demons. God forbid they were repeating my death sentence.

Then, without warning, he said, "Dr. Garnet, the voices you control didn't tell me to do this. That was a new voice. It's not here now, so you can't control it." The quietness of his speech made it seem to come from a great distance, as if his own voice was disembodied from him. It gave me the chills, but also put me on my guard. As he spoke I managed to slowly bend my right knee, and I was ready for him when he swung the scalpel at my face. I ducked my head to one side and delivered a vicious kick deep into his groin.

He let out a screech and, already leaning forward to reach me with the scalpel, doubled up enough that the force of the blow propelled him headfirst into the door behind me. His aborted swing buried the blade harmlessly into the wood beside my left ear, where it made a loud crunch.

He stayed arched over, groaning and gasping for breath. Before he could recover, I flexed both my legs, planted the soles of my shoes against his stomach, and heaved him off me as hard as I could. He staggered backward the length of my office and crashed into my desk, where he slumped down to join me on the floor.

I was first to my feet, blood running down my legs despite the pressure I was applying to where he'd cut me. Gingerly I moved my left hand and lifted the blood-soaked flap of my lab coat. Then, using the third finger and thumb of my right hand, I managed to get enough buttons undone on my shirt to grab a peek at the damage. Despite its length and the mess, I could see the laceration was only partially through the thickness of the skin. Reassured that I wasn't about to have my intestines fall into my hands, I reapplied pressure on my side and, despite a palm slippery from the previous cut to my index finger, managed to get the door open. Stumbling into the hallway, I glanced back to see if he was coming after me, but he was still doubled over on the floor and trying to recover his breath. Nevertheless, there appeared a spark in his eyes as he glared up at me, and they began to glow with a dark fury that hadn't been there before. It was time for a dozen orderlies and a syringe. I reached back around the door, retrieved the scalpel with a yank, then raced toward emergency.

Chapter 7

My arrival produced bedlam. Patients and visitors screamed at the sight of me dripping blood and running through the corridors while carrying the scalpel. Nurses and residents ran up and offered their help.

"My God!"

"What happened?"

"Get him a stretcher and lie him down."

A circle of helping hands tried hustling me toward one of the treatment rooms.

I ignored them all. "Every orderly in the place, get to my office. There's a violent psych patient there," I bellowed. "And I want a dozen more called on the P.A." Three men in white immediately spun around and dashed in the direction from where I'd come. "Be careful," I called after them. "Just keep him cornered until your reinforcements arrive." I eyed Susanne running to me, alarm all over her face. "We need enough haloperidol to stop a horse," I told her. "Get ten milligrams in a syringe, and as soon as someone has a clear shot, give him the works. Plus you'll need posy belts and leather ankle restraints on this one as well—"

"Dr. Garnet! We know what to do, now lie the hell down!" she barked at me, taking me by the elbow and propelling me to the nearest stretcher. More than a few eyebrows headed for the ceiling, including my own, at her unprecedented sharp tone with me.

"Yes ma'am!" I said, submitting to her authority.

She then gave a flurry of her own orders, sending anyone who was still standing around scrambling to do their tasks, and a whole bunch of things began happening at once. The call for help went out over the P.A. Seconds later more orderlies flew through the corridor on the way to my office. Two nurses, one carrying restraints and leather cuffs, the other a large syringe, quickly followed. Within minutes I was lying in a treatment room, my wounds cleaned and prepped, and a pair of nervous residents, one on either side of me, were starting to sew up my lacerations. As they worked I heard them wheel my assailant into another cubicle. Hospital regulations required that someone check him over to make sure I hadn't hurt him.

"He has the power over my voices!" he was screaming. "The power over my voices!"

By the time I'd gotten fifteen stitches in my side and four in my index finger, including one in a partially severed extensor tendon, his shouting still hadn't stopped. That was unusually long for the haloperidol we'd given him to act. After the dressing to my abdomen was secure, and Susanne had wrapped enough gauze around the finger to make it look like a stumpy white sausage, I exchanged my bloody clothing for a set of OR greens and joined the residents taking care of my attacker.

As soon as I stepped into the room and saw him struggling against his shackles—screaming, white-faced and sweaty—I felt a stab of alarm that perhaps something else was wrong with the guy besides his schizophrenia.

"What do we know about him?" I demanded, addressing the half-dozen residents gathered around his bed.

A young woman whom I recognized from a rotation she'd done with us a few months earlier handed me his chart from Psychiatry and explained that he'd been her patient upstairs. "His name is Martin Whitehead, he's thirty-three, schizophrenic, does well if he takes his meds, but over the last ten years has been subject to repeated relapses and admissions to hospital for going off them. A week ago he was admitted in his usual agitated state, screaming religious references . . ."

I let her voice become a drone in the background as I flipped through his chart. Quickly I ascertained he had no other medical history, particularly diabetes, and wasn't taking any medication in addition to his antipsychotics. Neither was he allergic to anything, nor did he have a history of alcohol or drug abuse. In other words, apart from his madness he was in perfect health.

". . . was kept restrained until he began responding to being medicated again . . ."

I flipped over to the section of his chart covering his many ER visits and confirmed that I'd been the one to treat him on several occasions, though not recently. On none of these did he demonstrate the violence I'd seen tonight.

". . . had begun to come around, and was allowed out of the locked ward to participate with floor activities . . ."

I put down the chart, leaned against the wall, and crossed my arms—wincing when the movement aggravated my fresh stitches. Meanwhile the resident piled layer upon layer of facts about the man, which meant she hadn't a clue why he wasn't responding to haloperidol as expected. I looked again at his sweaty pale face and felt something familiar suggest itself. Something basic and routine to ER when a patient arrives out of his head, confused, or comatose, and we have no history to help us. I stepped over to the side of his bed and felt his skin. It was cold. He didn't even seem to see me as his eyes darted about the room and his head thrashed from side to side. His screams and mumblings were incomprehensible.

"Did anyone here do the DONT?" I demanded, interrupting the resident's interminable recitation, which was going nowhere.

Five jaws dropped as her young colleagues betrayed their bewilderment at what I meant.

"Did we do the *what*?" the psych resident said.

"The DONT. Remember? You learned about it while doing your rotation with us. Dextrose. Oxygen. Narcan. Thiamine." DONT was an acronym for the initial treatment automatically given to patients presented with decreased mentation and with no one accompanying them to tell us what had happened. The routine addressed the most common causes for such a state—dextrose would correct hypoglycemia, or low blood sugar; oxygen would help reverse hypoxemia, whatever the cause; Narcan was the antidote to a narcotic overdose; and thiamine was the vitamin most likely to be deficient in alcoholics with a persistent confusional disorder called Wernicke's.

"But Dr. Garnet, he's already admitted . . ."

"Not on diabetic meds . . ."

"No drugs or alcohol . . ."

"What he is, people, is a patient in ER with an altered mental status, the cause of which we can't explain. And from the look of him—pale, sweaty, and on exam, cool to the touch—even if he isn't supposed to be taking pills that would make him hypoglycemic, I'm checking his sugar." I'd already stepped over to a nearby equipment tray and taken out a small glucometer. Using a lancet, I pricked the tip of Martin Whitehead's finger—he didn't seem to notice—and got a drop of blood for the test strip. Sixty seconds later I had my answer. "His sugar is two," I told my astonished onlookers. They knew the implications of the reading without my explaining further. It was a dangerously low level which could cause confusion, extremely aggressive behavior, and ultimately seizures. In a paranoid schizophrenic who was only partly controlled with his proper medication, the resulting behavior—as we'd just seen—could be explosive.

They stood around in stunned silence while I riffled through drawers under the counter until I found a resuscitation tray. I took out a large prepared 50cc syringe of concentrated glucose, removed the protective cap, and injected all of it into the side portal of the IV line Susanne had started on him when he'd been wheeled in.

The results were almost immediate. The agitated movements ceased, his incomprehensible yelling stopped, and his sweaty pallor pinked up to more normal-looking skin. The sudden quiet in the room was eerie as the young man stared at each of us, his gaze suddenly focused, yet his expression uncomprehending. "What happened?" he finally asked in a quiet, shaky voice.

Several times a day, day in, day out, the alarm is sounded at St. Paul's to respond to an agitated patient. Most involve people in Psychiatry, but a ruckus can occur anywhere. Most are minor, though the possibility of someone getting hurt is always there. But there's also the occasional, extreme case, when a patient heaves a metal fire extinguisher at a staff person's head, for example, or suddenly grabs them by the neck or flails at them with punches. Sometimes it's only by luck or chance that the intended victim isn't seriously hurt or killed. Martin Whitehead's eruption, on paper, seemed to be no different from other relatively rare cases of extreme violence involving patients.

There would be a case review checking how a medication mix-up could have occurred. I'd already spoken with the man's nurses upstairs and found that there were two diabetics on the floor who were taking oral hypoglycemics. It wasn't inconceivable that in putting each patient's pills into a dispenser cup, Whitehead had mistakenly received a drug that would make his glucose level plummet. Whatever had happened, by the time Martin Whitehead had been wheeled back to Psychiatry along with his chart he was considerably calmer, though continuing to babble the stuff of delusional thinking steeped in religious symbols.

Yet as I sat in the nursing station filling out my portion of the incident report, I remained troubled. At first I thought my unease was because I'd never come so close to being killed by a patient before, and I simply tried to shake it off. But other thoughts kept plaguing me as I wrote up what had happened. Most attacks on staff members that I'd seen seemed to explode randomly out of routine pieces of business by the caregivers—their checking vitals, drawing bloods, or doing a physical examination. Even such a little thing as ordering a patient back to bed could send him or her into a rage, but the event usually occurred on the spot. In this case, Whitehead had come looking for me, years after any encounter I'd ever had with him in ER, and had somehow found a scalpel on the way. That suggested a degree of intent that didn't jibe with an isolated psychotic breakdown fueled by hypoglycemia. Yet I'd seen the blood result and treated the man myself. There was no question of the authenticity of what he'd had.

I shuddered, then told myself that the thought of a psychotic patient specifically targeting me after such a delay was absurd. Shoving the notion out of my mind, I concentrated instead on getting my report done so I could go home.

The trouble was, I found it difficult to write, having to wedge the pen against my bandaged finger with my thumb. The sutures would come out in ten days, but the tendon would take three weeks to heal completely. In ER my ability to use a pen and scribble fast notes was nearly as crucial as being able to use a stethoscope, and the handicap was going to be a pain. "Damn!" I muttered, rereading my account of what had happened and seeing how indecipherable it was. At one point I'd slurred the letters so badly that it looked like I'd said Whitehead had slashed my *throat* instead of my *coat*. I was correcting the error when I thought of something that perhaps I should have questioned much earlier.

"Oh, my God!" I said out loud.

"What's the matter?" Susanne asked as she passed behind me on her way to meet a new patient.

"Oh, nothing," I dissembled. "Just that my writing isn't readable anymore."

She grinned at me over her shoulder. "What do you mean *anymore*? It never was, Chief."

I tried to smile back but my heart wasn't in it. An icy chill was encircling my chest as I wondered if a medication error had accidentally put Martin Whitehead into a similar state once before. And he had ended up cutting Hector Saswald's throat.

Chapter 8

The crowd of visitors at the elevator—all festooned with offerings of flowers and fruit baskets and appearing to be about the size of a block party—was unusually heavy for a Wednesday night. I took the stairs instead, two at a time until the stitches in my front yanked me back to a slower pace.

"Whitehead was admitted to a locked ward last week," the resident had said. Saswald had been killed two nights ago. The obvious question—had Whitehead still been under lock and key at the time of the murder—I'd only be able to answer after looking at his chart and talking to the nurses who'd been caring for him.

The first person I saw when I rushed into Psychiatry's nursing station was Peter Forbes. For once I could tell from his expression what he was feeling. He was flushed all the way from his shirt collar to his bald spot, and his frown this time was no faint affair, having pushed his forehead into more ridges than were usually on a snow tire. The object of his displeasure was in his hand—the familiar form of an ER resuscitation record filled in by Susanne's neat handwriting and clipped to the front of Whitehead's chart. Forbes looked up from reading it when he sensed me watching him. His high color went a shade darker. "What are you doing here?" he demanded. "And I don't appreciate the way you people in ER insinuated my department was responsible for a medication error."

"Easy, Peter," I admonished. "We're not accusing anyone of anything."

"Oh yeah! Your call to my nurses and the questions you asked about other diabetics being on the ward as much as blamed them for a mix-up——"

"I suggest you focus on what's happened, not who's to blame. I take it Whitehead's under you." As this month's admitting officer for psychiatric emergencies, he'd be supervising the resident I met downstairs.

His eyes flashed at my cutting him off. "What did Whitehead say to you that makes you so sure he was given something? Your glucose reading could have been wrong."

"He said that he was the power and I was the Satan. Come on, Peter, what do you think he said? He's your patient and we all know he's psychotic. But there was absolutely no mistake in his reading. All the clinical signs of hypoglycemia were there to back it up, and his abrupt response to dextrose was clear-cut."

Our hostile exchange was attracting the attention of the nurses working nearby. I stepped closer to Forbes and lowered my voice. "I strongly suggest we take this to your office. We may have a hell of a lot bigger problem than what happened tonight."

His red face began to blanch at chameleon speed. "What do you mean 'bigger problem'?"

"Your office," I insisted. "And bring Whitehead's chart."

Behind his closed door the mood between us didn't improve any. He didn't even offer me one of his fancy chairs and remained standing himself, across his desk from me, the furrows in his forehead undiminished. "Well, what's this more serious problem?"

I knew what I was about to suggest wasn't going to help his churlishness any, but there was no way to dress it up for him. "Was Whitehead still under high-risk security the night Saswald was murdered?"

The impact of my question on Forbes was as if I'd given

him a jolt from our resuscitation paddles in ER. "You're not serious?" he exclaimed, his color completing its transformation to pale. "Why that's . . . impossible!"

"Not unless you can guarantee that on the night of the murder he was on this ward between the time Saswald was last seen alive and nine P.M., when they found him."

"My God, the very idea's unbelievable. . . ." His voice trailed off as he seemed to collapse into his chair.

Visions of Whitehead's steadfast attack on me danced readily to mind, reinforcing that it was all *too* believable. "The record?" I pressed, tapping Whitehead's chart, my impatience clearly evident.

"Of course," Forbes said, as if snapping out of a trance, all trace of our quarrel gone from his voice. It was strange. I wasn't used to seeing the man so transparent about his feelings, but I could have sworn I saw his expression shift ever so slightly from disbelief to just a hint of relief. He quickly flipped open the chart and found the pertinent notes for the night in question. He scanned several pages of handwritten entries by nurses, each with dates and times, then, in another section, more notes on blue-colored paper, which I knew would be the resident's clinical observations. As he read I saw his frown return, and I expected the worst. But to my surprise, he looked up and pronounced, "No, you're wrong. He was still in the locked section for unstable newcomers. He was never out of our sight that evening. Here, see for yourself," he said, shoving the chart at me.

I skimmed through the same pages he had, using my bandaged finger to guide the way. There was no doubt about it. Martin Whitehead had never left the premises that whole day, let alone during the fatal hour in which Saswald had his throat cut.

I found myself exhaling a sigh of relief as I closed the file, for Martin Whitehead's sake. As awful as what had happened tonight was, it wouldn't be a police matter. Soon antipsychotic drugs would beat his voices back into submission enough that he'd once again be released into the streets, and he'd return to whatever life he was able to keep a grip on out there. Until the next time.

Hardly a scenario to celebrate, I mused, but it was the best he could expect to have. In my business, that sometimes had to be enough. "Well, good for Martin Whitehead," I said, getting ready to leave. I certainly didn't want to hang around Forbes any longer, in case he got riled up at me again for having suggested the medication error.

But he didn't reply, just sat behind his desk staring off over my shoulder at some point on the wall behind me, a worried look on his face.

Weird, I thought, turning for the door. It was probably a good thing that he normally didn't show his emotions. When he did, they were confusing as hell.

"Right," I heard him say as I left the room, his voice sounding vague and far off. "Good for Martin Whitehead."

On my way out of the department the nurses slid me a slew of dirty looks as I passed their station. I was thinking that my provisional diagnosis about their role in the night's meltdown hadn't made me any friends among them either, when up ahead the doors to the ward flew open. A portly middle-aged man hurried in, followed by a slim woman who seemed slightly younger. Even from that distance I could see the worry on their faces, and the man's features had a familiar wide-eyed innocence about them that made me catch my breath. The two raced by me and went directly to one of the nurses. "Excuse me," I heard the woman say, her voice shaking and breathless. "We were called to come right away to the hospital. What's happened to our son?"

I wanted to hurry out of there—my fatigue was settling into muscles I didn't know I had, and my cuts were finally starting to hurt—but the thought of them having to endure Forbes in his current distracted state, whatever the hell its cause, made me hesitate. Perhaps I would still have kept going if at that moment I hadn't heard the nurse's reply.

"Mr. and Mrs. Whitehead, I presume," she answered, sounding displeased, as if the distraught couple's not properly identifying themselves had put her out somehow. She then said nothing, while their expressions made it obvious they were imagining the worst. "Well, you'll just have to wait for Dr. Forbes about that matter," she snippily huffed after an interminable few seconds.

I wheeled around. "Martin's fine," was all I said, wanting to immediately let the parents out of their agony, but my eyes were fixed on that abominable nurse. Be angry at me if you must, I felt like screaming, but don't take it out on them. I kept her in my glare until she turned away and flounced off. Then I strode over to where the victims of her torment were standing, introduced myself, and explained as gently as I could what had occurred.

When I finally got home, Janet insisted on inspecting the needlework on my wounds after I'd told her of the night's events. "I thought the idea was that you teach the residents, not let them practice on you," she commented dryly, replacing the bandages after giving the sutures a critical once-over and pronouncing them "okay."

About how close I'd come to getting killed, she said nothing, yet I knew it was bothering her terribly. That night I repeatedly woke up to find myself held tightly in her arms as she slept, and reflexively she clasped me even closer if I tried to move. When I held still, I could feel her hold on me relax but not let go. Despite the laceration in my front smarting under the pressure of her grasp, I fell back to sleep each time, feeling blessed by the love of the fierce woman at my side.

"Get another blood gas!" I ordered, quickly placing my stethoscope at the bases of both his lungs. The air entry was good. One of the residents grabbed a syringe and removed a few cc's from an arterial line.

It was noon the next day, and I'd just intubated a fifty-two-year-old man who'd been brought in comatose after rising from a chair in a restaurant, clutching at his head, and collapsing. He was being ventilated, IV lines were in place, an arterial line was inserted to provide samples for blood gases, and his bladder was draining through a catheter inserted up his penis. He was also wired to every monitor in the room, and whatever signs of life he had left in him were showing grossly abnormal on the machines that beeped and blinked at his bedside.

"BP's two ten over one twenty," Susanne said, bending over his right arm and letting the air out of a pressure cuff. The data was also on the monitors, but all of us had been burned with bad numbers for vitals enough times that we still measured them the old-fashioned way.

A resident at my side was shining a penlight into the man's pupils. "Neuro signs are unchanged. Eyes deviated up and to the left . . ."

She was telling me that the motor nerves controlling his ocular movements to the right were gone and that the unopposed muscles opposite them, still intact, were pulling his gaze away from the paralyzed side. By the dictates of neuroanatomy, the brain damage causing this particular phenomenon occurred in the motor cortex of his left hemisphere. To keep things simple for the residents, and ourselves, we teach that these kinds of strokes leave their victims "looking at their lesions."

". . . decorticate posturing; increased reflexes; upgoing toes, mostly on the right."

Deprived of the upper brain, limbs then curl into flexed positions, muscles jerk wildly when we tap reflex sites, and stroking the soles of the feet raises the big toe toward the head on the affected side.

Snapping off her light she concluded, "Left pupil's dilated and sluggish."

Pressure from the bleed had incapacitated his nerve for constricting the iris on that side.

"What's the coma scale?" I asked her.

"No improvement there either. Still only a three."

The number was a measure of the patient's level of responsiveness. A three meant that he wasn't reacting at all to any stimuli—not to words, not to touch, nor to pain—and was the lowest number awarded. A common joke among the residents was, "Even a corpse would score three, just for being there."

"Again, vitals?" I said to Susanne.

This time she read the numbers off the monitor—they must have jibed with her previous manual check. "Two fifteen over one twenty and rising—pulse forty-six."

A slowing pulse and increasing hypertension—further signs of a buildup in pressure within the skull.

I turned to the woman with the penlight. "Okay, what's your diagnosis?"

"Left-sided intracranial bleed, likely from an aneurysm or an arterial venous malformation."

"Very good. And what's your treatment plan?"

"Neurosurgery stat . . ."

"Already called," Susanne piped up. "They'll be here in minutes."

". . . and for this instant, to slow the bleed, IV beta-blockers will lower the pressure, and hyperventilating him will lower blood CO_2, causing arterial constriction . . ."

In snippets like these we pulled together the man's clinical findings and scored what his nervous system could still accomplish, all according to the convention used in most ERs to establish the diagnosis, the status, and probable fate of stroke victims.

"Good work, Doctor," I complimented when she finished and the nurses had started to carry out her orders. "You'll be a bright star in the firmament of your chosen career." She'd used me as a reference in her application for a residency in neurosurgery.

Her ebony skin creased at the corner of her eyes, her mask

hiding the rest of the smile. Then she was all business again. "They'll probably want to go directly to the OR. . . ."

Soon the neurosurgeon arrived with his residents, and immediately huddled with the radiologist to arrange angiography— dye in the vessels to visualize on X ray the location and size of the bleed—before taking him to the OR to evacuate the blood and stop the bleeding. When they were ready to shoot the films, we all made final checks of our equipment, then hustled out into the corridor so as to avoid exposure to radiation. To my surprise, I was ambushed by Riley as soon as I stepped through the door.

The scowl on his face and repetitive pulsing along his jawline forewarned that he was upset. "I need to speak with you!" he ordered.

My first thought was that he'd finally gotten his hands on David's chart and discovered what I'd been keeping from him. "Jesus, Riley, not now!" I protested, gesturing with my gloved hands toward my patient. I then turned my back on the detective, hoping he'd go away, and watched instead the technicians and radiologist as they worked to get the shots we'd need. Images of the dye coursing through the man's arteries appeared on a monitor located behind a lead-shielded barrier. The radiologist peered at it, trying to pinpoint the leak. He kept asking for other views, and altogether the process was taking too long for us to be away from the patient's side, even with all the monitors.

"When can we talk?" Riley demanded, standing at my shoulder.

I couldn't hide my impatience. "When this guy dies, or we get him to Surgery," I snapped, not taking my eyes off the scene of total life-support that flashed, beeped, and hissed in front of me. I was particularly worried about the man's breathing as I watched and listened to his ventilator. It was meant to assist his still-present respirations—I'd done the final adjustments on the machine myself and set the alarms—but managing an airway in ER required being at the patient's head.

"Get me a lead apron," I said to Susanne, "I'm going back in there."

"I've got it, Dr. Garnet," one of our more aggressive residents volunteered as he grabbed the heavy body vest before Susanne could hand it to me. He pulled it on as he rushed back to the head of the stretcher. I saw that he glanced at the readouts for oxygen saturation, made the appropriate checks of all the tubing, and immediately listened to the bases of the man's lungs. "Good air entry," he called out, "and the O_2 sat. is ninety-eight."

I relaxed a notch. The young man seemed to know what to do, and for the moment the patient's oxygen level was fine.

"It's important, Doc," Riley continued, whispering near my ear. "I heard about what happened to you last night. The gossip's all over the hospital."

"I'm okay, if that's what you want to know—"

"Doc, doesn't the pattern strike you?"

"What pattern?"

"Look at it. You questioned Saswald about a clinic owned by Brama. He got upset about it, and less than an hour later he was murdered."

I felt a flash of annoyance. "Look, Detective, I really don't have time to revisit that—"

"Two days ago I asked questions about that same clinic, and also got a very annoyed response, this time from the good people of Brama. Yesterday you were attacked with a scalpel."

"What?" I exclaimed, spinning around to face him. "You can't be suggesting the two events were connected!" The abruptness of my reaction got the attention of everyone nearby.

Riley glanced uncomfortably at all the raised eyebrows staring at us over the top of surgical masks. "Step over here a moment," he ordered, moving far enough away from the group that we could resume whispering and remain out of earshot, despite everyone now straining to overhear what had gotten me so excited.

"Cops look for patterns in crimes, Doc," he resumed, "just, I suppose, like you look for symptoms or signs of a given illness when you make a diagnosis. I think we have to consider there might be a link between the murder and the attack on you."

"But last night's incident was the result of a medication error! I treated the patient myself."

"Maybe it was," he frowned, "or perhaps questions about that clinic are stirring up a very dangerous pot. Is there any way the error and the attack on you could have been part of a setup?"

I felt myself want to scoff at such a bizarre notion. It was so crystal clear what had happened. A mix-up in pills was all, something not unheard of in a hospital. I felt my stomach knot just thinking of our own recent close call with a potentially lethal dose of IV potassium. And medically it had made sense—accidental hypoglycemia in a psychotic patient already bombarded by voices. The explanations had been at hand. Yet Riley's question hit a nerve.

His frown deepened as he studied my silence. "Can I know what you're thinking, Doc?"

Instinctively I balked at telling him what had struck me as odd about the attack—the peculiar degree of intent in Whitehead's seeking me out and bringing along a scalpel—because it was beyond belief that anyone could have made him do what he did to me. He'd obviously been driven by his voices at that time, so bombarded by them, in fact—he'd referred to several, which was usual in schizophrenics—that he'd seemed too unpredictable to have been made to carry out any action, at least not reliably. I flashed back to my own futile attempt to overrule the hold his auditory hallucinations had on him as I lay at his feet watching the blade glint in the overhead light. The recollection made me shudder, but I remained determined not to risk setting the police on Martin Whitehead the way I had with David by revealing too much, no matter how frightening or unusual I found the incident. "Offhand I'd have to say there's no way that patient could have been sent after me," I told the waiting detective in a whisper, not wanting anyone to overhear even my denying such a surreal idea, in case they might feed it to the rumor mill.

Riley scowled his dissatisfaction at my answer.

"Look," I quickly added, "I don't see how anyone could have controlled him enough to make him do anything."

Over where the nurses and residents were shuffling restlessly at the door to the resuscitation room, someone murmured, "At last," and a few others started adjusting their masks. I figured that the technicians must have nearly completed taking X rays and we were about to go back in.

Riley also glanced in that direction, then quickly asked, "Will you at least think some more about how it could be done?"

"Yeah, but don't count on much." I turned and walked over to rejoin the others, molding the top of my own mask around my nose, to keep my breath from escaping upward and fogging my glasses.

Riley followed behind, his persistent whisper rasping in my ear. "I went to the psychiatric floor this morning and asked the doctor in charge if I could interview the patient who'd attacked you."

"Oh, Christ!" I exclaimed, snapping my head around to face him. "Goddamn it, Riley, that patient should have been left alone—"

"Don't worry, I wasn't allowed near him. But perhaps you could interview him, when he's better."

At that moment the X-ray team breezed out. "Okay everybody, he's all yours again," one of them announced. A radiologist had remained huddled over the monitor, going over the images. The surgeon joined him, flanked by a circle of residents. Susanne and the nurses surged back to the patient, surrounding his stretcher and scanning the readouts of his monitors with their eyes. My young resident with the pen-light broke off from looking at the angiograms and started poring over the man again, loudly saying his name, pinching his extremities, and prodding him once more with a reflex hammer.

I was left standing in front of Riley, my face burning. I was furious at his latest attempt to cross the boundaries of what was appropriate with patient confidentiality. I certainly didn't want a scene with him in the middle of my own department, but it took all my self-control not to raise my voice. "Now get this, Detective," I began, speaking through clenched teeth. "Despite your ideas to the contrary, that patient's first and only violent episode was probably caused by a careless nurse. If you or I go to him and suggest otherwise, both he and his family will start worrying he might pick up a scalpel and go after someone else in the future. Even if we never proved anything, we'd have disturbed the comfort of his caregivers to have him around them. That comfort, sir, with schizo-phrenics, is crucial to their having a life outside as opposed to their being in an institution. And you and I are not going to fuck with that delicate balance simply because *you've* got a head full of unsubstantiated suspicions."

Riley seemed rocked by my vehemence. Not waiting for him to recover enough to argue with me, I pivoted and strode away to rejoin my colleagues.

Minutes later Todd Robbins—I'd learned his name from the chart—was ready for the OR. As we'd mounted all his monitors and equipment onto his stretcher for the brief trip upstairs, the man's wife, an attractive woman who appeared to be in her late thirties, stepped in to see him for what might be the last time. While I secured the connections and made last minute adjustments to his IVs, I overheard her providing what background she could to the surgeon.

". . . he's always suffered from migraines, but three weeks ago he had a different sort of headache. 'Worst in my life,' he told me. It was, well, odd because we'd just made love"—she flushed—"and it came on all at once, with none of the usual warning signs. That's what he found different. And the pain being so bad. His usual pills didn't take it away."

"Did he see his doctor?"

"It was Saturday night, and his usual clinic was closed. He even thought of coming here, but his insurance company insists on authorizing any visit before they'll pay for it. The nurse on call said it was probably another migraine, but that if he felt it was something more serious, by all means go to Emergency. Yet she wouldn't guarantee payment if it was simply one of his usual headaches. What really put him off was her warning him that the type of tests he might needlessly be put through—a CT and a spinal tap, I think she said they were—could cost two thousand dollars. So we waited. I got laid off last year, and his job just gets us by, so it's always close to the line for us financially. By morning his pain was pretty well gone, so we figured that that nurse had saved us a bundle. . . ."

"Any other medical problems?"

Her eyes began to tear. "None," she said with a sob. "He always kidded he had to take good care of himself, because he wouldn't ever want to seem old. . . ." She reached for a tissue in her purse. "What's happened to him, Doctor? Will he . . ."

At that point I tuned out of their conversation in order to give instructions to the respiratory technician who'd taken over ventilating the man from the machine. But I couldn't tune out my thoughts. The tests he'd been discouraged from having might have saved his life. They would have picked up the small hemorrhage of blood from an abnormal bulge, or aneurysm, in one of his cerebral arteries, which had caused that headache three weeks ago. Such "warning leaks" often precede the catastrophic type of rupture that had occurred today. Immediate surgery to remove the deadly malformation back then would have given him a ninety-five percent chance of surviving intact. Now his chances of dying were four to one.

* * *

When I got back to the nurses station, I found that Riley had left me a note marked *Confidential*.

Dear Dr. Garnet,
 Sorry for how I acted. I understand your position, and I'm sure you can understand mine. I would have stayed to apologize in person, but I had to meet with Mr. Fosse—he wants an update on the progress of the investigation so far.
 Call me as soon as possible, if you figure out how someone might have pulled off what we discussed.
Riley

I crumpled the paper and tossed it into the nearest wastebasket, annoyed that the man wasn't taking no for an answer.

But neither could I shake the bug that he'd put in my ear about the attack being set up, and between seeing patients I found myself thinking about the purposefulness of it. Each time my wounds twinged, I remembered Whitehead waiting quietly outside my office—an hour, he had said—and wondered how that jibed with a psychotic rage. During a particularly quiet interlude around midafternoon, I even found myself sitting at the counter and doodling what in effect was a flowchart of the murder. Saswald was in the center, and around him, like planets, I added the names of David, Martin Whitehead, and Brama. It suggested nothing.

Later I tried again. This time I placed Brama in the center, made Saswald a planet along with David and Martin Whitehead, and, in keeping with Riley's thesis that I too might have been an intended victim, I added my name to an outer orbit. I stared at this design awhile, but the only thing I could see was what I already knew—that Saswald, David, and I all had a connection to Brama, albeit mine was a hostile one. Nevertheless, feeling very silly, I drew an arrow from each of our names to Brama's. Not wanting to leave out any of the players that I knew of, I then added the name Baines under that of the company. And off to one side, but still close to Brama, I wrote *clinic*.

I studied this version for a while. Absently I drew a line between David's name and *clinic*. I was about to join the line between Brama and the clinic when I thought of the pattern that had struck Riley—how both the people at Brama and Saswald had not taken kindly to questions about the clinic. Their mutual discomfort about anyone mentioning the place was interesting, I mused.

Thinking about that discomfort caused another name to float into my head. There was someone else who'd recently given me the impression he was unwilling to talk about the place, someone who, as far as I knew, had no connection to Brama. I penciled in Peter Forbes's name among the orbiting planets.

"Now that's new," I muttered, staring at my diagram.

Absently I added lines between the psychiatrist's name and those of his two patients. "But why would Forbes be uneasy about the clinic if he's got nothing to do with Brama?" I put a question mark between Forbes's name and the company's.

"Who's got nothing to do with Brama?" asked Susanne, who was passing.

I instinctively moved to cover what I'd written. "Nothing, just scribbling."

She arched an eyebrow, but left me alone.

When I looked back down at the paper, I realized what a mess of lines and squiggles it was, and started feeling silly again. Yet before wadding it up and throwing it away, I noticed the place where I'd left out what might be the most controversial line of all—the one between me and Martin Whitehead.

A psychotic episode or a planned attack?

I entered a question mark.

Chapter 9

"The surgeon said it was the best possible result," a pale and shaken Mrs. Robbins was telling me a few hours later. Her dark hair contrasted sharply with her white complexion, and her eyes were swollen and red. She wasn't crying, but she kept darting a tissue to them. "The best possible result," she repeated, forcing a brave smile that broke my heart. "And thank you for what *you* did for Todd," she added, then wheeled around and fled back upstairs to her husband.

Doctors sometimes use the phrase "best possible result" as code for "don't expect too much" rather than an expression of hope. I'd spoken to the OR earlier and learned that they'd retrieved a small bowlful of clotted blood from what was left of his brain before they repaired the rupture. The "best possible result" in this case meant making it off the operating table alive. Left unsaid was the likelihood that even if he lived, Todd Robbins might never score more than a corpse on a response test.

As I filled out the insurance forms that we'd omitted to do in the rush to get the man to surgery, I couldn't help thinking that we could have saved his life three weeks ago for the same amount of money it would now cost for having operated on what, to all extent and purposes, was a dead man. Wanting to scream at the people who were responsible, I flipped over to the letterhead expecting to get Brama's triage number, but was surprised to see the logo of a completely different company. "Son of a bitch," I muttered, dismayed that for the second time in as many days a firm that I'd mostly had logical dealings with in the past seemed to be engaging in Brama-style practices of intimidation. At that moment I also realized that I hadn't seen a familiar toothless grin since I'd come on duty. "Susanne, where's Maggie?" I called out, swiveling my chair around from where I was writing at the counter. "Did she finally get admitted?"

Susanne looked up from where she was charting. "No, she went home before you got in this morning. The overnight staff cleared her. She was feeling better, and it was perfectly evident her insurance wasn't going to cover anything more than the ER visit. Under those circumstances, she wanted out of here."

I exhaled my frustration. "She shouldn't have been discharged!"

"What else could you have done with her?"

"I don't know," I snapped, spinning back around to pick up the phone, "but surely to God we can do better than letting an insurance company push an eighty-year-old woman into a corner where she has to risk losing her house or not get any care at all." Frustrated by my helplessness to do anything for Maggie, I angrily punched in the phone number of the people who had played triage roulette with Todd Robbins. But instead of getting to try to blast some sense into someone at his managed care outfit who was responsible for authorizing ER visits, I spent the next twenty minutes being passed from secretary to secretary like a hockey puck. Finally a funereal-sounding vice president came on the line. He was courteous, he was sympathetic, but he sounded ice cold as he reiterated that it was the patient's choice, tragic as it was, not to go into ER.

"Would you have paid for his tests if they'd turned out negative?" I demanded.

"Our policy is to pay for whatever care a patient needs."

"Decided when? In retrospect, after the diagnosis is

known? Your triage people intimated you'll only pay for patients who turn out to be sick."

"Of course we don't encourage trivial visits to ER, but our medical panel is competent to decide what investigations are appropriate, and any necessary test will be provided—"

"That isn't the message Todd Robbins got!"

"I don't think you're in a proper state of mind for a rational discussion, Dr. Garnet," he declared with a chilling evenness in his voice, and rang off.

Left with the phone buzzing annoyingly in my ear, I was as disgusted by the man defending what his triage people had done as I was by his obvious comfort in doing so. He'd actually sounded practiced at it, as if such catastrophes had been anticipated—were part of their new way of doing business—and he'd readied, prepared, and rehearsed himself for dealing with the fallout. And by his manner, it also seemed pretty clear that from his company, at least, we could expect more of the same.

I made a quick swing through the unit, asking the physicians on call if they'd encountered any evidence of an upsurge in such tactics on the part of other HMO groups. Some had noticed increased paperwork in documenting the need for an admission, and others had seen a small increase in admissions being given only provisional approval, such as Maggie's. And most had recently come across several patients who'd delayed coming into the hospital because they were warned by HMO triage officers that their ER expenses might not be fully covered should their problem turn out to be trivial.

Until I'd raised the matter, the physicians involved had all thought these episodes were due to nothing more than poor judgment on the part of a few individuals in separate health care firms. It was disturbing to us all when we totaled up our cases and found that the incidents were common enough to have occurred at least once on all our shifts over the last week. And in some instances, I also learned, the delays had done harm.

". . . had atypical chest pain, and the postponed trip to ER definitely delayed thrombolytics . . ."

". . . had a full-blown torsion. Another hour and he would have lost the testicle . . ."

". . . was septic with pneumonia by the time we got her . . ."

Small numbers across the board—hardly noticeable in the hundreds of cases we see—but in this little group the consequences had been potentially lethal.

"You think something important's going on?" my associate director, Michael Popovitch, asked. A heavyset man with permanent fatigue etched in circles below his eyes, he always looked worried, but I thought I saw a deepening of the many lines crisscrossing his forehead. Like me, he was a veteran of the pit. Also like me, he'd been showing the dark-eyed signs of wear lately.

"Let's keep a watch on how bad it gets," I answered, addressing the bunch of us who'd huddled together in a quiet corner of ER, "and I want everyone to report any more such instances to me."

"The trouble with that," Michael said, looking grim, "is that we'll never know how many people have been scared off to the extent they never came in at all. What's happened to them?"

The irony of Brama's boycott was that with fewer semi-urgent cases, we had more than enough beds and personnel to handle the big emergencies—life-threatening catastrophes such as cardiac arrest, acute respiratory failure, multiple trauma, and penetrating knife or gunshot wounds. For those problems, the paramedics had complete discretion over which hospital it was best to head for, and since St. Paul's always had room these days, we were their favorite destination.

But between the major resuscitations I had too much time

to think and would quickly become preoccupied with the question that had begun to plague me most—planned attack or psychotic rage?

Over and over I tried to solve how anyone could have made Martin Whitehead try to kill me. During one of these sessions I remembered how he'd called me Satan while he was attacking. Had somebody played on the religious content of his delusions to convince him that I was some sort of devil, and then sent him to destroy me? Yet he certainly hadn't seemed predisposed to listening to anyone outside his own voices in my office. Hours later, nursing a coffee through yet another interlude, I wondered if somehow those voices could have been manipulated, and thereby used to control him by giving him instructions? I recalled how he'd appeared to be listening as he towered over me. But what had he said then? I'd been paying more attention to his scalpel than to his exact words at that moment. Something about "the voices" that I controlled not being the same as the one that had told him "to do this," and that I couldn't control that voice because "it's not here now."

Exasperated, I gave up trying to make sense of his madness. Schizophrenics often distinguished between their multiple voices, finding some pleasant to hear, and others frightening—the ones that tell them to do "bad things."

At home that evening, after a day of doing justice to a week's worth of caffeine, I found myself sitting at the kitchen table unable to sleep and thinking some more about the way Whitehead had sought me out. Although I kept concluding that his behavior prior to the attack just didn't fit the pattern of a psychotic rage, I was still a far cry from accepting that someone could have used him to target me. Nevertheless it was enough to keep me fretting over how such control over him might have been accomplished. Even when I took Muffy for a walk and tried to shove the puzzle from my thoughts I couldn't leave it alone. It kept popping into my head, like some annoying riddle I couldn't escape. I went to bed with it; I got up the next morning with it; I carried it around with me at work. I eventually grew so frustrated that I even considered breaking my resolve not to interrogate Whitehead about what had made him come after me. If it would be just the two of us talking, I reasoned, with no police around, and I waited until his medication had dampened down his voices, perhaps I could get some answers without traumatizing the poor man.

Riley seemed to be having an equally bad time. The fatigue in his eyes grew as none of his investigators, after questioning staff both in the hospital and at Brama for hundreds of man-hours, seemed able to come up with a specific lead. "I know Baines is nervous as hell about something," the detective raged during one of his many visits to my office, "and every instinct I have tells me the man's up to no good, but I'll be damned if I can find any hard evidence to suggest why he or anyone at that company would want Saswald dead."

I poured him a coffee—the nurses had given me my own maker by now—and offered him my visitor's chair. "Did your interviews indicate if someone noticed that Saswald himself was behaving any differently in the weeks leading up to his murder?" I asked, handing him a steaming cup so black and strong it made even him wince when he took a sip.

"Not really. We specifically asked the people who he'd worked with if he was particularly worried or angry about anything. Most said he seemed stressed in the few days before he was killed, but put it down to his wrapping up his duties as Chief of Anesthesia."

"What about any long-simmering feuds between him and another staff member? Every department has its share of those."

"Didn't uncover any. And the only beef that he'd had recently with anyone besides yourself, as far as I could find out, was a quarrel between him and your CEO the Wednesday before he died. Fosse's secretary told me about it, but their argument turned out to have no relation to the case."

"What happened?"

"According to the secretary, Fosse had called Saswald to his office at the end of the day, the anesthetist seemed very tense when he arrived, and they had a huge row behind closed doors. But Fosse explained it was because Saswald had suddenly announced he'd be resigning without having given ample notice for the hospital to find a replacement. The secretary confirmed that immediately after the encounter she'd been told by Fosse to arrange for the reception, despite her boss being so furious at the guest of honor. As I said, it all seemed pretty mundane, from a policeman's point of view. Except of course whatever the reason was behind Saswald being in such a hurry to get out of here. Unfortunately, no one could tell me that either."

The following afternoon, during my weekend shift, Riley showed up with a different lament. "I never even got those charts upstairs," he told me. "The court ruled instead that the hospital should contact all patients named Pearson and ask if they'd agree to talk to the police. Most of them have, but it's going nowhere. And some, I'm told, are out of town," he added, pointedly scowling at me. "We certainly haven't found any patient yet with a connection to the clinic in Mexico." He leaned forward in his chair. "Why don't you contact him for us, Doc, and ask if he's willing to speak with us. That way—"

"Forget about it!" I snapped. "I told you, that patient has nothing to do with the murder."

His eyes flashed and held me in their heat for a few seconds. I wondered if he'd try to haul me in front of a judge and force me to give him what he wanted. But slowly that fierce light subsided, and I saw the muscles along the line of his jaw release the clamp they'd put on his back teeth. "You better be right about that, Doc," he warned darkly, "because one way or another I'm going to get to whoever it is you're protecting and find out for myself what he or she has to do with this case. And heaven help you if you've obstructed justice, no matter how altruistic your reasons."

Shit, I thought after he'd left, wondering what "one way or another" might involve. Having checked out the majority of patients named Pearson to no avail, could he now convince a judge to be more sympathetic in granting access to a smaller number of records—those of the people who were out of town, for instance, or those of patients who'd had links with a Brama facility? Or perhaps this time he'd simply try to get the Mexican police to raid the clinic and arrest a patient named Pearson?

In any case, the encounter only reinforced my original decision to keep from him my growing obsession with Martin's attack on me. I'd figure it out first, I promised myself, and if the young man was used as some sort of pawn, I'd make sure he wouldn't suffer at the hands of the police.

By Sunday evening I was so preoccupied with it all that even in bed Janet was asking what was wrong.

"It's this Brama business," was my reply. Better to trouble her with an old worry than a new one, I figured, especially if the new one involved someone wanting me dead.

"But why is Brama bothering you so much more now?" she pressed, snuggling up beside me and dropping a long leg over mine. So I told her about Baines trying to badmouth me to Riley.

"Why, that's odious," she declared, beginning to stroke my thigh with hers. "But you couldn't be all that upset about something that makes Brama's executives look guilty."

Then I confessed about how the legacy of Brama was spreading to other health care companies, affecting people like Maggie and Todd Robbins.

"Now that is worrisome," she said, pausing in her movements as she became lost in her own thoughts for a while.

Monday morning Susanne met me at the entrance of the nursing station and led me aside to a quiet corner. "Just to warn you, the son of Dr. David Pearson is waiting outside your office." She hesitated, then added, "He looks upset. I hope it's not bad news."

When I stepped into the hallway leading to my door, I was staggered by the appearance of the young man seated on a chair. He was the image of David, but from the time when I knew him as a young, competent physician long before alcohol had taken its toll. I was also taken aback to see he was wearing the dark green jacket and trousers of a U.S. Marine. I suppose I shouldn't have been—the rules by which sons emulate or oppose their fathers have always proved inscrutable to me—but I would have thought a boy who'd grown up witnessing the physical and mental scars David had suffered from war might have come to a different choice. Three gold braid chevrons on his sleeve above an insignia of crossed rifles told his rank, but my own ignorance of military dress kept me from knowing for sure what it was. One thing was for certain—even if Susanne hadn't warned me, I would have known I was greeting David's son.

"Mr. Pearson," I said, approaching with my hand held out. I was unable to remember his first name. The last time I'd seen him, he'd been barely a teenage boy hovering frightened at the foot of his father's stretcher during one of the man's many admissions to ER. There'd been a younger sister as well, and the two children had made an indelible image on me back then, clinging to their mother as David suddenly began screaming about spiders. Thankfully, both children had stopped coming after that episode. Years later, so had their mother.

"Dr. Garnet," he said, rising. He was as tall as I was, and powerfully built, which was no surprise, considering the training he'd been through. Yet there was a shyness in his smile that was at odds with how formidable he looked.

"What a fine young man you've become," I enthused as we shook hands. His grip fit the rest of him, but what I noticed was the worry in his eyes, which dominated all else.

"I'd like to speak to you about my father, if you have a moment," he said quietly.

"Of course." Unlocking my door, I braced for the worst.

As soon as he was seated across from me he stated, "He's disappeared from the addiction treatment center he went to. They called me nearly two weeks ago to say he ran away, and no one's heard from him since."

My insides twisted into a knot. Apart from hearing he was dead, I couldn't imagine worse news. David had not only blown his last chance, he suddenly no longer had the clinic for an alibi as to his whereabouts on the night of Saswald's murder. Outwardly I tried to look upbeat, and started giving him reassurances I didn't believe at all. "Mr. Pearson, perhaps he'll turn up—"

"Please, Dr. Garnet, call me Allen. And I'm not a kid now. More than anyone, I know the mortality from alcoholism— I've been watching it kill him for years. If he's taken off, then he's drunk somewhere, or already dead." As he spoke his eyes narrowed and his previously quiet voice rapidly took on an edge. "Whether this binge is in Mexico, or he's ended up in a ditch full of rattlesnakes trying to cross back into the U.S. without proper papers, he's pretty well run out of luck, chances, or whatever name *hope* goes by these days. Personally, I don't possess any more of the stuff, having spent my lifetime's quota when I *was* a kid—hoping he'd make it, hoping that this time he'd do what he said and not drink anymore, hoping I'd get my daddy back. I've paid too high a price for learning what I know to let anyone imply I don't know the score, so you can cut the bullshit."

The bitterness poured out of him like acid, scalding me into feeling ashamed for not being more forthright. "I'm sorry, Allen," I quickly apologized. "I didn't mean to patronize you. Of course you know the reality of his drinking, and yes, you've every right to demand that I be up-front with you."

The fire in his eyes died back a little as he studied me.

"Please," I persisted, "let's start again. How can I help?"

He hesitated a few more seconds, then answered, "We—my sister, my mother, and I—need to know what happened. I'll be damned if I'll let that uncertainty hang over our lives. I know I want to get on with mine. I've already wasted enough time waiting around for things that never happened to be saddled with wondering if he's dead or sick or just around the corner and about to walk back in on us. Do you know what I mean?"

I nodded.

He studied me a few seconds more, then said simply, "I need your help to get by the red tape at the clinic."

"Red tape?"

"I can't get any straight answers. At first they were reasonable enough, advising my mother that he'd run off, reassuring her that it sometimes happened, that the isolated locale of the place made it unlikely he'd go far, especially since they still had his passport and money in their safe. They also claimed that they'd mobilized all the local authorities to look for him, and of course we were to call them immediately if he turned up here."

"When exactly did you say they reported him missing?"

"A week ago last Tuesday, but he'd already been gone three days by then. Apparently it's their policy not to contact the family immediately if someone runs away, but to complete the initial stages of a search first. Nearly a week later, the following Monday, I also got a call from their head office in San Francisco—the president of the company, no less, a guy named Baines—and he starts laying on the schmooze. How upset and worried they were, that if my father turns up in Buffalo to have him call immediately, that the clinic would readmit him, no questions asked—personally, I thought it was a con, stroking us in an attempt to make it less likely we'd raise a stink."

"Baines himself called you?" Now that was odd. I'd heard from patients how Brama was adept at smooth-talking the families of the people they'd screwed—part of their publicity budget, I always suspected. Because even though they couldn't be touched legally, they were still mighty sensitive about malcontent clients, relatives, and, needless to say, doctors like me mouthing off about them. But a call from the president of the company himself was extraordinary. Added to the suspicions Riley had already raised about the man, Baines's personal interest in David's disappearance was like an alarm going off.

Allen caught my incredulity. "Yeah, I thought the man was piling it on a bit thick myself. In fact, his reaction made me wonder if there was some kind of recourse we had that he was nervous about. I dug out my father's copy of the contract he'd signed—can you believe he insisted that I keep it? 'A reminder that I'm serious this time,' he told me—and showed it to a buddy of mine in law school. In effect, we had nothing, not even our own health plan anymore. When my father ran away, he'd rendered his entire policy null and void, including the coverage that extended to his family."

That sounded like the Brama I knew. "When did Baines phone you?"

"It was Monday morning around ten. I remember, because when the call came through at the base, I calculated it was only seven in San Francisco, and the guy being that eager to speak with me in itself seemed unusual."

It certainly was.

"But now something even stranger has happened," Allen continued. "Nobody at Brama will talk to me at all."

"What?"

"Since the day the clinic first called and I spoke with a Dr. Martinez, the psychiatrist who treated my father, I called back every few days to see if there was any news. Each time I was put through to Martinez, and was politely told that though the search was continuing, there were no developments. When I tried last Wednesday, he refused to take my call, and a receptionist told me not to disturb him anymore.

Angry at the brush-off, I called Baines's office in San Francisco, only to be told he was in Buffalo. But when I repeatedly left messages with several receptionists at the offices here, he never got back to me. I even went down to the building to try and see him in person, but couldn't get by the front door. Go figure. On Monday he can't get up early enough to speak to me. As of Wednesday, I'm persona non grata. I can't figure out what happened."

A murder, a cop named Riley pestering Baines with a lot of questions about the clinic, and the entire police force asking about someone named Pearson—that was what had happened. Though why it would make everyone at Brama suddenly not want to talk with Allen Pearson, I had no idea. Leaning forward in my chair, I asked, "Did your father ever mention being treated by a physician named Hector Saswald?"

"Wait a minute. That's the doctor who was murdered here last week. What's that got to do with my father?" Allen demanded, suddenly sounding wary.

"I don't think anything, probably, it's just that—"

"I told you to level with me, Dr. Garnet!" His voice was harsh again, and a look of alarm was spreading across his face. "My God, that's why the hospital already phoned my mother twice now, asking would my father please call them regarding a police investigation when he gets back. The biggest police matter at St. Paul's right now is the murder—"

"Allen, please, believe me, I mean it when I say that it probably hasn't anything to do with your father. The police have a lead on the name Pearson, and *all* patients of that name who have ever been at St. Paul's are being contacted." As his expression transformed into one of amazement, I asked, "What did your mother answer when they called for him?"

"Just that he's out of town. Even though he's gone public with his alcoholism in the past, she's still ashamed of it, and obviously didn't want to advertise where he was, or why."

"Good. Now trust me on this. If they phone back, stick to

that answer. Don't even say he's out of the country, and specifically don't mention Mexico."

"Why?"

"Because even if your father has nothing to do with this, that comment might give him problems with the police that he doesn't need or deserve right now."

His eyes narrowed again. "Tell me why, Dr. Garnet!"

Brother, I thought, I'm not handling any of this well. Still, I hesitated about how much to say. If I violated Riley's order not to reveal that *Pearson . . . too young* was written beside the body, and he found out, the good detective would have my head, if not actual grounds to carry out his threat of charging me with interfering in a police investigation. Then for sure I'd end up in front of a judge, forced to give him the name he wanted. I carefully worded my response. "Saswald worked for Brama. The police think his killing might have something to do with the place. They're liable to make a big deal out of your father being a patient in a Brama facility. It's the last thing he'd need right now."

"You talk as if you think he's still alive."

"I won't dress a grim situation up for you, Allen, but it is possible."

He exhaled long and hard, and for the moment let his shoulders slump out of their military bearing. He leaned forward in his chair and ran both his hands over his bristly haircut. "In some ways that's the possibility that haunts me the most. I keep thinking about him being helpless somewhere, and I want to know what's been done to look for him. How hard have they tried? If I could get leave, I'd go down there myself. But without the cooperation and help of the clinic personnel, I'd probably get nowhere. That's why I came to ask if you can help me get through to the people at Brama."

"Allen, I'm not very welcome at Brama myself right now."

He looked up at me and gave a little laugh. "I understand. 'No-fault murder,' right? You really plowed them good with that one. A lot of people I know felt you were right on the button. That's why I didn't bother you at first. I figured you wouldn't exactly be someone who Brama would easily listen to. But now, well, everything else I tried has come up against a stone wall."

"What about the authorities in Mexico?" I asked, hoping to at least suggest something useful.

"Again, without someone from the clinic to tell me who they've been talking to, I'm lost. All I know is the general area where it's located, just south of the border in the mountains east of Tijuana, but the one police station I could find through information for that district knew nothing about a David Pearson. I also checked with U.S. customs. They have no record of him."

"Have you thought of declaring him missing?"

"Yeah, but when I do, word of his running away is bound to reach both the radio station and newspaper where he works. His last chance to keep his job with them would be officially over, and despite what I said about being out of hope, I can't yet bring myself to write him off to the extent I'd slam a coffin lid on his career." He gave a sardonic chuckle. "I know I'm not exactly being consistent right now, but emotionally, one minute I'm cold as ice, the next I feel like that little boy I told you I wasn't anymore." His eyes started to brim with tears, and I saw him clamp his jaw tight and purse his lips, as though his holding them closed could stem the flow from his eyes. It worked, partially. Only a single rivulet spilled over the brim of his left lower lid and coursed down his cheek. "Sorry," he said, briskly wiping away the evidence of his lapse. "Besides, what could the police do here that would be of any help, since he's likely still down there?"

I hoped he was. And now that I thought about it, who knew how police files were circulated between departments? A missing person's report involving a man named Pearson who was last seen at an addiction clinic in Mexico might be passed

Chapter 10

"Fired for stealing records?"

"That's what his head nurse said."

"But that's—so bizarre!"

"Bizzzzzz," copied Brendan, waving his fork in the air.

Janet and I were having dinner in our kitchen. Brendan was thoughtfully picking through his cut meat and joining in our conversation.

"You bet it's bizzzzzzzarre," I said, putting my face close to his and making him laugh while feeling far from humorous myself.

"But would he do something like that—steal papers? And why?"

I flashed back to when we were rooming together in the late sixties. There were always members of various movements or popular crusades sleeping on our floor at his invitation, some of whom were draft dodgers and deserters he was helping escape to Canada. "Yeah, he'd take a few shortcuts outside the law, if he thought it was for a good cause."

As Janet frowned, Brendan studied her somber face, then cocked his head, leaned toward her, and gave her a goofy grin she couldn't resist. She ruffled his hair. "Thank you for cheering me up, my little man." He offered her a forkful of mashed carrots. As she took it from him, smacking her lips in a noisy display of appreciation, she turned to me and added, "You know, I like what you like in the man, even though I find him impossible to be around for any length of time."

"Really?"

"Of course. He's a fighter—a real-life Don Quixote—and thank God for nuts like him to take on the skirmishes the rest of us don't have time for." She picked up a spoon and offered some of the yellow mush to Brendan's open mouth. "I meant what I said at lunch today, Earl. He made a big difference for patients in his hometown, and the more I look at how we might have to fight the same fight here, the more impressive his feat seems." Her frown returned. "It's such an ignominious way to leave the field, for a guy who's already accomplished something that difficult to bring about, which is so important. And it's such a huge waste of his experience. Frankly, the thought of squaring off with these companies and not having the help of someone like Jack, who's been through it, intimidates the hell out of me."

Her words gave me an idea. "Hey! If I find him, why don't I offer him a job in ER at St. Paul's, and then he could lead us through what needs doing."

Janet grinned at Brendan, pointing her now empty spoon at me. "Your dad's a little slow, my sweet man, but eventually he can pick up a good idea if we give him enough hints. But of course later on he'll swear he thought it up himself."

On the car radio going into work the next morning, all the newscasts were reporting on a press conference being held by a local patients' rights group.

". . . HMOs deterring sick people from ERs with threats of reneging on their coverage . . ."

". . . an odious practice not previously seen in upstate New York, but one which has plagued the Southwest . . ."

". . . that current laws permit such behavior on the part of health insurance companies . . ."

Obviously the citizens of Buffalo had started to notice the trend.

By the time I arrived at St. Paul's, the same reporters who'd

"That's from *The Sound of Music*."

"So who cares? It's quest music, right? 'Swim every sea—' "

"The line's 'Ford every stream.' "

"Stickler!"

By the time she got to the chorus, I had sore sides from laughing and my stitches were in danger of coming out. But I suspected her levity was all show. Later that evening, when I came up to the nursery, I stood at the doorway and watched her rocking Brendan to sleep. Normally her face exuded peace during this ritual, but tonight I was startled to see her expression drawn and lined as she stared out the window.

The call came shortly after. Luckily I was the one who answered.

"Earl Garnet?" said a raspy voice.

"Yes?" We had an unlisted number, so I expected it to be someone from the hospital.

"We can get to your wife. Be smart, and shut the fuck up!"

"Who are you?"

"Your worst nightmare, Garnet! I'm a whole bunch of people who you've pissed off." The whisper grew in volume until it became a sibilant shriek. "Remember, it's your wife who'll pay!"

"Who the hell are you?" I yelled back.

A harsh chortling noise came through the line, then I heard a click and the dial tone.

I had Riley on the phone in less than a minute.

"I'll get a patrol car outside your house immediately," he stated as soon as I related what had happened, "and I'd like your permission to put a tap on your line."

"Of course."

"Do you think the threat is because of what you've been saying about HMOs?"

"Isn't that obvious?"

He heaved out one of his massive sighs. "Maybe not. Have you discussed your suspicions about the clinic in Mexico with anyone besides me?"

"No, not really." I tried to remember exactly what I'd said to Allen Pearson. I was sure I'd only warned him not to mention that his father had been a patient there.

"What do you mean, not really?" Riley snapped.

"I mean no, I didn't, period." Boy, he was quick on the uptake.

"Doc, this is not the time to hold back information, even if there is another of your patient-confidentiality issues at stake. Yours and Janet's safety depends on you being straight with me."

His bluntness about Janet made me wince. "I *am* being straight," I assured him.

His silence told me he suspected otherwise. Finally, after sighing yet again as if attempting to exhale his frustration, he elaborated. "Suppose I'm right that the questions I asked Baines and his CEO about the clinic precipitated an attempt on your life. That would mean the killer fears such questions, probably because he thinks they could expose what was behind Saswald's murder. It also means he knows you're the one raising the questions. Since that person's first attempt to get rid of you failed, it would be convenient for him that every HMO in the area has just declared you public enemy number one. A threatening phone call sounding like a response to what you've been saying to the media today would make any future attempt on you seem part of that business, with a lot of ready suspects at hand." He paused a few seconds, presumably to let me mull over what he'd suggested. Then he asked, "Have you told Janet about the threat?"

"No. I called you first."

"Are you going to?"

This time I let out the sigh. "It'll scare her."

"Damn it, Doc, she has a right to know. How else can she protect herself. Now you tell her, understand?"

His sudden fierceness caught me by surprise, then left me feeling sheepish for not knowing better. "Yeah, of course you're right. She has to know."

"Okay, then. Now this will sound trite, but try not to worry. That patrol car at your home will become a fixture day and night until this whole situation is settled." His voice was all at once gentle, and remarkably reassuring.

"Detective, I . . . I appreciate your help, and your setting me straight about Janet."

"Think nothing of it, Doc. There, I've got an advantage over you. When women started coming on the force, I took all the courses on how to treat them as equals."

When I told her of the threat, Janet took it as she always took difficult news—quietly, and with steely silence. I didn't expound to her Riley's theory that it might be tied in with the murder. Despite his advice to be forthright, I figured once she was warned enough to be on her guard, there was no point of adding further unknowns to her worry.

"Well, I guess it's started," was all she said after a few minutes. "And you're sure a marked police car will be parked out front from now on?"

From the alarm I saw in her eyes, I suspected she was thinking of Brendan's safety. She was too fearless personally to ever be that concerned for her own. "I have Riley's word on that, plus they're going to put a tracer on our line," I reassured her.

During the night, I woke to her holding me in her sleep again. Lying awake, I listened to her breathing and occasionally felt her stir against me. This time I hardly even noticed my stitches.

Martin's wide eyes stared up at me, beseeching acceptance the way a puppy might. His short black hair was neatly combed, and his massive shoulders which had so intimidated me now slouched submissively as he sat on the side of his bed. He was dressed in a polo shirt and slacks, having graduated from being restricted to wearing only a housecoat on the floor. Behind us Riley was leaning against the windowsill while Mr. and Mrs. Whitehead occupied the two sole chairs for visitors, each occupying a corner in the room. Having just arrived, after saying hello to the others I stepped up to Martin, my hand extended, and said, "Good morning. I'm glad to see you're feeling better."

His shake was limp, and I felt the clammy coolness of his skin that was an occasional side effect of antipsychotic medication. "Hello, Dr. Garnet," he replied so softly that I could barely hear him. He then looked down at his lap.

"May I sit beside you?" I asked, speaking almost as quietly. He nodded without looking at me, and I eased myself onto the bed as near to its end as I could so as not to crowd him. I waited a few seconds until I saw him take a quick glance my way from under his lowered eyelids, then spoke. "Martin, I know that what happened was not your fault. And please understand that Detective Riley and myself also appreciate your agreeing to answer our questions."

"Are the police mad at me, Dr. Garnet?" he asked, his voice void of any inflection.

"No, they're mad at someone else. Someone who perhaps deliberately mixed up your medication."

"You think someone did that? Who? And why would they?"

I didn't know how to answer without upsetting him. "Someone who wanted to hurt me, Martin," I replied after a few seconds' thought. "That person may have tried to trick you into doing something you'd never do on your own. A low sugar makes people violent. Martin—"

"I know, Dr. Garnet. After the nurses explained what had happened, I read about the hypoglycemic medication in some medical books I have—my parents brought them in for me from home. Glyburide, it was—peak onset of action three to four hours after ingestion. That means it was given to me between three and four that afternoon."

I very quickly realized that Martin was not only bright but

surprisingly literate. Some patients with his disorder isolate themselves even from reading.

"I'm impressed, Martin. Not many people can understand material—"

"I've read all about schizophrenia too, Dr. Garnet. I know what medications I take, and what happens if I don't stay on them. I figure the glyburide was slipped in with my usual pills given at three. I wouldn't have noticed. I usually down them all at once, not like some who take them one at a time."

"Who gave you the pills?"

"One of the nurses brought them to Dr. Forbes's office. We were having a session together that afternoon. I'd just gotten out of isolation the day before, so he was meeting with me to see how I was doing."

"How did you feel then?"

He looked at me sideways, then back at his hands, which he kept rubbing together. "Not good," he said softly. He remained silent a few seconds. "The bad voices were telling me things, swearing, saying everyone was going to hurt me."

"Did you tell Dr. Forbes about the voices?"

He started to rock. "Yeah."

"What did he say?"

"That they wouldn't do anything to me. That I was safe."

"Were the voices saying anything about me while you were with Dr. Forbes?"

"No. That voice came later."

"That voice? It was a single voice?"

"Yeah." His rocking and hand-wringing intensified.

"Did you ever have singular voices before?"

"Sometimes they shout in my head, and argue together, the good voices with the bad." He paused, then added, "That scares me."

"But the good voices don't?"

"Yeah. I like them. They sing nice songs, tell me I'm going to be okay."

"Do you have the good voices now?"

"A bit. I don't like it when the medication makes them go away completely. It's too lonely."

"When did you start hearing the voice which told you to attack me?"

His rocking picked up tempo. I noticed he was now looking over at the telephone on his nightstand. "In this room, after I got back. It told me that you were an agent of Satan, and that tonight you were going to slip into my room to cut my throat as a sacrifice to your master. The voice said you'd been fooling everyone for years, but that you killed people like me when we came through your Emergency. The voice revealed that you'd picked me to die years before, when you treated me yourself, but you'd waited, so no one would suspect. He ordered me to kill you before you killed me." The pace of his speech was speeding up. "He proclaimed that he was an avenging angel of God, that he'd chosen me to serve as his instrument of retribution on Earth. I didn't want to hurt you, but he said if I didn't, I'd burn in Hell. That he'd sear my eyes out. Melt my flesh off my bones." The back and forth movement was becoming forceful enough to shake the bed. His breathing quickened and he was wringing his hands so fast now that he appeared to be washing them.

Hoping to calm him, I quickly said, "We'll stop. If this is upsetting you—"

"I was scared!" he cried out, his voice as loud as when he'd shouted at me in my office.

"It's okay, Martin," his mother intervened, getting up and walking over to the other side of the bed. "Dad and I are here," she reassured him, starting to massage his shoulders. "You're safe, dear. Everything's all right."

The effect was immediate. His breathing slowed, his hands went still, and he leaned back against the woman, no longer rocking. After a minute of soothing him in this way, she calmly said, "I think you can continue now, Dr. Garnet."

"Are you sure you're ready to talk some more?" I asked, taken aback by how brittle his equilibrium was.

"Yes, Doctor." His tone was flat.

Despite what he said, I knew my questioning him further might unsettle him again. I proceeded, but very cautiously. "How else did you feel, besides scared?"

"Hungry," was all he said at first, while still staring at the phone. Then he added, "Dizzy too, and sweaty."

These were symptoms of hypoglycemia.

"What else did the voice say?"

"That I was to go down to Emergency, find the door with your name on it where the offices are, and wait for you to show up. When you did, I was to say that I was being discharged the next day and that I wanted to speak with you, until I got you alone. Then I was to cut you open and spill your blood, thereby sanctifying your evil ground." His voice was absolutely neutral. He might have been telling me how he was sent to a store to buy some milk.

"Had one of your voices ever given you instructions like that before?"

"No, never like that."

"But you got instructions."

"Yes."

"What kind?"

His eyes returned to his now-still hands. "Long instructions— how many steps to take forward, how many times to sit down, to bow right, then left—that kind of thing."

Schizophrenics could sometimes be seen carrying out long, involved repetitive rituals of movement and speech, dictated by their auditory hallucinations. But the sequence of detailed directions he'd described pertaining to me were unlike anything I'd ever heard from a hallucinating patient. Nor had I ever read of a psychotic episode where "voices" had set up such a carefully laid-out act of violence. The only case that sprang to mind was the famous Son of Sam killer who stalked

parked couples in New York City. But as much as I could remember from reading in the papers about it back then, not
even he got such specific advice from "Sam," his guiding
demon. Something very definitely didn't add up with what
Martin had experienced. "Where did you get the scalpel?" I
asked next.

"It was in the drawer of that table," he said matter-of-factly,
nodding toward the nightstand. "The voice told me it was the
chosen sword of the Lord."

"You found the scalpel in the bedside table?" I blurted, far
too loudly. At that same instant I heard Riley stir from where
he was sitting at the window and quickly come up behind me.

Martin cringed at the change in us, and he leaned back into
his mother.

"Sorry," I quickly apologized, lowering my voice. "I didn't
mean to startle you."

After a few seconds of looking from the detective to me,
and his mother murmuring comforting sounds in his ear, he
muttered, "Yeah. It's okay. That part of what happened has
been bothering me too. If it was all in my head, there wouldn't
have been a scalpel."

"You've got that right," I heard Riley mutter behind me.

"Do you remember at all being in my office?"

"What happened at that point starts getting pretty vague."

"Were you hearing the voice telling you to kill me then?"

"No, I don't think so. But I was afraid to disobey. It had
scared me so much. I just remember getting more and more
frightened, dizzy, and light-headed once I got you alone." He
paused and made repeated swallowing movements. A dry
mouth was yet another side effect of his pills.

While I waited until he found enough saliva to continue
speaking, my mind was racing. Increased effort can profoundly
accelerate the development of hypoglycemia in a nondiabetic
after his taking a product like glyburide. As he'd sat quietly
outside my office, the pill would have already been steadily

doing its work, lowering his blood sugar to subnormal levels, yet not necessarily enough to alter his mentation. But with the sudden effort of attacking me, his body's demand for additional energy would have plummeted his glucose to the exceedingly low range, thus setting off his violent behavior. Left unchecked, such severe hypoglycemia can result in seizures, coma, and death. With a shiver I realized that if Martin's hypoglycemia had been induced to help manipulate him into making an attempt on my life, then very likely my would-be assassin had intended him to conveniently die as well.

"Dr. Garnet," he resumed, "the nurses said I cut you." His articulation sounded labored from lack of spit. "I don't remember doing that at all." He looked up from his hands. Although his face was expressionless, his eyes no longer shared that same blankness. Instead they were full of pain, like open wounds, and I couldn't bear looking at them. "Did I hurt you badly?" he asked.

I tried for a reassuring smile. "No. They were superficial cuts. A little stitching fixed me up fine."

He continued to study me with that dreadful stare.

I changed tack and went on to less stressful matters.

"Did you tell anybody about all this?" If he had, I wanted to know what idiot hadn't reported what was obviously a bizarre account, to say the least, and clearly beyond the bounds of what could be explained as part of his psychosis.

"Nobody asked about it before you."

"Not even Dr. Forbes?" It would be awfully lax for a therapist not to explore other factors that might have contributed to his patient going berserk, over and above the effects of hypoglycemia.

"No. He never asked me anything."

"Not even about where you got the scalpel?" Riley demanded, speaking over my shoulder.

"No sir," Martin said, shaking his head.

I heard Riley suck in his breath behind me. Then he asked,

"Was there anything that struck you as odd about this voice that told you to attack Dr. Garnet?"

"Yeah. It was how the voice came over the phone."

"Over the phone!" Riley exclaimed, his voice rising. "How do you mean, 'over the phone'?"

"I mean this voice came out of the phone—whispering at me. I never had that before. My voices are always in my head."

Riley stepped over to the nightstand and picked up the beige, single-line affair that was connected to the wall by a removable jack. All telephones by patients' beds are arranged for easy removal in case they're too sick to receive calls. He looked at me and suggested, "Could a speaker have been placed inside, and the voice transmitted from a microphone somewhere?"

On this ward they gave syringes full of haloperidol for that kind of thinking. I might even have dismissed Martin's claim of hearing voices from an instrument as being part of the characteristic delusion of schizophrenics that messages were being beamed into them from electronic equipment. But I'd already heard enough to know this had been no typical auditory hallucination, and I was rapidly thinking along the same lines as Riley. "Maybe," I said.

"What was also odd," Martin resumed, "was that I shouldn't have had a phone at all then." His speech sounded increasingly thick, as if his mouth was full of glue.

"Pardon?" Riley said, looking up from his inspection of the receiver. He'd already unscrewed the mouth- and earpiece and was checking for added equipment.

"I'd just gotten out of isolation. No phones allowed. Yet when I got back from my session with Dr. Forbes, the phone was there, and a few minutes later the voice started coming from it." He stared at the cradle portion with the touch-tone dial which still rested on the nightstand. "But that phone was different from this one."

"Different in what way?" Riley asked, replacing one of the covers he'd removed.

"That phone was black, and had a lot of buttons. Someone must have changed my phone."

Riley looked up from the receiver he was working on, then resumed reassembling it. Obviously he'd found nothing there. "Was there anything else which struck you as out of the ordinary that afternoon?" he asked.

"No, sir."

"What about any of the nurses? Did any of them act strangely toward you?"

"No, not at all."

"And there was nothing about the voice that impressed you as being different from the usual voices you hear, apart from it coming out of the telephone this time?"

"It scared me lots more than usual. The things it said that would happen to me—going to Hell is my worst fear."

"But you never thought someone might be deliberately trying to fool you?"

"I was so scared, Detective. You have no idea how scary those voices can be, and this one, like I said, frightened me more than any I'd ever heard before." He looked down at his hands again. "I know it seems silly now, even to me, what with my being on medication again and knowing they're just in my head."

The torment of the disease is so great that one in five schizophrenics chooses suicide. When Martin and others like him are out of control and their voices rage ceaselessly at them, they sometimes live a daily terror the likes of which no so-called normal person could ever begin to comprehend. The thought of someone adding to Martin's already burgeoning terror by making him fear that I was coming to kill him sickened me.

Riley glanced in my direction. "Can you think of anything else to ask, Doc?"

I shook my head.

"You've been most helpful," he declared, turning back to Martin. "I appreciate how much courage you showed in revisiting very upsetting memories, and I promise you, if any of what happened to you was deliberate, we'll get the person or persons responsible." He then spoke to the parents. "I also want to thank you for taking the time and helping us with—"

"Time!" Martin interrupted. "Detective, I do remember another thing that was odd, after all. It was the time Dr. Forbes was late for our session. It struck me then because he's never late. And another thing. When I was sitting there in his office waiting for him, his phone started ringing. It wouldn't stop. I didn't answer it, of course, but the noise bothered me. Then when Dr. Forbes did arrive, he didn't answer it either. Instead he just took the receiver off the hook without speaking to whoever it was and put the whole phone in a drawer of his desk. So we wouldn't be disturbed, he said. I took it then as simply a thoughtful gesture—one that made up for him keeping me waiting—and I didn't think any more of it. But with all that talk of yours—implying how the phone might have been used to make me hear that terrible voice—I just remembered something about that incident. The phone he put away wasn't his usual big black one with all the buttons. It was a simple beige model like that," he said, pointing to the nightstand. "I think someone switched our phones that day."

"Forbes thinks it'll be a routine interview at seven this evening. The time's in keeping with how we've scheduled all our other meetings with doctors at the end of their working day so as not to interfere with their care of patients," Riley was saying, huddled over his coffee at a corner table in the cafeteria. "But in this case the intervening hours will give us a chance to interview every nurse who was on the floor the day in question, so we can have as detailed an account of his movements during that particular afternoon as possible. Then if the son of a bitch starts lying to us about his actions, we'll be on to him immediately."

"Won't he be suspicious, receiving all this attention?"

"We've simply stated that we're expanding the investigation and requestioning people since we have no leads, so I don't think he'll suspect we're coming after him specifically. But I'd like you with me, so he can't snow me with psychobabble . . ."

It was just before noon, and since our meeting with Martin Whitehead, the detective had spent the hours marshaling his officers to draw a noose around Peter Forbes. We'd agreed to meet for coffee so he could fill me in on the plan he'd arrived at, and this time I had no qualms about helping him. The scalpel planted in the nightstand had erased all doubt that Martin's "voice" had been fabricated to set him on me.

". . . figure the black phone with all the buttons had a speaker as part of its regular features. All he'd have to do is take it to Whitehead's room, plug it in, dial his own extension . . ."

As Riley elaborated on how "voices" could be made to come out of the phone, I was trying to figure out how the psychiatrist might have been implicated in Saswald's murder and why he'd want me dead. In the end, I hadn't a clue.

". . . when the session was finished, he probably told Whitehead to return to his room and rest. All he'd have to do then was take out the phone he'd hidden in his desk— the connection would still be intact—and start broadcasting his whispered threats and instructions to that poor, terrified kid . . ."

Perhaps we could frighten the fat little prick into telling us everything after we got him into custody and out of his four-thousand-dollar suits, I thought hopefully. After all, we had a charge of attempted murder to threaten him with. "I wouldn't miss being there to help you take the creep down for anything," I assured Riley when he'd finished talking. "And I'm particularly looking forward to seeing the misery in his face when you slap the cuffs on him."

Riley gulped down the last of his coffee and ran off to brief Fosse about what was happening, including the possibility that Dr. Peter Forbes could be led out of the hospital under arrest that very evening.

I downed what was left of my own cup—it would be all the lunch I'd get today—and hurried back to my office, where I was scheduled to do a phone interview on the abusive powers of HMOs with a well-known noon-hour talk show host.

Chapter 11

The program went well, I thought. My interviewer had a way of cutting to the bone of the issue, and I was primed to stomp on a few toes. Even the threat against Janet was fodder for my anger, and I threw it into the mix.

"You've had threats made against you for speaking out against the practices of these companies?"

"Against myself, and against my wife, Dr. Janet Graceton, which I thought was particularly gutless."

"Are you accusing any company in particular?"

"The police will be doing that."

"Obviously they've made a mistake if they thought they could shut you up."

"You bet they have. I believe the only response that works with people like that is to expose them, the way you lay open a cancer and cut it out."

"So what are you saying that's got them so upset?"

"For starters, let's talk about withheld care. Or better still, let's debunk the jingoistic claim of these companies that they don't withhold care but simply withhold payment. Let's discuss how doctors get bonuses if their patients cost the HMO less than the national average for whatever diagnostic group they fall into, and these same doctors lose up to twenty percent of their income if they don't. And let's not forget that hospitals also sign contracts with HMOs too. They have an interest in getting patients out quicker and cheaper as well."

"I think we've known for years that it pays doctors and

hospitals to keep visits, tests, and treatments to a minimum. What's so different now?"

"What's different now is that measures initially intended to eliminate unnecessary testing and to encourage optimal practices on the part of doctors are currently used by companies to give themselves greater leeway in improving profits and cutting costs."

"You mean the downsizing and cutbacks going on in other industries these days?"

"No, in my mind this has evolved into something far worse. Other industries are at least accountable for their cost-saving measures."

"How do you mean?"

"If a car company takes shortcuts to save money and it leads to events that cause injury or death, they're liable."

"And HMOs aren't?"

"You've got it. They can pressure doctors into making these savings for them with impunity."

"That is pretty strange."

"Now let me be clear on this. I'm not saying all physicians or hospitals yield to this pressure. And I certainly am not against efficient or cost-effective care. What I am opposed to is the profit motive having such a dynamic in making clinical decisions."

That set the tone. By the time we neared his signoff time at one o'clock, we'd covered everything from the tactics of provisional approvals for admissions and ER visits to policies for seniors which imposed such unpalatable choices on them that they'd rather risk dying at home.

"Before we conclude, let me ask you, Dr. Garnet: Are you claiming these companies behave like this across the board—with all their patients? If you are, that's a pretty sweeping indictment."

"Of course they don't. Even with the recent trend toward such methods in Buffalo, so far I'd estimate we're only seeing examples of it in about one out of every hundred patients."

"Let me be provocative here. Why should we be excited about something occurring on such a small scale?"

"Because the resultant delays, even on a small scale, are exceedingly dangerous. In my own ER over the last month a child has died and an adult has been left seriously disabled—permanently, I'm afraid. Even as we speak I know of an elderly lady who's risking her own death by staying alone at home because her HMO would only provide a provisional approval of her admission and she'd lose her house if, in the end, they reneged on covering the expenses."

"But why would these massive companies bother to pull such stunts on only one percent of their clients?"

"Because they probably figure they can get away with treating one percent of their clients this way. Look at your own reaction. A second ago you yourself asked why get excited about it."

"Good point," he conceded. "All right. You've shown me that they can get away with it. And you've explained how existing laws make them immune to lawsuits for any damages resulting from their pulling these moves. What you still haven't explained is why they bother."

I was ready for this one. "The other day our CEO at St. Paul's reminded me that health care is a trillion-dollar business in this country. You discourage one in a hundred people from seeking attention, and even if only a half of those are intimidated away from ever getting help, the resultant half-a-percent cut in expenses would still save these companies five billion a year. That's a lot of bonus money for the men and women who run them."

"Thank you, Dr. Garnet."

This broadcast had the hospital muttering, loudly, all afternoon. If my encounters with colleagues were any measure, half hated me and a quarter of them thought I was nuts. Men and women alike gave me their dirty looks, icy stares, and called me asshole under their breath as they passed. It got vicious enough that I found myself wondering whether last night's threat had come from one of them. That notion disturbed me even more than the thought that it might have been from some thug working for an insurance company.

But I also had reason to take heart. The remainder of doctors who reacted to my performance were alarmed enough by the growing impact of HMOs on their own practices that they stopped me in the halls and asked what we could do about it as physicians. Apart from encouraging them to speak out to their patients and the media as I'd done, I had no ready solutions. Organizing against the companies the way Jack MacGregor had in San Francisco was an impossibility with seventy-five percent of our physicians hostile to showing any opposition at all.

The retaliation from Brama came later that afternoon, and it was leveled against Janet. As opposed to what we'd been expecting—goons in the night—they resorted to a dirty trick that was absolutely legal.

Maria Naglia, a senior secretary in their contracts department, sat across from me at a small conference table in a seminar room near the birthing center. She looked in her late thirties, was plump in the midriff, especially for her short height, but had contrastingly thin arms which seemed to dangle out from the voluminous short sleeves of her oversized blouse. Her moon-shaped face beneath thinning dark hair already streaked with gray completed the picture of someone who probably suffered from Cushing's disease—a disorder leading to diabetes, hypertension, and brittle bones. She was obviously nervous, and kept glancing around at the mock-ups of female reproductive anatomy that lined the shelves on the wall in front of her. She was also a patient of Janet's.

Having decided to warn us after hearing me on the radio, she'd come to St. Paul's on her way home from work and paged us both. Janet was sitting at her side, a protective arm around the woman's shoulders while listening intently.

"If they found out, I'd lose my job," the woman was saying, "yet I couldn't stay quiet and not warn you, Dr. Graceton, especially after all you've done for me."

A key chain lying by her purse contained a baby's picture. I assumed Janet had gotten the woman through the rocky pregnancy that cushingoid women normally experience.

"At Brama they keep a list of physicians designated 'the undesirables,' doctors who repeatedly exceed their average costs per patient despite a repeated twenty percent cut in fees. But as you know, these doctors often are the ones who care for people in need of expensive treatments, such as those with AIDS, geriatric patients, or, as in the case of your practice, women like me, who are considered high obstetrical risks. This morning I got the directive to add your name to that list. When your current contract expires with them at Christmas, it won't be renewed."

"What?" Janet said, incredulous. "But those bastards came to me when they first arrived in town, pestering *me* to sign a contract with *them*, because so many of the women they were trying to sign up would only do so if I was one of their approved obstetricians. If I knew then what I know now about them, I never would have, but—"

"Dr. Graceton, I don't think it's got anything to do with you. It's your husband they're after," she said, looking over at me. "They can't get to him directly, so they're coming after you."

I was paid out of the hospital pool of emergency revenues. The reduction of our incomes due to their boycott hit me as it did everyone else, but it was limited to their ten percent of market share. They couldn't single me out as they had Janet because my contract was with St. Paul's.

"Have I got any options?" she asked, looking stricken. "Or more to the point, do my patients who have policies with them have options? How easily could they switch out of

Brama to one of the other carriers where I'm still under contract?"

"Not easily," the woman answered. Then she flushed, swallowed a few times, and added, "I'm afraid you're facing worse problems than that. Health care companies always deny doing this, but not only do a lot follow the policy of listing so-called undesirables, some even exchange these lists amongst themselves. A doctor dropped by one company as a high biller may soon find himself or herself dropped by others and, once stigmatized, unable to get new contracts anywhere else."

I interrupted. "Why would competing HMOs help each other?"

"To avoid both public and political scrutiny. Acting in concert this way, no one firm sticks out from the rest as they cut back or limit their exposure to certain high-risk, high-cost diagnostic groups. That means they can't be accused of discriminating against these particular patients. And if they all dismiss doctors from time to time, some of whom happen to be heavily involved in the care of these patients, the practice is less likely to attract attention to any specific company and more likely to appear as if it's simply part of employers' exercising their right to sign, renew, or let drop any contract they please. Since the collusion occurs at the level of CEOs and presidents, it's next to impossible to prove. Names arrive the way Dr. Graceton's did, and we let contracts drop. Even if I wanted to blow the whistle, which I don't, I couldn't prove anything. Hell, I'm not even sure the whole business is illegal, and perhaps they're keeping it secret simply because it's so odious. After all, if it ever became public that HMOs were using a loophole in their contracts with doctors to systematically exclude from care some of the sickest patients in the land, there'd probably be such a furor we'd get some new regulations damn quick that would put an end to their little game." Turning to me, she added, "Congress might even be forced to throw in some of those right-to-sue laws you've been talking about. Which brings me to my point." She returned her attention to Janet. "I don't know any easy way to say this, so I'll come right out with it. All the CEOs and presidents of health care companies in these parts are so mad at your husband, I'm afraid you can soon expect to become an undesirable across the board and have your contract dropped by all the other outfits in town."

"Those bastards!" Janet ranted, pacing circles around my small office. We'd retreated there after Maria had left. "Those filthy, rotten bastards."

"Easy, Janet. We'll fight it."

She swung around to glare at me, her eyes like blue fire. "Don't you patronize me. You know damn well there's not a thing I can do. No doctor can once this happens."

She was right. Under existing rules, no company was obliged to give just cause for dropping a doctor's contract, and since it was simply a yearly agreement renewable at the company's discretion, physicians had no recourse to claiming unlawful dismissal. And as Maria Naglia had indicated, neither could patients do anything, at least not right away, without paying a stiff financial penalty. Since most of them wouldn't have the financial means to change carriers in protest, they'd have to accept one of the many remaining doctors in the Brama plan, until their own policy came due for renewal, possibly years from now. Besides, if the companies acted in concert the way Maria suggested they could, there wouldn't be any carrier they could switch to and still retain Janet's services. No matter what we did, she'd be out of business, all because some CEOs wanted to shut me up and close me down.

I walked over and put my arms around her. She was trembling. "I'm sorry, Janet, so awfully sorry," I whispered to her, feeling my rage mount by the second. "But I swear, I'll find a way out of this."

As I held her, the cuff of my sleeve slid up my wrist, exposing my watch. It was 5:05, and I realized I'd already missed an hour of the board meeting.

A few minutes later I was in the wood-paneled domain of Administration and scuttling over inch-thick blue carpets. The secretaries and almost everybody else had gone home for the day, so as I hurried past the empty reception areas I could look into the open doors of all the plush office suites that were apparently necessary to run St. Paul's these days. To be fair, I'd never yet seen any hospital where this part of the operation wasn't first-class all the way, whatever their budget problems.

I had few illusions about the reception I'd get from the members of the body I was rushing to meet. They were primarily Buffalo's corporate elite, mostly men, some women, and CEOs all—a group too comfortable with the language of profit and loss for my liking, and they brought it so easily to the ongoing debate of how to keep St. Paul's abreast of current clinical trends, procedures, and equipment. All too often the first question they'd ask was, "Can we afford to keep up with what is best for the sick?" or, as I was starting to hear lately, "Can we legally get away with providing the minimum?"

Pushing through the ceiling-high oak doors to the boardroom, I came upon an even richer decor of rosewood-paneled walls, pastel green broadloom, and a mahogany table that could seat twenty at a side.

Fosse was chairing the meeting from the far end of the room, and his audience at the table mostly had their backs to me, having swiveled their chairs in his direction. I slipped into an empty place behind everyone else.

The discussion appeared lively, and it didn't take me long to figure out what the topic was.

". . . a disgrace to the hospital!" shouted a grandmotherly looking woman three places from me.

". . . admissions down ten percent with eighty beds now

empty!" howled a jowly middle-aged man who I remembered once treating in ER for gout.

". . . the gall of the man, using the media to stir up even more trouble. I got calls today from every HMO we have a contract with, and if even half of them make good on their threats to drop us—"

Fosse slammed down his gavel and brought the cacophony to a close. "I won't have you maligning one of our finest physicians that way!" he declared, his black eyes flashing defiantly as he cast a stern gaze around the room. But when he caught sight of me, I saw him start.

At first his declaration was met with silence. Within seconds the quiet was broken with groans and murmurs of disapproval. Then came angry mutterings, and finally, halfway up my side of the table, a small man with a huge mane of white hair jumped to his feet, waving his finger in the air, and shouted, "I move we demand Garnet's resignation!"

The rest loudly seconded the idea.

". . . no other choice but to get rid of him . . ."

". . . his continued presence means a loss in revenues we can't sustain. We'll have to close the beds and lay off staff . . ."

Fosse hadn't moved his eyes away from me. His gaze seemed to grow sadder and his frown deepened with each angry comment. A few other people turned my way, presumably to see what he was looking at. Soon they were nudging their more vocal neighbors and nodding toward my part of the table. In no time all the noise had died down and every eye in the place was on me.

In my white coat amidst all the dark suits, I felt like the last chess piece of a very one-sided game.

Fosse jumped to his feet and roared, "I'm disgusted with all of you!" His face grew flushed above his white beard, mimicking the colors of a beef on rye. "I'll have you know Dr. Garnet's stand against Brama and the other HMOs has struck a nerve in this community. You say you got calls from these companies? Well I've been inundated with calls of support for the man from our patients—the *real* lifeblood of this hospital. They're fed up with the likes of Brama jerking them around, maximizing profit by minimizing care, and crossing ever further beyond the bounds of decency in doing so. Dr. Garnet's a credit to this hospital as far as they are concerned, for giving a voice to their frustration, and you want him fired? You'd sacrifice one of our best to protect companies that represent what's worst in our business?"

Fosse caught his breath and surveyed the well-heeled group. A few looked away as he tried to catch their eye. He leaned forward, placing his palms on the table. "Look at me, all of you!" he ordered, his voice suddenly quiet. His abrupt drop in volume seemed to electrify his audience into listening more attentively. There wasn't a shuffle, a cough, or a whisper of disapproval to be heard. "Have you forgotten what happened to the little boy whose case precipitated all this? Do you even remember his name? I do. It *was* Robert Delany."

Nearly everyone in the room winced.

"Do you want your child treated like that?" Fosse pressed. "Perhaps you'd like the parents of that boy brought in here so they can witness which side of this fight you want the hospital to take?"

I saw the white-haired man who'd called for my resignation start to fidget with his hands. A few of the others who'd been his noisy supporters made little clearing sounds in their throats. They all kept their eyes on the table.

Fosse took stock of the impact he was having on his audience. "Yes, it's harder when we make it personal," he continued, speaking almost softly. "But I think it's our duty to keep issues like this personal. I've fought against the type of mentality that killed Robert Delany my whole career because I learned at a very young age what it's like to lose someone needlessly for want of access to good doctors. And at the end of a forty-year career in health care, I can say that there are few enough Earl Garnets around to keep the light on in ER for anyone who needs help."

He straightened, walked around to where I was sitting— the rest of the room absolutely still—and insisted on shaking my hand. Smiling down at me, he spoke over his shoulder. "There are at least a dozen of you who this man has treated personally at one time or another. I know, because you called me first to set it up. If you've a shred of self-respect, you will stand by him now, and protect him and his work from the travesty of Brama trying to silence him!" Turning back to face the table, he added. "As for any of you who still want to fire him . . ."

He walked over to a wastepaper basket and gave it a fierce kick, sending it clattering down the room. Gasps of disbelief filled the air, and those sitting nearest the missile leaped halfway out of their chairs. Even when it spun harmlessly to a stop on the carpet, jaws continued dropping to the right and left of me.

Fosse stood there with his hands on his hips and let the re-action to his outburst die down. "I'm in my retirement year, folks," he said, still ever so quietly. "That means I've got nothing to lose in any battle you want to wage here, and be-lieve me, I'll do whatever it takes to keep this hospital from knuckling under to the likes of people who think that what happened to little Robert Delany is an acceptable business practice." As he spoke he met the stare of anyone at the table who dared look at him, and in those seconds he actually seemed menacing, which was completely at odds with his stout Kris Kringle appearance. "Come on, Earl," he ordered, once he'd cowed every set of eyes in the room. "I'm sure you've got far better things to do than waste your time with this sorry lot."

No sooner were we outside the massive oak doors than he warned, "I can talk tough, but I don't know how long I can stall those creeps back there from dismissing you as chief. I'm sure you're aware there's a lot more than your job at stake here. If Buffalo's leading teaching hospital caves in to the HMOs calling the tune about which doctors can work and who will provide our medical leadership—"

"You're damn right I'm aware," I interrupted, having already decided that I'd found an ally to help with Janet, "and I suggest we go to your office to discuss how you and I are going to protect the latest physician to be targeted."

"Threats? 'Undesirables'? Putting a doctor like Janet Graceton out of business? It's a fucking outrage!" Fosse ranted while he paced a groove in his own taupe-colored broadloom. "I knew we were headed into this kind of crap, but it's twice as disgusting when it actually happens." Each time he pivoted to change direction, I thought he might leave divots in what was clearly the thickest carpet in the hospital. "You know what we're gonna do?" he challenged, spinning around and pointing at me. "Tomorrow morning you and I will pay the president of Brama a visit. The son of a bitch is here from the West Coast visiting the local offices. I'll set the meeting up, implying I'm coming in to discuss terms for ending the boycott, then we'll surprise him with the two of us and confront the hell out of him about what he's doing to Janet. Will she want to come as well? I've never seen anyone fiercer when it comes to fighting on behalf of her patients."

"Probably she will. I'll ask her tonight." I noticed he hadn't mentioned the occasion on which he'd learned Baines was in town. His apparent decision to keep his own counsel in matters regarding David Pearson reinforced my determination to do the same in front of Riley.

He started pacing again. "You know what might really scare them?" he said, waving his right index finger in the air. "What if we went to the media about them declaring doctors as 'undesirables'? Would Janet accept making her own case public? Of course I'd tie it in with attempts to silence you over the Robert Delany case, and I'd make the boycott against the hospital public as well. What d'ya think? Go on the offensive?"

I was staggered. "I . . . I like it," I finally stammered, then quickly added, "Of course, I'll have to run it by Janet."

"My bet is she'll go for it like the tigress she is," he declared, his eyes sparkling with excitement. "You've no idea, Garnet, how much it would mean to me to take that blood-sucking Brama down a rung or two before I retire. I meant what I said at the meeting. It drives me mad to see everything I've stood for come under such a sustained attack just as I'm about to head out the door . . ."

As he ranted he was striding up and down in front of a mahogany-paneled wall covered with photos that documented highlights from the lifetime of work he was alluding to. Most were pictures of him receiving oversized checks from private donors to finance special medical projects, but a few were of him in groups from years gone by—graduating classes, his military outfit, old sports teams—and off to the side of this gallery were some shots that looked more like family photos.

". . . convinced Brama's the key. They're the scourge of the profession. If we can make their sleazy practices into such an expensive public relations disaster that the bastards back off, there's an outside chance that the other goddamned companies will fall into line . . ."

His face had reddened again, and his dark eyes glinted as fiercely as they had in the boardroom, but what struck me most as I stood at close quarters to him was the force with which he kept slamming his right fist into his left palm. The man was in a frenzy.

". . . and that leech Baines is sure to be more than a little spooked by the investigation into Saswald's murder, which won't hurt us any, because he'll be worried about the bad PR on that front as well. Detective Riley briefed me about how jumpy the asshole gets each time the police show up to ask questions. Frankly, it warms my heart, the thought of him being scared shitless whenever he's interrogated by the law—"

"Mr. Fosse," I interrupted, bringing him to a standstill, "I simply want to say how . . . how . . . well, proud I am to be fighting alongside you on this. I don't know quite how to put it, but I never met an administrator like you before, and, well, you're very special. Thank you."

He stood looking at me, his cheeks growing flushed, his eyes watery. He abruptly turned away, ending up facing his wall of photos. He appeared to study them as he presumably composed himself. When he did speak, I had to strain to hear him. "As with all crusades, mine started with an old hurt. Maybe when you've time to listen, and I'm not quite so emotional, I'll tell you about it." He glanced down at the family end of the display, but said nothing more. When he did look me in the eye again, his color had returned to normal and a smoldering blackness had replaced any trace of tears. "I'm going to let you in on a secret, and you mustn't breathe a word of it, not even to Janet. If all goes according to plan, I've got a new weapon that will help us against Brama."

As I stood there and watched, a sly grin spread under his beard and mustache. When it reached the size of a smile, he glanced toward the closed door of his office, then whispered conspiratorially, "I'm on the verge of bringing in the largest endowment of my career, and it's fitting that you be the first to know." He'd lowered his voice even further, despite our being alone. "The benefactor wishes to remain anonymous, but it's going to be called the Robert Delany Fund, because the impetus for its creation was when you made that poor child's case public. Its sole purpose will be to combat exactly what we're talking about—the abusive policies by HMOs of the kind that led to that toddler's death."

This retiree-to-be was single-handedly adding a whole new dimension to my understanding of medical politics. "But why didn't you tell the board that?" I demanded when I got over my astonishment. "Surely that would have calmed them down."

"Are you kidding!" he exploded, slamming his fist into his palm again and starting to pace once more. "Because it's possibly going to take months to set up. And for it to work, if and when I do get the money, I have to spring it on Brama by surprise. We certainly can't count on our having it operating in time to get both you and Janet out from under the immediate threats to your jobs."

"But how would you use the fund when it is ready?"

A sparkle danced back into those coal-like eyes. "As I told you, we have to nail that particular company hard—hurt them—for pulling the crap they do, and make it a message all the other companies will understand. If a patient gets the runaround from them about emergency care, the fund will not only initially pay that patient's ER expenses, but will also finance a very public, very messy campaign to make the sons of bitches settle the account. Radio, TV, newspapers, billboards—every means of negative advertising possible about their every indiscretion will be brought to bear on them. Now that's the kind of pressure that could actually put them under and win us this war. Of course you can see right away another reason why I couldn't tell the board about it. No one in that bunch has the stomach for what's called for here, and most of them would try and stop me. I have to get everything in place and launch a campaign that's so quick and dirty they won't be able to do anything about it."

I found myself smiling. "Once more, Mr. Fosse, let me tell you that I like how you think."

"Really?" he said with yet another grin, this one quite sly. "Well let me introduce you to my teacher." He walked toward the section of the wall dedicated to what I thought were family portraits and stopped beside a faded, sepia-tinted, black and white photo of an old man standing with a young boy.

I leaned forward to look at it. The man, dressed in a safari jacket and puttees, was lean, and beside the boy, at least, appeared to be quite tall. He wore a handlebar mustache, had very hollow cheeks, but his eyes were the most arresting. They were dark, deep-set, and even in their faded rendition seemed to sear right into me. The boy looked about five, was holding up a medium-sized fish, and was smiling a little grin that looked half shy, half proud.

"That's me and my grandfather," Fosse explained from behind me, "taken sixty years ago. He was the black sheep of the family, a gangster from Chicago's East Side, though he was always very kind to me. It was only when I was a teenager and he was 'retired' that he began telling me about what he did, and even then it was in bits and pieces, exciting stuff about fights and guns that he knew would impress a boy who wasn't quite yet a man. When I got older, I put those pieces together enough to figure out that he was an enforcer for the protection rackets, and a pretty small-time one at that. Years later when I was an adult and he was frail and elderly, he'd sometimes talk frankly with me about the 'old days.' Once, I asked him about the violence and bloodshed of his business. He didn't make any apologies about what he'd done, but rather, told me how he'd kept it minimal. 'If you hit the leader hard and send a very clear message, everyone else pretty well starts to behave and you have no more trouble, for a while. But if you're half-assed about it, and the message isn't strong enough, the bloodletting goes on forever.' That's what you and I are going to do to Brama, Earl, using billboards and media coverage."

I shared a wicked chuckle with him, then glanced at my watch. It was six-ten, and I was due to meet Riley in my office for a final debriefing before we went to confront Peter Forbes at seven. "I'm sorry, Mr. Fosse, but I have a meeting scheduled in ER for a few minutes from now."

A cloud passed over Fosse's face. He said nothing, but after Riley's debriefing earlier, I figured he knew the grim business that I was off to do. We arranged a time to meet in the morning, shook hands, and I left. As I strode along between the lines of deserted offices, I wondered about what had happened "at an early age" to have instilled in Fosse such a magnificent, lifelong passion to stand up for the sick.

* * *

Riley arrived at barely five minutes before seven. "Sorry," he quickly exclaimed, "but my debriefing with the officers who questioned everyone on Whitehead's floor took much longer than I'd expected. Let's head up, and we can talk as we go."

The start of visiting hours meant large groups of people were waiting at the elevators, and we took the stairs instead. Though Riley appeared heavier and older than me, his conditioning was obviously superior. He talked easily as he took the steps two at a time, whereas I was left puffing heavily just trying to keep up. "We got all kinds of nasty little circumstantial tidbits against Forbes," he began. "First, the nurses remembered that he'd given them specific orders to bring Whitehead's three o'clock meds to his office, where he'd scheduled their session together. He told them he wanted to give the meds himself only at the end of the interview, in case he decided to change Martin's drug regime after evaluating his progress. After the meeting was over, Whitehead was told to rest in his room. The nurses recalled that Forbes left strict instructions not to disturb Martin, since he'd upped his sedation. What they found unusual, but not unheard of, was that Forbes said they were not even to take him his supper, but instead to let him sleep until morning. Now you tell me, doesn't that all fit with Forbes giving himself the opportunity to slip his patient the glyburide pill and then work on him with the whispered messages?"

"I guess so," I gasped as we rounded the first floor landing and headed toward the second.

"I figure it also increased the chances of the nurses not noticing that their patient had slipped off the ward when he headed down to ER. But here's the clincher. Forbes is connected to Brama."

"What!" My surprise nearly made me pull up, but Riley never broke stride.

"One of my men conducting interviews on the floor today

caught sight of him and remembered seeing the man going into Baines's office on the Tuesday after Saswald's murder."

"How the hell did he remember that?" I managed to wheeze. We were nearly up to the third floor.

"He'd come looking for me, except I'd already left, having finished questioning Baines and his CEO a half hour earlier. But while he was there he noticed this ugly fat man in a super-looking suit striding in to meet with Baines. At the time he didn't know who the guy was, but he remembers commenting to his partner about it, that expensive clothes could make even a toad appear handsome. When he saw Forbes upstairs today, he recognized him right away."

Riley was already on the fourth floor landing and holding open the door into the administrative wing of Psychiatry. "Think of the sequence," he was saying as I caught up with him. "Saswald's murdered Monday evening. My officers spend the night and all day Tuesday asking about the name 'Pearson,' and that afternoon I'm making Baines and his CEO squirm with questions about their Mexican addiction clinic. Then Forbes is seen trotting into Baines's office, and the next evening Martin Whitehead is manipulated into trying to kill you. Let me tell you, I'm *really* looking forward to hearing what this son of a bitch has to say about all that!" Riley's voice had dropped to a whisper as we stepped into the corridor and strode toward Forbes's office. He didn't hesitate when we got there, but stepped up and knocked firmly.

No answer.

He looked at me, lines of concern suddenly zigzagging across his forehead. He repeated the knock, and when there was no reply, he tried the handle. The door was locked. "Shit!" he muttered. "I've got men at all the exits from this floor, in case he made a run for it, but if he's bolted the hospital, then we've got our work cut out for us." He started to turn in the direction of the patients' wing where the nurses' station was located, then stopped in mid-stride, puzzlement replacing the concern on his face as he looked down at his feet. "What the hell?"

I'd felt something sticky pull at the bottom of my own shoes as I'd taken a step to follow him, causing me to also glance down.

My gut clenched like a fist.

Fresh blood was oozing out the bottom of the door and beginning to puddle where we'd been standing.

"Jesus Christ!" Riley exclaimed, leaping forward and hammering on the door again, this time twice as loudly. "Forbes! Open this door! Can you hear me?"

Silence.

"Shit! Run get a key!" he ordered, and began to throw his shoulder against it. From the solid thudding noise that echoed along the hall each time he made contact with the heavy wood, it sounded as if he might as well be attempting to batter down the tree that it had been cut from.

I ran up the deserted corridor, heading for the door leading through to where the patients were. I flung it open and began yelling, "Help!" as I continued my sprint toward the station. "I need a pass key for Forbes's office!"

The ruckus caused a few patients to stick their heads out of the entrances to their rooms. A pair of nurses also appeared, coming out of a doorway just ahead, where they'd presumably been attending to someone. Farther on, their supervisor stood and glowered at me from behind the counter surrounding the ward's central workstation.

"Someone's locked in Forbes's office and is hemorrhaging," I exclaimed as quietly as I could when I drew near the two nurses who'd stepped into the hall. "Get security up here fast with a key," I directed the one standing closest. To her companion, I ordered, "You keep the patients in their rooms." They hesitated as a look of shock passed over both their faces. One of them appeared about to speak. "Move!" I yelled, cutting her off.

They blanched but sprang into action. The first woman

stepped back into the room she'd come out of and grabbed the bedside phone. "Locating, this is an emergency . . ."

The other one strode down the hall, ordering, "Okay, you people, back out of the hallway! I want this area cleared . . ."

I shouted to the still-frowning woman at the counter, "Call a Code Blue for Forbes's office, stat!" I spotted a nearby utility cart, from which I grabbed some latex gloves and masks. Whatever we found, it was bound to be messy and wet.

Pulling on the protective wear as I raced back into the administrative wing, I heard the thudding up ahead suddenly end in a splintering sound, and Riley yelled, "I'm in!" But as I ran up to him, I saw he was having trouble pushing the door open more than a few inches, and already more blood was flowing over the sill and spreading on the linoleum floor around his feet. The office itself was in darkness. He shoved harder, making the gap wide enough so he could squeeze through. Disappearing inside, he switched on the lights. "Oh my God!" I heard him exclaim.

Even with my mask on I could scent the sickly metallic odor. Breathing through my mouth, I quickly followed him inside, my shoes squishing over the soaked carpet. As I peeked behind the door I saw Peter Forbes lying on his back, his head pointed to where I was standing, his right arm stretched up to the door handle, fingers still encircling the knob. His neck was slashed open, a deep clean cut identical to Saswald's, but where that laceration had nearly drained empty, this wound was still awash in blood, the vessels and structures within obscured from sight. A trail of red showed where he'd dragged himself from one of his overstuffed antique chairs—now coated in glistening crimson atop the maroon and gold. Everything else—his desk, the bookshelves, his journals, even the ceiling—had been caught in the spray.

Riley was kneeling beside him. "Mother of God, Doc, look!"

He was pointing to where small bubbles were forming on the surface of the yet-unclotted pool welling out of the trenchlike gash. I quickly stooped down beside him and stared. Amidst the dark, more static portions of the liquid, I could still see tiny pumping eddies of brighter colored currents swirling up from below. His heart was still beating. "He's alive!" I cried, more out of horror that he could survive in such a state than as a clinical pronouncement.

Then, as if to confirm what we were seeing, a soft gurgling sound came out of his neck, his eyes slowly slid half open, and ever so slightly his mouth began moving, making the shapes of noiseless words.

Chapter 12

My stomach lurched toward the back of my mouth.

"What's he trying to say?" Riley demanded.

"I have no idea!" Even if Forbes could have issued sounds, he would have been so delirious from blood loss that he'd have emitted little more than gibberish anyway. His half-opened eyes already were so fixed and lifeless that I doubted he could even see. But maybe he could still hear. As someone dies, it's the auditory sense that's the last to shut down. I leaned over him, positioning my mouth near his ear, and grabbed his hand that was nearest me. "Peter, it's Earl Garnet. If you can, squeeze my fingers."

No response. Perhaps he was too weak for even so minor a task. "Close your eyes, Peter! Close, then open them."

At first nothing happened. Seconds later, ever so slowly, as if they were encased in glue, his lids lowered, and after what seemed an interminable pause, opened again.

Riley immediately took over. "Blink once if you know who did this. . . ."

From the hallway behind me I could hear the approaching steps and voices of the trauma team. But I was transfixed by Riley trying to communicate with Forbes.

"Blink again if the person who did this is named Pearson. . . ."

My breathing slowed to a stop as I stared at those sightless eyes and waited for a response. Images of David over the years—his face livid and swollen by drink as he'd lashed out at me—flickered through my mind with the speed of a lightning flash. Could he have returned from Mexico in one of his alcoholic rages, this time blaming Forbes? But for what? Sending him to a clinic that had failed to help him stop drinking? Or for something worse?

"Blink, damn it!" Riley implored him.

But the psychiatrist's lids remained immobile and his lips no longer stirred. Instead his mouth hung slack, and he appeared to be giving a departing moan.

First through the door was Sean Carrington. "Holy shit!" he exclaimed. Behind him came Susanne, her nurses, and Michael Popovitch.

"Christ almighty!"

"My God!"

After them followed half a dozen residents from ER.

"Gloves everybody!" I ordered, my clinical reflexes taking over. "He's still got a heartbeat." In the credo of a trauma center, that meant he also had a chance, albeit a slim one.

We got to work.

As everyone scrambled to start IVs, I shoved a big wad of sterile gauze into the depths of his wound. The white material instantly turned crimson, soaking up enough blood that the sides of the trench-shaped cut became visible. Amidst the remaining wetness I could see torn strands of muscle and the open ends of lacerated vessels pouting from the lower half of his neck—but not the severed airway I was looking for. Using more swabs, I got the area sufficiently dry that I could make out the lighter-colored interior of two other orifices. One, I knew, would be the creamy lining of a transected esophagus, and the other had to be a cartilage ring in the open end of his trachea—the object of my search. But the openings were so recessed in the surrounding tissues, and the anatomy of the neck was so distorted that I couldn't tell for certain which was which.

"Tube them both," Sean muttered, peering into the twisted mess from his vantage opposite me. He reached and slipped the tip of an endotracheal airway into one of the two lumens. While he secured it in place I performed the same procedure on the other opening. We took turns giving the chatter of teaching, explaining what we were doing as the residents hovered over us.

". . . a few puffs of air with the ventilating bag will tell us which is the trachea . . ."

". . . if you hear gurgling, you're in the stomach . . ."

Soon we were sending volleys of oxygen into Forbes's lungs and letting the remnants of his most recent meal drain into a basin.

"Probably his last," I heard someone mutter.

Glancing behind me, I could see that Michael and Susanne had infusions of normal saline up and running through large bore lines in his groin.

"To the OR," Sean ordered quietly.

Lifting Forbes onto a stretcher, we raced for the elevator, Sean bagging him through his open neck, me supporting his head against its sickening, lolling motion, and a nurse holding his intravenous bags aloft while riding on top, her knees astride his legs. Despite repeated shouts of "Stand clear!" our macabre little float was constantly slowed by the parade of visitors arriving at that hour. In our wake I could hear a steady stream of stifled screams and loud gasps.

At the operating room more nurses, technicians, and residents—all shouting orders—swarmed our near-lifeless cargo. They drew bloods, started O-negative transfusions, and inserted additional lines, then wired him to so many monitors that an entire wall lit up with screens displaying digital readouts and luminescent tracings. A masked anesthetist took command of his breathing and quipped, "Quite an airway," saluting Sean and me with a pair of raised eyebrows. A pair of nurses finished cutting away his finery, leaving him naked, with his white belly dominating his skinny limbs. Others went to work between his legs, skewering his limp manhood with a thin red catheter. If past rumors were true, more than one of the women present had had intimate en-counters with that part of him before.

Pulling on sterile garb, I watched Sean—already masked, gowned, and regloved—as he picked up a scalpel, anointed the left side of Forbes's chest with a swab of disinfectant, and made a sweeping incision along his sixth rib. Into this opening he inserted a pair of hinged metal claws which he used to pry the ribs apart. With a few popping sounds the moist connecting cartilage gave enough that a half-foot-long gap several inches wide appeared in the chest wall. It was big enough to admit a hand, and I reached inside. The shiny wet surface of healthy pink lung tissue bulged out around my wrist with each inflation by the anesthetist.

"Whatever other habits he indulged in, he was not a smoker," Sean commented wryly as he turned to begin re-pairing the severed neck vessels.

I slithered my hand past the expanding and deflating lobes until I felt my fingers close around his barely beating heart. Gently I began compressing and releasing the ball of muscle at a rate of once a second to augment its feeble pumping action.

But my thoughts were neither caring nor professional. How could they be—the man whose life I had in my grasp had tried to kill me. For his willingness to sacrifice Martin Whitehead in the process, I loathed him, and I was growing more con-vinced by the minute that he'd also wronged David, knowingly sending him to a facility with such terrible secrets as to require murder to keep them hidden. While every squeeze of my fist determined his chances of survival, Forbes's malevolence so revolted me, I fantasized that what he really deserved was my ripping the organ from his innards.

By any ethical standard, my frame of mind should have compelled me to request another physician take my place, but I didn't. Because what overrode my detesting him was my de-sire to keep him alive in order that he could provide some an-swers. Given who was available in that room, I knew my own resuscitation skills—among the best in the hospital—were his only hope. You won't get away from me, you bastard, I kept telling myself, continuing to pump. You're going to talk to me before you die.

The surgeons moved back from his neck to observe their work and scan for leaks in the vessels they'd rejoined. The still-unsutured portion of the slash gaped at me, seeming to leer at my resolve. Forbes so resembled a corpse on a slab that the resident behind me murmured, "This isn't surgery; it's an autopsy."

Twenty minutes later his heart simply went still in my palm. Neither repeated countershocks nor injections of epinephrine and atropine could start it again. The myocardium, or heart muscle, was irreversibly damaged by lack of oxygen due to his loss of blood.

Calling off a resuscitation is always an admission of defeat, but it had never felt like this. Walking out of the OR, furious at my having let him slip away, I had none of my usual pity or sorrow for the dead. Instead my raging at Forbes for what he'd done went on unabated, and the questions left unanswered by his dying continued to pepper my brain. Who was his killer? David Pearson? But was he also his victim?

Ripping off my surgical mask, I strode past rows of mostly darkened operating suites and felt the fatigue of the last few hours settling heavily in my back, in my legs, and in my soul.

Riley and Fosse were waiting just outside a pair of swinging doors that bore the sign CAPS, GOWNS, AND BOOTS MUST BE WORN PAST THIS POINT.

Fosse looked pained as he said, "For the sake of hospital security, Earl, I don't think we can avoid any longer letting Detective Riley look at the chart of one patient. You know whose I mean. A judge is already being asked to grant the necessary subpoena, and for that single file, given what's happened, there's a chance this time that the ruling will be in favor of the police. Now, I've already alerted the family as to what's about to happen, and suggested they get legal representation, to protect this patient's interest, even in his absence . . ."

Fosse's words faded into the background as I beheld the withering expression in Riley's eyes. He didn't say a word. He didn't have to. His searing stare cut into me like a blowtorch and was more than enough to reignite my guilt. *If only you'd confided in me earlier,* his black gaze seemed to accuse, *maybe Forbes would still be alive.*

Chapter 13

Half an hour later I got a call that made all the legal wrangling unnecessary.

I'd returned to Forbes's office at Riley's insistence, and was standing in the hallway outside, where a group of his officers were reconstructing how the murder had occurred. Despite Riley being furious with me, he'd wanted me to observe the proceedings, "In case something important might catch your attention," he curtly informed me. When I heard my name coming over the P.A., I excused myself and picked up a nearby wall phone.

"Mother reached me here at the base right after Mr. Fosse spoke to her," Allen Pearson blurted as soon as I identified myself. His speech was pressured and his voice rose to a higher pitch than what I'd heard a few days ago in my office. "I appreciate his advice about counsel, but we sure as hell don't need lawyers. They'd only delay things. I figure that since the police will be investigating my father's whereabouts anyway, why not tell them about his being at the clinic in Mexico. Maybe then they'd get after the authorities down there to finally mount a proper search for him—"

"Jesus, Allen, cool it!" I hissed at him, speaking behind my hand into the mouthpiece and hunching over the receiver. Riley was near enough that he might overhear my end of the conversation. "What the hell's the matter with you? You could incriminate your father in this murder more than he already is if you're not careful. Even if he's got nothing to do with it—"

"If? Come on, Dr. Garnet. My father may be a drunk, but I know he's certainly not a killer. Suppose by some miracle he hasn't boozed himself to death and they do find him. Surely it'll be a simple matter to clear him of these killings since he was thousands of miles away at the time. Besides, in a high profile murder case like this one, if I don't volunteer the information, there's bound to be a frenzy of publicity about the police department suing for access to his psychiatric file. That would be devastating for my mother and sister—"

"Allen, listen to me!" I interrupted. "Don't you realize that at the time of the killings he may have already been back in Buffalo—that he could be in the city as we speak? It's that possibility the police are going to be looking at, and lord knows what kind of motive—"

"And my father not contact me or my sister and mother?" he interjected. "No way. He'd have had to be reasonably sober to make the trip, and then we would have heard from him. He loves us, Dr. Garnet, whatever mess he made of his and our lives—that one truth is constant—and he would have phoned us if he could."

Not if his alibi required you and everyone else to think that he was still in Mexico, I very nearly retorted. I found the young man's faith in his father's innocence strangely naive, and at odds with the cynicism I'd heard in nearly everything else he said about David.

But the headstrong Marine was giving me no more time to argue. "Look, I'm meeting with the police tonight," he declared, "whether you approve or not, but if you could be there with me, I'd appreciate the moral support." Before I could protest further, he hung up.

"Damn," I muttered, as puzzled by his rashness as I was troubled by it. Replacing the receiver, I passed under a curious glance from Riley as I rejoined his investigators. Focusing

exclusively on a young woman in uniform who was reading
from a pad, I tried to ignore him.

". . . probably the killer was waiting in the dark for his
target to enter the room. From behind this door he could
have grabbed the psychiatrist, sliced his throat with a single
stroke, then kicked the door closed while keeping hold of the
still-flailing victim. This administrative wing is usually deserted by seven P.M., so there wasn't much chance he'd be
seen . . ."

As she spoke, despite myself, I pictured David carrying
out the savage execution she was describing, and a swirl of
nausea reeled through my head.

". . . we found the imprint of a rubber boot on the carpet,
suggesting again that this killer wears protective gear against
the spatter . . ."

My mind's eye couldn't help but visualize David drenched
in blood as he clasped the dying psychiatrist to him, restraining the man's bucking and lashing until the death throws
subsided.

But David was also a victim, I argued to myself, if Forbes
had first done to him anything nearly as evil as what he'd
done to Martin. Not that I was suddenly condoning vigilante
justice—a lifetime in ER trying to patch together the human
remnants resulting from that kind of rage had left me permanently sickened by it. But I was more ambivalent than ever
about helping the police track David down.

The policewoman pocketed her notes, reached through the
strands of yellow tape designating the murder scene, and
shoved open the door to the office, which, fortunately for us,
she'd kept closed until this point in her report. I hung back
as the others looked in—I had seen all I'd wanted of the place
the first time. But I couldn't escape the smell. It wafted from
the room, filled my nostrils, then caught in my throat.

Exsanguinated blood first congeals, then, as does any other
body tissue once it's dead, begins to decay. But the breakdown of semifluid clots gives off a smell quicker than more

solid organic matter. The process had already started in that confined space, releasing bit by bit a cloying sweetness into the air and adding it to the biting, sour scent of the iron in plasma that was already so evident.

". . . once the victim was too weak to crawl any distance or to help himself, the killer left, locking this door behind him with the victim's keys. We think he slipped in and out unnoticed by using the rear staircase . . ."

Christ, I thought, breathing through my mouth and barely managing to keep the odor tolerable, Riley and I might have run into him if we'd come looking for Forbes ten minutes earlier.

When the call for the detective finally came through, he scowled at the interruption as he strode over to use the same phone that I had. While he spoke, his gaze abruptly swung over to me, and the jaw he'd been clenching so tightly dropped open.

After hanging up, he motioned me aside and whispered, "As you probably already know, that was a Sergeant Allen Pearson of the U.S. Marines. He's meeting me in Fosse's office half an hour from now to tell me everything I want to know about his father, a Dr. David Pearson, who was your patient. He assured me that I wouldn't need a lot of legal rigmarole, but he requested you be there. How about it?"

"Of course," I replied, feeling sick at heart and fearing that we were about to do David great harm.

Allen, in uniform, sat erect on the front edge of a wingback chair as if he were at attention. He'd taken less than fifteen minutes to relate his father's story to Riley—telling him all about David's addiction, his admission to the Brama clinic in Mexico, and his subsequent disappearance.

Riley occupied a small sofa a few yards from Allen, and occasionally jotted notes on a pad as he listened. Two of his officers stood lounging against the wall behind their boss, and Fosse was perched on the corner of his oversized desk, watching the proceedings attentively and frowning over what he'd heard so far. I'd taken what was left—an overstuffed Victorian love seat that was a lot more comfortable than it looked.

Allen went on to describe his own attempts to track his father down, including his initial meeting with Fosse, his phone conversations with the psychiatrist Martinez at the clinic, and his first encounter with Baines via the early morning call from the man a week ago Monday.

"The morning of the day Saswald was killed," Riley made a point of noting.

Allen then quickly summarized how he'd suddenly found himself shut out—the clinic repeatedly hanging up on him; Baines and Forbes refusing to meet with him; and later, Baines rebuffing even Fosse's personal intervention on Allen's behalf. As I listened, his voice remained devoid of any emotion, and he sounded more like a medical resident reciting the complex medical history of a stranger than a son talking about his father. I found the detachment unsettling.

Riley studied his notes a few seconds when the young man had finished, then asked, "About this abrupt unwillingness of anybody at the clinic or at Brama to talk with you, it started last Wednesday?"

"Yes sir."

"And in the case of Baines and Peter Forbes, their refusal to meet with you also began on that day?"

"Not exactly. Forbes refused to see me the day before, early Tuesday afternoon. But the big freeze from Baines began on Wednesday."

Riley tapped the end of his pencil against his chin and shot me a cold stare across the expanse of taupe-colored carpet that separated us. "The timing is interesting, don't you think, Doc? Do you have anything to add to this sequence of events?" He sounded polite, but I could tell by the strain in his voice and the swell of his jawline that he was clamping his teeth together again, probably in an attempt to control his anger at my having kept so much from him.

"About Forbes, I'm afraid I do," I admitted, and described my visit with the psychiatrist last Tuesday morning. The detective's eyes grew even blacker when I related Forbes's peculiar reaction to my questions regarding David being at the clinic.

"What's going on?" Allen demanded, looking from one to the other of us.

Riley kept his gaze aimed in my direction, letting me have his silent fury full blast.

"Please, tell me what you suspect has happened to my father," Allen persisted. "That's why I came forward, so I could learn what's become of him." His voice was once more rising sharply, revealing his underlying anxiety, yet his expression remained rigid and under control enough not to betray his feelings. Having gotten no reply from Riley, he turned to me. "Dr. Garnet, you promised to give me straight answers!"

I felt a surge of sympathy for him. "As I told you before, Allen, there may be some connection between Dr. Saswald's murder, Brama itself, and Forbes's death—"

"We don't know anything for certain," Riley snapped, speaking solely to Allen while making it clear that I was to keep my mouth shut. "But I would appreciate getting the phone number of the clinic in Mexico, if you have it handy."

Allen's eyes flashed. For a few seconds I thought he was about to give the detective the same sort of dressing down I'd received two days ago when I'd been evasive, but the soldier's self-control won the upper hand. "Zero-one-one-five-two-six-five-seven," he recited, making the eight digit area code sound like his serial number. He followed this with the local exchange, also by memory. Neither his voice nor his eyes now held even a hint of the resentment he'd shown only seconds ago, but I figured it was still there, buried deep within layers of discipline.

The detective finished scribbling the number in his notepad, then said, "I have one more question, Allen, again about the sequence of events. What day was it exactly when you spoke to Mr. Fosse the second time about Brama stone-walling you?"

"Last Friday," Allen replied.

Riley turned to Fosse, who was still half leaning and half seated on the corner of his desk. "And that's the day you pressured Baines to be more forthright with the Pearson family?"

"Yes it was," Fosse replied. "I was surprised to learn he was in town, but leaped at the chance to give him hell personally for how his company was handling young Allen's problem. Not that it did any good."

"I appreciated your effort, sir," Allen quickly interjected, his expression softening.

Fosse's bearded face broke into a smile. "Why, thank you, son," he said gently. "And I assure you I'm not letting go of what happened to your father, whether his disappearance has anything to do with this other business or not. I never met him, but I've always been a fan of his writing."

On that calming note, Riley turned to Allen and thanked him for coming in. "One of my men will see you out past the guards at the door—"

"Detective, there's something else I want you to have," Allen interrupted, reaching inside his breast pocket. He brought out a standard-sized snapshot. "To help in the search, here's a photo of him. I know you could get the one they used for his column in the paper, but it's more than five years old, and frankly, he looks much more haggard now, on account of his drinking. This is the latest I have, taken just last spring when I got my sergeant's stripe. For the occasion, my father put on his old army uniform—it still fit him—and Mom took the shot. I figure you can blow up the part with his face in it and make copies for the Mexican police to show around. But I'd like the original back."

Riley studied the picture for a few seconds, then, without showing it to Fosse or me, put it inside the notebook he'd been writing on. "You're the spitting image of your father," he said absently.

Allen, getting up to leave, smiled for the first time since he arrived. As the two men shook hands he told the detective, "That's what everybody says."

No sooner was he out the door than Riley started pacing the length of Fosse's office. "I could have stopped Pearson from killing Forbes," he declared, wagging his index finger at me. "I fucking could have stopped him!"

"Now wait a minute," I protested, "I did what I was obliged to do and protected my patient's rights—"

"You withheld critical information!" he cried, wheeling around and stepping up to where I was sitting.

"It was medically confidential, which you keep denying."

"It implicated Forbes! I could have put the heat on him days ago—maybe even arrested him—but thanks to your delaying, the killer got to him before me."

"Hey!" I sprang to my feet and went eye-to-eye with him. "You don't think I did whatever I could, *legally,* to help nail this killer? I've been pointing you at Brama and that goddamned clinic in Mexico since the beginning. That's where the real crime was probably committed in the first place, and Pearson is likely as much a victim—"

"A victim who's maybe hacking heads half off—"

"Cool down, both of you!" Fosse barked, flashing an admonishing scowl as he slid off his desk to move between us. He reinforced his edict with a you-should-know-better look, then added, "Your going at each other seems to have blinded you to an altogether different scenario which strikes me as being pretty obvious."

The pulsing movement in Riley's jaw stopped. "Let's hear it," he sighed, giving an impatient wave and wandering over to stand behind the chair where Allen had been sitting. He grasped its back with his hands, his thick fingers indenting the upholstery with their strength.

"As you suggested, Detective, it's the chronology that's key," Fosse continued. "Now correct me if I'm wrong, but from the debriefings you've been giving me, later the same day that Allen Pearson and Dr. Garnet were upsetting Forbes with questions about David Pearson and the clinic, you were visiting Baines and his CEO in their Buffalo offices with identical inquiries of your own, leaving them equally upset. In addition, you told me earlier this afternoon that within an hour of that meeting, one of your men saw Forbes striding into Baines's office—summoned or showing up on his own—we don't know yet. Have I got all this right so far?"

Riley simply nodded.

"But the following day no one in Brama will have anything to do with Allen Pearson, and Peter Forbes apparently attempts to manipulate a patient into murdering Dr. Garnet. It all leads to some pretty interesting possibilities, doesn't it?"

Riley's disappointment showed in his face. So far this wasn't anything he and I hadn't already covered. "What's your point?" he demanded, sounding weary. "We already know that questions about David Pearson and the clinic make everyone at Brama nervous."

Fosse continued, undeterred. "Whether Baines ordered Forbes to try and kill Dr. Garnet to prevent his asking any more questions about David Pearson and the clinic, or the attempt was the result of Forbes panicking about what those questions might lead to and acting on his own," Fosse turned to me, "either way, his bungling your murder must have left Baines mighty uneasy."

"Holy shit!" Riley exhaled softly.

"It could have been Baines who had him killed!" I burst out.

"To keep him from talking," the detective added, "because he'd become a loose cannon."

"Baines could have feared that we'd eventually figure out how Forbes had tried to kill me," I elaborated, picking up the thread of thought, "and then decided he couldn't risk our arresting Forbes for murder."

"Exactly," Fosse said, leaning back and looking triumphant, the way a teacher might after making a breakthrough with slow students.

Riley frowned again. "But how did Baines know we were about to arrest Forbes? Christ, he or whoever he'd hired to do the killing must have gotten to the psychiatrist barely minutes ahead of us."

Fosse shrugged. "Maybe Forbes was frightened enough about your wanting to talk with him that he phoned Baines to ask what he should do. Maybe he even found out that you two had been interviewing Martin Whitehead, and he figured his jig was up. If he'd called Baines in a panic, babbling about facing arrest for attempted murder, Baines could have determined then and there to do away with him."

Riley's frown deepened as he digested the possibility. "Perhaps," was all he replied.

"What's troubling you?" I asked. "You look a hell of a lot less enthusiastic than you did just a few seconds ago."

The detective started to pace again, his index finger once more moving in the air, but this time as if he was doing math in his head. "If Baines is behind Forbes's murder, we also have to assume he's behind Saswald's. But from the airline records, we know for sure that Baines didn't leave San Francisco until after Saswald was killed."

"So?" I shrugged. "You just said he could have hired someone."

"I know I did, but if I think about it, the savagery of these kills goes against them being the work of a *professional* hit man. In particular, the method's too messy and prolonged. It requires the killer to hang around until the victim can't crawl or get help, and that delay increases the chances of his getting caught. Whoever did it took a lot of risks to make sure that Saswald and Forbes died slowly, in agony, and aware."

I'd always presumed that the butchery we'd seen was the product of an insane rage. That anyone could be so calculatingly savage chilled me to the bone.

"But couldn't Baines have ordered that the killings be

made to look like revenge slayings," Fosse suggested, "to make us think of someone like David Pearson? You said from the beginning, Detective, that the scrawled message might have been left by the killer himself to misdirect the police toward a scapegoat."

Riley seemed to go back to his silent calculations again, frustration written all over his face. I heard him murmur, "If Baines ordered up both murders and is that clever . . ." He trailed off, stared at his hands, and began kneading his knuckles the way arthritics sometimes do. Without warning, he slammed his fist into his palm, the force of the blow making me wince. "Christ!" he exploded, coming to a standstill. "Until I find out what Baines and his crew are up to at Brama or in that damn clinic, everything else is pure speculation." He threw his arms in the air and flopped down in the fancy love seat, his features sagging into a show of exhaustion. "Can *you two* tell me how an American health care company, an addiction clinic in Mexico, a psychiatrist, and an anesthetist can be used for something so illegal that it's worth killing over?"

His question sounded like the preamble to a weird joke.

Fosse looked contemplative but didn't offer up an answer.

I scarcely fared better. But watching the detective sprawled over that expensive piece of furniture as I considered the riddle he'd asked got me to thinking about Forbes's taste for pricey chairs. "Whatever the late psychiatrist was involved in, I bet it put money in his pocket," I said absently.

"You've got *that* right," Fosse readily echoed. He sounded relieved that I'd at least thought of something.

The lines of fatigue etched on Riley's face rearranged themselves into a show of exasperation. "Come on, give me stuff that's less obvious and more useful," he growled.

Fosse grimaced and admitted that he was still out of ideas. I quickly tried to come up with a different line of thought, but found myself drawn back to thinking some more about Forbes's lifestyle—of his receptiveness to perks for his *me too* research, perks that FDA regulations had curtailed over five years ago. Then it popped into my head that the trappings of wealth Forbes was in the habit of providing for himself—high-priced clothes, top-of-the-line cars, and travel—hadn't shown any corresponding decline. I hadn't given the matter any thought before, but now I wondered if he'd found another way to supplement his income. "You know, if research is involved," I speculated out loud, "I just thought of a scam that's unethical as hell, but unfortunately still occurs. Maybe Forbes was getting kickbacks for providing human subjects. When this goes on, the money involved is usually disguised as a 'consultation fee,' and the consultant simply persuades his colleagues to provide subjects from their practices. But one thing that's a complete no-no, and absolutely illegal, would be to take money for coming up with subjects who were your own patients."

Now Riley seemed mildly interested.

Fosse's expression, on the other hand, brightened, as if it had been caught in a spotlight. "Suppose their recruiting methods weren't the only things that were out of line," he piped up, his voice filling with excitement. "As you know, Earl, I sit on our own committee which screens proposed studies for the hospital, and it's especially tough on any clinical trials involving human subjects. One reason this Brama bunch chose to operate in Mexico might be that their research wouldn't pass muster under either U.S. law or national ethical guidelines."

This idea set Riley's eyes alight. "You know, there was a case somewhere in the Midwest," he began, leaning forward in his chair, "where a hospital was giving kickbacks to a ring of psychiatrists for bogus referrals of Medicaid and Medicare patients. Basically, those crooks would lock them up and put them on drugs for a while to generate false claims. Nobody listened when a few of the victims got out and complained—these people were officially diagnosed as crazy, right?—but finally the FBI got involved when the accusations started popping up in more than one state. Could this be something similar, but involving bogus research? An isolated setting in Mexico would be an ideal place to avoid scrutiny by American law enforcement agencies, in case anyone from this side of the border tried to raise a stink."

"Why would Baines be involved in generating false claims against his own company?" I asked. "That doesn't make sense."

"And I doubt the research would be entirely bogus," Fosse added. "A man like Baines wouldn't risk a dime on whatever they're working on, illegally or otherwise, unless it promised big profits."

Riley thought a moment. "Okay, let's come at the problem with a different set of questions. Why focus on research into alcoholism, and, although I can see a psychiatrist being involved, why use an anesthetist?"

"Maybe they chose alcoholism because it's such a massive problem crying out to be solved," Fosse suggested.

"Give me a break," Riley retorted with a groan. "I doubt this bunch is much motivated by the betterment of humankind."

"No, but that need makes the business of treating addiction worth a pretty good buck these days," Fosse replied. "As many as fifteen to thirty percent of hospitalizations are related to alcoholism, if you count the secondary admission diagnoses—cirrhosis, GI bleeds, multiple trauma—at a cost well over one hundred billion a year. A breakthrough on existing treatment methods could be worth a fortune for HMOs if it significantly reduced the amount they currently have to pay out for the problem."

"Forbes come up with an innovative idea for a disease as complex as alcoholism?" I hooted. "No way! He was a mental midget in the realm of original thinking. Any research he'd be involved in was bound to be derivative. And the only new development he could have tried to pirate are anticraving drugs—naltrexone, for one, and two similar agents still under study. But even if he'd had a copycat version and was trying to run quickie trials on it that he never would have gotten away with in the U.S., he wouldn't need Saswald for a scam like that, so it's unlikely that that's what he was up to. As for new clinical work on alcoholism that *does* involve an anesthetist, *I* certainly haven't heard of any." Yet as I spoke, something stirred at the back of my brain, as vague as a sensation of déjà vu. I tried to dredge up a more specific recollection of whatever it was, and after a few fruitless seconds decided it must have come from a lecture I'd heard or something I'd read long ago. But casting through distant memories of all the marginal medical information I'd been exposed to in the course of a lifetime was never a profitable exercise. "Nevertheless, let me see what the Net turns up if I plug in those key words," I suggested to Riley.

Fosse loosened his jacket, stretched, and wandered over behind his desk. He started opening drawers as if looking for something. "What are you going to do with all this speculation, Detective?"

Riley stood, arched his back, and groaned. "That's the trouble with having only speculation and no hard evidence. I couldn't use what I've got to pin so much as a parking ticket on either Baines or Pearson. And as far as investigating the clinic goes, look at the runaround Allen Pearson got, trying to make local Mexican police launch a search for his father. Unfortunately, our people are going to have just as much trouble getting anything done in that neck of the woods—cooperation isn't a watchword when it comes to cops and international jurisdictions."

Fosse asked, "Will you be questioning Baines about tonight's murder?"

"In a general way. I can't justify getting too heavy-handed with him."

"And have the media found out yet?"

"We haven't issued a statement," he answered, walking over to a corner window overlooking the grounds. Tendrils of mist played against the outer panes of glass, and I doubted he'd see much. "I'm sure reporters are down there, some-where, waiting in their remotes," he said wearily after taking a glance into the night. "They'd hear the 'possible homicide' call go out on the police band, and with all our cop cars coming and going, they'll know it's for real. Even with our ordering all the hospital workers not to discuss what's hap-pened until we finish questioning everyone, word's sure to leak out after the eleven o'clock shift change when people head home."

"So specific news of the murder, including Forbes's name and how he died, will likely break within the hour," Fosse said quietly as he pulled out what resembled a household phone directory with small index tabs along the side. I recognized it as the log where he kept all the chiefs' private numbers, in-cluding those when we were at conferences or away on vaca-tion. He always insisted that he had to know our whereabouts in case of emergencies, and what he was holding we'd long ago christened as his "mother hen" book. I assumed that he would now contact the Chief of Psychiatry and inform him of Forbes's death. Life must go on, and a replacement to take over the dead man's patients would have to be found tonight.

But instead of picking up the phone, Fosse placed both his palms on his desk and leaned toward a gloomy-looking Riley. "How would you like to bushwhack Baines at his office early tomorrow morning? It ought to be very interesting to see how he's reacting to the psychiatrist's death, especially if he hasn't had a chance to compose himself and prepare for a chat with the police."

"How do you mean?" the detective asked.

Fosse turned to me. "Earl, after our discussion about Janet this evening, I set up a meeting with Baines for eight A.M. to-morrow. He thinks I'm coming cap in hand with some 'con-sultants, in order that we might settle this Garnet trouble once and for all,' was how I put it."

Riley looked mystified until I quickly explained about un-desirables and what Brama had in store for Janet. "Although it all seems small potatoes now," I admitted, feeling foolish to even be discussing the problem in the wake of what we'd just witnessed, "I still have to do something about it."

Fosse's infectious grin once more parted his white beard as he turned to Riley. "Why don't you join us, Detective?" he invited, sounding as gracious as if he were putting together a table for one of his many fund-raisers.

"You're not serious," Riley exclaimed, looking surprised. "As odious as what they're doing to Janet is, it's not a felony and it isn't something that justifies a visit from the police."

"But a threatening phone call is," Fosse persisted, his eyes narrowing as if he were drawing a bead on a quarry. "Question the son of a bitch about that, and at the same time see for yourself if he's behaving like a man who's just murdered Peter Forbes."

Chapter 14

Brama Tower—a gleaming stone, steel, and glass structure—
had been erected near the shores of Lake Erie on the former site
of a rusted-out factory. It easily dominated the landscape—an
otherwise forlorn, scruffy section of town still littered with the
ruins of Buffalo's once great industrial era—and local com-
mentators had predicted the area would stay that way, thanks
to the garishness of the HMO quarters scaring off other de-
velopers. Certainly the company had the place to itself.

Not that there hadn't been an attempt on the part of the plan-
ners to blend in. The architectural design of the windows—row
upon row of slightly curved, silvery panes set in peaked concrete frames—had been an obvious try at mimicking a style
found in another celebrated local landmark, the nearby city
hall building. But the latter was a layered, bulky, thirty-three
story tribute in stone to Art Deco, and the try at melding the
two just hadn't worked. The taller, newer structure ended up
making the city hall appear stumpier than ever, and the only
effect of all those highly reflective, specially contoured sheets
of glass was to make the Brama building look as if it was
made from a stack of giant, one-way sunglasses.

As for me, I always thought the facade was perfect, for a
sleazy outfit with something to hide.

As I pulled onto the grounds, the prospect of a face-to-face
showdown with Baines had me pumped with excitement.
Janet was immediately behind me, having driven her own car
in case she was called to a delivery. Minutes later Fosse ar-

rived by cab. He spotted us easily enough, as at this hour there were no other cars in the section reserved for visitors, nor were there many anywhere else in the parking lot. It appeared that Brama felt it could afford giving doctors and hospitals a head start each morning before resuming the daily business of telling us what they were and were not going to pay for.

At five to eight a chauffeured squad car pulled up to where the three of us stood waiting, and Riley climbed out. He greeted us with a terse, "Let's go."

While the sun was already making the upper half of the building glitter silver and gold against a faultless blue sky, down here we were still in the shade, our breath trailing behind us on the cool October air. As we strode toward the main entrance, I shivered and sank my hands deeper into the oversized pockets of the coat I was wearing. Off in the distance I could see the flashing waters of Lake Erie dancing and sparkling and seeming to mock the coming winter which would soon smother it with ice.

It took but a minute for Riley to outline the final details he'd worked out by which he could convert our visit into official police business and use it "to soften Baines up, then pluck him clean," as he put it.

I liked what I heard.

Half a dozen security guards were positioned inside the front doors. "They weren't here last week," Riley muttered as he flipped out his badge and got the bunch of us waved through to the foyer inside. It was a massive, high-ceilinged space enclosed with glass—two-way at this level—and filled with ornamental trees. The centerpiece was a small landscaped waterfall that filled the air with the sounds of a running brook.

Looking around her, Janet murmured, "It's like a goddamned hotel!"

Fosse led us to a circular reception counter staffed by two more guards, who were sipping coffee and loudly debating this year's chances of the Sabres, Buffalo's extraordinary hockey team. Showing his card, he announced, "We've a meeting with Mr. William Baines."

"Ah, yes," one of the guards responded, putting down his cup and shoving a sign-in book at us. "We've been told to expect you."

Riley smiled at the other man. "Best goaltending in the league, I figure," he schmoozed, then pulled out his badge and summoned the startled fellow to meet him a few feet away, where he briefly huddled with him.

Seconds later as we waited for the elevators the detective quietly informed us, "The extra security was ordered an hour ago, by Baines himself."

"Because of Forbes's murder?" Janet asked.

Riley shrugged that he didn't know.

"It's a pretty defensive response if it is," I commented.

A few Brama early birds on the way to their offices joined us, and no one spoke as we were whisked noiselessly to the upper floors in less than a dozen seconds.

When the doors slid open, we stepped into as lush a reception area as I'd ever seen. A spread of pastel-blue carpet the size of a putting green led to a variety of sitting areas, each furnished with beige sofa chairs and a richly finished coffee table. Everywhere there were plants, and on three sides of the room hung an abundance of prints, none of which I recognized and most of which seemed to have been chosen for their colors, which matched the decor. But most stunning was an end wall entirely of glass. The view over Lake Erie from this height was such a startling sweep of deep blue that nothing else in the room could compete with its beauty.

Yet Baines's secretary, her desk set off to one side, obviously had gone to the trouble of giving it a good try. Her model's looks were enhanced with gold-speckled powder, her casual cascade of black hair had been carefully arrayed in place with mousse, and her long nails, exquisitely painted a soft pink, must have commanded at least an hour's worth of attention that very morning. While Fosse announced himself,

I caught her eyeing Janet's natural complexion and boyishly coiffed blond hair with what could only be called a competitive once-over.

When the woman finally did take in the rest of us, she said, "He's expecting you—" but at the sight of Riley, who'd made it a point to be last off the elevator, cut herself off and demanded, "Detective, what are you doing here? He didn't tell me anything about your coming—"

"I'm with them," he quipped, and strode over to a double set of doors set in the wall behind her. She started to protest, her makeup exaggerating the look of alarm in her face. With a disarming grin, he quickly added, "Don't worry, I know my way."

We followed after him before she could say or do anything more. Once inside, we were facing a very startled, very slender, immaculately dressed man who'd already sprung to his feet behind a desk that would have dwarfed even Fosse's. "What the hell?" he uttered, silhouetted in front of another wall-sized window overlooking the lake.

He had closely cropped blond hair verging on white, a lean, handsome face, and, even though he was of medium height, his compact physique made him an imposing figure. But then I got a good look at his eyes. Though they were the same color as the lake behind him, they lacked its brilliance, and even as a dark scowl spread across his forehead, his anger failed to ignite a spark in them.

"Mr. William Baines," Riley began, his voice coldly officious. "I think it appropriate that before we start this session, I read you your rights."

"My rights!" he gasped, growing flushed despite his California tan.

"Yes, your rights, because if I'm not satisfied with the answers you give me today, you may be leaving this building under arrest."

"Jesus Christ!" he uttered. "What are you talking about?"

"You have the right to remain silent. You have the right to an attorney being present . . ."

As Riley intoned the familiar refrain, Baines's expression quickly changed from fury to one of full alarm. Yet his eyes remained lusterless, as if they were switched off from what was happening. And from the way the skin below them sagged in tiny, dark pouches, I could tell that the man whom more than anyone else I held responsible for the death of little Robert Delany wasn't sleeping.

". . . anything you say can and will be used against you . . ."

I found it strange. I'd arrived thirsting for my chance to have at him and bring him to account, yet I'd been expecting a fiend in full roar who'd be brimming with arrogance. Instead I was confronting someone whose gaze was dull and full of dread, almost haunted. Nevertheless, once Baines started squirming and looking indignant under Riley's interminable warning, my anger at him for what he'd done returned with a vengeance—and waxed and waxed.

". . . if you cannot afford an attorney, we will appoint one for you . . ."

Yeah, right, I scoffed, looking around at the lavish surroundings. Knowing the price that patients had paid so he could afford the decor served only to jack up my fury a few notches more.

Turning from Riley, Baines pointed at Fosse. "You set up this meeting to settle the Garnet business," he accused. " 'Once and for all,' you said!"

"That's what we're doing," Fosse replied quietly.

A look of genuine confusion swept over Baines's face. "What the hell has your bringing the police here to do with Garnet?" He then gestured toward Janet and me. "And who the fuck are these two?"

Fosse suddenly bristled. "That's Dr. Earl Garnet and Dr. Janet Graceton," he snapped. "You should at least know the faces of the people whose careers you set out to destroy. Oh, but that's not your style, is it, Baines? You never *do* see the faces of the people you mess with! Did you ever even bother to look up a photo of the Delany infant?"

Baines's color went from red to white, and a sheen of perspiration appeared around the follicles of his short hair. He kept glancing from Janet to me, stammering, "I—I—I've done nothing illegal, nothing, you hear me? And if you think you can bully me with false accusations—"

". . . and do you understand these rights as I've read them to you?" Riley concluded, raising his voice enough to cut Baines off and grab his attention.

"I understand nothing!" Baines protested.

"Then get your lawyers in here," Riley replied, his voice smooth and cold as ice. "They'll explain it to you."

"Explain what?"

"Are you waiving your right to counsel?"

"Counsel about what?" Baines cried, his voice halfway to a shriek.

"You mean you don't have any idea what this is about?"

The beleaguered CEO sank back into his chair, repeatedly trying to swallow, but he didn't seem to have enough spit. "No, I don't," he finally replied, sounding shaky.

"Do you want me to tell you, without your lawyers here? I warn you, in front of these witnesses, that I'll use whatever you say in a court of law."

Baines looked up at us, his pupils so dilated that the irises around them had become thin blue rims. My God, he was afraid, I marveled. Was it solely of us—that we knew what he'd done? Or had it something to do with whatever was robbing him of his sleep and put that look of dread in his eyes before we'd ever walked in on him?

"We're investigating a threatening phone call placed to Dr. Garnet's home three nights ago, on Monday evening," Riley continued.

In the parking lot he'd confided to us that after "softening Baines up by reading him his rights," he intended to keep him guessing about how much we knew through a series of "carefully planned, insinuating questions."

"Now, Mr. Fosse here attests that you have demonstrated a great deal of hostility toward Dr. Garnet recently. Would you care to comment on that allegation?"

"He what?" Baines exploded, swinging his full attention over to the normally kind-looking sexagenarian, only to be greeted by a steely glare.

"Given that you've strong-armed our entire board to fire Dr. Garnet," the older man retorted without hesitation, "I figured the police should be made aware of anyone carrying that big a grudge."

Baines mouth curved south in a sneer. "Why, you meddling old fart—"

"It makes you or someone working for you a prime suspect for having initiated those calls," Riley cut in.

Baines was starting to resemble a man watching a tennis match. "You can't be serious!" he snapped, swiveling his head back around to face Riley again.

The detective stepped up directly in front of him and leaned across the desk. "You bet I'm serious. Two physicians at St. Paul's have already been murdered. There's also been an attempt made against Dr. Garnet's life, or do you already know about that as well? Make no mistake, Mr. Baines. Anyone suspected of threatening Dr. Garnet is in a lot of trouble."

In less than a heartbeat the pinched lines of rage in Baines's face widened into a show of startled, opened-eyed surprise. "An attempt against Garnet's life? What are you talking about?"

"You claim to know nothing of that?"

"Of course I don't. Someone tried to kill Garnet? My God!" He darted a frightened glance in my direction.

If he was lying, he was stellar at it, I decided. But a corporate sociopath would be, wouldn't he?

"You don't deny your hostility toward Dr. Garnet?" probed Riley.

"My battle with Garnet had nothing to do with anything personal!" Baines proclaimed. "It was because the man was attacking the very foundations of managed care and threatening to undermine the confidence of the millions of Americans who rely on us for the maintenance of their health . . ."

"Gimme a fucking break, Baines," I butted in. "I attacked Brama because you let a child die!"

His only response was to up the volume.

". . . thereby jeopardizing a system that has finally offered unprecedented access to health services."

I nearly puked. "So this is the pitch of the man whose company more than any other in America plays and espouses the game of 'withholding payment,' " I fired back. It was all I could do to keep from lunging at him.

Riley kept the pressure on him, giving the man no chance to start arguing with me. "You of course know that Peter Forbes was murdered last night."

Baines caught his breath and appeared to have trouble swallowing again. His pulse was fluttering at the base of his neck, his face was still pale, and his pupils remained as dilated as before. Each was a sign of his surging adrenaline levels—what physiologists call the "fight or flight state"— our most primitive response to fear. I couldn't tell whether he was preparing to bolt or mount an attack. "Yes. It's awful," he said. "I caught the news on the radio this morning—that poor man, dying so horribly." Baines spoke in breathless spurts. "I even ordered extra security, because, like Dr. Saswald, Peter Forbes also worked for us. I couldn't help but think that other physicians associated with our company might also be at risk of becoming targets." He stole another glance my way. "But now you tell me this killer tried to murder Garnet?" He was almost whispering, as if he preferred that I didn't hear the question.

Riley cocked his eyebrows and treated him to an inquisitor's silence. Baines resumed his squirming again, until the detective softly asked, "And why would you expect that someone would want to harm doctors who worked for Brama?"

Baines literally choked on whatever spit he'd managed to muster up. "Why, uh, well . . ." he stammered, then, flicking another glance at me, leaned forward to Riley, as if he was once more attempting to keep me out of their conversation. "Detective, I was actually going to call you about that matter. You see, we've had trouble before at our other offices, particularly in San Francisco, where local extremists have gotten patients' groups all lathered up and made them hostile as hell toward us." His voice grew louder. "As a result we've received obscene phone calls, bomb threats, even extortion attempts."

"What's your point?" Riley demanded.

Baines swung his gaze back toward me, his face flushed with anger again. "My point, Detective," he blasted at full volume, motioning toward me with his index finger, "is that troublemakers like Garnet here stir up the public and instigate these kinds of attacks. He's the one you should blame for what's happened to Saswald and Forbes! If he hadn't mouthed off about that kid—"

I lost it. "You creep!" I roared, and lunged across the desk at him. I yanked him forward by his necktie until my face was inches from his. "You killed Robert Delany, and you think that's just fine because legally no one can touch you for it."

"What the hell!" he sputtered, making a grab for my hands.

But I hung on. "And of course you must be laughing your head off that my wife and I don't have any legal recourse to stop you from destroying our careers."

"Jesus Christ! Detective, stop him," he called out, struggling to free his tie, and himself, from my grip.

I gave him another hard tug, and watched his pupils swell even larger. "But you're frightened, Baines. Why? Have you also done things that we *can* catch you on—illegal, terrible things? Is that why you look scared shitless?" So much for pussyfooting around with "a series of carefully planned questions." Better to bombard the creep with accusations.

"Doc, stop it!" Riley growled, grabbing my shoulders.

"Earl! What the hell are you doing?" Janet yelled.

I was beyond listening. "You know that Forbes tried to kill me, don't you? Maybe you even ordered him to. Is that the reason he's dead now, to keep him from implicating you?"

"What?" Baines squeaked.

Riley's grip tightened. "Shut up, Doc!" he ordered.

I not only held on, I pulled Baines close enough that I could smell the sweat off him and see his pupils pulse wider still. "It's the clinic in Mexico that's got your dark secrets, isn't it? What are you up to down there? In particular, what happened to David Pearson at that place?"

His eyes dilated further. "Shut up and get away from me," he shrieked, trying to ply my fingers open, with no success. To Riley, he hollered, "Get him off me, damn it!"

"Let him go, Doc!" Riley commanded again. But this time his grip remained the same.

"Earl Garnet, you idiot! Stop it!" added the love of my life.

I took a measure of the alarm in Baines's face. Not enough, I decided, and pushed harder. "And why was Saswald killed? Because he had something to do with research in the place that wasn't exactly legal?"

Baines's mouth dropped open. I was sure I'd hit a bull's-eye.

Riley racked up the pressure in my shoulders a nudge, but it suddenly flashed in the back of my mind that this was but a shadow of what those powerful hands of his could inflict. He could have had me off Baines in seconds. "Now, Doc! Drop the tie," he thundered convincingly just as I grasped that he must be actually *letting* me have a go at the man.

Instantly spurred on by having the cop's permission, I screamed into Baines's face, "What happened to David Pearson?"

Once more his pupils pulsed wider, to the point where the blues of his irises were barely visible, then constricted a bit. I knew I must be probing near whatever had him so frightened, and I was about to press him with more questions when Riley unceremoniously dug his thumbs into my armpits, and currents of numbness swept into my hands. "Let him be, Doc!" he said into my ear.

I had no choice. My fingers went paralyzed and my grip released by itself. Baines flopped back in his chair with a startled yelp and stayed put. Riley then hefted me easily to one side and took my place in front of the shaken executive, leaning over the desk at him. "You know what I think frightens you most of all, Mr. Baines?" he said. "It's the possibility that this killer is someone who's escaped from that clinic, and now he's returned to get even with the people who sent him there. That means Saswald is one, Forbes is two, and before you know it, maybe you'll be number three."

As Riley spoke, I watched Baines's pupils finally expand the rest of the way until his eyes went fully black with fright and stayed there. We'd hit the core of Baines's nightmare.

But the detective wasn't finished with him. "Do you know what it will be like, Baines, when he gets to you?" he continued, still standing over him and speaking in little more than a whisper. "Even when this killer's blade slices as deep as we've seen, it probably won't make much more than a soft whisking noise. What you'll hear is yourself sucking air through the slash in your neck. And as for what you'll feel, knife cuts sear you at first, like a line of acid. But then the real pain will come, waves of it, along with the blood. I've been with men as they've died from a knife wound—it's agony heaped on agony. Dr. Garnet figures with this kind of slash to the neck, you'll take ten minutes to go."

I thought his eyes would bulge out of their sockets. "You bastard!" he croaked, his voice breaking. He fought to control his breathing, then gave a sob. "Christ! You're a fucking bastard!" His eyes brimmed over with tears.

* * *

"Nobody could ever fake being that scared," Riley asserted from the backseat of my car. "As far as I'm concerned, the man truly believes he's next in line to have his throat cut."

"He was afraid, that's for sure," agreed Fosse, who was in the passenger seat beside me.

The three of us were returning to St. Paul's, having left a very unhappy William Baines surrounded by a pack of equally unhappy lawyers. They'd all been threatening to lay charges against me for assault and against Riley for police brutality.

"The only thing that got assaulted was your tie," Riley had told Baines as we were leaving, "and I never laid a finger on you."

"You intimidated me!" Baines had yelled after him.

"I simply made sure you understood what you might be up against," Riley countered, "in case you might want to disclose everything you know about David Pearson, to help us protect you from him."

His lawyers had wanted to continue the fight, but at the mention of David Pearson again, Baines signaled them to be quiet and ordered us off the premises.

"The minute I saw how frightened he'd become," Riley continued, "I figured he couldn't be behind the killings, but I had to press him to be sure. By the way, Doc, you zinged him nicely about the clinic." He leaned forward and gave me a friendly nudge on the shoulder. "His reaction, as far as I'm concerned, told us that our guesses came pretty close to what's going on down there."

Pulling up to a red light, I smiled at the acknowledgment, thinking that we sounded like members of a sports team complimenting each other after a successful game. But Janet hadn't been thrilled by my performance. "You idiot!" she'd berated me later in the parking lot. "If he had sued you, and won, you'd have lost your license." She'd then given me a hug and raced off to a delivery.

"But how could you tell that he was afraid of being murdered," Fosse asked Riley, "as opposed to his being afraid that you'd find him out for whatever scam he's involved in?"

"Did you ever see a man who's afraid for his life?" the detective replied. "It's the biggest fear there is—the sort that settles into the eyes and stays there—the kind that I saw in him today. His look reminded me of men I've seen on death row or people who know there's a contract out on them."

"Or in a patient who knows he's terminal," I quietly added, confirming Riley's observation.

We rode in silence for a while.

We were at the next stoplight when Fosse asked Riley, "So you were serious when you suggested that it's David Pearson who's gone on a rampage?"

"I guess so," the detective replied after considering Fosse's question a few seconds. "But I'm back to my old refrain. If we're going to make a case against Pearson for Saswald's murder, we need solid proof—not only of the anesthetist being at that clinic, but also of his having had contact with Pearson. So far we have neither."

We sat in silence again, waiting for the light to change.

"Wait a minute," Fosse declared, "I just thought of how I might get you the proof you need. Hell, I may even have had it in my hands last night!"

"Proof?" Riley said, sounding skeptical.

Fosse ignored the detective and instead tapped me excitedly on the shoulder. "Earl, it's my directory where I keep track of departmental chiefs when they're away."

His mother hen book.

"All those weekends Saswald was off working at Brama facilities," Fosse continued, "I have their phone numbers."

"My God!" I exclaimed.

"Hey!" Riley broke in. "One of you better tell me what the hell you're talking about."

Out of the corner of my eye I saw Fosse give the detective a grin. "As soon as Earl gets us to the hospital, I'll give you the link you're after," he promised.

The light changed and I gunned the accelerator. With Riley on board I didn't think a speeding ticket would be a problem.

By the time we pulled through the gates of St. Paul's, Fosse had already explained to Riley his insistence on knowing where his departmental chiefs were when they were traveling. "And I don't accept calling them on their cell phones. Half the time they turn them off, and just as often they're in a dead zone," he continued as we rushed into the hospital. "They leave me numbers from all over the world—Asia, Europe, South America—and an exchange from Mexico wouldn't even have made me think twice. In fact, Saswald was away so routinely over the last year, most times he simply told my secretary where he could be reached, and she'd enter it into the book."

Minutes later we reached the hushed domain of Administration and trooped into his office. "Now, to cover his tracks, he may only have given the Brama number for their headquarters in San Francisco, expecting them to forward any call from me," Fosse continued, pulling out the familiar directory from his desk as Riley and I crowded around. "But since he was away mostly on weekends, outside regular office hours, I'm hoping he felt he couldn't rely on anything less than leaving me the actual clinic's exchange." Flipping it open, he asked, "When did Pearson get transferred to the clinic?"

I gave the date, remembering it from when I'd checked his chart.

While Fosse found the appropriate page, Riley pulled from his pocket the pad where he'd written the number. With it came the photo that Allen had provided last night, and it fell onto the desk. While I waited for Fosse to find what we wanted, I found myself staring at the image of the young Marine and his gaunt-looking father.

"Here!" Fosse exclaimed excitedly. "Saswald was away

four and a half weeks ago," and he quickly read out a long stream of figures that sounded familiar.

"Bingo!" Riley cried out. "They match."

"Do we call the clinic," Fosse asked eagerly, picking up the receiver, "and see if they'll verify knowing him? My Spanish is pretty good."

The detective laid a restraining hand on Fosse's arm. "I already phoned yesterday evening, after leaving here, but only got the night staff. The manager of the place and the psychiatrist who took care of Pearson won't be in until eight o'clock their time." He glanced at his watch. "With the difference in zones, that's not until eleven this morning, another hour and a half."

"What are you going to say when you do speak with them?" I asked, looking up from the picture.

His forehead creased. "Good question. They're sure to follow the same party line as Baines—that Saswald's never been there. And after what we put Baines through this morning, the warning's certainly going to go out, if it hasn't already, ordering them to beware of American cops, particularly ones asking about Saswald and research. Now if you'll excuse me, I've got to call my office." He stepped over near the window and punched in a number on his cellular. Before he lowered his voice out of earshot I heard him order, "Let the hounds loose—everything we prepared overnight. It's Pearson we're looking for. But keep it solely a missing person's angle. I don't want to connect him publicly with the killings just yet . . ."

While we waited for him to finish, Fosse picked up the snapshot and casually looked at it. "You know, I really don't think you hurt your own cause any by pressing Baines the way you did. It'll buy us a bit of time, and maybe I can get the Robert Delany fund operational sooner than expected." He glanced up and caught me looking at him in amazement. "What, you think I'm obsessed with this Brama business?"

"I think the relentlessness of your opposition to Brama is remarkable."

He grinned. "You left off, 'for an old fart.' " Then his eyes sparked darkly and his face folded into a scowl. "It's not remarkable at all, Earl," he said curtly, and I felt as if he were scolding me for saying so. "My mother died of breast cancer, and my father worked himself into a heart condition trying to pay the bills. After my mother's death, he got progressively sicker, and I watched his doctors treat him with the same sort of indifference and dismissive arrogance that HMOs now institutionalize and make into a business. Then my grandfather and a few of his 'colleagues' paid some of those doctors a visit. After that, my father received first-class treatment all the way, except 'their care' came too late to help, and what he really got was a first-class trip to his grave. My grandfather helped whenever he could, but I basically ended up raising my younger brother and sister on my own, so I know what sickness and medical expenses are all about, in spades. Years later I got another taste of that same arrogance. This time it cost me my wife and an unborn son—an obstetrical resident dismissed her complaints of headache and heartburn as unimportant, and she died of eclampsia—" He checked himself, falling silent, but fiery bitterness remained in his gaze. "Sorry," he quietly murmured. "As I said last night, I shouldn't talk about this when I'm emotional. But everything I've stood for in my professional life is rooted in that family history of mine, you understand. So it isn't likely that my commitment to stand up against the likes of Baines and Brama *could* be anything less than total."

I stood motionless, feeling uncomfortable and saying nothing. I'd known Fosse was a widower, but little else of his personal life. I'd had no idea that he'd fashioned his professional avocation out of such tragedy. I also hadn't a clue what to say about such a string of misfortune that happened so long ago.

To my relief he shrugged and indicated the topic was closed by looking once more at the photo of David and Allen, which he still held in his hand. "Boy, they could be twins," he muttered, tossing it back on the desk, "except of course the son is too young."

"Pardon?" I queried, suddenly gaping at him. "Can you repeat that?"

"Look, I didn't mean to embarrass you with details of my past, and I really don't want to talk about it anymore. All I meant to explain was that if you find my commitment to stand up against Baines rather extreme, it's that way for a good reason—"

"No! I understand that perfectly. I meant what you said about the Pearsons."

The space between his eyes furrowed. "Why, just that they looked enough alike to be twins, except of course the difference in ages. It was a silly comment, really."

"Oh, right," I answered, trying to make it sound as if it were of no consequence—that I had simply misunderstood him in the first place. But his "silly comment" had just sent my thoughts snapping through a 180-degree turn, and the words scrawled beside Saswald's body in blood had abruptly taken on an entirely new meaning. Worse, their implications were rapidly making me feel ill.

At that moment Riley completed his call and rejoined us. Had he overheard Fosse? Would he also pick up what I'd just realized? I didn't want him to, not yet, maybe not ever. First I had to think it through. Maybe on closer scrutiny the idea would seem so farfetched that I could dismiss it.

The detective arched an eyebrow my way. "You look startled, Doc," he said. "Did you think of something else?"

I gave a little laugh. "No, not at all."

He skeptically raised both brows, but then turned back to Fosse. "I'm going to need that book of yours as evidence . . ."

Their conversation faded into the background as my mind raced. If Saswald had known only David, and hadn't been aware that David had a son, it could be possible, I reluctantly concluded.

What the dying anesthetist may have been attempting to tell us was *Pearson, but too young . . .*

That his killer looked like David *Pearson*, except that he was *too young*.

He may not have known his name, nor even who he was, but he could have been describing Allen.

Chapter 15

Recheck the facts, I kept telling myself. Make sure I hadn't made a mistake.

But once the idea took hold that Allen could have been the murderer, it made frightful sense. Because he might have been avenging his father, either acting in concert with David on his behalf or extracting his own revenge for whatever Saswald and Forbes had done to the man. Being a trained Marine, he'd know how to cut a throat. As for his whereabouts at the time of the killings, the police could check that out at his base. Pray to God he's got an alibi, I thought, appalled by how readily my thinking the worst of him was gathering its own terrible momentum. But his motive had come so easily to mind and seemed so credible that the rest of the scenario practically wrote itself.

And then I realized that maybe I wasn't the only one to have suspected him. When Martinez, Baines, and Forbes had suddenly not wanted anything to do with him, had it been because they also believed he was the killer?

I looked over to Riley, who was still talking earnestly with Fosse. At one and the same time I dreaded the detective suspecting Allen and yet wished he would. Because as long as I kept the prospect of Allen's guilt to myself, and neither Riley nor anyone else thought of it, I was covering up for the son exactly as I had for the father.

I looked back at the photo and stared at it for a few seconds. Damn you, David, I cursed. When will I ever be free of you?

"Jesus, Doc, are you sure you're all right?" I heard Riley ask.

Snapping out of my daze, I saw both the detective and Fosse staring at me, their brows creased with concern.

"Yeah, what's wrong?" the older man added. "You don't look good at all."

I had an ER to run. At least that's what I'd said to Riley and Fosse after assuring them that I was only overtired, so as not to make my quick exit seem too conspicuous.

But I had a lot of trouble keeping my mind on the job. Even seeing patients with routine problems required all the concentration I could muster, and my ineptness in performing administrative duties soon had Susanne fit to be tied. "Everybody's as distracted about Forbes's murder as they were about Saswald's. In fact it's worse," she warned. "What with all the rumors that a maniac's loose in the hospital and stalking our staff. Your not being here didn't help any either. For God's sake talk to them now, like you did before."

But what could I say? Telling them at this point that Forbes and Saswald were probably involved with something illegal and that they were killed in some kind of revenge slaying was out of the question. Riley would go ballistic, and the media would have a field day. "Susanne, I don't think anybody here is in personal danger, but the details are police business, and I'm not at liberty to discuss them."

"Then please, at least tell them that!" she snapped, her growing frustration evident. "We're having close calls again."

I made the rounds and said what I could, but whenever anyone asked a question, my evasiveness obviously made them even more uneasy.

To make matters worse, more HMOs than ever were only giving provisional approval for admissions, and increasing numbers of patients were signing themselves out against medical advice.

". . . too big a risk. If they don't pay the bill, it would bankrupt us . . ."

". . . that's our food money . . ."

". . . hey, man, clothes for the kids, gas for the car—you know how it is . . ."

Not only did the incidents increasingly involve HMO providers other than Brama, after a few phone calls to other hospitals, I discovered that the trend was citywide.

"Collusion!" cried some of my staff.

"Monkey see, monkey do!" the others insisted.

"What are you going to do about it?" a worried Michael Popovitch asked.

I didn't know.

By early afternoon I'd argued myself hoarse to no avail with triage officers from over half a dozen HMOs.

"We simply issue payment guidelines. The medical decisions, and the responsibility, remain with you, Doctor," they'd all parroted, ever so sweetly.

"Nice try!" wheezed a fifty-year-old asthmatic who couldn't risk being hit with a bill for the few days I felt he needed to stay in the hospital. As I presented him with a release stating that neither I nor St. Paul's could be held accountable for whatever happened to him if he left ER, Susanne muttered, "Why not ask him to sign his own death warrant?"

Riley phoned shortly before two. "As expected, everyone at the clinic denied knowing Saswald, and all of them kept reciting the line that an addiction center had no need for an anesthetist," he reported. "By the way, did you have a chance yet to check out the Net for any experimental stuff that might make the connection?"

I'd been so preoccupied with our problems in ER, and wrestling with what I should do about Allen, that I'd forgotten. "Sorry, I'll get to it as soon as I can."

"Okay, Doc. But I hope you'll find me something. I need a definite lead on what that place could be up to, or I'll never get the local cops to give it so much as a glance. Already they're doing the jurisdictional jitterbug about our request that they issue an APB down there on David Pearson in case we're wrong about him being back in Buffalo. All I got them to agree to was their notifying us if he turns up. I know young Allen's going to be disappointed, but even I've got to admit that a full search on their side of the border, under the circumstances, doesn't seem justified."

I thought of how adamantly Allen had wanted that search. Had his insistence been a ruse, an attempt to fool us into thinking he'd had no contact with his father up here? Or perhaps it had been an attempt to keep alive, for our benefit, the possibility of what would be his father's best alibi—that he was still in Mexico. In fact, Allen coming forward and making a voluntary statement right after the murder might have been a carefully planned move intended to deflect suspicion away from himself.

"And, Doc, I finally got to look at David Pearson's chart. I've been thinking. Perhaps you should continue to be careful."

"Of David?"

"Of course I mean David. Who's to say he's only going after the doctors affiliated with Brama who took care of him? I'm warning all the physicians who are listed in the dossier to be careful. Your name appears more often than any of them."

It was evening by the time ER fell quiet enough that I could retreat to my office and log on to the Internet. As the machine repeatedly attempted to dial me through, I sat and listened to the sound of rain against my solitary window—a postage-stamp-sized affair that allowed light to come in but was too opaque with grime to let me see out. Tonight it lit up with the occasional flicker of lightning, and I had barely counted three steamboats before the thunder rolled overhead. Obviously, after such a bright start to the day, the weather had turned for the worse—like my state of mind.

I clicked into the Med-Line program—a service that indexed all major medical publications—entered my four key words—*alcoholism, research, anesthesia, psychiatry*—and requested a search spanning journals from the last five years. Within a minute I had three pages worth of abstracts to scroll through. Most pertained to new protocols for anesthetic problems during emergency surgery on alcoholics, some dealt with recent competency issues for doctors obtaining informed consent preoperatively from inebriated patients, and none of them were of any use to me.

Perhaps what I'd so vaguely remembered was from more than five years ago. I punched in the instructions to extend the search period back in time. To narrow things down, I changed my key words to read: *addiction research, anesthesia, psychiatry.*

This time I got absolutely nothing.

Further back still? I knew Med-Line only included titles from 1980 on. I punched in the request and let the computer prowl through the cyberspace equivalent of ancient memories. This took longer, and I had time to appreciate that the storm outside was crackling and booming more fiercely now. One particularly strong shot of lighting made the computer protest, but the tenacity of the microchips won out, and the connection held. Not that it did me any good. Once again my screen came up blank, a flashing marker on the blue emptiness inviting me to enter another question. But I couldn't think of anything else to ask. Whatever Forbes and Saswald had been up to, it was beyond the ken of the computer world.

Before signing off, I checked my e-mail to see if Jack Mac-Gregor had gotten back to me yet. After four days, there was still no reply.

I was soaked through before I'd gotten halfway to my car. The lot was barely a quarter full, the visitors having gone home hours ago, so I could sprint more or less a beeline across the open asphalt. But my late arrival this morning meant that I was stuck in the outer limits of regular parking, and the deluge was so strong that to get there, I had to skirt entire areas where the pavement was submerged in inches of water. Already loud, the downpour teemed into these pools with such force that I wouldn't have heard a shout from ten feet away, nor would anyone have heard mine.

I paused at the edge of a particularly large flooded section and debated plowing through or finding a way around. My clothes wouldn't get much wetter than they already were if I took the longer route, but at least I'd spare my shoes and myself the unpleasantness of a "soaker." I hurriedly took the detour.

When I finally had my car in sight, I deactivated the alarm with my remote as I ran toward it, then flung open the door and squished into the driver's seat. Removing my glasses, I proceeded to wipe away the water streaming off my hair and into my eyes. The drumming on the roof was even louder than the noise of the storm outside, and the windows were so awash that I could barely see out of them.

Shivering as cold rivulets ran down my back, it took me half a minute more to clean my glasses before I retrieved my keys from my coat pocket and reached for the ignition. In the process I glanced in the side mirror on my left, and froze.

Three dark figures blurred by the rain were approaching the car, fast.

At first I was too taken by surprise to move. I wasted another instant thinking they might simply be people running for their vehicle just as I had. By the time I grasped that there were no other cars around me and made a quick stab for the power locks, the door behind me flew open and a gruff voice ordered, "Don't move!"

My keys still in hand, I jammed them into the ignition and started the motor. Immediately my upper arms were grabbed from behind and yanked backward as I strained to reach the stick shift and get into drive. Both doors on the passenger side of the car opened in unison, and I could see two people in black ski masks and rain wear. *This killer wears protective gear against the blood* was all I could think of.

My rocketing fear gave me the strength of a madman. I managed to twist and get my right leg up to deliver a few kicks toward the one coming at me through the passenger door. The one entering by the rear reached over, grabbed me by the hair, and pulled my head back over the top of the seat. "Behave!" he barked, applying more tension, but the pain in my scalp was nothing to the terror I felt with my neck so exposed and ready for slicing. I started to flail and kick so hard that I nearly wrenched free of the one behind me who was holding my arms, and felt the toe of my right shoe make contact with what I thought was the chin of the attacker in the front seat. For my trouble I got a round of curses and my head yanked even farther back.

But what was a little hair loss to a man about to be slaughtered? I whipped my trunk and neck forward, letting out a roar, while both feeling and hearing the roots rip from my scalp.

"What the fuck!" uttered the one left with a handful of hair.

This time my forward momentum also broke me free from the man directly behind. "Stop him!" he yelled, trying to regain his hold on me as I grabbed the door latch with a quick pull and lurched to my left, evading his grasp. At the same time I drew up my knees and delivered another kick at the face of the man in the front seat, who was also reaching for me again. The force of the blow sent him flying backward until his head hit against the top of the door frame, and the recoil was enough to shove my head and shoulders out the open door at my back. I propelled and wiggled myself the rest of the way from the car, sliding onto the pavement and eluding the two trying to grip me from over the backseat.

"Get him," screamed the guy who'd sampled my hair.

I saw the rear door on my side start to open as I scrambled to regain my feet and run. But my shoes slipped on the wet surface and I went down again, while the man coming out of the car launched himself at my legs. I managed to roll on my side, draw up my knees again, and deliver another kick just as

he was about to land on me. My shoes caught him on the side
of his head and he roared with pain, his neck snapping back
as he fell to my right.

I once more tried to get to my feet, but could see the other
two already coming around each end of the car toward me.

If I could just keep my footing this time, I prayed, rising on
my hands, and pushed off in a slipping attempt at a sprinter's
start. My right sole caught some traction, my left a little less,
but I was started.

"Stop, you fucking asshole!" screamed one of the pursuers
above the din of the rain. I knew there was no chance of
anyone but me hearing him. I doubted a passerby near the
hospital could even see our little drama in the dark. I had to
get closer to the building.

A different voice bellowed, "We're taking you to Jack!"

Jack the fucking Ripper's more like it, was all that clicked
in my head as I lurched forward, picking up speed. But my
feet were sliding far too often. I paid no further heed to what
they were yelling, pumped my knees as hard as I could, and,
still accelerating, thought only of getting away.

Nearly upright, I felt an outstretched hand sweep down my
back, missing me, then heard another volley of curses, but
didn't risk a glance over my shoulder. Instead I poured on the
speed, and began to think I might actually make it.

The rain was so heavy that I was inhaling water and choking as I ran. From barely a few steps behind me I could hear
the labored breathing of my pursuers, and knew they were
having the same trouble I was.

Directly in my path lay the large pool of water I'd skirted
on my way over, the rain teeming across the reflection of the
hospital lights on its surface. Would it slow me down? No
more than it would them, I decided, and splashed through it.

It took me a few seconds to realize I had only one runner
behind me now. Peripherally I could see the dark shapes of
the other two going around the water, one on either side of
me, and they were pulling abreast. I could already tell that by

the time I got back on unsubmerged asphalt and on an even footing, they'd be slightly in front. Could they then angle back toward me in time to cut me off? The thought of once more being in their hands jolted me to new speed.

No one was yelling anymore. All I continued to hear above the sounds of the rain and splashing footsteps was my own noisy breathing blended with that of the man behind me. A flash of lightning illuminated the two side runners as they began pulling ahead. The staccato flicker sent their smooth movements into the jerky motion of a film at fast-forward. Then the darkness returned, and a roar of thunder passed over us.

I ran free of the water seconds later, but they'd already adjusted their course and were closing in to intercept me. I tried to gauge the point up ahead where I'd either be by them and free, or tackled and captured. One way or another, I'd know in a matter of seconds.

I started a count to help me time my moves. I'd covered ten more yards and reached the number two by the time they were near enough that I could see their eyes behind their masks as they lined me up.

The one on my left flew at me first. I managed to straight-arm him in the head and swivel by his outstretched hands. But the maneuver had given his partner the edge in speed that he needed.

His leap was timed perfectly. He crashed into me waist high, seizing me in a viselike grip that didn't lessen any as we hit the ground. The impact knocked what little wind I had remaining out of my lungs, leaving me unable to move, and I wondered if my stitches hadn't opened. The third man was on me in an instant as well, binding my legs with what felt like tape. It took a little longer before the one who'd missed his tackle joined in, planting his knee in my back and resuming his grip on my hair. I felt my arms pulled behind me, where they were given the same treatment with tape as my legs. Nobody spoke. We were all too busy puffing and heaving.

Finally the one at my head managed to gasp, "Now, Garnet, we're going on a trip."

They rolled me over on my back and extended my neck.

Oh, Christ, I thought, this is it.

I knew begging was useless. I had seconds to decide how I would die. Screaming curses at them? Shutting them out and thinking only of Janet and Brendan?

The one at my head reached inside his voluminous rain gear. I readied myself to see him extract the knife.

Instead he pulled out a black case the size of a pen box, and from that he took a prefilled syringe containing a clear fluid.

"What the hell?" I exclaimed as he snapped the cap off the needle and pressed its tip into the side my neck.

"This is midazolam, Garnet, standard dose, and I assure you that I'm as good at hitting the jugular as you are, but if you struggle while I'm injecting, and the damn point snaps off, well, you know the consequences of a two-inch spear floating through your bloodstream."

I felt the sting of the needle as it slipped through my skin. I didn't try to jerk away, but my thoughts were going through a blender.

Midazolam was a short-acting, rapid-onset benzodiazepine, or tranquilizer. Was he putting me to sleep before cutting my throat? I didn't have more than seconds to figure it out. I was plummeting into darkness as swiftly as if I'd been dropped down an elevator shaft. The last words I heard sounded vaguely like, "MacGregor's going to be pissed."

"These days he's always pissed," someone replied.

The next thing I remembered was listening to Jack MacGregor arguing with someone, and thinking that I was back with him during my residency days in New York.

"Christ, I wanted him cooperative, not comatose, you assholes," he was saying.

Probably to some junior intern, I thought. Jack rarely lost

his temper, except when the junior interns did something really stupid.

"Now give him more flumazenil," he ordered.

They had to be treating a benzodiazepine overdose. Fluma-zenil was the antidote.

"What do you expect, Jack? You can't snatch a person and expect him to cooperate," someone answered back, far more angrily than was appropriate for a junior intern addressing his senior.

"You didn't have to jump him with masks on," Jack persisted.

"Oh, yeah? You were the one who insisted he wasn't to be trusted with a prearranged meet."

"Hey, I didn't say he wouldn't cooperate—"

"That's the trouble with you these days, Jack," interrupted a second voice. "You've been seeing so many traitors everywhere that none of us is ever sure which of your alerts are real, but neither can we afford to ignore them."

"Yeah!" agreed the first speaker, sounding increasingly belligerent. "We sure as hell couldn't risk letting him see our faces, in case for a change you were right about not trusting him. Maybe *you* can fly from place to place and stay safe, but we have to live here."

"Goddamn it!" Jack snapped. "You don't think I've got cause to be especially careful?"

"Hey, take it easy, friend," rejoined the second speaker, sounding hostile and not at all reassuring. He also seemed to have moved closer to me, and immediately I felt a tingling along my left arm.

"*You* dare tell *me* to take it easy?" Jack countered, his tone jarring, almost whining. "You've still got a license. I don't."

"For Christ's sake, get hold of yourself" exclaimed a third man. He spoke firmly, yet not as loudly as the other two, and managed to sound almost kind. "We've got less than two weeks to go, and frankly, your drinking isn't helping—"

"Shut up! I'm not so drunk that I can't still do my job,"

Jack yelled back defiantly. "After all, it's not like *I'm* still working in ER. You try sitting around for months on end—"

"Jack, do you want to take Brama or not?" this third speaker interrupted. "This is *your* baby more than anyone else's, but so help me, if you don't smarten up, sober up, and toughen up now, I'll cut you from the operation myself."

"No!" shrieked my former classmate. "Nobody's fucking taking that from me, y'unnerstan'! Nobody!"

This wasn't the Jack I knew.

"Shit," the second voice muttered. "He's not even in good enough shape to debrief Garnet."

Nor was this part of our residency, and that meant we sure as hell weren't in New York.

The flumazenil hit and catapulted me out of my stupor and into the middle of a nightmare.

First my eyes flew open, and I saw the hollow-eyed, unshaven face of my oldest friend staring at me. A garish light from somewhere behind my head painted his gaunt features in black and white, throwing harsh silhouettes of him and his three hooded companions, who were also hovering over me, against the far wall. We were in some kind of car garage, surrounded by lifts, racks of automotive repair tools, and loops of chains dangling from hooks high in the ceiling. The elongated shadows in the place cast everything in duplicate, and it all resembled a Marquis de Sade playground. I quickly became aware of the grease and oil smells, and soon realized that the rushing noise in my ears was actually rain pelting onto what sounded like a metal roof.

"Hi, Garnet," Jack said quietly, pulling up a wooden chair, turning it around, and straddling it, keeping the back between us.

I simply stared at him, aghast at how skeletal his usual lean, good looks had become. Only after digesting his appearance for a few seconds did I try to speak, yet even then I found I couldn't get my mouth to work. I was also feeling perpetually on the verge of dizziness, and had the beginning of a headache that kept threatening to set up residence above my eyes. All, I knew, were effects from the anesthetic agent. Glancing down, I noticed that I was propped up in an old car seat, its upholstery chewed into holes the size of rats.

After several more seconds of experimenting to see what movements my feet and hands could make—they were no longer taped together—I once more tried talking. It took a few tries, but this time I finally got my jaw disengaged enough to slur, "Jack, I swear to God, there better be a goddamn good reason for this, and even then I may still use your guts for a bungee cord. What the hell's going on with you anyway? You look like shit!"

He said nothing at first, then ran a hand over his stubbly face. "You mean this? Why, it's my new look. Best disguise in the world, being a homeless drunk." He forced a phony-sounding laugh, but the gathering gloom in his bloodshot eyes belied his attempt at sounding cocky. "And sorry about the rough stuff," he added, as breezily as if he were apologizing for some minor social infraction. "Since there are warrants out on me, I can't take any chances, but I'm afraid my men *were* a bit overzealous."

"My men were a bit overzealous?" I echoed incredulously. Part of me wanted to laugh, but I was too angry. Somewhere in my half-anesthetized brain it registered that this was the second time in two weeks that some idiots had scared the shit out of me in that damn parking lot. "Simply saying 'Sorry' doesn't begin to cut it with me," I began, my voice quickly gaining volume. "And as for *your* daring to talk to *me* about not taking chances, you don't think jumping me like that and shooting me into a coma with midazolam wasn't a teensy bit chancy?" I was roaring at him now. "Why the hell didn't you just call me? And what kind of trouble are you in anyway?"

He flashed me a grin, but there was no merriment in it. "Hey, Earl, the reason I didn't call is that, frankly, I don't trust you or anybody else right now. When I talk to people these days it's face-to-face, so I can see all the little gestures and clues that help me know who's lying and who isn't. Besides, though I know I'm not on *America's Most Wanted*—yet—I still don't give advance notice to anyone I meet. After skipping bail, failing to appear in court, and crossing numerous state lines, I'd make a nice small-time catch for any cop who might get a tip about where I was scheduled to show up."

"Wait a minute. You seriously thought that I'd have turned you over to the police—"

"Don't take it personally, pal, but there's simply too much at stake for my risking the cops nabbing me. Other doctors that Brama targeted—some of them calling themselves friends—have been willing to make deals with the bastards— me and my group in exchange for their careers. Oh, I didn't think you'd set me up to save your own skin, but now that they're using Janet to get at you, well, I know there's nothing you wouldn't do for her."

I couldn't believe what I was hearing—neither the paranoia in the words nor the resentment in his voice. "How do you know about Janet?" I demanded. "And what are you talking about, 'you and your group'?" I glanced at the other three men, who had withdrawn into the shadows and not said a word. Did I know them? Were they afraid that I'd recognize them by their voices in spite of their masks?

"You tell me what we want to know," he continued, "and maybe I'll let you in on what we're organizing. As for how we found out about Janet, let's just say we've got friends inside Brama who feed us the names of doctors who've pissed them off so badly that they've become undesirables. Then we show up and say, *Wanna join us?* That's how we got the one who stuck you with the needle."

His continuing glibness about the attack irked me. "Join what? Kidnappers Incorporated? And are you saying one of these bozos who presumed they had a right to abduct and drug me is a doctor?" I waved vaguely toward where the trio were standing, and only then did I notice a small intravenous line and syringe taped to my arm. I went to reach for it and

Jack quickly grabbed my wrist, a whiff of body odor and alcohol accompanying his sudden movement.

"Not so fast, friend," he cautioned, his grip tightening.

The hint of menace in his voice dismayed me. "Friend?" I said incredulously, and met his tormented stare head-on. "That's right, Jack. You are my oldest friend, and you're frightening me. Tell me, as one friend to another, how frightened of you should I be? What are you about to do? Twist my arm? Tie me up again? Maybe worse? Tell you what. I don't know why you're here or what you're up to, and I sure as hell don't know who your new buddies are, but I'm walking away from this place now. Whether you and I can salvage anything between us after this crap depends solely on your letting me go—"

"Oh, don't give me that holier-than-thou horseshit of yours, Garnet!" he snarled, shoving me roughly back in my seat. "First of all, you might need another shot of flumazenil before the midazolam wears off entirely—I'm friend enough not to risk letting you leave before it's safe—and secondly, everybody in this room, including you, wants to see Brama brought down. Isn't that in itself cause enough for you to stick around and chat?"

His face had turned an ugly shade of crimson as he glared down at me. My God, I thought, alarmed by his sudden show of temper. *Could* he actually turn violent? In all the time I'd known him, I didn't ever remember seeing his face so livid. I had to get out of there.

As soon as he took his hand off my chest, I defiantly attempted to stand, but abruptly felt my brain go into a spin cycle, and flopped back onto the car seat. I spent the next sixty seconds leaning forward with my head in my hands and trying not to throw up. Above the noise of the rain overhead I could hear an occasional roll of thunder, and something else. At first the sound blended in with the storm, but then I recognized it had a steady crescendo and fadeaway that was far too even to be thunder. It was an airplane—a jet, small, I guessed, by the pitch of it's engines—passing low above us.

Suddenly I couldn't fight the nausea anymore, and retched loudly, but nothing came.

"I won't say I told you so," Jack said, his voice jocular. "Do you want a bucket?"

His mood swings were making the doctor in me despair, as they suggested a mind working in fragments, unable to offer an appropriate affect, or feeling, with any consistency. But I felt so rotten myself that for the moment I couldn't care about anything except trying not to throw up. "I don't think so," I replied weakly, staring at a grease spot on the floor between my feet and swallowing my spit over and over.

"Anyway," Jack continued, "enough about me. Let's talk about you. And my my, haven't you become quite the fire-brand, old friend, joining the battle against Brama the way you have. I must say, I liked the expression 'no-fault murder.' A real grabber, that one. Our group followed your press with interest . . ."

As he talked his forced gaiety cut through the spinning in my head and continued to set off alarm bells. His voice, strained to the point of sounding brittle, had a desperate edge to it that I'd sometimes heard in smiling depressives, just before they'd attempted suicide. Swallowing extra hard, still feeling at risk of vomiting, I looked up, intending to say something therapeutic, such as, "Cut the crap, Jack!" But he appeared so agitated, up on his feet now and pacing in front of me while he ranted, that I held my tongue. Better to handle him with kid gloves, I decided.

". . . we keep track of newspapers, and cases like Robert Delany's. That's how we find our real soldiers. Of course there are traitors . . ."

His unbuttoned raincoat streamed out behind his six-foot frame like a cape as he strode back and forth. In happier times we might have laughed about how he cast a huge silhouette resembling a very campy Count Dracula each time he passed in front of the light. Tonight the spectacle only added to my sense of disorientation.

". . . one of our informants in Brama headquarters did me in—after they caught her sneaking out files. She could save her ass, they told her, by agreeing to set me up. When she made her next delivery, the cops were there as soon as I took possession . . ."

He'd abandoned all pretense at being flippant now and was pouring out his words, as if he couldn't unburden himself of them fast enough.

". . . Now we're willing to go outside the law, and we'll bring Brama down—"

"Wait a minute. *Bring Brama down?* And that means what, exactly?" I interjected, startled to hear the threat amidst his meandering rant.

He abruptly halted, then spent at least a dozen seconds staring at me, wearing the quizzical look of a man who seemed to need reminding about why I was there. His three buddies off in the darkness started exchanging urgent-sounding whispers.

Jack ran his hand over his unshaven chin, appeared to collect himself, and returned to sit once more in the chair before me, this time turning it the right way around. "What I need from you, Earl, is information," he implored, leaning forward. "It's better for you that I don't explain why." His manner was all at once as calm and reasonable as if we were discussing a case in ER. This unexpected return to normalcy was perhaps his most unsettling change so far. It was as if he'd decided that we'd both simply forget what had gone before.

"Did a patient from St. Paul's or someone close to a patient kill Saswald and Forbes?" he bluntly demanded, his voice still quiet. "In particular, a patient with an alcohol problem?"

My head promptly cleared. "Pardon?"

"You heard me."

"Why did you ask that?"

He sighed and gave a wave of exasperation. "I told you that for your own good, I can't give you details."

"Look, Jack, for reasons of confidentiality, I can't tell you who's involved, but yes, there is a suspect who's got problems with alcohol. I want to know how you knew to ask."

"Shit!" he exclaimed, creasing his forehead and ignoring my demand. Off in the dark I heard the outbreak of more excited mutterings. "Can you give me his name?" he entreated.

"No, of course not. He's my patient, and besides, the police told me not to discuss anything about the killings, so as not to compromise their investigation."

He leaned back, opened his arms, and grinned. "Hey, you know you can tell me," he wheedled, "doctor to doctor."

I felt my anger flash again. "I don't know shit about you anymore, Jack! I sure as hell don't know if I can trust you after what was pulled here. One thing I *do* know is that I'm not telling you squat until you level with me. And no more shit about your not telling me for my own good."

He studied me for a few seconds, his scowl darkening. "Like I said, pal, we have good cause to be wary of you," he declared softly, his voice hardening.

I bristled. "That crack you made about me turning you in to save Janet was an insult!"

"We have other reasons," he coolly replied. "You've been observed working closely with the detective in charge of Saswald's and Forbes's murders. That's why we figured you'd know who the main suspects were, but it could also mean you might be so cozy with the cops that you'd be a danger to us."

"Observed? Wait a minute! You've been watching me—"

"Fuck your goody-two-shoes outrage, Garnet," he bellowed, jumping up from his chair and knocking it over. "We intend to destroy Brama; they intend to stop us; the winner will be the one who fights dirtiest—it's that simple. I'm not about to let you or anyone you might talk to screw up what has to be done simply because you have some selfish, puritanical need to keep your lily-white hands clean." He paused, his face crimson. "That's always been your problem, Garnet," he added, "being hung up on the rules, and frankly, I don't have time for it now. So tell me what I want to know—who's being investigated for those murders—and then you can go back to your ER, your wife, and your kid, and let people who *aren't* scared of getting their hands dirty take care of Brama for you."

I felt my own cheeks burn. Jack seemed to transform into a stranger before my very eyes. So Janet had been right about his being jealous of her after all, I thought sadly, and my take on his accepting my having a home life over the years had been wrong. What else had I been mistaken about? More specifically, what was he capable of doing that I wasn't aware of? But I had to admit that one thing hadn't changed with Jack. Despite being so distraught, half inebriated, and raving, his criticisms still had the power to cut me to the bone.

As I sat there trying to compose myself, he stood watching me. Then his shoulders dropped and his face softened. "Earl," he said, his voice all at once weary, "have you seen Robert Delany's parents since the night he died?"

Stunned by his unexpected question and the softness in his voice, I hesitated, then answered, "No, and even then I'd only met his mother. Why?"

"How do you think they're handling it?"

I unwillingly thought of Brendan. "I think they're probably in hell."

"Are they aware that their boy might have been saved if the mother hadn't been tricked into waiting?"

I started at the word "tricked." It was brutally more accurate than anything I'd ever used. "Yeah, they know."

"Have you had similar cases lately?"

I simply nodded.

"And the people who have tried to get solace or justice through the legal system, how do you find they cope after the courts have told them that they've no recourse?"

"Not well," I answered tersely, beginning to grow impatient with his Q&A routine.

"Now imagine how Robert Delany's mother and father would react if someone approached them at this moment and offered them a chance to get even, to get justice, to pull down those most responsible for their son's death, and prevent such an evil tragedy from ever being inflicted on other sons."

"Oh, my God! Jack, you didn't?"

He ignored the question. "Also imagine your other cases like this one added to all the similar cases of other doctors—not just from your hospital or from your city, but from the whole country." He paused, then added, "As I said, we find the more sensational ones through the press, using the Internet to scan every print media outlet that has a listing, and we study the numerous websites that are rich with horror stories involving HMOs. But with Brama we have—or at least had, until I got busted for it—a very special edge. One of their secretaries—her mother had died from a heart attack as a result of their triage-two-step—became sympathetic to our cause and had access to their more sensitive records. Did you know they actually review the morbidity and mortality figures for unexpected trips to ER following triage advice? It helps them keep their deterrence of visits at a level sufficient to generate savings between one and two percent, yet not kill or maim so many as to provoke too big an outcry for them to keep under control."

"No, I didn't," I admitted, nevertheless taken aback at how close to the mark my speculation about their motives and tactics had been.

He looked at me, exuding only sadness now. "That's what we've been doing, Earl, for the last few years, tracking down and approaching the survivors of people on that list, offering them proof of why their loved one died, and a chance to do something about it."

I simply gaped at him.

His revelation, so terrible in its simplicity, yet so logical, and the sweep of what he intended to do, had staggered me to the point that I found myself holding my breath.

"Not all of them respond, naturally," he continued, apparently unaware of the impact he was having on me. "Some are too numb to do anything; others, by some strength I'll never possess, are actually managing to cope, but a good half are so racked with anger, pain, and frustration that they find what we offer them to be a godsend, sometimes for their very sanity."

I remained too flabbergasted to speak. Finally I was able to ask, "Do you not realize the emotions you're playing with?"

"Oh, I know, Earl," he replied, his eyes growing dark with excitement. "It's a fierce and terrible rage that I'm tapping into. And it's all going to be directed at Brama. But when they suffer the justice we intend to bring down on their heads, there won't be an HMO in the country that'll dare to continue the practices that killed the likes of Robert Delany, because we'll be there watching them too, gathering information, and ready to strike."

A cold sweat crept over my skin. His zealotry to engage in such an odious form of mass manipulation drove a coup de grace to the heart of whatever I'd once liked in the man. Was this the sales pitch he used in order to rally his followers and hold them to his purpose? I wondered. Or once he'd unleashed their fury, did it simply feed and perpetuate itself, keeping them all at the ready to do his bidding?

I carefully tried to keep all traces of judgment from my voice and face. If I made him hostile again, he'd clam up and I'd learn nothing more of what he planned to do. "How many of these survivors have you recruited?"

"Admittedly it was slow at first," he replied, showing no hesitation. "But as we got more members, and they in turn fanned out to go after yet more candidates, soon we were growing with the speed of a chain letter. After two years' work, we've established chapters all over the country, and our numbers run in the thousands." Unchecked pride showed in his face and sounded in his voice. "Different people want to help in different ways, of course," he continued without prompting. "Some provide funds, others who are well-placed in the health care industry provide us with information, and still others are more prone to direct action."

This was the opening I was waiting for. As evenly as I could, I asked, "And what direct action will all these people take?"

In an instant he was as alert as an animal who'd heard the warning snap of a twig. His eyes flared, he held his head up as if he were sniffing the air, and the lines in his face once more pinched together, gathering into a mask of anger and suspicion. In the silence of his gaze I became aware again of the thunder rumbling and growling overhead and the rain teeming onto the roof. Once, the lightning was so close that I actually heard its searing snap, and the building shook under the impact of the boom that followed on top of it, but Jack didn't waver from his study of me.

Then he caught me totally off guard, and winked.

For a marvelous moment I saw in his forlorn face and eyes the old fire from days long ago when we had trained together on the most desperate patients in ER. That spark, a sign of Jack's own confidence, had always been there when he'd insisted we not shy away from the worst lost causes who came through the door. I had teasingly called it his St. Jude's fire and deemed him patron of the hopeless cases, but in truth that special glow that suffused him when he took on the impossible was contagious. Time and time again, when I'd been on the verge of succumbing to my own feelings of hopelessness and inadequacy, he'd used it to ignite my own confidence and exhort me to heights of courage and skill that I'd never known I possessed.

"Well, Garnet," he grinned, "as I keep saying, I can't tell you that, for your sake and ours, but I promise you, it'll be one hell of a show."

Before I could protest, the magical moment was gone and

his expression had clouded over again. "And now, it's your turn to fess up," he told me sternly. "For our plan to work, there can't be any loose cannons in our group taking matters into their own hands. That's why I have to know who the police suspect. If it's anyone from our group, we've got to weed them out now."

I started to feel ill again. "Jack—oh my lord—you haven't set up some kind of death squad—"

"Of course not!" he snapped, the hostility in his voice soaring. "But someone else may have. There's a lot of anger out there, and as you know, rage can sometimes make people go over the edge. Our credibility demands no loss of life but our own!"

My state of mind surged toward panic. "What the hell are you saying?"

"Look, are you going to give me the names I need or not?"

"The answer's no, Jack! I won't! I'd never help you manipulate people already deranged by grief into doing God knows what. It's monstrous. You just admitted you can't always control the effects of that kind of meddling. And what the hell does 'no loss of life but our own' mean? Some kind of protest involving mass suicide?"

He stared at me, his eyes slowly refilling with a cold, black anger. But it was his failure to deny any of my charges that really disturbed me. "So this has been a total waste of time," he finally declared.

I gathered my strength and stood up. After a few weaves and staggers, I managed to stay on my feet. "No, Jack. This hasn't been a waste of time," I said, ripping out the syringe and IV. "This has been an education. You're certifiably out of your head, a danger to yourself, and from the sounds of it, to a lot of other innocents as well!"

He spat on the ground between us. "Fuck you, Garnet!" He pivoted on his heel and strode away.

"You're playing God with other people's lives, Jack!" I bellowed.

Over his shoulder he yelled, "So's Brama, damn you! And you don't know half of it." He waved the others to follow and headed toward a door at the far end of the building.

I stumbled after him. "You're always so righteous, Jack. Always so sure that you're more on the side of the angels than everybody else. It makes you blind to means different from your own."

"You're an innocent, Garnet. A useless innocent!" he replied without breaking stride.

Determined to stop him, I quickened my pace. "Jack, wait! I know another way to bring down Brama that's not going to get people hurt. I think they're into something illegal, and they're scared as hell I'll find out about it."

He spun around to face me, continuing to back away as he talked. "Ooooh, I'll bet you've got them trembling in their boots," he mocked. "Like I said, Garnet, you don't know half of it," and he turned again toward the exit, reaching for the door handle. The three other men were right behind him.

I could barely keep up. "Damn it, Jack. They have an addiction clinic in Mexico, and I'm sure we can nail them for whatever they're up to there."

I might have fired a gun in the air. All four men froze. Jack already had the door open, but shoved it closed again.

I stopped dead in my tracks.

"Shit, he knows!" one of the three men in masks declared.

"No, he just said he thinks they're up to something illegal," Jack corrected. "He doesn't know shit. But he could do harm."

The others waited by the door while Jack strode over to where I was standing. "Garnet, you leave that clinic alone, you hear me? Take my word for it, there's no good you can accomplish by poking your nose into their business, but you could put them on alert if you try. The consequences could not only be deadly for you, but lethal for a lot of other good people as well, and there'd be nothing to show for it."

Damn, I was fed up with his elusive talk. "What are you

saying, Jack?" I challenged, hoping to provoke him into revealing something specific. "Not five minutes ago you gave
the impression that you were setting your followers up for
some sort of noble sacrifice. Are you trying to tell me now
that it's okay for people to die as long as their deaths help
your cause?"

I'd expected him to be furious with my defying him again,
given how he'd been behaving, but his features softened and
that terrible sadness I'd seen earlier flooded into his eyes. "It's
bad that we end this way, Garnet. I know that I'll never convince you about the rightness of what I'm doing, nor will
your arguments ever persuade me to back off. But maybe I
can help you to at least understand. Remember my favorite
book? I used to keep it on my desk back in our apartment. Revisit it if you can. You might think kinder of me." He paused,
then pointed a finger right between my eyes. "But whatever
you do, Earl," he uttered, as softly as if he were speaking a
prayer, "heed my warning about the clinic."

With that he turned and was out the door, along with the
others.

I didn't run after him this time, knowing it was pointless,
just as he'd said it was. I instead walked over and stood in the
exit, feeling the cool night air laden with rain rush over me.
Outside I could see a floodlit junkyard cluttered with the
rusted remnants of trucks and cars. Nearby I spotted my own
vehicle, parked in the shadow of a huge tree. In the distance,
where the front of the property opened onto a road, I saw the
taillights of what must have been the kidnappers' car flash,
then turn right and disappear into the night. On the other side
of the road was a chain-link fence, and beyond it a darkness
broken by lines of runway lights receding into the distance. I
was at the far end of the Buffalo airport.

I stepped outside. The rain was much lighter now, and I
found it refreshing as I walked toward my car. The keys were
in the ignition, but I didn't feel up to driving just yet, so I
strolled the rest of the way out to the highway. A few flashes

of lightning lit up the distant sky, but they were so far away that now I could barely hear the thunder.

At the roadside, I stood and watched the rotating beam atop the control tower about a mile off. A plane was taxiing toward this end of the field, blinking green and red as it slowly drew near.

Then I spotted him silhouetted in the glare of the plane's landing lights—a solitary figure running across the field at full speed to meet it. Instantly I knew it was Jack, by the cape effect of his raincoat billowing after him. When the plane slowed to turn and face back up the runway, I could make out that it was a small jet, but couldn't see the markings. As I watched, a rear door opened on the side nearest me, out of sight from the tower, and hands reached out to haul Jack on board. The hatch closed, the engines roared to a high-pitched whine, and the winking craft sped away. It was airborne in seconds, and as I stood there staring after its diminishing green and red flashers, the title of Jack's favorite book popped into my head. He'd always kept Dickens's *Tale of Two Cities* on his desk, and read it whenever he needed to relax. "Theirs was the perfect friendship," he would say, referring to the relationship between the two lead characters, Charles Darnay and Sydney Carton. Then he'd add with a laugh, "Just like ours." He'd been especially fond of the story's closing lines, attributed to Sydney Carton as he mounted the steps of the guillotine in his friend's place, and I could recall the sound of Jack's voice when he'd quote them, as he often had, sometimes facetiously, but always lovingly: *"It is a far, far better thing that I do than I have ever done. It is a far, far better rest that I go to than I have ever known."*

Shit! I thought, feeling I'd been tricked into remembering the words. Whatever he was up to, had the self-aggrandizing son of a bitch just tried to glorify his *own* suicide to me?

As I continued to track the green and red dots moving across the sweep of black sky, there was another distant flash of lightning, and I caught sight of the little plane illuminated in its entirety against a high bank of clouds before the sky returned to darkness. It had been enough to let me see the red cross insignias on the fuselage. He was hitching a ride in an emergency air ambulance.

It was a vintage Jack move, and I found myself grinning, in spite of everything. Those pilots were notorious cowboys who flew in conditions no one else would consider even remotely safe. And they'd never refuse a favor to an emergency physician, not even one who was in trouble, because it was mainly ER doctors upon whom they depended to man their flights.

The plane seemed to settle into a southwest course before the running lights winked out for good.

"What have you unleashed, old friend?" I muttered, needing the reassurance of hearing my own voice.

But all I got for an answer was silence.

I stood a long time staring off in the direction he'd gone, my questions gathering and expanding, until they seemed as vast as the night and were as far-reaching as the great distance he was now flying over.

Perhaps answers couldn't be had here, I finally told myself, and headed home.

Chapter 16

"Mass suicide! How can you be so sure?" Janet demanded.

"From what he said. From what he didn't say. From the look in his eye," I replied. "He was so fragmented there's no one thing I can pinpoint."

Yet by the time I'd driven home from that accursed garage, I'd grown nearly as certain about what he was up to as if I'd laid out his plans myself. "You should have heard him," I continued, "saying things like, 'Quite a show,' and 'Our credibility demands no loss of life but our own.' I've got to tell you, on the way back here in the car, those words kept giving me flashes of people strapping themselves with dynamite, occupying Brama offices all over the country, and, after sending out the staff, blowing themselves, plus the company, out of existence—all in the name of lost loved ones."

"Good God, Earl. That's too hideous to consider!"

"Not for him it isn't. Not now. ER was his life. With that gone, he's got nothing left, except this crusade of his. And if he's as suicidal as I think, why wouldn't he sacrifice himself to bring about Brama's downfall? Look at the allure. He'd be destroying not only the company's property, but also the reputations of Baines and his cronies, probably to the point they couldn't even think of rebuilding. Brama would probably be out of business for good, and it isn't likely there's an HMO in the land that would dare ignore a message that brutal. They'd all change their ways—especially if they feared that Jack had made good on his threat to leave some of his people behind to serve as monitors, ready to act again if necessary. Believe me, the idea of his leaving that kind of legacy would appeal to him."

Janet gave a shudder. "You make it all sound so effective, but it's madness."

Too damned effective, I thought, to ever expect that I or anyone else could simply persuade Jack not to put the scheme into play. "My only hope of making him back off would be to come up with a better way to get at Brama." Even as I said it, vestiges of a plan to do just that started popping into my head.

"Hold it, buster," Janet declared, her expression immediately shot full with fresh alarm. "All I expect you to 'come up with' is an assault and kidnapping charge against this so-called friend!" Her voice was shaking. She'd already been on edge for several hours, having had no idea where I was. My walking in the door all muddied, bruised, and missing a tuft of hair hadn't helped her state of mind any. But her continuing to be so upset now, I suspected, wasn't solely on account of all that had just happened or what I'd told her, but also because she had no idea what I might do about any of it. It wasn't that she didn't trust me. But she had a long-held conviction that my *so-called friend* was the one person on the planet who could even come close to matching her influence on me, and in her mind, not always for the better. Ever since I'd once arrived home driving his Harley, having had no more training in motorcycle driving than Jack perched on the back yelling out the occasional instruction, she'd never been entirely sure that I'd act sensibly whenever he was around. Except this time I had to admit that she had cause to be worried.

"Earl, we tell Riley!" she insisted when I didn't agree right away. "Is that understood!" It was an order, not a question.

"Of course we tell Riley," I reassured her, quickly determining the parts of the story that I'd leave out. They pretty well corresponded to what I hadn't told Janet—that Jack was using an air ambulance to move about, and that he may have already tried to recruit Robert Delany's parents to his cause. I was protecting the pilots because they probably knew nothing of Jack's plans anyway, and besides, for what I had in mind, I needed Jack out there, in a position where he could call off his followers. As for causing the Delanys any more grief or harassment—that was out of the question. "But do we have to call the detective now?" I asked, glancing at my watch. It was after one in the morning, and we were seated at our kitchen table sipping tea, both of us dressed in bathrobes and nothing else. Even under the loose white folds, the shape of her tall form easily aroused in me a desire to lose myself in her.

A strand of blond hair fell across suspicious blue eyes as she asked, "What are you up to, Earl Garnet?"

"Nothing." I grinned, draining my cup and refilling it from the pot she'd made us. Then I toasted her with it. "But since we're full of tea, wide-awake, and suitably undressed, surely we can think of something better to do right now than talk to the cops."

Janet's frown deepened. "What aren't you telling me?"

"That you're a beautiful woman, mother of my child, and altogether too suggestive under that robe for me not to get at least a few ideas."

"You've got to be kidding. After what you've been through?"

"Why not? Nothing like a little terror to fan—"

Janet leaned forward and silenced me with a finger against my lips, then ran it gently over them. "Just don't get any crazy, dangerous ideas about trying to save Jack from himself, Earl. You owe that to me and Brendan. We're the ones who love and need you." She got up off her chair, took my cup from my hand, and straddled my groin, letting her robe fall open. "Now, as you love me, Earl, promise me that," she commanded, reaching down and gliding me into her, then taking my breath away with a fierce, hot thrust.

I promised.

* * *

I don't know which brought Riley running faster, Janet's promise of a good breakfast or my informing him over the phone that I'd been kidnapped. I knew virtually nothing of his personal life, but since he was the only one who ever answered his phone whenever I called him at home, I presumed he lived alone.

He arrived by seven, and by seven-thirty had gone through two omelettes while listening to my story, and was now sitting in our front room with Janet and me, sipping his third cup of coffee, his pad balanced on one knee. The morning light streaming through the window behind him was filtered by the remaining leaves on the trees and filled the room with the golden colors of late fall. Brendan, having finished his own breakfast mash, played with some blocks in a patch of sun on the rug that he always sought out at this hour. Muffy dozed at his side.

I was well into my abridged version of events, telling only what I wanted the detective to know while leaving out the rest, and leading up to my pitch for the scheme I had in mind. At the beginning Janet had monitored my every word, "In case he editorializes," she'd growled at me as she slipped Riley's first plate of eggs in front of him, but now she was staring off in the distance, apparently lost in her own thoughts.

Hoping to sell the detective my idea before she could tune back in and start to protest, I said to him, "Look, surely the real priority now is to stop Jack before he gets God knows how many people killed. Our best hope of accomplishing that would be to publicly expose whatever is going on at the clinic and hopefully bring about the downfall of Brama before Jack can act. Then I'm sure he'd stand down—"

"Impossible!" Riley interrupted. "I told you it's already a jurisdictional quagmire. By the time we get it sorted out enough to accomplish anything, if we ever do, it'll be too late."

"But if I went down there, as a private citizen, there's a way I could get into the place—"

"No!" Janet shrieked. "No! No! No! Goddamn you, Earl Garnet, you promised me there'd be none of your going off on some wild-goose chase because of Jack MacGregor. And you will keep that promise, do you hear me!"

Brendan started to cry at her outburst. Janet scooped him up and quickly comforted him, while Riley, his muscular jaw hanging totally slack for one of the few times since I'd known him, gaped at my normally reserved wife.

"Focus on Jack MacGregor, Detective," she told him coldly. "That whole spectacle last night, with all his noble talk about 'no loss of life but our own,' might have been a sham to mislead you through Earl. After all, he admitted they'd apparently spied on my husband enough to learn that he was working closely with you on the murder investigation."

Riley shot me an alarmed glance.

"What?" I exclaimed.

"Come off it, Earl," Janet rebuked, continuing to nestle Brendan, who'd immediately fallen quiet. "You know he's always been willing to go outside the law while promoting any cause he thinks worthwhile. You think he'd balk at using your friendship? He and his group of fanatics might *very well* be assassins, trying to find out from you what the police have learned, if anything, about their activities, and then pretending to abhor the killings. He'd know you'd report verbatim what they said to Detective Riley."

"How can you think that about Jack?" I protested. "He's no killer."

Janet leveled a blue stare at me that could have brought on an ice age. "Judging from your description of the shape he's in, I don't think you can tell anymore *what* he is."

The normally cozy room suddenly seemed cold.

"And as for you, Detective Riley," she added, pivoting around to give him his share of the freeze, "if I find out you've so much as discussed my husband going to Mexico on some seat-of-his-pants investigation, I'll report you to your superiors for unlawfully enticing a civilian to engage in an unauthorized police operation in a foreign country."

Riley nervously flicked another glance at me, then hastily pocketed his notebook and got up to leave. "Thank you, Dr. Graceton," he said graciously. "I agree with you that we should go after Jack MacGregor, first and foremost."

I suspected he probably would have said anything to get out of there in one piece at that moment, but his agreeing with Janet, I knew, was sincere. He'd come to appreciate the soundness of her judgment while investigating the series of deliberately caused infections that had closed her former hospital. Her insights at that time had been closer to the mark than anyone's, including mine.

"We'll charge MacGregor with kidnapping," he continued, giving her his warmest of smiles, "and unless I'm mistaken, the FBI will be *real* interested in making him answer a whole lot of questions about his group, the murders, and especially what he knows about the clinic in Mexico." He then chuckled, and added, "As a result, I can assure you that we won't be needing your husband's services as some kind of half-assed foreign agent."

I was pretty shaken when I set out from home for St. Paul's.

You're wrong about him, Janet, I kept reassuring myself as I threaded a way through the heavy traffic. You have to be. Surely I couldn't have been fooled to that extent. And no way could the events of last night have been part of an elaborate ruse. Still, once she'd set my doubts simmering, I couldn't entirely cool them down.

I also had other worries. As he left, Riley had indicated that agents from the FBI might want to interview me themselves. Accelerating up the ramp to the freeway, I found myself having second thoughts about my initial impulse to withhold how Jack was traveling around the country. This time I'd be facing a different league of cop, and while all I had to do was keep as silent on the matter as I had with Riley, it was one thing to withhold evidence from the local police regarding my own kidnapper, and quite another to keep that same information from the FBI. If they did deem it appropriate to launch some kind of search for Jack, the prospect of my being found out for concealing the information, especially if it was after they'd been watching train stations, bus terminals, and airports to no avail, rattled me.

But worse than *my* getting caught would be if they captured Jack, making it impossible for him to contact his group and have them back off—*if* I could find out Brama's secret and it was devastating enough to shut them down. During the half hour it took me to creep through the crowded streets, I kept churning over the details of how I might penetrate the clinic.

It was halfway through my morning shift in ER when Fosse got me on the phone.

"Earl, the first installment for our Robert Delany Fund is in the bank," he told me excitedly. "You can start using it today. I've already arranged for an official dedication service at four this afternoon. The press have been invited, Mr. and Mrs. Delany have consented to be present, and of course I'd like to have you there as well."

"How big is the fund?" I asked curtly, unable to keep my foul mood from sounding in my voice.

"Why, it's a good size," he answered, startled. "What's the matter? I thought you'd be thrilled."

"Sorry," I quickly apologized. "It's not been a good day. What's wrong is that all the HMOs are playing Brama's triage game now, big-time, and the numbers appear to be growing. Yesterday alone half a dozen people had to sign themselves out, and we've had that many again already today—all because they couldn't risk getting hit with an ER bill. How long can you cover those kinds of expenses?"

His silence on the line spoke volumes. "Is Brama leading the pack?" he finally asked.

"No, actually. It's pretty ironic. I haven't been fighting with them on the phone at all. Maybe our visit yesterday shook them up a bit. They certainly seem to be behaving themselves, at least for the moment."

Fosse said nothing for a few seconds. "Well, that's something," he finally muttered, but he sounded deflated. "Maybe the other companies won't be so cocky either, once the negative publicity part of the program starts nailing them," he reassured. "And we'll just have to convince our donor to be more generous," he added before hanging up. Yet the worry in his voice confirmed that the Robert Delany Fund hadn't been designed to handle what was happening now.

All the same, cash was cash, and I immediately knew who I wanted to be the first recipient. I had the clerk get me Maggie's chart and called her number myself, imagining the toothless grin she'd probably flash when I told her that she'd not only be admitted and tuned up at our expense, but would then qualify for a stretch of home care.

An intercept broke in on the line. "The number you have dialed has been disconnected," intoned the recorded voice.

I stood with the receiver in my hand, eyeing the number listed as her next of kin. It was her son in California.

On impulse I dialed it.

I reached her daughter-in-law. The woman told me that her husband, Maggie's son, was already in Buffalo, settling his mother's affairs. Maggie had died Sunday night, in her bed.

Riley called half an hour later. "A buddy of mine at the regional office of the FBI in Niagara Falls has agreed to drive down and meet with you at one this afternoon."

My stomach squeezed into a ball and unleashed a load of acid. "I suppose his quick response means their finding MacGregor will be a big priority for them," I replied, bracing to carry on with my lie of omission about Jack's travel arrangements.

"Actually, it was my offer to buy takeout that got him moving so fast. Chinese okay with you?"

I got him to agree on using my office. I'd need all the advantages I could get to pull off what I intended, and home turf would be clearly less stressful for me than one of Riley's interview rooms in the downtown branch of the Buffalo police station—a place where the city's *really* tough guys got taken for questioning.

By quarter to one I'd cleared my slate of cases and lugged a chair from the hallway into my office, as was my custom when I expected two visitors.

Agent Bill Watson was a middle-aged, leanly built man with closely cropped salt and pepper hair. His dark ebony face easily broke into laugh lines when he smiled his hello as Riley quickly made the formal introductions. We then helped the detective lay out a half-dozen take-out containers on my desk, and soon my small work space was filled with the aromas of sweet and sour chicken, barbecued ribs, and steamed vegetables.

Riley had briefed the agent well, so we didn't spend a lot of time going over old ground. Despite this newcomer's disarmingly easygoing good humor, I could tell by his questions and comments that his mind was lightning quick. "I want to know why you dismissed your wife's allegation that this man MacGregor could be setting up assassination squads," he demanded without ceremony at one point. "Why couldn't he be the one responsible for the deaths of Saswald and Forbes?"

"Because Jack's not a killer."

"But your scenario has him enticing possibly hundreds of people to take their own lives. Isn't that a type of killing?"

"Yes, but from his point of view, giving your life for a good cause isn't murder; it's a noble sacrifice. And since he's probably including himself among those who will die, I think he's capable of rationalizing a mass suicide."

Watson didn't even pause to think over what I'd said, giving me the impression that he already had his own answers to the questions he was asking. "Now, Dr. Garnet, from what you told Detective Riley, these other three men who actually did the kidnapping were probably locals, and at least one was a doctor who'd been put on this list of 'undesirables' that Brama keeps."

I simply nodded, having just taken a mouthful of rice to try to settle my stomach.

He turned to Riley. "You've arranged for us to meet Baines at three?" he asked.

While tearing a piece of meat from a rib with his teeth, Riley made what was clearly an affirmative noise.

"Good," Watson acknowledged at the sound, "and the first order of business will be to ask him to produce a complete list of these so-called 'undesirables,' not just the ones from Buffalo, but from the whole country. Since, according to your story, Dr. Garnet, MacGregor's recruited most of the physicians who have joined his cause from that group, if we interview them all, we're bound to rattle a few in his organization enough that they'll admit as much."

"But a lot of innocent doctors have been declared 'undesirables,' " I exclaimed, completely taken back by the sweep of what he was proposing, "such as my own wife!"

Watson's gray eyes abruptly shone like gunmetal and his kindly features hardened. "Dr. Garnet, the United States government does not tolerate threats of terrorism in any form, and the Bureau will do whatever is necessary to bring anyone uttering those threats to justice—whatever their profession, be it doctor, lawyer, or Indian chief. As for those men and women who happen to be innocent, they, of course, have nothing to fear."

I didn't reply, but felt a chill run through me.

He released me from his stare, and once more assumed the demeanor of someone no more threatening than a crossing guard as he laid out the rest of what he intended to do. "I figure what I'll need next will be harder to obtain, but Baines might agree with our request for it, if he figures his cooperating will put an end to MacGregor's army."

"And what could he give you that would accomplish that?" I asked, my mouth so dry I could barely speak.

"All the names and addresses of the patients whose files were stolen and passed on to MacGregor," he replied cheerily. "Right there I figure we'd be on to his biggest source of recruits. Our questioning them is bound to turn up some of his followers, and once we have a few, we can probably persuade them to give us the names of others, who in turn will give us more names still. Now the third item we'll be taking up with Baines will concern this clandestine clinic in Mexico which seems to be so central to everything, but even for us the jurisdictional problems—"

"Mr. Watson," I interrupted, "how long do you think this operation you've just outlined—tracking down all these people—is going to take?"

He frowned at me, making it clear he didn't appreciate my cutting him off, then answered, "What with cutbacks and the agents available, maybe a month or two."

"But Jack's men said it would be less than two weeks before they launched whatever they're planning."

His sudden smile was condescending, and a quiver away from becoming a smirk. "Of course we'll be advising Brama officials to up security at all their offices," he told me with barely disguised impatience. "If MacGregor's bunch do strike before we hunt down their members, we'll be ready. Actually, that might be the easiest way to tie up this problem. I agree with your hypothesis about how they might attack—individuals or small groups making a simultaneous move against Brama facilities all over the country. Hopefully they'll try to carry out MacGregor's promise that there be no loss of life but their own, and give people in the buildings a chance to get clear. We can use that time to demand they surrender, or take them out before they detonate whatever device they're carrying. Now, back to the question of the clinic in Mexico—"

"But they won't surrender," I protested. "They're all suicidal."

This time he outright scowled. "Look, Doctor, we're on a tight schedule. I've tried to inform you how we intend to act on the information you've provided out of courtesy, not because I'm prepared in any way to discuss Bureau strategy with you, and certainly not because I need your permission to carry out what needs doing. Now I only have one more question, and then Detective Riley and I can move on. Did your friend MacGregor let slip how he was flying around the country—which airline he was using or what name he was traveling under? We already know the commercial carriers have no record of him."

I was so staggered by everything else he'd said that I blurted out the truth with no hesitation whatsoever. "Jack never said a word about any of that to me."

"This helpless toddler's name will become a rallying cry in our institution," Fosse proclaimed loudly, "as all of us come to use the Robert Delany Fund to redress the excesses of what managed care has become today. I call on all of you who work in Emergency to use it like a sword of justice against those who would visit such wrongs on the sick at their weakest and frailest hour . . ."

He was in full flight—eyes flashing, voice crackling with eagerness—but as noble as his purpose was, I found his words embarrassingly bombastic. He was holding the dedication in the waiting room of ER, and while my own staff were obviously delighted at being handed such an innovative weapon, however short-lived it might turn out to be, I found myself watching the Delanys, and flinching.

I was sure Mrs. Delany was on some sort of antidepressant. Her countenance was dazed, and while she appeared to approve of the proceedings—nodding repeatedly at Fosse's rhetoric—when she looked around the room, her dull eyes and placid expression seemed to float over the crowd, as if disconnected from what was going on. But it was her husband's painful appearance that I found more troubling. His eyes were darkened and hollowed by lack of sleep, his cheeks deeply sunken from not eating, and his face possessed of a punched-out quality that I doubted any medication could re-sculpt. Even more discomforting was how he otherwise showed no trace of emotion, standing rigid, staring into space, and keeping his grief securely locked within him—where it could eat him alive.

He'd need help, some sort of grief counseling, the doctor in me noted, while in my heart I cringed at the thought of ever having to endure such agony myself.

Mercifully, Fosse's speech was as short as it was over-blown, and the ceremony was over in less than five minutes. As reporters bombarded him with questions about whether he was declaring war on managed care, I walked over to the Delanys and once more offered my condolences.

"Thank you for coming." Mrs. Delany smiled, shaking my hand. Her stare was so blank and her voice so flat that I wasn't sure at first if she even knew who I was. But then she turned to her husband, who'd remained unflinching at her side, his arms still as rigid as a sentinel's. "This is Dr. Garnet, dear, who I told you was so kind that night."

Her calling attention to me was more than he could manage. He looked into my face like a man awakening from a dream, and his wan features crumpled up like a used tissue as he let out a huge sob. Doubling over, he clasped his head in his hands, then, in slow motion, buckled at the knees until he was on the floor. After struggling to breathe in again, he emitted a bloodcurdling wail that silenced the room. With his wife kneeling at his side, her vacuous expression now shattered with alarm, and me crouched over him with my hands around his shoulders, he continued to cry, his face pressed to the floor, his body racked by each convulsive catch of his breath. No one else moved or uttered a sound. Even the reporters, normally ready to leap on such scenes, were too shocked to react. It took at least ten seconds before the first flash went off.

In the end it was Robert Delany Sr.'s display of agony that persuaded me to go. Or rather, it made me accept what I'd probably known all along—that I couldn't not go. And once I'd resigned myself, the consequences—defying Janet, acting behind Riley's and the FBI's back, ignoring even Jack's warning to stay away—seemed but painful yet necessary steps that I'd have to take in order to get the job done.

I turned to the one person who I knew would have the nerve to help me.

Chapter 17

"I think we're ready." Fosse beamed, grinning mischievously as he hung up his phone. He'd been talking with his counterpart, a Mr. Brad Parker, at City Hospital in New York, my, and Jack's, old stomping ground. "Calling in a few favors" was how Fosse had put it. In the last three hours he'd also made contact with the CEOs of several other hospitals in that area. He'd always been immediately put through, always addressed them by their first names, and inevitably had gotten the special cooperation we needed. I knew the man was known for having extensive contacts in the health care network, but it was impressive nevertheless to witness his putting those contacts to use.

"Parker's personal secretary will route us through her switchboard," he continued, "and any number-display device they may have on the Mexican end of the call will show the New York exchange for City Hospital. The only physician around your age with blue eyes who's leaving on vacation within the next few days is a urologist, Dr. Arthur Kane. Now, I figured you knew enough about the emergency end of his field to talk the lingo if it came to that, so I said that he'd do fine." Fosse shoved a pad at me where he'd scribbled down the man's birth date, mother's maiden name, street address, and a number of other personal details that I might have to provide off the cuff. "Kane's sending you his birth certificate and a few other pieces of nonphoto ID—his urology association card, state physician's license, automobile association, that

259

kind of thing—by courier for delivery to this office tomorrow morning. In case anyone in Mexico tries to call Kane's home or office to double-check his whereabouts, his answering service will state only that he's on vacation. He said it was an honor to lend his name to any venture aimed at taking Brama down a peg."

As had several psychiatrists and directors of labs at the other hospitals he'd contacted.

Fosse then glanced at his watch. "It's six-thirty. That means three-thirty at the clinic. Since it's Friday, if you think you're ready, I suggest we phone them now and set things in motion before that psychiatrist, Martinez, and anyone else that matters, goes home for the weekend. Otherwise we're liable to be stuck until Monday."

We'd already gone over in detail what we were going to say in our respective roles. I glanced at the scrap of paper that held all I knew about the man whose identity I was about to usurp and drastically alter. It was precious little, but probably enough for this first contact. If they asked me any other easily verifiable facts that I didn't have, I figured I could slip into the kind of belligerent paranoia alcoholics so often display, and loudly demand, *What do you want to know that for?*

I nodded for Fosse to proceed, took a few deep breaths, and, while he was being put through, waited for my cue to become Dr. Arthur Kane, longstanding alcoholic who was willing to pay any price for one last chance.

Fosse began, "Hello, this is Brad Parker, CEO of City Hospital in New York calling. I'd like to speak with Dr. Martinez, please." After listening a few seconds, he declared, "No, he can't phone me back. It's urgent that I speak with him now." There was another pause, then he added, "Thank you," and mouthed to me that they were getting him. As we waited in silence he doodled on his pad for what seemed about a minute. Then he sat at attention. "Dr. Martinez, how kind of you to speak with me. My name is Parker, and I need your help with a delicate matter regarding one of my staff at City Hospital, a Dr. Arthur Kane, who's also a family friend . . ."

As Fosse settled into his part, I found myself thinking about the problems we'd anticipated, and worrying whether the precautions we'd taken would be enough. The first difficulty would be if Martinez tried to verify that he'd actually been talking with the CEO of City Hospital in New York. Parker's personal secretary was supposed to field any such attempts and if necessary contact Fosse. But what if the psychiatrist got someone else to direct dial Brad Parker's office and request to speak with him under false pretenses, then listened in on the real CEO's voice?

". . . Dr. Kane has run around to various hospitals, but attempts to treat him have been sporadic and unsuccessful. He even tried one of the new anticraving drugs, but it didn't work. One of the last psychiatrists who attempted to help him had made contact with a Dr. Peter Forbes about the possibility of sending Dr. Kane to your clinic—apparently, word is getting out about the remarkable results you're getting—but we've just heard of Dr. Forbes's tragic death . . ."

Fosse and I had taken advantage of the tendency for physicians not to seek help, or, if they did, to do it sporadically, and we'd created a confused medical record that wouldn't be easy to check out—but not impossible. Once Fosse had paved the way with their respective CEOs, I'd actually asked the psychiatrists at the various institutions to create a file, assigning them each a fragment of Arthur Kane's history. I'd then spoken to their respective lab directors, indicating what blood results I'd need from each of them to create the overall biochemical picture of an alcoholic who was engaging in ever more frequent episodes of binge drinking. But would the fabrication stand up if Martinez contacted any of these people and questioned them in person?

". . . Dr. Forbes had given this psychiatrist your number, saying you might want to make a special arrangement for Dr.

Kane. You see, he'd prefer to pay cash, so there's no record of his condition being so severe he couldn't lick it on his own . . ."

The most important piece of our plan relied upon their greed. Both Fosse and I agreed that we should mention money as often as we could.

". . . Yes, I understand. I'm sure that that price and those arrangements would be most satisfactory. In fact, I happen to have Dr. Kane here with me, should you wish to speak with him. Let me put him on."

Fosse handed me the receiver and made a thumbs-up sign. I was on.

"Hello, Dr. Martinez," I began, talking fast. I also shook my free arm rapidly back and forth, to transmit a hint of tremor to my voice. I'd decided to play Arthur Kane as a man who wasn't falling-down drunk, but was keeping one swig ahead of the DTs. "Please, you've got to help me. I'll pay anything you ask. My job, my family, I'll lose it all this time—"

"Easy, Dr. Kane. Of course we will try to help you," Dr. Martinez said, with the perfect syntax typical of those who have mastered English as a second language. What little traces of a Spanish accent remained served only to make him sound suave. "But please understand, ours is as yet an experimental program. There are certain releases you will have to sign, and an agreement of absolute silence on your part regarding what you will experience here is mandatory, to protect against anyone stealing our methods before we publish them. We make it clear from the outset that we would impose very heavy financial penalties on anyone who violated this agreement. I'm sure, as a physician, you can understand our need for such strict secrecy to prevent plagiarism."

"Yes, yes, I understand!" I exclaimed, making myself sound impatient with such details. "Will you take me?"

"The final issue *is* one of finances," he went on, ignoring my question. "As I told your CEO, we sometimes do make special arrangements for certain upscale clients. And as I also told him, the fee for such consideration is fifteen thousand U.S.—a cashier's check made out to the clinic for five thousand to be sent immediately to us by courier, as a deposit, and ten thousand in cash that you will deliver to me and me alone on your arrival. And you are not to discuss these terms with anyone else who is here. Is that clear?"

"Yes, I say nothing to anyone, while giving the cash to you and you alone," I replied for Fosse's benefit. He rolled his eyes at the ceiling, then gave me two thumbs up.

"One other thing," Martinez continued. "You must be detoxed before you come. How long do you think that will take?"

This was a standard requirement of addiction treatment centers, and I'd been counting on it being enforced. While it was possible for me to imitate over the phone a man who was about to go into a state of delirium tremens, all the accompanying physiologic changes—sweating, rapid pulse, metabolic acidosis—couldn't be faked. When I did finally stand in front of them, I intended to be simulating a patient in a weakened, postwithdrawal state—a condition that had no telltale clinical signs. "No problem. I'm checking myself into the hospital tonight," I declared, trying my best to mimic the overly sincere urgency that most drinkers used when declaring their good intentions. "I should be straight enough to travel by Tuesday morning."

"Fine," he said coolly. "We'll need your medical file attesting to this, along with all your past records. Call me when you've confirmed your travel arrangements. Will you be renting a car?"

"No, my permit's been revoked," I told him, attempting to sound morose. The scenario I'd prepared avoided above all my needing a driver's license, or any other identification with a picture on it.

"Ah, yes, I understand. Then plan to arrive in Tijuana well

before three P.M. That's when the last bus leaves for our region—the nearest village is called La Rumorosa. By the way, no cellular, or we'll confiscate it, and dress warmly. We're in the mountains, and this time of year you can get caught in a freak snow squall. Just last weekend six migrant workers froze to death trying to cross over into *your* country from here." He hung up before I could reply.

I looked across at Fosse. "I'm in," I said in disbelief.

"What's 'in' is the cash," Fosse replied with a sarcastic laugh, "and from the way he had his price ready, plus the instructions—could you believe that 'deliver it to me and only me' shit?—I suspect he makes it a habit to accept special 'upscale clients.' Hell, I bet he pockets the ten grand portion without anyone else knowing."

"Sounds like it. Still, it seemed mighty easy to get accepted."

Fosse shrugged. "He obviously wanted the money."

"But he didn't even ask me my mother's maiden name."

When I came down to breakfast the next morning, I found Janet at the table sipping coffee. Beside her was the Saturday paper, and on the front page I could see the photo of Robert Delany's father huddled on the floor, with his wife and myself trying to comfort him. BEREAVED FATHER COLLAPSES AT MEMORIAL FOR INFANT SON was the headline. Under it, in bold print, was the statement CEO AT ST. PAUL'S INDICTS TRIAGE PRACTICES OF MANAGED CARE.

I poured myself a coffee and sat down opposite her, taking my cue to say nothing from Janet's own silence. She hadn't even acknowledged my coming into the room. The evening before she'd also not said much, but it had been a frostier quiet than the thoughtful stillness she now seemed lost in, and I hadn't dared to even mention Mexico.

"It's not because of Jack that you want to go," she said absently, sounding as if she was thinking out loud more than talking to me. She glanced toward the picture. "But because of him, and what he's lost," she continued, lifting her blue stare to catch me full in its clear light, "and for others like him, isn't it?"

I nodded.

"Because you think there's a chance that you can keep the ones whom Jack recruited from destroying themselves," she declared softly.

"Yeah, I do," I answered.

She continued to study me, her finely etched features making her seem as fragile as porcelain. "You know I've every right to expect that you'd chose Brendan and me over Jack MacGregor," she asserted.

I nodded again, and added, "As you said, it isn't about that."

"You've already decided?"

"Yes, I have."

"When will you leave?" she demanded, sitting a little straighter and brusquely wiping away a strand of blond hair that had strayed across her forehead.

"Tuesday morning." I'd bought my tickets to L.A. on the way home last night.

She started as if I'd slapped her. "What were you going to do, leave me a note?" she snapped, her lips hesitating between being pursed into a thin hard line and remaining open, full, and soft.

"Janet, don't," I said, quickly moving around the end of the table and sitting beside her. She turned her head away and stiffened when I tried to pull her to me. Then she seemed to slump in my arms.

"Damn you, Earl Garnet," she muttered. "I know you're right, but damn you."

We sat there awhile, neither of us saying anything, until Janet asked, "What exactly are you planning to do?"

I began explaining what Fosse and I had set up, immediately generating another hurt outburst followed by a barrage of questions about what I intended. As I answered those, there were even more queries, until before long she'd gotten a pad of paper and shoved it, with a pen, in front of me. She tapped it with her finger, looking every bit the angry schoolmarm. "I want to know your plan, every item of it, in writing," she declared. "Then you and I are going over it, again and again. It doesn't surprise me that Fosse helped you—he's always been a zealot if he thinks the cause is right—but he's a little too ready to take risks for my liking. If you *are* going to stick your nose into God-knows-what, I'll be damned if it will be with some half-baked scheme that I haven't checked out every which way, including sideways. Now let's get busy."

Soon the anxiety in her eyes and her hurt expression evolved into the familiar focused look her face assumed whenever she brought her fierce intellect to bear on a problem. We worked side by side well into the morning, itemizing all the preparations and contingency plans that we still had to make. By the time Janet got through adding on what she considered I'd overlooked, it was a very long list.

Around noon Fosse called to say that all the documents we needed had arrived from New York. "By the way," he added, "that Martinez was a lot more cautious, and trickier, than we thought. He waited until after hours to phone City Hospital back, and requested that the switchboard put him through to Brad Parker's home. Fortunately, Parker had warned his wife to take a message should any calls for him come in from Mexico, but it was a close shave."

"You didn't call Martinez from a Buffalo exchange, did you?" I blurted out, alarmed that we might have made our first slipup.

"No," Fosse quickly reassured me. "Parker left orders with his hospital operators that they're to still forward any of my long distance replies."

I felt myself relax a bit, but remained on edge about how easily our whole scam could go wrong.

"What did he say he wanted?" I asked, curious about how clever the greedy psychiatrist really was.

"Something he'd obviously trumped up. He claimed he'd forgotten to ask you if you had a history of heart problems."

I never could lie outright worth a damn—my eyes always shifted or my voice went up half an octave and gave me away. So I was surprised at how well I'd been lying by omission to Riley so far. In fact I was finding the practice not much different from my keeping medical confidences, and I figured when I next talked to him, that more of the same would suffice to conceal my plans for Mexico.

He called later that afternoon. "Baines half cooperated with Watson," the detective announced without preamble. "First, as CEO, he readily agreed to have his San Francisco office provide the FBI with a list of all the patients whose files MacGregor stole and to immediately step up security at all the Brama regional offices. But he denied outright that there even was a list of 'undesirables,' and when the clinic came up, *then* he raised the issue of medical confidentiality to justify not talking about it."

"Has Watson changed his plan any?"

"Not substantially. He's surprised that he got the patients' names so easily, but now that he has them, he's more convinced than ever that the surest way of putting MacGregor's army out of commission for good is to track all those people down. And with so many potential leads in hand, he's not even that upset at Baines's denying him the 'undesirables.' Certainly nothing's changed with regard to his decision that it'll be Brama's private security forces which will meet any immediate attack, and that the Bureau will then back them up with lethal force, if necessary. About the clinic business, he figures we've got enough to focus on, and he's letting it drop, for the moment."

I suppose part of me was still faintly hoping that Watson, having seen the error of his ways, would already be hastily pulling the international strings necessary to raid the place and make his own attempt at exposing Brama's secret in time to stop Jack. But on hearing that the agent's thinking had hardened in exactly the opposite direction, I abandoned any illusions that I'd get a last minute reprieve from doing the job myself. "And what do *you* think of that strategy?" I asked softly.

"It's a textbook response to terrorists," Riley replied in a flat tone that gave no inkling of how he was taking the prospect that so many people would die. "Even our own tactical manual says contain them, confront them, and if they don't surrender, shoot them."

When, years ago, Riley had been the only cop who would listen to me about who had killed our former CEO, I'd also learned something not so noble about the man—his reluctance to suffer the political consequences of speaking out against his bosses—and had nearly lost my life in the process. As soon as I sensed he was yet again retreating into that same peculiar passivity, I felt angry, frustrated, and once more let down. Yet instead of challenging him to do better—my previous attempt two years ago had gotten nowhere—I found myself sadly writing off his chances of ever being secure enough to act differently. The bitter truth of the matter was that the detective, despite his tenaciousness in the field, simply wouldn't commit the heresy of telling an FBI agent, even one who was a friend, that in this case their tried and true methods of dealing with terrorists were wrong.

When I didn't comment right away, he sent a heavy sigh through the line. "I'll keep you posted next week about what's happening," he quickly offered, probably because he knew damn well what I thought of his refusal to speak out and was trying to make amends.

But I wasn't in the mood to let him. Even though his failure of courage occurred away from the mean streets and in the domains of bureaucracy, it could still have lethal consequences.

"Sure, Riley, you do that. I'll be in ER as usual," I told him coldly, my voice remaining smooth as ice, and, if he'd been able to see me, without so much as a flicker of my eyes.

Chapter 18

The bus emerged from a thick gray mist into a burst of golden sunlight. Up ahead, against a darkening eastern sky, I could see the craggy, high summit ridges of the coastal range where La Rumorosa was located. Behind them, as if behind a jagged wall, loomed towering storm clouds the color of eggplants.

"Get off at the clinic road—about a mile before the village. The driver will know the spot," Martinez had instructed me. "There's a phone booth there. Call me when you arrive, and I'll fetch you myself. We're about two miles away, due north, near the American border."

I indicated the stop I wanted; luckily for me the word for clinic in Spanish was *clínica*.

"Gracias," I called back to the man at the wheel as I stepped onto the gravel shoulder of the road. The blast of cold wind that whipped my raincoat was more what I'd expect in Buffalo than in Mexico.

"De nada," he replied, closing the doors and releasing the brakes. A loud hiss nearly drowned out his cry of *"Hasta luego!"* and the vehicle lumbered away, leaving me in a cloud of fumes that quickly blew off.

The steep crest of the mountains rose another four hundred feet above me—the bus had already climbed four thousand since leaving Tijuana—and the thunderheads I'd seen before were still massing. Directly overhead, however, it remained clear blue, and to the west a span of overcast sky the color of lead stretched into the distance, until it met a thin molten streak blazed across the horizon. At my feet the landscape sloped away from me, gilded but not warmed in the dying moments of a late-afternoon sun slipping beneath the cloud cover and vanishing into that same crimson line. In the foreground, lakes of fog filled the numerous hollows and twisting deep gulches that we'd passed on the way up. Scattered among these were dark bluish stands of giant conifers—evergreens on steroids, had been my first impression as we'd driven through them—alongside groves of deciduous trees—all of them wind-lashed.

I walked across the highway to the phone booth that stood like an abandoned sentry box at the mouth of a dirt road. Apart from a string of hydroelectrical poles running in each direction, there wasn't another man-made structure in sight.

"I'll be there to get you in ten minutes," declared a cheery Martinez when I called.

I spent the time huddled in the glass box, feeling the bite of cold air as it whistled around my ankles. Outside it was blowing with enough force to surround me with a mournful howling and send a nearby grove of trees into a tossing frenzy. From beyond the ridge above came erratic flickers of lightning followed by a low rising rumble. The sound echoed off the surrounding rock formations and was still going on when the next set of flashes occurred. The incessant growls made it easy to imagine this place as the origin of mythic tales involving great beasts prowling hungrily just over the rise and out of sight.

I pulled out a flask of whiskey that I'd bought in Tijuana and took a mouthful, swishing my mouth with it before letting the amber liquid dribble down my chin onto my clothes. I knew from years of watching alcoholics leave ER for rehab centers that it would have been outright peculiar for Arthur Kane not to have tried giving himself a bracer. And I needed to have more than whiskey just being on my breath. In case the clinic had a blood lab, I wanted at least enough in my system to register an alcohol level, and had been sipping it since I'd gotten on the bus. Twenty minutes earlier I'd also swallowed a niacin pill to help Arthur Kane really get a glow on. Over the years, whenever a patient complained of unexplained flushing, that over-the-counter vitamin supplement was often the culprit. It causes the blood vessels to dilate, and already I was feeling my cheeks growing warm as it took effect.

Martinez arrived in a flashy, black Japanese four-by-four, which I knew from having priced one in Buffalo—before rejecting it as far too expensive—cost over $65,000. The tall man who uncoiled himself from the leather-lined driver's seat looked approximately my height and age, but there the similarities ended. He wore a beige full-length coat which I suspected was cashmere. When it caught the wind and flapped open, immaculately pressed tanned slacks and a navy blazer caught my eye. He flashed me a brilliant smile that was all the more dazzling set off by his bronze face and black mustache. His teeth were too perfect not to have had a lot of help from his dentist, and I suspected his jet-black hair came from a bottle. If I threw in the sparkling diamond that adorned the hand he extended to me, my first glimpse of the man had taken in about a hundred grand worth of personal wealth.

"Dr. Kane," he greeted me warmly as I stepped out of my shelter. "Come, let's get you out of the cold." He took my valise and accompanied me around to the passenger side.

"Why, thank you, Dr. Martinez," I said far too effusively to be appropriate. I made sure I was close enough that he could smell my breath.

After he threw my bag in the backseat, he waited until I was halfway in the passenger door before he quickly reached inside my breast pocket and relieved me of the mickey. He cocked an eyebrow at my choice of beverage—it wasn't expensive—but instead of throwing it away, he smiled kindly, saying, "This will do perfectly for your treatment," and slipped it into his own coat.

I rode in silence, attempting to re-create the withdrawn quietness I'd often observed in alcoholics who'd recently dried out. About five minutes into the drive Martinez gestured at a rise about half a mile ahead. "That's our pride and joy," he said.

I leaned forward and caught sight of a long, curved, three-story structure with oversized windows, rose-colored stone walls, and a red-tiled roof. The building was perched upon a soaring outcrop of stone at an elevation high enough to still catch the dying light. "It's beautiful!" I gasped, finding it resembled more a villa than any clinic I'd ever seen.

"That's the benefit of starting from scratch outside established, and therefore old, American institutions," he enthused. "We can offer a setting that's physically designed to engender a sense of well-being in our patients as opposed to simply housing the facilities for our clinical program." He sounded like a brochure for the place.

Still, I saw an opening. "I must say, I'm intrigued to know what that clinical program of yours is. From the rumors that I've heard around New York, your results here are rapidly becoming the talk of the health profession."

He gave a start. "Rumors?" he said, his easy charm vanishing and his face clouding over. "What kind of rumors?"

Easy, Garnet, I cautioned myself, reel him in slowly, and don't spook him by saying too much. "That you're on the cutting edge of treating alcoholism; that you're the first people in fifty years to clearly improve on the current ways of keeping drunks like me dry." I paused, to see how he reacted to the praise. Even if his group hadn't achieved the results that Fosse and I had surmised, I doubted that the ego of the man at my side, given all the trappings he'd adorned himself with, could resist hearing that he was the object of such tributes. And if I whetted his appetite for compliments enough, I figured, maybe I could make him boast a bit about exactly what it was that he did here.

The look of alarm that had seized his face drained away.

"Oh?" he said simply, giving me the distinct impression that he'd love to hear more, yet he remained silent.

Perhaps if I assured him that the details of his secret remained safe, I thought, despite all of New York pitching him accolades, he'd open up. "I'll say this about your security, though—it's airtight," I began. "No one who I've talked to, not even the psychiatrist who recommended your place to me, had a clue about your breakthrough. What have you discovered anyway, a wonder drug?"

His smile reappeared like a sun sliding out from behind a passing cloud. "Patience, Dr. Kane, patience. We'll get you settled, give you supper, and then I personally will do your admission physical. After that, later this evening, we may have a chat about what we have in store for you."

Figuring I'd primed him to spill the information I needed as best I could for the moment, I again retreated into my pose of being withdrawn, not wanting to risk any unnecessary small talk by which I might trip up and give myself away.

The road climbed steadily, emerging from a grove of trees and curving along a steep drop-off. I found myself peering over gravel edges, and at the bottom of what seemed a five-hundred-foot gorge spotted the rusted remains of a pickup truck that must have skidded off the road long ago. As we wound back and forth over a series of switchbacks above the site, the crushed frame remained in view, serving as a grim reminder that if it did snow up here, driving back down, even with four-wheel drive, would be treacherous. We then continued upward on a straight stretch covered in asphalt, the vehicle swaying under the merciless bombardment of the wind, and the thunder continuing in the distance like a kettledrum solo.

"Do you know what La Rumorosa means, Dr. Kane?" Martinez called out happily over the sound.

"I have no idea."

"A loud, noisy rumbling."

When we got closer to the clinic, I was surprised to see

that behind its frontal facade, parts of the place toward the rear were still under construction. The entire right wing at the back was largely a frame of timbers, and the rear walls on the left, although completely erected, hadn't yet received their outer coat of stucco. Like a movie set, was what came to mind.

"As you can see, we're in the process of finishing the building," Martinez said as he swung into the parking lot and saw me looking at the uncompleted sections. He pulled into a slot with his name on the curb.

Except something didn't jibe. Even though it was after five and the workers would normally have gone home, there were no overturned wheelbarrows, bags of cement, or shovels lying about. In fact, I didn't see any supplies at all—no lumber, no piles of sand, not even scaffolding—to indicate that people would be resuming work tomorrow or any time soon. The site simply looked abandoned. A sudden lack of cash flow? Or perhaps all the questions I'd been asking about the place had rattled Baines even more than I thought, and he was having second thoughts about continuing whatever they'd started here. Well well, I thought, pleased at the prospect of having troubled him to that extent.

"Uh, Dr. Kane, about our agreed-upon terms," Martinez said, interrupting my reverie, "I take it you have the money with you."

"It's in my case," I replied, "as you requested."

Fosse had provided the cash from the Robert Delany Fund. "We're doing something that is certainly within the spirit of the endowment," he'd insisted as I'd stored the bills in my carry-on bag. I'd never let it away from my side since leaving Buffalo.

"Perhaps I should take it here," Martinez continued, "before we go in, so as to keep our business arrangements private from the rest of the staff and patients."

Just like a whore, I thought, getting your payment up front.

Except in this instance I'm probably the one who's going to get fucked.

Hiding my disdain with the greatest of difficulty, I affably replied, "Of course," and reached to get him his money. He beamed effusively as we completed our transaction, making it even seedier. He then locked the stack of bills in his glove compartment and set his antitheft alarm. Given the total desolation of where we were, I figured the precautions were to avoid being robbed by the people inside his place of work.

As I climbed out I noticed that the car beside us, in the place marked CEO, was a new-looking green Mercedes. By contrast, the other dozen or so vehicles looked run-down and could be only described as early American. They all had Mexican license plates, and I presumed belonged to the clinic's staff.

Huddled against the wind, I followed Martinez up what looked like a recently laid sidewalk. The black earth on either side was level, as if it had once been made ready for sod, but it now hosted a growth of weeds instead.

I waited at his side while he rang the buzzer on a massive white, windowless door. From a distance I'd assumed it was made of wood; standing this close I could see that it was metal. Above me a security camera whirred as it swiveled around to point at us, the door handle emitted a harsh buzzing noise followed by a loud click, and we were inside.

"State-of-the-art security," the psychiatrist crowed as the heavy barrier clanged shut behind us. "We run the place on a locked-ward principle, given the nature of our clients, and we've never had anyone escape yet."

We headed off down a pristine white corridor with a gleaming black and white linoleum floor. A pair of security guards at a control console filled with video screens greeted Martinez with polite smiles. Less friendly looking were the revolvers holstered on their belts.

The result of Baines ordering beefed-up security even here?

I wondered. It made sense, especially if the FBI had passed on my report of Jack's special interest in the place.

Martinez cheerily pointed out the various rooms we passed—his offices, an adjacent examining cubicle, a classroom, a nursing station, a small laboratory. "For doing basic hematology and biochemistry workups, including blood alcohol levels," he informed me. It was all standard fare for a rehab center. Except when several ladies in crisp white uniforms swept by and showed Martinez a bowing deference that American doctors hadn't seen from nurses since the fifties.

Next we visited a modestly equipped, six-bed infirmary, "Where anyone who came down with an acute illness during their stay would be cared for," he assured me. My cursory look at their medication supply told me they had the standard agents used for cardiac, respiratory, and gastrointestinal emergencies, but their antibiotics included none of the more recent-generation drugs. I then got a peek into the dining room—a large spartan area with wooden tables and benches where half a dozen men sat glumly eating their evening meal. After following him up a few flights of stairs, I was shown the common washroom facilities, including showers. I finished my tour by being ushered into my room, a windowless cubicle with a simple metal bed, a nightstand, and a small bathroom.

The harsh contrast between these jail-like interiors and the luxurious outer appearance of the place begged for an explanation, but he didn't volunteer any, nor did I ask him for one. Because for me there was only one question that had mattered since I stepped into the bizarre facility: If what Martinez had said about no one ever having run away was true, then what really happened to David Pearson in this place?

The next few hours gave me little time to think. On Martinez's instructions I left my bag in my room, first retrieving from it all my identification papers and past medical records. "We lock our patients' important documents in the safe," he informed me as he flipped through them. "Where's your passport?" he added, suddenly frowning.

I'd used it to cross the border as Earl Garnet, knowing that the customs official would probably run it through a scanner and thereby create a record of my entering Mexico—a key component of Janet's contingency plans. Another precaution was to lock that passport along with all other paper traces of me in the trunk of my rented car, which I'd left parked at the Tijuana bus terminal—in case she needed access to more proof that I was still in the country.

"I'm afraid I've let my passport lapse," I replied sheepishly, "as I have just about everything else in my life. Luckily my birth certificate was acceptable to the customs officer."

He found the laminated card among the sheaf of papers, then commented, "Crossing our border without photo ID is unusual, Dr. Kane. After all, a lot of people have blue eyes."

I grinned at him. "As I said, I was lucky."

He studied me for a few seconds, and I felt my skin prickle with sweat. Then he shrugged. "Come, let me take you to get some food."

Exhaling with relief, I slipped into another of my planned responses, again modeled after the behavior of patients I'd seen who had quit drinking only a few days before. "Actually, I'm not that hungry," I protested, and given the cabbage aroma I'd been inhaling all along the corridors, it wasn't a lie. "But I could sure use some coffee."

"Of course," Martinez said, nodding knowingly. "We can have some together in my office."

We set off along a different corridor—"A shortcut," he explained—the white walls and checkered linoleum still the dominant motif. On the way I caught sight of what seemed like a small resuscitation facility. Inside were a monitor-defibrillator unit and an anesthetic cart alongside a stretcher, and on the walls were oxygen outlets. I'd no sooner stuck my head in to get a better look than Martinez hustled me out again, as opposed to showing it off, the way he had everything else.

"We better hurry," he urged, "because our lab tech is staying late this evening specifically to draw your bloods and process them."

I politely acquiesced, but not before I'd spotted a glass cabinet full of familiar-looking vials I recognized as a variety of anesthetic agents. Feeling the hairs stir at the back of my neck, I chose my words carefully. "My, you certainly seem prepared for every medical eventuality, including cardiac arrest. I'm very impressed. Do you also do minor OR procedures under general here, or is awake sedation for scopic examinations the limit?" Get him boasting again, I thought, this time about how they might use an anesthetist, and he may let slip why they'd brought in Hector Saswald.

Martinez still wasn't biting. "What we do with our patients, as I told you before, Dr. Kane, you'll learn in good time."

Over coffee, and under the guise of chitchat, he put me to the test about Arthur Kane's background, deftly exploring and probing the man's personal history as any psychiatrist would. Thanks to all my practice sessions with Janet, I made no errors. Then he casually quizzed me about my hospital and working in New York. My previous knowledge of the city got me through that. Finally he ordered me to prepare for my promised physical. Minutes later I was in his adjacent room lying on an examining table—stripped, cold, and at my most vulnerable so far.

"You have none of the usual stigmata of excessive drinking—telangiectasia, spider nevi, a medusa's cap—not one, Dr. Kane," Martinez commented as he inspected my skin for the telltale vascular markings.

"Yeah, I've been lucky that way," I said with a nervous laugh. It was unusual but not impossible for a heavy drinker to be without them. I kept studying Martinez's face for any indication that he was growing suspicious.

"But what are these fresh scars from?"

"A fight with another drunk who had a straight razor, during my last bender."

He raised his eyebrows at that, then returned his expression to neutral as he moved on to poke and prod the rest of me. "You also seem to have gotten to us in time before you did yourself much hepatic damage," he said dryly while palpating and tapping out with his fingers the shape of my normal-sized liver.

"Thank God!" I exclaimed, as if grateful for the miracle.

By the expert way he was going over me, I could tell that unlike a lot of psychiatrists, he hadn't lost his ability to do a thorough assessment of a patient's physical state of health. "Just my luck," I muttered, pulling my clothes back on when he'd finished. I followed him back into his office and sat opposite him at his desk. He remained hunched over my fabricated record, frowning while riffling through its contents. From the color of the papers he was concentrating on, I could tell he was paying particular attention to the biochemical profile of my liver function. I'd concocted results that returned to normal after each binge, and documented my latest drinking episode as having been nipped in the bud, before even transient damage had been done, but it might not fool him.

My pulse kicked up a notch as I quickly searched his expression again for any signs that he was on to me. But I could read only puzzlement in the piercing dark eyes that roved beneath his furrowed brow as he continued to pore over the bogus reports.

"Very lucky indeed, Doctor," he finally said, sliding into his smiling self once more. He then called for his long-waiting technician, ordered her to draw blood samples, including a specimen to be tested for an alcohol level, and presented me with a medical release form to sign. "You know the formality, Doctor. It basically states that you agree to participate as a subject in our experimental program."

Besides specifying the staggering financial penalties that would be levied against me if I broke silence about the secret study, the form was so blatantly in violation of any U.S. informed-consent norms that no physician, not even a drunk like Arthur Kane, would agree to the terms without at least some protest. "It doesn't indicate what I'm letting you do to me," I objected after reading it through, improvising what I thought would be my character's response.

Martinez's eyes widened in a show of surprise. "Dr. Kane, it's you who came to us—begged me in fact to let you into the program. I already warned you over the phone that we had stringent conditions in force to guard against plagiarism. You told me that didn't matter, as long as we helped you. But if you've changed your mind," he said, glancing at his watch and suddenly flashing me his happy face again, "a bus going to Tijuana passes our road within the hour, and I'll drive you to meet it. Of course, I'm afraid I cannot refund your fee, as we already have gone to considerable expense in making special arrangements to include you in our study."

I was getting sick of that easy smile of his, especially the way it seemed brightest whenever we discussed money.

After whining a few more times about the unfairness of it all, I made a show of begrudgingly agreeing to stay, leaned forward, and sullenly penned "Arthur Kane" on the appropriate line. Janet had had the foresight to make sure I'd practiced the man's signature until I could replicate how it appeared on his various cards and documents.

"Fine, Dr. Kane, fine," Martinez enthused, slipping the paper into the rest of my file without so much as a glance at it. He then tilted back in his chair and eyed me for a few seconds.

As far as I could tell, I'd fooled him every step of the way.

But given his reluctance all evening to divulge anything, I was expecting to be dismissed, no wiser about David and resigned to staying that way at least until morning.

Instead he announced, "Now, how about a demonstration of what we have in store for you?"

Chapter 19

"You've heard of the works of Pavlov, haven't you, Dr. Kane?" Martinez asked, leading the way through the dimly lit corridor, his white coat flowing out behind him.

The unexpected question startled me. "Of course."

"And you recall how Pavlov's famous experiment—making dogs salivate at the sound of the dinner bell instead of at the sight of food—was the first demonstration that physiological reflexes in animals could be conditioned to respond to a secondary stimulus?"

I wanted to tell him to quit patronizing me, but held my tongue and simply nodded while hurrying to keep abreast of him. He hadn't said where we were going, but we seemed to be heading back through his shortcut. The sameness of the passageways made it hard to tell.

"And I presume your medical school training gave you at least an introduction to the works of Skinner?"

Skinner had been the father of modern behavioral science and had developed during the fifties and sixties the theory of conditioning behavior through associative rewards, again using laboratory animals, mostly rats running a maze for food. He was required reading for even premed students. "That's right," I answered, remembering back to those early courses.

"And are you also familiar with his work done during the sixties on the next step: negative reinforcement?" Martinez continued.

"Yes," I snapped, irritated now by his not getting to the

point. "Skinner's rats could be made *not* to do a specific type of fundamental behavior, such as eating, by associating that activity with the repeated application of electric shocks," I elaborated, hoping to demonstrate he needn't review the basics. I may not have thought much about basic psychology since medical school—a doctor's mind files away colossal amounts of information that is learned early in training yet never needed in practice—but I did remember it.

He led us past the resuscitation room—the door was closed and I could hear the murmur of voices inside. Instead we entered a small adjacent cubicle that was bare of furniture but had a set of dark green curtains drawn across one wall.

"Do you also recall the controversy the work of that period caused?" he asked, flicking on the light and shutting the door behind us.

Now I was getting interested. "Mind control," the critics had called it. "A powerful tool to modify aberrant behavior," advocates had trumpeted. A famous British film director had even made a popular movie in which he prophesied its use in the treatment of sociopaths. But ultimately all the hoopla had died when the technique proved far less effective in permanently modifying people's actions than anyone had first hoped, or feared. "Sure," I replied. "It was very topical, and a whole flourish of scientific debate appeared in the various medical journals of the time—all about the ethics of using such techniques with humans."

"And are you aware of the first human trials which applied the principles of negative reinforcement to inhibit drinking in alcoholics?"

I caught my breath. His question had made me remember a solitary seminar on a sleepy, autumnal afternoon from over thirty years ago. "Oh, my God!" I involuntarily exclaimed, all at once recalling what it was that a psychiatrist, an anesthetist, an alcoholic, and an addiction center had in common.

A team of psychologists from Canada and England had

been visiting major U.S. medical schools. They were attempting to enlist participation in a multicentered trial aimed at using an extreme form of aversion therapy to stop alcoholics from drinking. "There is no greater drive in the human body than to breathe," their key spokesman had claimed. "Choke that function off with paralytic agents, in association with the subject taking a drink of his or her favorite beverage, do it often enough, and soon the very sight, smell, and taste of the drink itself will become the secondary stimulus that will produce in our subject the same extreme terror associated with suffocation. In short, fear and pain will overcome the craving, and the subject will be unable to imbibe."

Despite his optimistic hypothesis, no American centers had agreed to participate in the study. Later we learned that the Canadians hadn't produced any better results with the technique than those achieved by the methods of Alcoholics Anonymous. And though the group in England managed to reduce a community's use of their local pub by seventy percent, few of those participating drinkers, on closer analysis, had really been alcoholics. The investigators abandoned their trials shortly afterward, one of our professors subsequently told us the following year. To me, it meant one less thing I had to remember.

Martinez had come to a standstill in front of the green curtains, his arms folded, his brow arching toward his jet-black hairline. "I take it from your reaction that you have heard something about that early work. I'm surprised. It was pretty esoteric stuff," he commented.

If you have to improvise a story, Janet advised me before I left, *make it your own.*

I related an account of the seminar, casting Arthur Kane, aspiring urologist, as the overworked, overtired student who'd vaguely paid attention.

When I finished, Martinez leaned back into the green folds behind him and against what I presumed was a one-way mirror. He casually crossed one leg over the other, flashed me a grin, and asked, "Do you know why those trials yielded such poor results, Doctor?"

My God, that smile of his *was* insufferable, I thought while dutifully admitting, "I haven't any idea."

"Think about what we've learned from PTS disorders. That's where I found the answer."

"What?" I wasn't sure I'd heard him correctly. The initials PTS stood for post-traumatic stress, a condition we were seeing all too frequently in military personnel, thanks to places like Iraq, Somalia, and the Balkans. "But what's that got to do with alcoholism?" I had no idea where he was going with this.

Martinez took a breath, puffing himself up like an opera singer about to deliver an aria. "As in all therapies, dosage was the key—the amounts given, the interval between successive administrations, and the total duration of the treatment," he pronounced. "In the British and Canadian study, those parameters were woefully inadequate, and the ethics of that time would not tolerate those researchers making the necessary adjustments. Now, however, it's a different matter. 'Effective, efficient, and cheap,' is the new ethos of the health care industry, and that reopens the door to therapeutic modalities previously regarded as completely unacceptable." He was talking so fast that he had to pause for a gulp of air. "That's where my understanding of post-traumatic stress disorders came into the picture."

Martinez uncoiled himself and began to pace in front of the curtain, his eyes eager. "I became experienced with the syndrome when I was working for the penal service. It used to strike me how prisoners, after a series of vigorous interrogations, actually relived the sessions, over and over, as opposed to simply remembering them. It was as if their recall of the trauma had bypassed the part of the brain that normally distinguishes between an event that is being remembered and one that is actually being experienced . . ."

Shit! I thought. He's talking about torture.

". . . I also noticed that these flashbacks could be triggered by a sound, a smell, or a sight associated with the original interrogations, much the way a secondary stimulus had tricked Pavlov's dogs into salivating," he continued, his eyes afire. "You can see the logical progression. Negative inhibition taken to its extremes could be considered nothing more than the induction of a very specific post-traumatic stress disorder—in this case, a flashback of prolonged suffocation triggered by the sight, smell, or taste of alcohol."

Disgust was all I could feel. It grew like a slowly cresting wave and caught in the back of my throat. Still, I had to learn more. Swallowing bile and managing to feign respect, I asked, "So how have you altered the original protocol used in the sixties?"

In answer, he strode over to a dimmer switch, lowered the lights, then, with a flourish befitting an artist unveiling his masterpiece, threw open the curtains.

The harsh light in the white resuscitation room made it easy to see. A gaunt, middle-aged man with a terrified look on his face was sitting on the stretcher wearing nothing but a johnny shirt. His skinny legs dangled nearly to the floor, and his thin arms protruded from the white, half-length sleeves, appearing not much more substantial-looking than those of a frail puppet. And though there were no speakers turned on to let me hear, he seemed to be pleading with a nurse who was starting an IV on him.

From behind me Martinez said, "I've upped the duration of induced apnea by fifty percent to eighty seconds, reduced the interval between reinforcement sessions to a matter of hours, and extended the whole process to be repeated for five days straight." His matter-of-fact tone sounded as trouble-free as if he'd been describing how he'd souped up his car. "This man, along with those whom you saw in the dining hall, will be finishing their final sessions tomorrow morning, after you start yours. They'll be heading home by noon."

My insides turned to ice. "I start in the morning?"

Those thin limbs began to flail and kick. A second nurse and an orderly moved in to restrain the man, grabbing his arms while the first nurse slipped an IV needle into a bulging vein below his elbow.

"Of course. That way you'll be returning home yourself, to New York and a new life, by Sunday. Did I mention our success rate that you're going to benefit from? Eighty percent of our subjects are still dry since the program began two years ago. And thanks to Brama's recruiting efforts, we've been processing six patients a week—that's six hundred subjects so far. I figure we'll need a thousand in our sample before our statistics will be bulletproof enough to override the moral outrage that's bound to arise in your country . . ."

By that point I'd tuned out. I only had eyes for the struggling figure on the other side of the mirror. All I could think of doing was to say I'd changed my mind and then get the hell out of there.

". . . you know yourself that well over a hundred billion—some experts say it's more—is spent each year in your country treating alcohol-related illnesses—GI bleeds, liver failure, trauma—and what we're offering has the potential to reduce that amount by eighty percent. Imagine an eighty billion dollar savings in health care expenditures, and the subsequent boost to HMO profits . . ."

A man wearing a surgical mask had stepped up to the head of the table and was checking a tray full of intubation equipment, indifferent to the struggle going on beside him. Martinez continued to spurt statistics into my ear.

". . . Brama, of course, was the first to grasp the promise of these benefits when they provided our start-up capital. But once the rest of the health care industry latches on to the scope of those savings, especially when they see how effective, quick, and economical our methods are compared to current treatments—for instance, we've got the anticraving drugs beat hands down . . ."

His voice sounded so breathless that I glanced back at him.

He'd become flushed, and as he enthusiastically continued to expound his vision to turn the treatment of addiction on its ear, his eyes remained riveted on what was happening beyond the one-way mirror, a miniature of the ordeal reflected on their glazed surface.

". . . there'll be no stopping the demand for access to our program from any number of HMOs. We'll of course offer it through facilities like this one—more outlets on our side of the border are in the plans—since Mexican regulations are far more progressive regarding clinics offering innovative therapies . . ."

I was both repelled and fascinated by the spectacle of him. He was so aglow with what seemed like genuine pride, so swept away by the prospect of his success, yet so steeped in the trappings of science, that I found myself wondering if he could even fathom the monstrousness of what he'd become—a torturer in a white coat. I looked back through the mirror in time to see the man on the table lash out with one of his spindly legs and deliver a feeble kick at his tormenters, the whites of his eyes bulging as he strained his head away and the orderly forced a glass of amber-colored liquid to his lips.

". . . we feel coercion is justified rather than let a patient face a return to drinking and a twenty percent risk of sudden death. All those subjects who initially rebel against the procedure are therefore restrained and forcibly subjected to the ordeal . . ."

So much for *my* refusing treatment, I told myself, breaking into a cold sweat and feeling my pulse rocket. But as I watched, I realized the worst of what Martinez had been saying. There'd be many in the business of medicine—doctors included—who'd find his arguments compelling. In fact, it suddenly dawned on me that as long as patients were desperate enough to sign that wretched release form and they agreed to the treatments on Mexican soil, everything that he'd described was not only doable, it was probably legal.

". . . our use of American anesthetists can only add to the credibility of the study. And there are other applications of behavior modification to consider—we could condition drug addicts against needles . . ."

The anesthetist picked up a large syringe filled with clear fluid, reached over the writhing man, and unceremoniously injected the contents into his IV line. The people restraining him stood back. The man looked disbelievingly at them, his eyes wide, his mouth open in dismay as if he still couldn't quite believe what they'd done to him. He suddenly began taking great breaths of air, his chest heaving, until, seconds later, the muscles in his arms and legs started to quiver and he fell back on the table, his body crumpling as lifelessly as if he'd been shot through the brain. His mouth hung slack; his eyes stared straight ahead; his limbs swung loosely above the floor.

I forced myself to stand there, watch, and not give myself away. Yet every instinct I had was shrieking at me to move in and resuscitate the man. I was also desperately trying to figure how I could get myself out of there. But if no one else had ever escaped, how the hell was I going to?

". . . of course, against a disease with that kind of mortality, our own one percent rate associated with the procedure itself falls within the norms of acceptable risk compared with other lifesaving operations. We certainly rival the mortality numbers associated with carotid endarterectomies for embolic stroke victims, or cardiac transplant procedures for patients with end stage heart failure. By the time people in your country realize this risk, they'll be reaping such fantastic benefits from the procedure that the chance of an occasional mortality will seem more than acceptable—"

"Wait a minute," I interrupted, turning to face him when his words finally registered. "A mortality of one percent?" I'd been so horrified by what I was seeing that at first I missed the significance of what he'd said.

"Yes," he replied enthusiastically. "Isn't it wonderful? Compared to the twenty percent chance of a sudden alcohol-related death, that's a ninety-five percent relative risk reduction—"

"Dr. Martinez," a curt voice interrupted from the doorway behind us. I swung around to see a stocky, middle-aged man who'd entered without knocking. In the partial light coming through the mirror, I could make out his swarthy complexion and that he was every bit as well-dressed as the psychiatrist. When he stepped closer, I noticed a key chain bearing the Mercedes logo dangling from his right hand, leading me to presume that I was looking at the owner of the green car in the CEO's spot. I had no idea how much of our conversation he'd heard, but by the dour look on his face, I could tell he wasn't happy.

He let loose a furious stream of Spanish at Martinez, which I hadn't a hope of following, then turned to me. "Dr. Kane, I am Mr. Vásquez, chief executive officer of this facility." His English wasn't nearly as good as Martinez's, but it was a hell of a lot better than my Spanish. "You should return to your quarters and get some sleep," he continued, then gestured toward the mirror. "As you have seen, tomorrow you face a harrowing ordeal."

I glanced once more at the man on the table. Holding an airway and a ventilating mask, ready to resuscitate, the anesthetist stood over him. I shuddered, unable to imagine the agony he was enduring behind those dead-looking eyes.

"Now if you'll excuse us, Dr. Martinez and I need a word in private," Vásquez concluded, abruptly inviting me to leave by gesturing toward the doorway with his outstretched left hand.

Martinez gave me an embarrassed shrug. "Mr. Vásquez is correct. You need your rest."

Just like at home, I thought. CEOs outrank doctors.

"You'll find an open kitchen in the dining hall where you can prepare coffee, tea, and light snacks," the psychiatrist added, "but I remind you that since we start tomorrow morning, you should have nothing to eat or drink past midnight."

It was the standard warning given patients who were facing an anesthetic procedure, intended to guarantee an empty stomach and thereby prevent the aspiration of vomit. I'd pronounced it myself a thousand times to patients headed to the OR. To hear the familiar caution given in preparation for my being tortured seemed surreal.

Over Martinez's shoulder I stole a final glimpse at what was happening in the next room. The anesthetist had finally started to help his victim breathe.

Trying not to show how rattled I felt, I said good night. But as I passed in front of Vásquez I caught sight of at least one thing that made him different from CEOs at home, and accounted for the slight bulge I'd noticed beneath his blazer. Under his outstretched arm I could see that he was carrying a gun.

Before the door had even closed behind me, Vásquez resumed his argument with the psychiatrist, in Spanish. A few words caught my ears—*"Baines . . . teléfono . . . paciente . . . privado . . . se prohibe"*—enough to make me slow my walk and linger in the hallway. For a few seconds I could only hear the murmur of their voices, then Vásquez began shouting, *"Cinco mil,"* and Martinez screamed back, *"Dos mil."* After they yelled the phrases at each other a few times, Vásquez unleashed another blistering torrent of undecipherable Spanish, this time from just inside the door. Fearing he was about to come out at any moment, I scooted down the corridor and out of sight around a corner, praying that the CEO's threat to phone Baines about the "prohibited private patient" was simply part of his extorting a bigger share of Martinez's secret take.

I listened as the two men came into the hallway, still arguing. Then Vásquez hissed, *"Silencio!"* and I heard a single set of steps walking away toward the front entrance. I carefully took a peek, and saw a scowling Martinez just as he entered the resuscitation room and closed the door behind him. The sound of Vásquez's steps going the other way continued.

I listened until I heard them stop, and the hollow sound of distant men's voices came drifting back down the darkened passage as if from some faraway swimming pool.

He was speaking to the guards. Then I heard a harsh buzzing noise, and seconds later the sound of that big metal door shutting after him rang through the halls like a gunshot.

I initially retreated to my room to try and digest what I'd seen and heard. Minutes later I fled back into the corridors, feeling too claustrophobic to think straight and needing to pace. Soon I found my way into one of the unused sections still under construction, but even as I strode here and there, pursued by my thoughts and trying to find an exit, my wandering those passages with their white walls and checkered floors felt like I was running a maze on a chessboard.

David Pearson was surely dead. So were five other patients who'd come here. Martinez had as much as confessed that he'd killed them when he let slip the real secret of this place— a one percent mortality rate among six hundred subjects. That's what Baines, and before him Saswald and Forbes, had been so determined to keep hidden. Those deaths, covering them up, and continuing to recruit unsuspecting patients into a one-in-a-hundred chance of dying meant they'd conspired to commit and get away with murder. But these weren't clever no-fault murders. Neither their having set up shop amid a haven of lax regulations in Mexico nor their unscrupulously worded disclaimers and release forms could protect them now. They were guilty of killing people, pure and simple. And I could nail them for it.

I could also be killed for my efforts. I doubted that men facing six murder charges would hesitate about a seventh to save their skins.

As I continued scurrying this way and that through the semidark passageways like one of Skinner's rats, I kept watch for a quick exit, but to no avail. Despite the incomplete construction, not only were the windows and doors locked, they were all wired to an alarm system. And even if I broke the glass in one of them and crawled through, I could see enough security cameras on the floodlit grounds to realize that the guards would spot me immediately.

I slowed my pace, tried to steady my nerve, and reined in my impulse to make a break for it. Besides, a glance at my watch told me the bus to Tijuana that Martinez had mentioned had long since passed by on the highway below.

I reached the end of the building and pulled up before yet another set of locked windows. Before long the panes in front of me were so awash with rain that the scene beyond dissolved into vertical streams of light and dark. As I stood there I kept telling myself that I'd found exactly what I needed to put an end to Baines, to Brama, and even to Jack's mad scheme. I just had to continue in my role as Arthur Kane and survive the next forty-eight hours. That's when Janet's ultimate contingency plan would kick in if she hadn't heard from me, I thought reassuringly, and she'd be notifying Riley that I was in trouble.

Outside, the wind moaned, lightning ripped the black sky to shreds, and a growl of thunder made itself felt as well as heard, its impact on the surrounding rocky terrain vibrating up through the floor. La Rumorosa was living up to its name tonight.

I tried finding the route back to my room, but the uniformity of it all—the whiteness of the place, the dull light, the checkered floors—continued to confound my sense of direction. I kept having to backtrack after going up a series of cul-de-sacs lined with cubicles no bigger than my own, but none of them were mine. The accidental tour at least served to show the scale on which Martinez and Baines planned to "treat" victims once they were fully operational. But how could they cover up a one percent mortality rate on such large numbers? They couldn't simply claim they'd *all* run away.

Then I thought about what Martinez had been saying just before Vásquez interrupted. How had he put it? *By the time people in your country realize the risk, the benefits will far outweigh an occasional mortality. . . .*

"Of course," I murmured, breaking the creepy stillness all around me between the rolling rumbles of the storm. They wouldn't have to conceal it. They'd probably counted on covering up only the initial deaths in order to publish their treatment as being absolutely safe as well as effective, to help ensure its acceptance. But once the treatment came into demand and was more widely used, they could simply claim that the problems being encountered hadn't arisen during their research. And since all new treatments have more side effects once they're in general use than during clinical trials, Martinez and Baines would most likely get away with the lie. Certainly Martinez was right that not just Brama, but the entire HMO industry had an incentive to accept the program. And he was also right that once those other companies got a taste of that eighty percent savings, extreme aversion therapy would have a hell of a good chance of becoming their treatment of choice for alcoholism, *despite* the consequent controversy and a one percent mortality rate.

I rounded yet another corner and ran into a severe-looking security guard making his rounds. *"Qué hace usted aquí?"* he demanded sternly.

"I can't find my bedroom," I replied, having no idea what he'd asked.

"Ah!" he said, smiling, and beckoned me to follow. He led me to the dining hall.

"Gracias," I told him anyway, figuring I could use at least a cup of tea and some toast. I still wasn't hungry, but from the burning I could feel in my stomach, I figured it was churning empty on pure acid. And I'd far rather get my thoughts together here, I thought, than in that oppressive little chamber I'd left over an hour ago.

There were only three men sitting at the benches, each one

by himself, and not one of them appeared likely to bother me. They all had the same hollow-eyed stare that I'd seen in war photos of GIs after they'd been in battle. I shuddered when it struck me that by tomorrow I'd look like that.

I walked over to a table where an urn of coffee and another of hot water stood ready. A toaster was beside them, a loaf of homemade bread, butter, and pots of jam arranged in front of it. On a nearby shelf I found a canister of tea bags and prepared myself a cup. The simple routine was soothing.

I then found the sugar in dispensers on the tables, but couldn't locate either creamers or pitchers of the real thing. "Excuse me," I said to one of the silent men at a nearby bench, "could you please tell me where the milk is?"

He slowly turned to look at me. His cheeks and nose were crisscrossed with enough webs of red and blue veins to make him appear sixty, but he still had the lean frame of a young man. "Try the fridge," he growled, pointing into the kitchen, then returned his attention to the bottom of his cup.

I retrieved what I wanted, made some toast, and took a seat off in a corner. I'd just taken my first sip of the warm sweet drink and was waiting for it to work its usual magic on my stomach when the gruff man I'd spoken to suddenly let out a huge sob. The sound of it echoed through the silence of that big hall with the volume of a shout. Startled, my cup still suspended halfway to my mouth, I watched his whole body begin to shake, then listened to him give a succession of hoarse cries as if he were in a paroxysm of coughing. Within seconds he settled into a steady wailing, which he muffled somewhat by burying his head in his arms.

I looked around, expecting at least one of the other two men in the room to react and come to his aid, since they probably knew him. But it was as if they didn't even hear his cries. Their inaction left me unsure myself of what to do—comfort him or leave him alone. As I watched, still uncertain, he raised his head, wrapped his arms around his chest, and began to rock, muttering something as tears rolled down his ravaged face. At first I thought he was praying, perhaps saying his rosary, but then the words became louder and I could make them out. Over and over, like a curse, he kept uttering, "It feels like death . . . It feels like death . . . It feels like death . . ."

Chapter 20

Five steps and turn; five steps more and turn again—I was doing the jailhouse shuffle back in my room. The place was growing colder by the hour, the night taking back whatever heat the previous day had provided. Neither did it help that here on the third floor all six sides of my little stone cubicle reverberated with the percussion of the mounting tempest. "Just like my skull," I shouted into one of the booming crescendos. To make matters worse, the cups of tea and innumerable slices of toast I'd downed, instead of having soothed my stomach, remained a lump amidst its tightening coils.

I'd gone to the sobbing man in the dining hall and managed to get him calmed down. The other two patients then drifted over to join us, and all three men eventually proceeded to describe in detail their own experience of what I'd seen earlier. Talking about the ordeal seemed to help them—treatment for PTS involves discussing the underlying trauma—so I'd listened quietly. Now in the darkness—the lights had gone off at midnight, the moment the automatic lock clicked shut in my door—I couldn't stop dwelling on their descriptions of asphyxia, and felt all the more confined for it. Images loomed out of the dark—apparitions of David stretched out on a table, paralyzed, staring, and turning blue as he died. These instantly transformed, and it was me I saw lying there. "Only one-in-a-hundred chance," I uttered over and over like an incantation, trying to dispel the troubling prophecy. My mind quickly obliged by changing to a less personal but no less horrific venue, conjuring scenes of a raging Allen as he dispatched Saswald and Forbes with a stroke of his knife. Yet in the middle of this whirling tumultuous free-for-all of visions, a very simple question posed itself. How had Allen found out what they'd done to his father?

I forced myself to stop pacing and sat on the side of the bed, fumbling in my bag for a portable radio I'd brought. Using the earpiece, I found an oldies station out of San Diego, and blasted it into my brain, hoping to force it into neutral. But even up against the sounds of Wilson Pickett belting out "Ride, Sally, Ride," my thinking wouldn't stop.

I kept dwelling on the fact that there was no way to explain how the young Marine could have penetrated the secrecy of this place, no matter how I tried, without evoking improbable scenarios involving someone from the clinic passing him information. Yet it seemed equally improbable to consider that he hadn't killed Saswald and Forbes. The idea of *Pearson* . . . *too young* being a killer's diversion intended not only to incriminate David, but encrypted to ultimately cast suspicion on Allen as well, was the most farfetched possibility of all.

"Shit! Shit! Shit!" I yelled above the music and thunder, but my mind still refused to quit. What if Janet was absolutely right about Jack MacGregor? it screamed back. What if he had become an assassin, and everything else he said was a lie?

I cranked up the volume on my radio as far as it would go. Otis Redding filled my head with the strains of "Try a Little Tenderness."

". . . the bombing occurred at two A.M., causing extensive damage to the company's head office in San Francisco. Brama has had a turbulent history with patients' rights groups, and most recently has been in the news because of controversy over their aggressive triage policies regarding approval of payment for ER visits. Critics say their practice of withholding full authorization often intimidates patients and leads to fatal delays in their receiving care . . ."

I woke up to complete darkness, wondering who the hell was screaming in my ear. Then I felt the plug and wire from the radio.

". . . all the other attacks seem to involve well-coordinated *home invasions* at the residences of various CEOs from the company. These occurred simultaneously in at least twenty states, timed to coincide with the bombing, leaving no doubt that it is a well-organized terrorist operation the scope of which this country has never seen. There are still reports of similar home invasions coming in from other cities . . ."

In a flash I was awake and sitting bolt upright.

". . . in all cases the houses have been occupied by members of a group calling themselves the PDL, which we've been told stands for the Patient Defense League. Details remain sketchy, but it appears that in the cases we know of, the families of each CEO have been let go while the company officers themselves are being detained as hostages. No direct threats have been made against these captives, but there is an ominous pattern developing. In every incident, the hostage-takers have issued a typewritten statement in which they declared their readiness to die and then the details of how the insurance company, they claim, has killed a loved one. We are getting copies of these as I'm talking to you, and from those I've glanced at, if half their charges are true, it seems that Brama is facing a very determined and angry group of Americans . . ."

For the rest of the night I lay awake listening to the bulletins and half-hour reports as they came in.

". . . a warning was given prior to the explosion, giving authorities time to evacuate the building before anyone might be hurt. Police suspect that a car bomb was left overnight in the underground parking garage by an employee . . ."

". . . the terrorists resorting to attacks on the homes of

CEOs may have been the result of increased security at their offices due to recent threats against Brama . . ."

". . . a detailed list of demands has been e-mailed to major media outlets, basically stating that unless Brama abandons its current triage policies and makes financial restitution to the survivors of those who have died, more attacks on facilities and responsible personnel will follow . . ."

The broadcasts were all the more compelling as the identity of the captors became known and the people who knew them—friends, relatives, neighbors—began giving interviews.

". . . he's been devastated since his wife died. Suicidal, even . . ."

". . . his son's death seemed to finish him . . ."

". . . they're a religious, law-abiding couple, but when they lost their daughter . . ."

Then William Baines gave a statement as he was intercepted by a reporter at the airport in Buffalo.

". . . the leader of these fanatics is a longtime troublemaker named Dr. Jack MacGregor. He's already wanted by the police for the theft of medical documents from our San Francisco office, and last week I understand he added kidnapping to his list of crimes when he drugged and briefly detained a former colleague of his in Buffalo. Clearly he's a disturbed individual—"

"But Mr. Baines, the people who took your chief executive officers hostage have reputations as reasonable men and women. And their claims of what your company did to their family members are a pretty damning indictment—"

"It's reporters like you who give encouragement to crazies like Jack MacGregor," Baines barked. "Let me tell you the facts. First of all, we never withheld care from anyone. It's the doctors who are responsible for deciding what treatments are or are not necessary for any given patient. Second, wherever Brama sets up shop, we not only provide medical services to millions of Americans, we also ensure it stays in business, able to continue meeting that obligation, by discouraging frivolous visits to hospitals. That vigilance results in a one percent savings, and as little as this sounds, it's the difference between going belly up and defaulting on our responsibilities to all our clients, or remaining solvent, fully capable of serving people who have real problems. And what's wrong with that? You wouldn't want a health care provider that looks after its finances so poorly that you can't be sure it'll have the money for the care you need when your time comes to be sick or injured. As a CEO, it seems to me that I'd not be performing my civic duty if I allowed that to happen."

"So what's your point?"

"My point is that Jack MacGregor is manipulating people who are genuinely ravaged by grief. And to those misguided individuals who have been swayed by this madman, I say stop now, before someone gets hurt or dies."

"But what about their charges against Brama? Their demands for compensation?"

"Brama always acts within the law. If anyone has legal arguments against us, let them make it in court, not through vigilante action. Now if you'll excuse me, I'm heading to San Francisco and have a plane to catch."

"But they have been to court—"

"I have no further comment!"

"Isn't it because you're unaccountable for these deaths in a court of law that you've been accused of committing no-fault murder—"

"That's a crock!" he snapped, abandoning his controlled, public-relations voice for tones of raw anger. "And I'll see you in court, along with anyone else who repeats that charge!"

"In court?" the interviewer said incredulously, completely losing her own neutrality. "I'm simply quoting other—"

"In court, you understand, damn you! That insidious phrase has been used by the media to systematically libel me, my company, and the HMO industry at large. I personally won't have it anymore."

"How is the phrase 'no-fault murder' libelous to you personally—"

"You're a disgrace to objective journalism!" he shrieked. "Go away! I have nothing else to say."

As the interview was cut off, I ripped out my earplug. "You'll have a lot more to say, you self-serving son of a bitch, if I've got anything to do with it!" I yelled aloud, elated that he'd just made such a fool of himself. As my words cannonaded around the absolute darkness of the room, my mood quickly grew somber.

If even one of Jack's group lost control and a hostage died as a result, they'd all be charged with murder. Worse still, a single death like that, if it provoked the police to move in on all the other hostage-takers, could spark the mass suicide I'd so feared.

I got up and started pacing again. Maybe I could still limit the damage. Get Baines arrested for the murder of David Pearson before a disaster happened, even accuse him of complicity in the deaths of the five other patients whom I assumed had disappeared. The president of Brama being led off in handcuffs on national media might still be enough to convince at least some of the hostage-takers that they could back down and let justice take its course. But I had to get out of here now!

Absently I noticed that the closed space was no longer filled with the feel and sound of rumbling. The storm must have stopped.

As for Jack, I thought, there'd be no helping him after this. Even if by some miracle not a single life was lost and his people ultimately called off their campaign, he faced a life in prison for what he'd instigated. I strode back and forth in that black, cold dampness, surrounded by a quiet befitting a crypt, and knew he'd kill himself before he'd submit to rotting in a cell.

* * *

At seven the overhead lights clicked on and the lock on my door snapped open.

"Attention all patients," a voice in accented English announced over a P.A. speaker in the ceiling. "You are reminded not to eat or drink before your treatment session. Those of you who are leaving at noon, have your belongings packed and ready . . ."

I clicked on an idea. Perhaps I could slip a note to one of the men whom I'd met last night and ask that he call Janet's cellular number collect once he reached the phone booth at the highway—to say that her husband needed help. It was a long shot, and even if he reported me, it was the kind of plea that even a desperate and frightened Arthur Kane might make. I didn't have to say Janet's last name, and the only thing that might give me away would be the Buffalo area code instead of the one for New York City. But I'd have to risk it. After the sessions, I decided, in the dining hall, that's where I'd make the attempt.

I shunned the public nakedness of the showers, feeling too vulnerable as it was, and chose instead to wash with a wet cloth at the sink. I also shaved and put on a clean shirt, in the tradition of the condemned.

At 7:45 an orderly knocked at my door and indicated I was to follow him. In the hallways a few nurses scurried by us. *"Buenos días,"* they said politely to my companion while nodding pleasantly to me. If they knew or cared about the events overtaking their clinic's parent company north of the border, they didn't show it.

Neither did Martinez. "Good morning, Dr. Kane," he greeted me matter-of-factly at the door to the resuscitation room. "Now we change your life for the better, no?" He stepped inside and ushered me with his outstretched arm to lie down on the stretcher.

A nurse with her back to me was at the counter in front of the medication cabinet. I could see in the reflection of the glass that she was breaking open a vial and drawing the contents into a large syringe. She then turned and handed the filled needle to the masked anesthetist I'd seen last night. As before, he was standing beside an assortment of airways on a steel tray beside the head of the stretcher. He said nothing, didn't even acknowledge me with his eyes as I lay down and looked up at him. His gaze, cold as the wave of sweat that broke out over my back, was fixed on the needle while he held it up in the air and tapped the clear cylinder to remove air bubbles. He then capped it and placed it on his tray, ready for use. I heard Martinez begin explaining what they were about to do with me and felt the wet coolness of rubbing alcohol as the nurse swabbed a vein in the front of my left elbow. A stinging prick followed as she inserted the IV. But I kept my eye on the one who would inject me.

". . . thirty seconds after the succinylcholine is given, you will feel your muscles twitching, and then the paralysis will occur. The transmission of neuroelectrical impulses through the nerve ends to striated muscle will be blocked, and all movement, including respiration, will be stopped. It is the extreme unpleasantness of mounting air-hunger that will, in the end, condition your response, and so you will be allowed to endure it for eighty seconds. At that point, the anesthetist will start to ventilate you and will carry on making you breathe until the drug wears off, in about four minutes. Your heart will continue to beat, and the drug won't affect your sphincters, so you won't soil . . ."

It feels like death, was what I kept thinking as I ignored the droning words and strained my eyes farther back to keep the anesthetist in view. All I managed to see now were his hands as he deftly snapped the blade of a laryngoscope open to make sure the light worked. Then he glided his gloved fingers over an assortment of rubber tubes and black curved airways arranged on his tray like an array of hors d'oeuvres. He adjusted a few of these items so they'd be easier to reach. Close by, also near enough to him that he could pull them into position when he needed them, were portable oxygen tanks connected by green tubing to a black bag and thick rubber mask.

". . . you will pour a small amount of your usual drink into a glass. First, smell it, then take a sip and hold the . . ."

The nurse moved up beside the anesthetist, bringing with her a small steel table on wheels. It held a clear bottle the size of a large pickle jar and a vacuum pump to provide suction. She verified the motor was plugged into a wall outlet, then uncoiled a beige-colored catheter with a metal tip and connected it to a tube dangling from a stopper which sealed the bottle. The anesthetist flicked a switch on the table and adjusted the force of suction until it was adequate to clear vomit from an airway. A nod to the nurse, and they were ready.

I felt myself start to sweat again as I sat up and watched the psychiatrist reach down into a briefcase and pull out the small green bottle I'd bought in Tijuana—flat, contoured to fit in a hip pocket, and with a familiar yellow label. Some of his subjects even at this point gulped the contents greedily, the three men had told me last night. Others were too overwhelmed by fright to drink anything. If I didn't play this part just right, someone might see through me, and I could end up dead.

I saw the anesthetist pick up the syringe. The nurse dabbed a little rubber side port on the IV line with an alcohol wipe, readying it for the injection. At least my fear should pass muster, I tried to reassure myself. It was absolutely genuine and mounting by the second.

I took the bottle of whiskey from the psychiatrist when he held it out to me, but my hands started to tremble and I fumbled with the cap. Once I got it open, the nurse pressed a glass into my right hand, then steadied it for me while I poured myself a mouthful of the amber liquid. The familiar bouquet mingled with the medicinal smell given off by her fingers. I felt the anesthetist move up to my left arm and turned in time to see him jab the syringe into the rubber portal. His thumb was poised on the plunger.

"Now take a sip," Martinez commanded, "then swirl it around in your mouth."

I needn't have worried about giving a convincing performance. My hands began to shake so badly that I was afraid I'd slosh the contents over the sides of the glass. The nurse again steadied them and helped me raise the drink to my lips. As the fluid entered my mouth, I barely sensed the warmth on my tongue. Instead I kept straining to see the syringe, watching the plunger. My whole body was trembling now. *It feels like death!* I tried to swallow but gagged, and the whiskey dribbled down my chin.

I couldn't continue. I had to stop this. I heard myself start to moan.

"Swallow it!" the psychiatrist snapped, startling me with the sudden harshness of his voice.

"Noooooo!" I wailed. "I changed my mind!" I tried to twist my left arm away from the anesthetist's grip.

But it was too late. He'd shoved in the plunger before I could pull the IV away from the syringe.

I sat frozen, staring at my arm. The nurse quickly took the glass and bottle out of my hands, but I was so transfixed on the IV site that I barely noticed. The anesthetist moved to the head of the stretcher, ready for what came next.

I felt a tingling sensation pass through my elbow and rise toward my shoulder. I started to panic. "No! No!" I pleaded, looking first at Martinez, then at the nurse. "Stop it, please stop it!" But their returning gazes were cold. I tried to yank the IV out, then clutched frantically at the upper part of my left arm in a futile attempt to prevent the injection from reaching the rest of my body. I was sobbing when the twitching started. The muscles in my arms, my trunk, and finally in my legs gave a few feeble jerks, then failed me, going completely flaccid. I flopped back on the stretcher, not breathing, still as death, yet fully conscious.

I caught my reflection in the large circle of stainless steel that encased the overhead light. My eyes—open, unmoving, the pupils dilated by terror—appeared unseeing and lifeless. But I saw all too well, and the expressions on the faces of the three who'd done this to me were chillingly indifferent as they leaned over to check my pulse, to document my loss of reflexes, or to simply stare down at the effects of their work.

Eighty seconds. It had sounded not so terribly long, like nothing much more than holding my breath. But I had no breath to hold because I hadn't timed my breathing properly, and when the succinylcholine blocked my respiratory muscles, what little air I had taken in was lost as my lungs deflated. The smothering pressure in my chest, unbearable at the outset, increased steadily. In my mind I bucked and strained against the grip of the paralysis, but my muscles remained slack, useless. I felt entombed, buried alive while locked inside my body.

"Ten seconds," the anesthetist said dryly.

It was beyond enduring. To be suffocating, and yet be so brutally clearheaded. There was no welcome slip into unconsciousness, not yet. I couldn't even close my eyes and escape the cruel scrutiny of the three onlookers. What's more, my senses seemed unmercifully heightened. I had to listen to the sounds of their breathing as I felt the pain of no air encase my chest and crush in on me like hardening cement.

Yet as horrible as it was, the ordeal was what the others had led me to expect. What came next wasn't. Suddenly I felt burning at the back of my neck and throat as vomit flowed up my esophagus from my stomach then poured unopposed down my windpipe. Oh, my God! I thought in alarm. The tea and toast I'd taken before midnight—it normally should have been digested by now! But obviously not by my stomach, churning as it had been on the levels of adrenaline I'd been pumping out all night.

"Thirty seconds," the anesthetist said, oblivious to the forming disaster.

The food particles in my windpipe filled me with the horrific urge to cough and gag, but the impulse went nowhere, the lifesaving reflex that might have cleared my airway fully blocked by the effects of succinylcholine. Instead I lay there, enduring the convulsive sensation of choking to death while being unable to move.

"Fifty seconds," the anesthetist intoned, methodically opening the valve on the oxygen cylinders and readying the bag and mask.

My eyes, though unblinking, could still cry. I felt the tears forming, welling up behind immobile lids and flowing down my cheeks. But my vision was dimming, the lack of oxygen finally, and mercifully, clouding my conscious state. Slowly I was freed from the sight of my tormentors; slowly I lost feeling; slowly the extreme pain of anoxia in my chest and limbs subsided somewhat. But the sensation of choking remained intact. It kept coming in waves. And I could still hear.

"Seventy," a distant voice said.

I felt the anesthetist roughly extend my head and flex my neck, as though forcing me to sniff a flower. I also could still sense enough to know he'd plopped the mask onto my face, covering my nose and mouth.

Then, from even farther away, I heard him mutter what I feared would be my epitaph.

"Shit! The son of a bitch aspirated!"

Chapter 21

At first the darkness was absolute, admitting no trace of light. Nor did sound penetrate to the levels where I floated.

I was neither conscious nor unconscious. Rather, I simply drifted with only the most primitive of my senses—touch, pain, temperature—intact and ready to be probed. But nothing was out there to impinge on them.

Then suddenly I felt movement around me, and the blackness issued up shadows for me to see. Immediately I accommodated, and acquired the power of sight as the shapes approached, loomed over me, then withdrew.

When distant voices broke the silence, sounding far off as if through water, my sense of hearing developed next.

"*Pulmonía . . . asfixiar . . . oxígeno . . . medicamento . . . antibiótico,*" a man was saying.

I tried to speak with him, but my throat clamped around something caught in its midst and I immediately jackknifed at the waist, caught in the clutches of a cough that wouldn't let go. My mind surged in panic the rest of the way toward the surface, until I breached it and remembered everything. My chest hurt, my limbs ached, and I kept gagging, launching myself into another cycle of hacking while still struggling to breathe. For a terrifying second I thought my lungs must still be plugged, but when I finally gasped in a breath, the whooshing noise in my ears made me realize that I was choking on an endotracheal tube in my windpipe.

Then I did something really hard, and opened my eyelids.

I immediately recognized the infirmary. Martinez was giving instructions to a uniformed nurse at the foot of my bed. *"Sedativo,"* he barked, gesturing in my direction but barely giving me a glance as he walked away.

No! Take the tube out! I tried to cry after him, but only managed to produce a whistling sound, the inserted airway having bypassed my vocal cords and rendered them useless. The nurse picked up a prefilled syringe, leaned over the intravenous line that was still in my left arm, and slowly injected me, until I fell back into the darkness.

This time I floated between black and gray while the shadows continued to come and go. Sometimes I felt them take my pressure; other times I could tell they were administering medication, from the tugging at my IV site. Whenever the sedation began wearing off I'd desperately want to know what they were giving me. The proper antibiotics for a lung full of vomit—clindamycin and a third-generation agent, such as cefotaxime—had been nowhere evident in their medicine cabinet the previous evening. Worse, I could feel a burning deep within my right lung. Gastric juices are acidic and full of enzymes, as well as bacteria. They not only infect the lung, they digest it. If the anesthetist hadn't suctioned me out adequately, I knew I could be in for a nasty, potentially fatal pneumonia.

Then all at once they'd inject me again, and I'd be too sedated to give a damn.

As I yo-yoed back and forth, I couldn't regain any sense of time. Now and then I recognized Martinez's voice. At one point I heard him order, *"Traiga su radio,"* and shortly afterward the tinny sounds of the portable penetrated my netherworld.

"The voice of San Diego!" brayed a manic-sounding DJ. "Bringin' ya hits from the D list with Dylan, Donovan, and the Doors." Another *sedativo*, and I drifted off to the accompaniment of Dylan's eerie "Ballad of a Thin Man."

The next time I began surfacing, my rise through limbo

seemed to be going quicker than usual. Like a diver coming up from the depths too fast, I felt that something was wrong. First of all, the place was deadly quiet. Next I realized that the shadows were no longer coming and going in their ministrations. And from the way I was coughing, I could certainly tell that they hadn't sedated me in quite a while. My eyes flew open and I saw that the room was empty.

Was everyone at lunch perhaps? But even the lights were off, and the illumination from the only window in the room was so gloomy that it suggested day's end.

Instinctively I raised my left hand to look at my watch, and was startled to see blood seeping back into the clear intravenous tubing from my arm. Glancing up, I saw that the bag suspended above me was completely collapsed, having been allowed to run dry. What the hell? I wondered.

Out of reflex I quickly reached overhead to turn off the flow valve. But the attempt to raise myself from the bed shot my entire upper body into spasms, and I flopped back with a shriek of pain. My muscles had been so deprived of oxygen that, like a marathoner's at the end of a race, they'd become full of lactic acid and useless.

Yet it was the hose in my throat that quickly became my biggest agony when the remainder of the sedation rapidly wore off. I began gagging on it again, and had to struggle through several tries at sitting up before I got myself perched on the edge of the bed. Still retching, I rummaged through the contents left by the nurse on the nightstand until I found a syringe. Quickly I connected it to a slim catheter flopping out of my mouth alongside the larger breathing tube. Pulling back on the plunger, I deflated the rubber cuff that lodged the device in my larynx and extubated myself, with much sputtering and spitting onto the bedcovers.

My watch showed nearly two-thirty. The men I'd met last night would be long gone, along with my chance to get a message to Janet. But where was everybody else? I wondered if something had happened in the standoff back home that had made them abandon the place, and me with it.

I grabbed the radio and, using the earplug so as not to alert anyone who might still be around that I was up, caught the news at the half hour. "The Siege of Brama," as the announcer now called it, was the lead story.

". . . the situation remains tense. From what we know to this minute, none of the hostages has been injured. But apparently there are new fears that the safety of Brama's president, Mr. William Baines, might also be in jeopardy. Baines arrived in San Francisco on a commercial flight just before noon, surrounded by armed guards, but instead of proceeding to the site of his heavily damaged head office and holding a press conference as his secretary had scheduled, he was promptly whisked away to a private jet, which then took off to an undisclosed location. It's rumored he's gone into hiding to foil a possible attempt on the part of the PDL's ringleader, Dr. Jack MacGregor, to take him hostage as well. But a company spokesman, insisting on remaining anonymous, indicated that Baines is now flying to the site of yet another Brama installation the PDL has targeted, where he intends to intervene personally in the crisis. Hiding out, or heading for a showdown, only time will tell. This is the voice of San Diego . . ."

I yanked out the earpiece and once more looked over toward the window. As far as I could see, it wasn't raining, but an occasional flash outside began to revive the familiar growls, sending them to new volumes. The thin gray light had dimmed even further in the last five minutes, until it seemed to be already nightfall.

"Oh, my God, Jack," I murmured, "what the hell are you up to now?"

Outside my door, during lulls in the rising noises of La Rumorosa, the hallways were completely quiet. It was understandable that they'd send most of their staff home, since there were no more patients besides me, but this silence in that echoing maze seemed to be total, as if no one at all was walking around anywhere. It became unnerving as I strained to hear at least something in that soundless place, until I almost welcomed the intermittent loudness of the storm to counter the spell.

Had they discovered who I was and simply abandoned me there to die?

I struggled to my feet and tested my legs. They nearly buckled, but after a few attempts I managed to take a dozen steps. The effort drenched my flimsy hospital gown with sweat and propelled me into another spasm of coughing. Except this time the ever thicker sputum was tinged with blood.

Alternately pushing my IV pole and leaning on it, I made my way unsteadily to the nurses' workstation, where I picked up the phone and tried to get an outside line. The call was instantly blocked by a busy signal. I tried again. Same result. It was hardly a surprise.

I was standing holding the receiver near my ear and wondering if one of the phones I'd seen in Martinez's office would be any different when I heard the click of someone else coming on the line.

I instinctively held my breath. On the other end no such precautions were taken, and I could easily hear the listener breathing. He or she—it was impossible to tell—must have seen an extension light up when I first tried to dial out. But who was it, and where in the building was their phone?

"Shit, he must be awake," said a voice that I easily recognized as Vásquez's.

"Get him!" another voice in the background ordered before the receiver slammed down in my ear.

With soaring alarm I ripped out my IV and stumbled for the doorway, determined to try and reach Martinez's office before Vásquez could stop me. But I was barely halfway across the room when I heard running footsteps in the distance.

I froze and realized it was at least three people, and the footsteps coming closer were louder by the second. *Hide!* my instincts screamed.

I looked around but saw nowhere to go—not a closet, not even a large-sized cupboard.

Praying there'd be a place in the hallway where I could conceal myself in time, I hobbled the rest of the way through the infirmary, stepped into the corridor, and glanced both ways. It was still empty, but the steps sounded as if they were just around the corner to my right. Wheezing heavily and trying like hell not to cough, I wheeled left and started running.

Immediately I started to choke. As my hacking reverberated along the walls, the steps behind me grew quicker still.

I kept going, heading for a series of closed doors about ten yards away, but was so weakened and slowed by my breathing that I felt as if I were moving underwater. If I could just fool them for a few minutes, I kept telling myself as I got nearer the first entranceway. Make them think I'd gone down another corridor. That's all the time I'd need to get behind them and sneak back to the front office, where hopefully I could dial Janet's number.

I reached for the handle and pulled. If it had been unlocked, I might have made it inside. As it was, I was still tugging on it when I saw Martinez, Vásquez, and William Baines turn the corner and head toward me.

"Hurry up with that damned IV," Vásquez snapped at Martinez, who was clumsily setting up a new intravenous set. "The sooner we get this done, the better."

Martinez's bronze coloring paled to a sickly beige. "Look, both of you, I am a scientist, a physician," he protested, looking from Vásquez to Baines. "I never agreed to help you do anything like this—"

"What you are, Martinez," Baines shot back at him, "is the greedy dumb fuck who let Garnet in here. Now you're going to help get rid of him!"

The three men had hauled me back to the resuscitation room and tossed me onto the stretcher. They then proceeded to dress me in my own clothes, including shoes and socks.

As they manhandled me, my face was pressed into the rumpled sheets and my nostrils filled with the sour aroma of stale sweat.

Baines paced as he ranted, his eyes staring darkly from the new folds of puffy circles that he'd accumulated since last week. The psychiatrist stood to my left, nervously unwrapping the cellophane from a new intravenous set and trying, it seemed, to avoid catching my gaze. Vásquez loomed to my right, not paying me the slightest attention as he kept a vice grip on both my wrists with a single hand. Not that I was in much shape to run off. Repeatedly I curled into a ball because of my coughing, and the muscles in my legs were reduced to little more than spastic knots, thanks to my premature attempt at a sprint.

Baines abruptly leaned toward me over the foot of the bed. "You hear that, Garnet, you fuck!" he shouted. "I head here to make sure our tracks are covered, and lo and behold, I find you. That means you're a man without much of a future." His haggard face reminded me of Jack's.

"And you look like a man who's not sleeping very well," I shot back, albeit in a croak. "Problems with the hired help?" I added, jerking my thumb toward Martinez and nodding toward Vásquez.

Baines recoiled with a snort of surprise, clearly annoyed at my insolence, and Martinez's jaw dropped an inch. But Vásquez started as if I'd slapped him, and his face colored to crimson. I thought he'd punch me as I watched him cock his fist and draw back his lip the way a dog would to show his fangs. Good, I thought, figuring that I'd hit a nerve. If he was defensive about his place in working for the American, I could exploit that.

"Easy, Vásquez! Get control of yourself," Baines warned sharply. "Remember, we have other plans for his face. It's got to look like a fall."

Vásquez remained poised to strike for a few seconds more, eyeing me and breathing almost as hard as I was, but he held back. Finally his thick features transposed into a leer. "That's right, we do have other plans, don't we?" he told me softly through clenched teeth. But then he lashed out at Martinez, jabbing accusingly at him with his finger. "You and your fucking private patients!" he roared, unleashing the fury that I'd stoked. "I told you that bringing him here was crazy."

"We were on guard for terrorists," Martinez fired back, "not some wimpy urologist from New York. Besides, you were quick enough to cut yourself into the take."

They lit into each other in Spanish, going eye-to-eye across my legs.

"Shut the fuck up!" Baines shrieked at them. "I can't be-lieve you two! That maniac's launching an all-out attack on us up north, everything we have is at stake, and yet you put us all at risk to pad your pockets with a few extra grand . . ."

The two Mexicans stopped shouting at each other and glared at Baines, both of them looking furious as he con-tinued to give them a dressing down, but they took it in si-lence. I'd gone into another fit of choking and was straining to hear his words. He must be talking about Jack, I thought, seeing the frustration written large all over his face.

". . . don't you realize what we're up against? He's bleed-ing us dry with his blackmail—thirteen million I've paid him so far—but he may still go to the cops. And his slicing Saswald's throat when I balked, then Forbes's—he could do that to you, me, any one of us, yet you haven't the sense to be careful—"

"Thirteen!" Vásquez interrupted. "I thought he'd extorted eight! You had to pay him another five million?"

Their words hit me like a head-on collision.

Baines wheeled away and resumed his pacing. "Yes, I had to fork over *another five million*. He started threatening to ex-pose this place—again!" he raved, waving his arms in the air.

I felt my universe start to turn upside down. All I could think was: They couldn't mean Jack!

"Jesus Christ!" Vásquez muttered. "You mean he milked you some more, then set his fucking PDL on us anyway?"

Baines answered by pivoting around and screaming into my face. "Your precious Jack didn't tell you that he was a blackmailing murderer before he sent you here, did he?"

My mind went reeling for the sidelines, too sandbagged by what I was hearing to think clearly. No, you're wrong! I wanted to scream, but before I could recover enough to say anything, Vásquez suddenly pinned my right arm to the bed with his knee, and I howled with pain instead.

He threw the rest of his weight across me and grabbed my left arm with two hands. "Get on with it!" he barked at Martinez.

The psychiatrist's eyes bulged as he swallowed a few times. "Listen, why don't we wait—"

"Do it now!" Baines ordered.

Martinez swallowed once more, then took the needle he was holding from its sheath and brought it up to a vein in my forearm.

"You bastard," I rasped at him while starting to struggle. But Vásquez's grip was too strong. I felt the sting of it going in.

Martinez averted his eyes as he taped the line in place and started the flow from a bag of saline. "I'm sorry," I thought I heard him whisper when his head was near mine. He then strode to the medication cupboard, picked up a glass vial—succinylcholine, it looked like—and snapped it open. I gaped at him as he deftly started drawing the contents into a syringe, incredulous that he could be so absurd and obscene as to apologize while preparing to kill me.

Suddenly Baines was at my ear. "Give MacGregor to me, Garnet," he said, speaking softly. "Besides you, he's fooled all those other poor idiots who he's got poised to die for their loved ones. You owe him nothing now. All he turns out to be in the end is a greedy con man on the take for himself, using them as unwitting enforcers. Why, he's like a mobster running a protection racket . . ."

My attempts to break out of Vásquez's hold had exhausted what little strength I had left. As I lay there, helpless to resist and my mind in a tumult, I still refused to believe what I was hearing. I also had a fleeting hope of turning to my advantage his belief that I knew how to locate Jack.

". . . where is he, Garnet? Give me MacGregor, and I'll sedate you before we do what we have in mind. Otherwise you're going to tumble into that deep gorge beside the road out front while wide-awake and full of succinylcholine . . ."

To shut out the words I focused back on Martinez, only to see that he'd finished drawing up a second syringeful from a smaller, different-colored vial—midazolam, it looked like—and was walking toward me. He held the cylinders of both needles upright in his hand, their points glinting in the light. The sight of the larger one was enough to send my heart pounding, and I began taking extra gulps of air, to get ready for what was coming.

". . . the fall won't necessarily kill you, but the lack of breathing certainly will. The idea is that the rocks on the way down will rip your skin open and bust you up inside while your heart is still beating, so you'll bleed awhile. On autopsy it'll look like you died from the trauma. Tell me where he is and you'll take the ride the easy way."

"Too many people know why I came here!" I protested, desperate to stop him. "You won't get away with it."

"Oh really? We'll say that you sneaked in here under a false name, wanting treatment. When Dr. Martinez kindly obliged, you got scared, ran into the storm, and fell—your tragic end brought on by yourself, the outcome of a misguided obsession with Brama. At least that's what I'll tell the media, as well as suggest that since you were here as part of MacGregor's terrorist group, maybe he sent you to blow up yet another Brama building."

"*That'll* never fly!"

"It won't have to fly. Just float around, like a shadow of doubt."

I knew it was futile—trying to convince him that he'd be caught—as though that would keep him from killing me. Yet, compelled by fear, I continued arguing with him. If nothing else, my striving to make him change his mind let me trick myself out of facing the inevitable, for the moment, and helped me keep my panic in check. "The police will go over this place with a microscope."

"We were eventually going to reveal what we're doing here anyway. The publication of our work will be a little early, is all. And no one can prove we killed Pearson or the others because they'll never find the bodies. Someone finding yours, on the other hand, will add credence to the story that the rest ran off."

"But why kill me at all?" I implored, barely able to speak, my mouth having gone so dry. The instant I spoke and heard the pleading in my own voice I thought, Oh, God, don't let me slide into begging for my life and give him the satisfaction of that. "After all, it's still just my word against yours," I added, desperate to sound as if I were simply pointing out the logic of his sparing me.

He gave a sarcastic snort. "My dear Dr. Garnet, you know way too much! Combined with how dogged you are, I'm afraid it makes you far too dangerous to be left alive. Besides, even before you came here you'd made yourself a plague to my company. You have no idea the added gratification my eliminating the man who coined the charge 'no-fault murder' is going to give me. That little ditty has become a PR nightmare for us. So how about it? The easy way or the hard way?"

My skin grew clammy. Fight him some more! I screamed to myself. Argue about something else; say anything at all to delay him and prevent me from thinking of my own demise. "You're wrong about MacGregor!" I shouted to keep him squabbling with me.

He didn't bite.

Instead he looked up at Vásquez, who was still on top of me, and asked, "Has everyone on staff been sent home?"

"Even the guards," the burly man answered, his grip tightening on my left arm. " 'On account of the roads and a risk of black ice,' we told them."

"Then bind him down and let's roll."

Vásquez pushed. Martinez scurried behind, carrying the two syringes, looking as dazed as if he were sleepwalking at a fast pace. Baines strode alongside, an Iago at my ear, continuing his effort to convince me about Jack.

". . . when the blackmail started after Pearson died, I was unable to even imagine it was him—at first. Because all those years in San Francisco when he'd been a thorn in my side, I'd at least believed that his patient advocacy, though misguided, was sincere. See my point? If he could fool his enemy, why shouldn't he be able to trick a friend . . ."

His words became an echoing noise as the white walls and ceiling went sweeping by my head, the landmarks from my entrance on the previous day—the dining hall, the infirmary, the lab—flashing by in reverse.

". . . so why protect a person like him? Look at his greed. The demands for money were small at first, but when he killed Saswald—the name 'Pearson' may have stumped the cops, but I sure as hell got the message that our blackmailer was the murderer—his price became two million . . ."

Whether from our moving so swiftly or my beginning to hallucinate, the ceiling tiles gave me the illusion of racing under an undulating checkered flag. Fighting a surge of dizziness, I bucked with my torso against my restraints and thrashed my head from side to side in an attempt to break free, until my mind snapped back to the times I'd tied David Pearson down and how he'd writhed to no avail before his hordes of oncoming spiders.

". . . at the height of the police investigation, particularly if they were pressing hard, MacGregor kept demanding two million more. When I balked and tried to bargain, he doubled his demand to four, and even then said he'd just as soon cut *my* throat . . ."

At the main nursing station the lights had been left on, making it appear as if they were expecting someone to return at any second. But nobody came.

". . . I still resisted, hoping that whoever it was, he'd slip up and I'd nail him. But all I ever dealt with was a husky, disguised voice calling from different pay phones in Buffalo—I know because I tried to have him traced. Then he murdered Forbes and threatened me again with more of the same unless I gave him six million. I paid—I was too terrified not to—and I've been paying him virtually on demand ever since . . ."

Wait a minute, I thought. How could Jack have used pay phones in Buffalo? But the question popped out of my head as quickly as it came. Thinking such puzzles through wasn't something I could do right then.

Seconds later we were past the abandoned guard station, through the automatic door, and out of the building. The daylight had turned as murky as smoke, and we plunged into a wailing wind so cold that I felt I'd been cast into ice water. Although the rain hadn't started again, everything was coated—the pavement beneath us, the asphalt in the parking lot, and the road ahead—with a slick, gleaming surface. We rattled over the sidewalk, the stretcher sliding sideways and its wheels nearly slipping into the black earth covered with weeds. Vásquez cursed as he brought it under control.

Through it all, Baines continued his harangue.

". . . when he called me this weekend, teasing, once more insisting he'd reveal the secret of La Rumorosa unless I paid, he took great pains to describe how he'd enjoyed watching Saswald and Forbes trying to talk once he'd cut their heads half off. Believe me, I again wired the money as soon as I could—to yet another offshore account—they're always different . . ."

I stared straight up at the sky and tried to get control of my rapidly unraveling nerve. Overhead a tree tossed its foliage like a mane as a strong gust swept through it, rustling its wet leaves and making them sound as if they were concealing a thousand snakes. Baines had to raise his voice.

". . . face it, he's a sadist, a murderer, a blackmailer, an exploiter—you've been used . . ."

I forced myself to tune him out, my mind still too addled to logically tackle what he was saying anyway. But my gut instincts had remained intact, and they held firm that it wasn't Jack. Because in the end, whatever Baines was claiming, I knew that Jack's fierce sense of justice would never let him surrender the high ground in his attempt to be the nemesis of the man. He'd break the law to pillory Baines with the PDL because he'd see that as righteous. And if he had resorted to blackmail as part of inflicting punishment on Baines, he'd have done so solely because hurting Baines in the wallet would be apt, not because he'd want the money for himself. But not for all the riches of the world would he ever debase himself with killing, of that I was certain, for it would betray everything he'd ever stood for as a doctor and, in this case, made him too much like the man he was after. Jack simply loathed Baines far too much to ever give him that kind of satisfaction.

Yet I only had to look at Baines's haunted expression to believe that *someone* had put him through the hell he was describing. If not Jack, then who? This question flew to mind like an arrow, staying the chaos and galvanizing me into a few more seconds of coherent thought.

We moved onto the smooth asphalt of the parking lot, passing behind Martinez's four-by-four and the green BMW—the only vehicles there. How had Baines arrived? I wondered fleetingly. Wherever the nearest airport was for his private plane, he wasn't the kind to ride a bus.

As we neared the point at which the lot narrowed into the beginning of the road, the grade sloped downward and Vásquez, sliding with every step, had increasing difficulty controlling the bed in the descent. I raised my head and could see the first of the drop-offs barely a hundred yards ahead, the dark sweep of the mountains lying beyond it.

". . . so tell me how to find him, Garnet," Baines once more cajoled. "Let me bring him to justice. You owe it to your cause and all those people he's deceived, and you'd be leaving the world with one less serpent in it—"

"All right! I know where Jack is," I lied, my voice breaking as I made no attempt to hide how afraid I felt. "But I don't want your thugs to hear me betray him. Come closer. I'll whisper it to you. And then you'll put me out, right? You promise me that? You'll put me out now?"

Baines looked surprised at hearing me beg. "Sure," he said suspiciously, and started to bend down near my mouth.

"It's too slippery," Vásquez interrupted, bringing the bed to a stop and setting the brake with his foot. "If he goes over the side on a runaway stretcher, they're liable to tell from the marks at autopsy that he was in restraints when he died." He started unbuckling my legs. "Here, help me!" he ordered Martinez. "We're going to walk him the rest of the way."

Baines had paused with his head turned sideways about a foot above mine, looking down at me the way a bird eyes a worm. "Well?"

"Closer. It's hard to talk," I whispered.

He leaned down another six inches. Martinez was stepping toward Vásquez and had slid the capped syringes into the pocket of his white coat. It was fully buttoned, but flapped noisily as its hem caught in the wind. I whispered low enough that the continued snapping drowned out my words.

"What?" Baines said impatiently, moving closer still.

I lunged at his ear with my teeth, clamped down on skin over cartilage and wrenched.

I felt it give.

Blood spurted over my face as Baines's shriek filled the air. His fist shot into my upper gut, exploding the breath out from my lungs and releasing my jaw.

He reared back, his hand cradling the half-severed appendage as blood continued to flow out between his fingers. "Son of a bitch!" he roared, his voice full of terror.

Martinez and Vásquez remained where they stood, mouths open, expressions of shock frozen on their faces.

Baines continued screaming. "Christ! What have you done to me, you bastard!"

Martinez moved first, grabbing a handkerchief from inside his coat as he stepped up to Baines and forced the man's hand far enough away from the tear that he could wedge the white cloth against it. "You'll need a plastic surgeon to repair that," he said loudly over the howling gale and Baines's cries.

"That's right, asshole!" I yelled. "You're going to need an ER. But out here, hours from anywhere and with the roads slippery as hell, your only sure way of getting sutured in time to save it is with me. My life for your ear! How about it? Unless of course you'd prefer going through life doing a Vincent Van Gogh imitation." I knew he could have me killed the second I finished, but for the moment I seemed to have gotten enough of the upper hand to win at least a temporary reprieve.

Baines appeared to get a grip on himself—he had stopped bellowing like a wounded animal—as Martinez's improvised compress slowed the bleeding. Still grimacing and moaning, however, he reached with his free hand inside his jacket pocket, took out his cell phone, and pushed a single redial button. "Get ready to take off and set a flight plan for San Diego," he ordered into the mouthpiece. "Have an ambulance meet the plane. I'm going to need a hospital. I'll be back up at the strip in twenty minutes . . ."

"It's our private airstrip near the American border," Vásquez taunted me from behind my head. "I guess loose-lipped Martinez forgot to brag about it."

Baines finished talking, then watched me deflate in front of him. Even with his face etched in pain and covered with blood, he managed to look triumphant as he enjoyed my defeat. Behind him loomed the half-built structure of the creation he'd soon unveil to the world, its dark ribs pointing skyward against the massing purple thunderheads. Except in the thinning light it might just as easily have been taken for an abandoned ruin left to rot, like the carcass of some prehistoric mammoth.

"You know, Garnet, it's guys like you who inspire guys like me to come up with ideas like this," he said, gesturing over his shoulder. "Because I figured that sooner or later the zealots on your side might just win the right-to-sue argument, and we could lose the one percent margin we now enjoy. That prospect drove me to come up with another moneymaker—in this case, it's aversion therapy. Brama's share of the savings alone in treating alcoholics will move at least eight billion from expenditures into our profit column. In other words, as you go over the edge, Garnet, know that the very cause you're dying for has, in a way, instigated our creating everything you've seen here, and a huge boost in earnings to boot. Kind of makes your sacrifice seem a waste, doesn't it?" He paused, then softly ordered, "Do it the hard way," addressing Vásquez while continuing to eye me.

Helpless under his stare, I tried my damnedest to keep from shaking in the cold. It suddenly mattered to me that he not think I was trembling because I was afraid. "Also, you better clean him up," he added, "in case the cops get creative and do something smart, like analyzing the blood on him."

Vásquez shrugged. "Why bother? It'll rain soon, and cops in La Rumorosa aren't exactly world experts in DNA testing."

"You'll do as you're told," Baines snapped, and strode back toward the building.

I raised myself up, craning to watch where he went. After crossing the parking lot, he passed the sidewalk and kept walking until he reached the far side of the sprawling edifice, where he disappeared around the corner.

The two men finished undoing the straps and yanked me off the table. Neither made any attempt to get Baines's blood off my head. Vásquez pinned my arms from behind and, with Martinez holding the IV bag aloft, frog-marched me the remaining hundred yards along the roadside where the footing was better.

I struggled every step of the way, then dug in my heels when they veered me toward the edge of the drop-off. But I remained weak as a kitten, and my efforts only managed to set off another round of coughing. Within less than a minute I stood shivering in the half-light between the two of them, looking down a steep rocky grade about two hundred feet high while the wind slammed into us with the force of a wave.

I sought refuge from seeing where I'd fall by closing my eyes. In that private darkness the shrill sound of the gale filled my ears, inviting me to leap into it with arms spread wide, to let it carry me up and away from there. I grasped at the fantasy, and had the fleeting illusion that there was charity in letting the condemned retreat into the blackness of a hood during the final seconds.

I sensed Vásquez reach across my chest to Martinez, who bracketed me on the right. "Give me the needles," he ordered.

My fantasy of flying crashed. My legs buckled. My brain dived to the level of a terrified animal's. I opened my eyes in time to catch Vásquez lifting both syringes from the psychiatrist's pocket. "Which one's the succinylcholine?" he asked.

"Martinez, for Christ's sake!" I blurted, suddenly desperate enough to want the easy way out. "You're a physician. At least put me under!"

"The smaller one with two cc's in it," he replied to Vásquez, continuing to stare straight ahead, looking at neither of us and swallowing about once a second.

That was the midazolam.

Vásquez studied the smaller syringe, and then Martinez's profile. "You lying wimp," he snarled. "I've seen what they've used often enough." Without ceremony, he shoved the larger needle into the injection portal and brought down the plunger. Within seconds I felt the tingling rising up my arm.

"You bastards," I screamed, my heart rate shooting into triple digits.

Martinez jerked his head around, finally looking me straight in the eye. "I'm so sorry," he repeated, his voice breaking while he still kept a firm hold on my wrist. "But they'd have killed me." His pupils grew tenfold with fright and his face distorted as if he were about to weep.

I spat at him. Except I had no spit.

Vásquez roughly yanked the tubing from my vein and flung the entire infusion set on the ground. Grabbing my other arm from Martinez, he once more pinioned me from behind and adjusted his stance, readying himself. For an instant we stood there, as three men might stand on a platform waiting for something as inconsequential as the next train.

My legs sagged again. Vásquez cursed something in Spanish, but held me up. Martinez abruptly turned away, his shoulders shaking, and I thought I heard a muffled sob. Then I felt the tingling pass up through my shoulders to my neck, and I started gasping in air as fast as I could.

My name floated to me from behind, faint against the wind.

At first I thought it was a hallucination, but I heard it again.

"Gaaarnet! Gaaarnet!"

I swung my head toward the sound just as the muscles in my shoulders started to quiver.

I saw figures running down the road toward us. Accelerating in front of them, riding the stretcher on his hands and knees with his coat streaming out behind him, was Jack hurtling at me, his face a howl of rage.

Chapter 22

Vásquez's grip on me shifted as he and Martinez also turned toward the sound. "What the hell?" Vásquez exclaimed when he saw what was heading toward him.

The fasciculations reached my legs. Knowing I'd be paralyzed in a matter of seconds, I deliberately dropped to the ground, becoming a dead weight in Vásquez's hands.

"Shit!" he exclaimed, stumbling with the unexpected load. He gave a quick heave, partly tossing, partly rolling me toward the edge until my legs dangled over the chasm below. Clinging to the rocky shelf, I dug in with my elbows and wiggled my torso, quickly gaining the inches needed to be more on than off. I kept scrambling and clawed up a foot more, all the while still trying to gulp in extra air. I raised my head in time to see Vásquez reach inside his coat and bring out his gun.

"Look out!" I screamed at Jack, who was hurtling nearer by the second. He'd already pulled himself into a surfer's crouch, the loose bed sheets billowing up around him as he drew a visual bead on Vásquez and prepared to jump him. But as the gap between the two men closed, Vásquez leveled his pistol to fire.

The paralysis hit, my head dropped, and the right side of my face plopped into the dirt. My breath ran out of me as softly as a sigh, blowing a fine dust into my still-open eyes, which I couldn't blink, and the squeezing sensation in my chest began to build. But it was when my lower legs flopped straight out behind me, still in midair, that the shift in weight made me slowly lose my perch and I started to inch down.

The rattling of the stretcher sounded almost on top of us. "Noooo!" I heard Martinez scream above a roar from Jack. Then a gunshot blasted over my head.

Martinez's shouting trebled into a screech, and Jack let out an even louder bellow. I heard a thud, followed by snapping twigs, scraping stones, and a stream of curses from Vásquez. The clattering of the stretcher grew so close that I was convinced the heavy steel table would bash into my head, then I felt its wheels brush along my right side as it raced by, and I heard it no more.

Martinez continued his shrieking, leaving me desperate to know what was happening as I continued to slide. Dirt grated against my chin. A salty metallic taste filled my mouth as tiny stones pulled my lip into a sneer and abraded its inner lining. Bristly tufts of underbrush and other potential handholds slid tantalizingly under my palms. But most of all I felt the pain of having no air, and it kept mounting.

Behind me, far below, I heard a distant crash. From above, Martinez's cries became a terrible gurgling noise, while sounds of punching and grunting replaced Vásquez's cursing. Floating over it all came the shouts of the people who'd been running after Jack as they drew closer.

Friends or foes? I doubted I'd have time to know. My descent quickened, and the rocky edge I was sliding off had already cut into the top of my thighs. It bit into my pelvis next, giving my bony prominences and other vital appendages a good scraping as they passed. Then my legs dropped straight down, and for a few seconds I teetered, the sharp stone digging into my waist, the approaching footfalls and shouts growing louder.

"Get him off me!" Jack hollered.

"Grab his fucking gun!" someone else yelled.

"I'll get Garnet!" a third voice volunteered.

But I slid again, this time all in a rush, and over I went.

I dropped like a rag doll, hitting the first narrow ledge of rocks ten feet below, and remained there, collapsed in a heap. Had I been a foot farther out or struggling to keep my balance, I doubt I could ever have stopped myself on such a small outcrop.

The next seconds seemed like an eternity as the agony in my chest grew, yet I was still conscious when Jack rappeled down, suspended from above by the bed sheets tied in a loop under his arms. "It's okay, Garnet, we've got you," he reassured me, purchasing a knee hold beside me on a space little more than twenty inches wide. Gently supporting my head and neck, he unfolded me, laying me faceup with my back on the stones, and, sealing my mouth with his, he blew the delicious relief of air into my lungs.

After four quick puffs he settled into a regular rhythm, his face looming over mine. I could see that his sleep-starved eyes and gaunt features hadn't improved any, but he was clean-shaven and there wasn't so much as a whiff of alcohol on his breath. "You and I . . . have some repair work . . . to do up top," he informed me between respirations. "That crazy Mexican in a white coat . . . stepped in front of a bullet for me . . . and I think the least we can do for him . . . is to save his life."

He settled into breathing for both of us. I began getting used to the idea that I was going to live. But instead of relief, I felt shame. In those last few seconds they'd broken me, snapped my will like a twig.

La Rumorosa gave a menacing growl, and the rain, driven by the wind, started to pelt us. Jack tilted his head back and glared defiantly at the heavens. "Oh, shut up!" he yelled, then flashed me a grin as bright as the lightning that was branching sideways across the sky above him. I felt my courage surge back at the glory of that smile, the way it always had whenever, in the middle of a hopeless case, his own crazy confidence and fearlessness had ignited the same in me. And the sight of him—cocksure, balanced on that tiny ledge, keeping me alive breath by breath as the rocks beneath us vibrated so much in the storm's roar that I feared they'd shake loose—was enough to make me believe that, together again, we'd have the knowledge and nerve to win this thing.

Minutes later a shiver rippled through my muscles, and the paralysis was gone, leaving me once more convulsed with coughing and shaking with chills. Jack eyed the thick yellow sputum I was hacking up. "Jesus Christ, man," he exclaimed. "Have you got pneumonia—"

"Jack, they've killed six people here," I gasped. "That's the real secret of this place, and we can charge Baines, plus his cronies, with murder!"

He started, his eyes shooting wide in amazement. "I knew it! There had to have been deaths," he exclaimed excitedly, "but we never could prove anything. Even our sources inside Brama who tipped us off about the clinic couldn't find evidence to crack that damn lie about patients running off and subsequently dying of alcoholism—"

"Look, Jack, I've got a witness who I think I can persuade to talk," I told him through chattering teeth. "He's the one up above with a bullet in him."

Four of Jack's men used the bed sheets as a litter and rushed Martinez to the resuscitation room. Red foam was bubbling up from the psychiatrist's lips each time he exhaled, and his face had grayed to the color of ash. All the hideous noises he'd been making previously had petered into weak, incoherent whimpers.

As Jack trotted alongside he eyed a pair of crimson stains on the psychiatrist's white coat—one expanding over the right upper chest, the other spreading out in an enlarging circle from his back, but lower down. By the time we reached the parking lot the stains had joined to become one. "A bank shot off a rib going in, and the exit wound a foot below," he commented, determining that the bullet had ricocheted downward, traveling the length of the lung and creating a much longer path of destruction than if it had passed straight through horizontally.

As good as Jack's and my ER skills were, I knew Martinez needed a thoracic-vascular surgeon and an OR within the hour. "Maybe we can stabilize him, then fly him out of here," I puffed, the brisk pace uphill taxing me heavily and forcing me to speak in short gasps. My previous burst of confidence was waning fast.

"Sounds like a plan," Jack acknowledged, his voice filled with the easy calm I'd always heard him adopt in the worst of times. "My plane's still at the strip, the crew keeping Baines's pilots company." But a frown capped his face when he looked back to where I was struggling to keep up. "Are *you* going to be okay?"

"Sure!" I bluffed, forcing myself to speed up and pull abreast of him. I grinned through the pain as my muscles rebelled, but my wheezing gave me away.

He shot me his best *Yeah, right!* look, yet said nothing.

When we reentered the building, it seemed that every phone in the place was ringing. "What the hell?" I exclaimed.

"Media," he said curtly as we scurried over the checkered floor. "The minute we touched down, our people back home issued a communiqué saying we'd seized the clinic and would be making a further statement. We intended to expose that Brama was basically torturing patients here, the disclosure hopefully adding so much to the company's infamy that this clinic would become a symbol of all their wrongdoing."

"But that means the police will already be on their way as well!"

"Afraid so. It was all part of our campaign. We knew they'd show up anyway, with a vengeance—cops don't negotiate with terrorists down here—so we needed to give the TV reporters a chance to arrive first. Except the storm's made it unlikely any newscasters will be flying in anytime soon, and of course we sure as hell didn't expect to find you, not after I warned you to stay away, nor Baines, especially since we moved up the date of our attack—" He broke off, suddenly speechless as he gawked at the austere surroundings. "Jesus Christ!" he burst out. "Who the hell decorated this place, Stalin?"

As I led the way, he stopped clucking in dismay and resumed briefing me on his strategy. "We meant to declare a twenty-four-hour deadline on Brama to settle up, and figured cameras would keep the local cops and Federales in check, giving us the time we'd need to continue broadcasting our case to keep up the pressure. Otherwise the forces of law and order in La Rumorosa might have turned our stand into another Waco before we even got started." He added a sardonic chuckle. "Hell, they still might."

"What are you talking about? I thought you just agreed that we get out of here!" I was still short of breath, as we were practically running.

He gave me a hard glance, without slowing down. "Think about it, Garnet! If we can't keep your pal here alive, or he doesn't give the testimony you'll need, there's no reason for any of my people to abandon our original plan. In that case, we'll all be staying put with our captives until either Brama accedes to our demands or the deadline passes. Except at this site I'll have Baines as a hostage instead of the psychiatrist, which is even better."

"And if Brama doesn't capitulate when your deadline runs out?" I asked, dreading what he'd answer.

"Don't worry, we may never get that far. If Martinez dies, then once word gets out the police will probably assume we shot him, no matter what anyone says. I think in that case we're likely to kiss our asses goodbye well before any deadline of ours is up, at least in La Rumorosa, even *if* CNN is watching."

His flippancy made the prospect sound all the more chilling. It was also a hedge against giving me a straight answer.

"Jack, please, be serious."

"What do you *think* we're going to do if Martinez doesn't come through, Garnet?" he snapped, a look of contempt abruptly curling into his darkening face. "Like I've said all along, none of us is afraid to die. Some may go by their own hand. As for the others, let's just say if the police did come in shooting, they'd be doing most of us a favor."

"What do you mean?"

"Use your imagination, man! Those of us who can't do it ourselves, we intend to provoke the cops into killing us. Hey, it's the latest fad in L.A."

Even though from the beginning I'd feared that Jack was mounting a suicide mission, to hear him admit the method of it so callously left me feeling sick to tears. "Why?" I forced myself to ask, my voice croaking from a throat that had suddenly gone dry. Though I'd already figured out his reasons from our encounter in Buffalo, I had a desperate hope that my forcing him to explain such an atrocity would somehow make him face the insanity of it, and he'd recoil from the idea.

"To cause public outrage and unleash it at Brama, Garnet," he replied with an easy coolness that implied I should have known better than to ask. "A public outrage of such a magnitude that the company will never survive it."

I hurried along in silence after that, unable to think of anything to shake the hardness of his resolve. It didn't help my plummeting hopes any when Martinez's blood started to drip through the sheets, leaving a brilliant red slash across the black and white floor.

For the next quarter hour Jack was the doctor whom I'd known of old. Before we even rolled to a stop and deposited our cargo on a stretcher, he'd pried the man's airway open with a laryngoscope, suctioned off a head of bloody froth that was rising up from the back of the pharynx, and with ease slipped a tube into the trachea. "There's a carotid pulse, but barely," he calmly reported as he palpated the neck.

That meant a pressure not much over sixty.

Having already dug out infusion sets from the wall cabinets, I had one in Martinez's left arm and was starting another on the right. "Does that flying hospital of yours carry O-negative?" We could give him all the volume of saline we wanted, but he'd hemorrhaged too much to ever survive a flight to San Diego without blood.

"Six units," Jack answered, hooking up the oxygen.

We both knew it would be barely enough.

He grabbed yet another intravenous set and proceeded to slip a large-bore needle into the veins under Martinez's left clavicle. A minute later we also had saline rushing into him through a pair of IVs in his groin and I was checking his pressure with a cuff and stethoscope. Seventy over zip, I got, and a pulse hammering at 130. By jacking up his legs I won a few points more, when a particularly loud boom of thunder set the room rattling.

Jack was hunched over the right side of Martinez's chest. "Jesus, is it always this bad?" he asked without looking up. With a small lurch he shoved a chest tube between the psychiatrist's sixth and seventh ribs. Seconds later it was evacuating a liter of blood from the pleural cavity into a suction bottle, restoring a space for the intact segments of his lacerated lung to expand into as they filled with air. I helped things along by grabbing a ventilation bag, hooking it up to the endotracheal tube, and pumping hard. Now at least we'd oxygenate what blood the man had left. But it was time to move again. We'd done what we could for him here.

Jack snapped off his gloves and pulled out a cellular phone. "We've got a gunshot wound for you," he said into the receiver. "Will you to be able to get him out of here?"

I quickly rechecked the pressure. Repeated boluses of fluid had lifted it into the eighties.

". . . are Baines's pilots giving you any trouble . . ."

But this was the crucial moment. Sometimes our draining off blood from a bleeding lung only served to dislodge clots and increase the rate of hemorrhage, causing the pressure to drop.

"Rev it up. We'll be there in twenty minutes," Jack declared. Then he eyed me and added, "I'm also sending you a walking corpse who claims he's a doctor but is too stubborn to lie down. Make sure he gets clindamycin, then cefotaxime, and put it on my tab."

I took Martinez's pressure a third time. It was holding.

At the front entrance the light had dimmed further, casting everything in gray, and the storm was hitting us with all its fury. We had Martinez once more on a litter of sheets supported between four men, but this time a fifth person was holding his IV bags up in the air and I was bagging him, a portable bottle of oxygen tucked in among his covers.

I'd had no success trying to convince Jack to abandon his idea of remaining behind. On our way out of the building he seemed to take a disturbing amount of pleasure in having Vásquez and Baines as hostages, glaring down at them lying propped against a wall in the corridor near the empty guard station. Both were bound with masking tape at the wrists and ankles, while someone had also applied a dressing to Baines's torn ear, having wrapped the entire upper half of his head in gauze until he looked like a partly clad mummy. They'd stared back up at us as we passed, but where Vásquez was sullen and silent, Baines's lips quivered under our scrutiny and then he sniveled at our backs, begging, "Please, Dr. Garnet, don't leave me here with MacGregor. Have pity. Take me with you." He broke into a series of uneven sobs after that, wailing, "And what will happen to my ear?"

A look of distaste had crossed the face of Jack's sixth man, who was holding Vásquez's gun on the pair. "Shut up," he growled.

We'd taken no more than a few steps outside when we pulled up short. In the distance a line of red and blue flashing lights was snaking up the road toward us.

"About a mile away," Jack said softly.

"And moving slowly," I added. "Probably because of the slippery roads. Still, they'll be here in a few minutes."

The others eyed the scene below in grim silence.

"You head for the plane," Jack said bluntly. "I'll keep them busy when they arrive. Otherwise you'll never make it carrying Martinez."

"No, Jack, let me stay. They won't hurt *me*, and I can fool them into thinking you're still inside the clinic—"

"No more arguing about my staying, Garnet. We've already been through that. Besides, from a practical point of view, you're the one with the best chance of getting Martinez to talk, presuming he lives. How could I hang around a hospital trying to convince him to do the right thing without the cops nabbing me and sending me to jail?"

"Jack, you said yourself, these guys don't negotiate—"

"Head for the plane, damn it!" he ordered his men, ignoring me.

They nodded and, without a word, began moving off, making it necessary for me to step away with them if I was to keep bagging Martinez.

"Jack, this is crazy—"

"Shut up, Garnet, and listen!" he barked, walking alongside. The look in his eye was steel. "As soon as I go back inside I'm going to answer one of those goddamned phones. I'll announce that we're about to produce a witness who can testify that Baines and his company were committing murder here. I'll also issue a statement instructing all my people to stand down as soon as it's confirmed that the witness has survived and given the necessary testimony to have charges brought against Baines. Anything less, there's no deal, and the PDL reverts to its original strategy. Is that clear?"

Swallowing hard, I nodded.

We'd reached the path leading to the airstrip, and Jack continued to talk as we turned and started along its narrow, pebbled surface. "One more thing. I don't know what's happening back in your hometown, but from what I could find out, none of my people had anything to do with the murder of Saswald and Forbes. And as far as this blackmail stuff that Baines was going on about—I take it you heard it from him too?"

"Yeah," was all the response I could muster as I desperately racked my brains for a way to make him get out of there.

"I have no idea what that's about either, except that it must be part of some other game that's afoot. So you be careful, Garnet, once you get back, until you find out what it is."

"Look, Jack," I protested, "leave Baines and Vásquez, grab Martinez, and run for it. Take Baines's plane and make the pilots fly you somewhere safe."

"No!" he shot back, his face again clouding over with anger. "For the last time, stop bucking me on this!" And he drilled me with eyes so black and scathing that it was all I could do to keep from looking away. "You and I, Garnet, we're out of time," he added, his voice all at once soft and imploring. "The least you can do for me is quit pretending that I can somehow cut out from here."

"Jack, for God's sake, listen to reason—"

"Damn it, man! One reason I can't back off is because I have nothing left *but* this fight, and you know it! So *please* spare me any more crap about my getting away. Bullshit like that only makes what I have to do harder."

In the ensuing silence between us he held me with that searing gaze of his. It was such a window to his torment that I found it painful to endure, yet I sensed that he *wanted* me to peer through those unblinking fathomless pits, in order that I might bear witness to what resided there. Reluctantly I returned his stare, and in its depths thought I saw such an obsession with taking this business to its conclusion that I felt certain it had him in a death grip from which I could never free him.

Yielding to his wishes, however reluctantly, I surrendered

to his despair, and felt as though a cold fist grabbed me around the heart.

He, on the other hand, took a few deep breaths and appeared to compose himself until his expression unfurled, the way a man might after he'd finally been relieved of a heavy burden. But his steely regard remained. "And just so you're forewarned, in case you want to distance yourself from me when you talk to the police, if Martinez doesn't make it, whatever justice is dealt out in this place, I intend to make sure that Baines and his thug get a piece of it."

"Oh Christ, Jack, no—"

"Hey, Garnet, whether it's through Martinez or the PDL, I'm making certain that both Baines and Brama are finished. With any luck, their fate should give every other HMO in the land that was scrambling to be just like them serious second thoughts about changing the way they do business. You want to guarantee nobody dies in the process? Then make sure Martinez talks. Now move out, finish the job, and don't let me down."

With that he turned away and strode back toward the building, his coat blowing in the wind.

"Jack, wait!" I called after him, stumbling backward on the trail as I kept up with the others and continued to bag Martinez.

He gave me a wave without turning around.

Chapter 23

Hunched low and leaning into the wind, the six of us stumbled along with our passenger, the rain stinging our faces like needles. Overhead great varices of lightning snapped across the sky, coloring the jagged landscape a molten yellow that left us half blinded in its flicker. Then we'd plunge back into a brown-gray limbo the color of rock.

And all the time, we kept looking back, expecting to see the Mexican police racing after us.

The small jet had its engines running, and one of the pilots was leaning from the door, waiting to lend a hand lifting Martinez on board. Even stationary, the plane was rocked to and fro in the wind.

"Can we take off in this?" I asked incredulously as we transferred our patient to a stretcher that was welded to the floor and strapped him in.

"We'll soon find out," he replied with a grin, turning back to secure the door.

Oh, Christ, I thought, having dreaded every commuter flight I'd ever taken, and busied myself strapping Martinez in and hooking him to all the banks of ICU equipment that lined the walls of the converted passenger compartment. Only when I inadvertently glanced up and saw one of the other men start down the retractable stairs and the rest waiting to follow did I realize they weren't coming with us. "Wait a minute! Does Jack still expect you to stay?"

"It's what *we* want to do, Dr. Garnet," the next man on the steps quietly informed me, "as testimony to the ones we lost."

"And to make sure Jack isn't alone up here," the fellow behind him added, his eyes and cheeks gouged hollow with the same haunted look I'd seen in the face of Robert Delany's father.

The five of them ranged in age from a young man who couldn't have been more than thirty to a balding, lean gentleman who had to be at least sixty, and they all had features similarly laden with grief. The revelation startled me. Until then I'd only exchanged brief instructions with this nameless group as we'd gotten Martinez safely along the trail together, and had been too preoccupied to see the torment that drove them.

"Please, for God's sake, don't go back. It won't accomplish anything," I protested, recognizing in their empty stares the kind of cold calm that was often a prelude to suicide. None of them paid me the slightest heed.

"Gotta go!" the pilot snapped, wresting down the door and levering it sealed as soon as the last of them were out. Seconds later we were taxiing to the end of the runway, passing Baines's plane where it sat parked on the sideline. I could see two men watching us from its well-lit cockpit.

"What about *them*?" I called to the pilot, who'd finished buckling himself into the captain's chair and had taken over the controls from his partner.

"From what they told us, I think they're just air jockeys who don't want any part of Baines's trouble," he shouted, bringing the plane around to face into the wind and shoving the throttle forward. The light craft shot ahead. Above the roar of the engines he added, "They'd be hightailing it out of here now, if they had the guts." Seconds later he pulled back on the wheel and we lurched up into the air, then slammed into a sharp right turn with all the g-forces of a roller coaster ride.

"California, here we come!" I muttered as I steadied the wildly swinging IV bags and turned my attention to Martinez.

* * *

By the time we sighted San Diego Airport, I'd started him on the last of the plasma. Before we even touched down on the runway I was doing CPR.

"We've got a welcoming committee," the pilot declared as he finished taxiing off the landing strip and pointed us toward the flashing lights of the ambulance waiting at the edge of the tarmac. Nearby, a clutch of media vehicles was surrounded by a crowd of people with cameras and microphones. They in turn were cordoned off by an equally large mass of blue uniforms.

That they all were waiting for us, I figured, meant that Jack must have given his interview while we were in the air.

When we rolled to a stop, a pair of paramedics leaped aboard and the police kept everyone else at bay.

"How is he?" screamed one of the reporters as we hurriedly transferred Martinez to the waiting ambulance.

"Not good!" I yelled, continuing to pump his chest and ventilate his lungs.

Our mad dash through evening rush hour bounced us around nearly as much as the plane had. The only time I looked up, we were hurtling toward a busy intersection against the traffic and accelerating as we went, sirens screaming at full blast.

Within three minutes of our arrival in emergency, the ER doctors had his chest open, a resident was pumping his heart with her hand, and he was on the way to the OR. "He's got a pulse!" she called out hopefully as the elevator doors closed behind her.

"I think we better have a look at you as well," the Chief of Emergency hurriedly insisted, walking over to where I was slumped, wheezing and coughing, against the corridor wall. After a quick listen to my chest with his stethoscope, he ordered me to bed and arranged for a technician to X-ray my chest. "By the way," he said with a wink, "Jack MacGregor has a lot of friends in this department, and that means you do as well."

Five minutes later he was holding my films up to the viewing screen and raising his eyebrows at a white patch the size of a tangerine in my upper right lung. "Clindamycin and cefotaxime, I'd think?" he said, as if I were a conferring colleague and not a patient at all. It's the way doctors often behave when treating other physicians.

"That'll do just fine, thanks," I replied, grateful that he obviously knew what he was doing, and within minutes one of his nurses had the infusions up and running.

I used the next few minutes to make a collect call.

"Long distance from San Diego, California," intoned the operator. "Do you accept a person-to-person collect—"

"Yes! Yes! Yes!" Janet shrieked.

"I'm out, and I'm okay," I told her quickly. "But I'll have to phone you back. A pile of people are waiting—"

"They'll just have to wait," Janet declared, her voice cracking. "Oh, my God, I've been frightened out of my mind since this morning when the news about the PDL broke, and then about La Rumorosa. I even called Riley. He was so upset by what was happening that he was going to fly to Tijuana—"

"Janet, it's okay now, and I'm fine—"

"Plus I heard Jack's interview just now. I was so wrong about him."

Police officers had started to gather around my bed.

"Janet, I've got to go. I'll call you back."

She gave a long sigh. "Damn you, Earl Garnet. You better. And be prepared for a long conversation."

"That's a deal. I love you."

After I hung up I got to talk with more people wearing badges than I'd ever want to see again in a lifetime.

Martinez had recovered consciousness after surgery, barely, but after a few words from the hospital priest, he indicated that he was ready to make what his doctors and all the readings on his monitors predicted would be a deathbed confession. He'd also requested that I be present, and I readily consented to be brought to his room in a wheelchair.

Still intubated and unable to speak, he managed to scrawl an admission that his treatment had led to the deaths of six Americans. To my surprise, those deaths had been significant enough to him that he'd carried the people's names in his head, the way most physicians, myself included, might remember for life their patients who'd died on account of an error in judgment. For each case he was also able to list the anesthetist who'd been in attendance. The sixth and final pairing on the paper read DAVID PEARSON–HECTOR SASWALD.

When he finished, he waved me to approach his bedside. Reaching for my hand, he made an attempt to beam me that million-dollar smile, but the black tube sticking out between his lips rendered the attempt pathetic. Before I could recoil from his touch I realized he'd slipped me a tightly folded piece of paper. Then the priest moved back in and I was dismissed.

Out in the hallway, with the holy man's incantation still audible behind me, I looked at what Martinez had written:

I've not much time left, Dr. Kane. At least I had a moment of courage in me after all. Maybe you helped me find it. Don't be so stupidly righteous now as to completely ignore my work. It could save lives!

I crumpled the note into my fist, as furious at its content as I was at its effect on me.

Let the priest forgive you, I thought, unable to find any mercy in my own heart. As far as I was concerned, there was no redemption in a torturer trying to flush his soul clean at the last minute. And his so-called *work* would get no help from me, not that I'd be able to keep it from the plenty of others who'd be willing to take a look at it.

Monster that he was, however, there was no denying his having taken a bullet for Jack. Yet even this redemptive act failed to temper my judgment of him any. If anything, I resented the incongruity, and the way it left me uneasy over the depth of my inability to forgive the man.

I was still slumped in the wheelchair when a voice startled me from behind. "You look like you could use a friend."

I glanced up and saw the priest standing over me.

"I'm Father Rodriguez," he introduced himself with a smile, extending his hand. I absently shook it, and his firm grip vouched that the physical strength suggested by his robust, fit appearance was authentic. The lines about his eyes suggested he was in his forties. "Can I be of any help?" he asked.

I started to feel embarrassed. "No, I'm all right, thanks—"

"I cover ER here. They told me all about you downstairs. And you can't really be 'all right,' given what you've been through."

"Well, no—"

"I know Jack, by the way. We used to do a bang-up lecture together about grief counseling in Emergency at conferences out here. He's a good man, and a hell of a ski buddy. I pray to God he gets out of this safely."

This priest was starting to impress me.

"I take it you must have pretty mixed feelings about Martinez," he stated, gesturing back to where the psychiatrist lay dying.

"You've got that right!" I declared through clenched teeth.

"Let me give you a word of advice, Dr. Garnet. Get back to doing what you do best, and, as we ER priests say, leave the triage of souls to God."

With that he squeezed my shoulder and strode off down the hall.

The ER people admitted me to a private room so I could follow events on television and not disturb other patients.

Soon the networks were broadcasting images of the indicted anesthetists being led away from their homes in the middle of the night, some blinded by the glare of camera lights, others with raincoats over their heads, and most still wearing pajamas.

Funereal-sounding reporters gave the obvious commentary.

". . . an indictment of the entire company . . ."

". . . the downfall of Brama . . ."

". . . vindicates the PDL . . ."

Within hours Jack's soldiers began releasing their hostages and surrendering.

But there was no further word on Jack.

". . . Mexican police continue to keep reporters from both sides of the border away from the scene . . ."

". . . local storms make it impossible to fly over the clinic . . ."

". . . two pilots working for Brama who are grounded by the poor weather on a landing strip near the facility reported by radio seeing an orange glow in the sky in the direction of the building, but then radio contact with them was lost . . ."

"Son of a bitch!" I screamed, driven to distraction by the infuriating snippets that suggested the worst yet confirmed nothing. Unable to sleep, I started to pace, pushing my IV pole as I went and desperately wanting to talk with Janet. I'd already made innumerable attempts to reach her again, but as luck would have it, she'd been called into the OR on an emergency.

I must have been well into my second mile when a wind-swept reporter huddled in rain gear appeared on the TV screen. Though behind her nothing was visible except the black of night, I could tell by a familiar low rumbling in the background that finally someone was broadcasting live from La Rumorosa. One look at her shaken appearance and I knew the news was bad.

". . . we've just learned that there has been a tragic end to the remarkable PDL-Brama saga. I'm reporting from the site of the clinic where charismatic PDL leader Dr. Jack MacGregor had been holding hostage Mr. William Baines, the company's now disgraced president. Mexican authorities have only just confirmed that much earlier tonight, around six-thirty P.M., Pacific time, local police from the village of La Rumorosa, along with military advisors based at a nearby army post outside Mexicali, launched a bungled raid on the facility in an attempt to free Baines. Apparently, incendiary grenades were used, and some landed in a part of the building still under construction. Exposed wooden frames caught fire, and the flames quickly spread to a nearby storage area where the clinic's own security forces had stored their ammunition. According to officials, when bullets started exploding, the Mexican police and soldiers mistakenly thought they were being shot at and returned fire. Nine people are dead, including Baines—who, ironically, a few hours later would have been charged with conspiracy to commit murder—and the charismatic Dr. Jack MacGregor, who is now being credited with uncovering the scandal at the HMO giant. Mexican officials claim that the local officers were paying little attention to the developing story in the U.S., and reacted as they would with any terrorist threat. When their ultimatum to surrender was ignored . . ."

The screen was suddenly filled with a shaky, slow-tracking shot along a row of bodies that had been laid out side by side. The harsh white lighting made the images appear black and white. Though some of the dead had cloths covering their heads, one corpse had a long flowing coat spread out over him.

Showing the image of his remains, the television became his coffin. By it, I sat down and wept.

"This flight will be a lot smoother, Dr. Garnet," the pilot called over his shoulder as he leveled off, pointing the plane away from the sunset and toward the gathering darkness in the east.

"If you need anything, there are sandwiches and juices in the galley fridge," the copilot added, gesturing to what amounted to a hot plate and a cooler stashed below a countertop. "We should be in Buffalo by one in the morning, their time."

The two men had phoned me in the morning and offered to fly me home. They had a pickup in Boston, but could drop me off on the way there. I'd jumped at the chance, wanting nothing more than to get to Janet and Brendan.

"Nothing for me right now, thanks," I answered, and settled back in my seat, eyes closed, only to become lost in my thoughts.

When the news of Jack's death broke while I was in the hospital, it had been another half hour before Janet could extricate herself from the OR and reach me. By then I was numb and practically monosyllabic, but she'd patiently coaxed me to talk, and bit by bit I'd told her everything that happened at La Rumorosa. When I tried to describe how Jack had rescued me, I broke down again.

"I'm so sorry, Earl," she'd consoled me over and over, until I'd been able to pull myself together and continue with the story.

"Look, get up and go down to ER," she'd gently ordered when I finished. "Be with people who knew him. As their chief told you, you've got friends down there now as well."

She'd been right. Even though work in the department had to go on as usual, the staff sadly welcomed me to park my IV at the nursing station and have some coffee. And busy as they'd been, conversations would gravitate to me about Jack, until I came to realize the extent of my old friend's influence there.

A resident who'd rotated through Jack's former hospital in San Francisco gushed about his greatness as a teacher. The doctor on duty who'd known him through ER associations in California spoke of his leadership. Even Father Rodriguez had shown up, seeking solace as well as giving it over the loss of a friend.

"Here, Dr. Garnet," the copilot said now.

I gave a start, breaking off my reverie and opening my eyes to see that he'd left his seat to hand me a blanket and pillow.

"And if you need to phone anyone," he added, "we can patch the call through our radio."

I smiled. "My wife knows I'm coming, and frankly, I don't want to talk with anyone else. But hey, you guys run a great airline." I positioned the pillow, spread the blanket over me, and once more began picking through the day's events.

The previous afternoon, to my surprise, I'd received a call from Riley. "I got the number from Janet," he'd explained. "I wanted to say how sorry I am for your friend's death." His voice sounded quietly sincere.

"Thanks," had been all I replied. My sharing stories and talking about Jack in Emergency had comforted me, because it was a fitting wake among friends and colleagues. The detective, on the other hand, sympathetic as he sounded, was an outsider, and not someone to whom I'd show my grief. I also had to resist snapping at him that if he'd stood up to the FBI and persuaded them to raid the clinic a week ago, maybe Jack would still be alive.

The subsequent pause between us lengthened enough that I had time to wonder whether Riley was going to complain about my going to La Rumorosa behind his back, when he suddenly demanded, "Doc, did he give you any idea before he died if one of his people might have killed Saswald or Forbes? Fosse's got a bug up his ass that it must have been a rogue member of the PDL after all, and the brass have me under huge pressure to solve this thing, no matter what. I don't have many other ideas, and was hoping maybe you'd turned up a new lead."

Always the plodding detective, I'd thought, once more resigning myself to the fact that he was the man he was, shortcomings and all. I'd then proceeded to relate yet again an account of what had happened at La Rumorosa, including Baines's claim that the killer was blackmailing him, and Jack's denial that the killings in Buffalo had anything to do with the PDL. Although the detective had pestered me for details of Baines's and Jack's exact words, my not having slept all night made accuracy a hit and miss affair.

"And after all this, you still have no idea who it could be?" he'd finally asked, sounding weary.

I'd decided then to reveal the suspicion I had kept to myself long enough. "Look, I hate to say this, but maybe you should check out Allen Pearson's whereabouts on the nights of the killings—"

"He was on duty at the base, both times," Riley had brusquely interrupted. "His alibi's ironclad. I checked out that possibility right after our session with him last week."

"Oh," I replied, taken aback. After a second of feeling relieved for the young man, I realized that we were as much at a loss for a suspect as we'd been at the beginning of the investigation.

"Dr. Garnet," the pilot called out, snapping me back to the present again. "What's been really bugging me is that I can't figure why the hell Jack didn't just surrender once we had you and that psychiatrist off the ground. Why, for Christ's sake, did he hold out like that?"

There was pain in the man's voice. As there had been in Father Rodriguez's when he asked me the same question back in San Diego and his eyes had filled with a very secular torment.

I repeated what I'd told the priest. "Because he didn't know yet if Martinez would survive, or if he did, whether he'd make a statement strong enough to indict Baines for murder. One way or the other, Jack was determined that the president would get the justice he deserved." It was a simplistic explanation that glossed over the agony of a complex man who'd been driven to obsession. But I wanted to keep private that aspect of what Jack had done, lest someone use it to give him a diagnosis and attribute his acts to a pathology of character rather than courage, thereby lessening him.

A solemn quiet broke out between me and the two men as they seemed to mull over what I'd said. I began to suspect that their generous hospitality was a prelude to getting me to talk about Jack, and that in time they'd want to ask more questions, or tell the stories of their own friendship with him. That was fine with me.

I spent the next minutes gazing down at the snowy ridges of the coastal mountains that separated California from the rest of the country. The low sun cast the western slopes in gold and the eastern sides in a blue-green shadow. But I found myself looking south, toward where the sinewy landscape of La Rumorosa lay. I didn't believe in ghosts, but if ever there was a place for an angry spirit to roam, I wouldn't be surprised if the locals started to report sightings of a tall figure striding through the clinic ruins, a long coat flowing out behind him.

Rainy days and frosty nights had left Buffalo coated with ice and glittering like a rhinestone cowboy. But the bite in the air along with the added chill of freshwater dampness blowing off Lake Erie were familiar discomforts, and I felt welcomed by them as I walked through the deserted parking lot at the airport. It took a few yanks to get my car door open, the earlier storms having frozen even the locks.

Driving was equally tricky. I'd intended to pick up a further supply of antibiotics to continue medicating myself at home and was heading for the hospital, but it was slow going. I also managed to get myself worked up about a solitary pair of headlights that seemed to be following me, staying a steady few blocks behind. Since there were virtually no other vehicles on the road, whoever it was remained easy to keep track of. In the end, however, it proved to be a false alarm as the car turned and headed up a side street when I got to within a block of St. Paul's.

"Hey! It's the famous Dr. Garnet!" the receptionist exclaimed as soon as I walked into Emergency.

"Welcome back!" the triage nurse declared. "When I saw you on CNN, I couldn't believe my eyes."

"They could have killed you along with those other poor men!" another added.

By then half a dozen people had dropped what they'd been doing, gathering around to inquire if I was okay while patting me on the back and giving me hugs.

"And what's this about pneumonia?" the charge nurse asked.

"How'd you know about that?" I demanded, somewhat surprised.

"Janet phoned and warned us you'd be dropping by to pick up the clindamycin and cefotaxime you'd be needing." She gestured to a medium-sized box on the counter. "We got it ready for you, plus the IV equipment to inject it with."

"Why, thanks," I said, stepping over to pick it up. "I'll be back to work in about a week—"

"Not so fast," she interrupted, reaching for the phone and punching in just four numbers. "Unfortunately, Mr. Fosse also found out you'd be coming in, and left strict orders that you were to see him immediately."

"Now? It's nearly two A.M."

"I know, but orders are orders."

"Forget it! I'm too tired!"

"Mr. Fosse," she exclaimed into the receiver, ignoring me. "He's here. We're sending him up."

I grabbed the receiver from her and started to tell him, "No way—" but he'd hung up. When I dialed the extension back, the line was busy. "Christ," I complained to the nurse, "you could have given me a break and simply not called him." I had half a mind to ignore the summons anyway and head home.

She winced at the rebuke. "I'm sorry, Dr. Garnet," she said remorsefully, "but I have to do what he says, because he *is* the *big boss.*"

"As are all CEOs everywhere," I muttered, equally as mystified as I was resentful at his insistence on seeing me. "Ah, what the hell," I said, then turned and strode toward the elevators. Walking up a staircase, I'd discovered earlier back in San Diego, was enough to leave me wheezing and coughing.

Fosse's eyes were dark with fatigue, and he appeared strained when he greeted me at his office door. "Come in, and thank God you're safe!" he exclaimed, gripping me by the shoulders. "I apologize for hauling you up here, but I waited up after I found out from Janet that you were flying in tonight. She told me you'd be stopping by to pick up your medication. How are you feeling, by the way, besides tired? She said you had pneumonia." He was speaking rapidly, the way people often do when they're nervous, and the pitch of his voice was a notch higher than usual. Whatever he was worked up about, it was unusual for him to let his stress extend even to his vocal cords.

"Physically I'm a wreck, but of course my pneumonia *will* get better, in about a week," I replied. "And yes, I'm tired, in fact exhausted is more the word I'd use. As for how I am mentally, given what happened to Jack, I quite frankly am not in good shape at all."

He looked taken aback at my curt greeting. "Of course, Dr. Garnet. I'm sorry to have spoken so stupidly," he quickly countered.

I hadn't intended to be quite so blunt, but had meant every word and figured it was the best way to make sure he knew to keep whatever he had in mind mercifully short. His addressing me formally, however, warned that I'd stung him harder than I should have.

"How else would you be feeling but devastated," he went on. "Please excuse my lapse of sensitivity."

I said nothing, there being nothing to say.

"And what a stupid, unnecessary tragedy," he added, starting to sound awkward. Get to the point, I was about to tell him, when he continued, "But it's his death that made it urgent I speak with you tonight. I'm afraid it may have placed you in very grave danger."

"Me?" I exclaimed, taken aback. "But why?"

"Here, sit down. I've made tea." He gestured to one of his many chairs. A tray with cups and a steaming, sterling silver pot sat on a nearby end table.

Without thinking about it, I chose the love seat, sitting well forward on its edge.

"I've already expressed my fears to Detective Riley," he continued, "and suggested that you receive official protection again, resuming tomorrow. He agreed—"

"Protection from whom?" I demanded, refusing to endure any more of his beating around the bush.

"From the person who killed Saswald and Forbes."

"What?"

"Because if the killer is a rogue member of the PDL, then who knows how he'll react to his leader's death? My worry is he might blame you for leaving MacGregor there."

"But Jack said he'd investigated his own people and didn't think they had anything to do with those deaths—Wait a minute! What are you insinuating? That I abandoned Jack?" I felt as if he'd slugged me. I'd been swept by a wash of emotions since Jack's death—grief, despair, shame at my own terror—but mercifully, I'd been spared guilt, at least so far. I certainly was in no condition now to even hear the suggestion that I'd *run out* on him.

"Oh, my God, Earl, of course not!" Fosse immediately protested. "Don't for a minute think that I or anyone who's sane would even consider that you're in any way responsible for how things turned out down there. I'm referring to how some unhinged maniac in the PDL might react."

But his belated reassurance that I wasn't at fault did little good. My doubts, once unleashed, seemed limitless. Should I have refused to leave La Rumorosa? Rushed out and met the police myself? Insisted more forcefully that Jack go with us? "I told you, Jack assured me that he'd checked out his own ranks," I asserted almost absently. "He was convinced there was some other game afoot." This time, invoking his exact words, it hit me that I'd never hear his voice again. Already profoundly rattled, I felt tears welling up in my eyes and had to fight them back.

"Don't you think he could have been mistaken?" Fosse pressed, speaking quietly as he poured and then handed me a cup of tea.

I cradled the warm drink between my palms. "He seemed pretty sure, and it's not like he'd have needed to check out his whole organization coast to coast. From what Baines told me, the killer always called him from Buffalo, which makes it likely he was a local."

"Ah yes, the blackmail. Riley told me all about that. It's quite a story."

I took a long sip of the warm amber fluid and felt its heat travel all the way into my stomach. "It surprised the *hell* out of *me*!" I said, taking a second mouthful and still trying to get a grip on my emotions. Fosse wasn't usually so clumsy when it came to not saying the wrong thing, but I doubted he could have gotten me more shaken up if he'd tried. I was finding it hard to concentrate.

"But why couldn't that blackmailer be from the PDL?" he continued to insist. "MacGregor still might easily have been wrong about one of his people here, even though there weren't a lot of them."

"Because there were other things about this killer that Baines let slip. Things that point elsewhere than the PDL, such as the *way* the blackmailer timed his harassment of Baines and the demands for more money."

"What do you mean?" Fosse asked. He hadn't served himself anything or sat down, and was slowly pacing in front of his photo gallery of pictures. The image of his younger self in his military uniform peered down at him.

"How did Baines put it? 'Whenever the police were pressing particularly hard, he demanded more,' I think were his words. My head wasn't too clear at the time."

"And you think that's significant?"

My mind was almost too drained to keep track of my own

logic. "I don't know. I'm probably making a lot out of nothing, but it suggests that the blackmailer knew exactly what the police were doing and when they were doing it with regard to their putting pressure on Baines and Brama, and could time his extortion attempts accordingly. That's also consistent with his knowing that Riley was about to arrest Forbes and then getting to the psychiatrist just minutes before us. Jack, on the other hand, made it clear the PDL didn't have a good line on what the police were up to—that's why he grabbed me for questioning. No, I think it's a person outside the PDL and that Jack was right about there being something else going on that we don't know about."

He looked disappointed that I'd shot down his idea. "Yes, I suppose you're right," he said softly. "I take it you've informed Riley about what Baines said."

"Not about the *timing* of the blackmail attempts. I'll tell him that tomorrow."

"I see," Fosse said, remaining motionless.

I looked up at him, and was again taken by how hollow-eyed he looked as he stared at me. "Christ, you need sleep as much as I do," I exclaimed, getting to my feet as my legs threatened to go into spasm again after being immobile. "And I'm so racked I can't add two plus two right now, let alone put together all these bits and pieces—"

"Of course, Earl!" he exclaimed, immediately apologetic again, and he gave me his best grandfatherly smile. "I'm sorry I hauled you in here, but I just *had* to make sure you understood my concerns and took them seriously enough to be careful. Hell, Detective Riley certainly assured me that he thinks it's important. He offered to cancel some annual hunting trip that he takes his men on this time of year, in order to personally supervise the operation of keeping you safe. So, despite your skepticism about the killer being from the PDL, promise me you'll accept the protection."

Oh Jesus, I sighed, quickly resigned to the fact that I was

going to be *mother-henned* by the police as well as Fosse for the next few days. "Okay, I'll be careful," I promised.

But my acquiescing failed to lessen his worried expression. In fact he seemed to grow more uneasy, repeatedly swallowing and pursing his lips as if he was reluctant to say something. "Will you indulge an old man a few more minutes?" he finally asked.

"Sure," I replied as pleasantly as I could, thinking only of falling asleep in Janet's arms.

"Because I've just had a brain wave, except I'm hesitant about confiding it to you, it's such a strange idea."

I waited for him to elaborate, but he continued to look indecisive about saying anything more. "Try me," I told him, attempting to hide my impatience with his keeping me here.

He took a breath, as if bracing himself. "Earl, once your own protection is assured, I want you to consider that it might be better if this killer is never caught."

"What!"

"I know it sounds crazy," he hastily added, motioning me to stay calm with his outstretched palms, "but I don't share everybody's optimism that Brama's collapse will make the other HMOs pull in their horns and behave, at least not in the long run. Hell, I'm so sure of it that I've decided to postpone my retirement awhile in order to be here when they start messing with St. Paul's again."

"You're staying on? Why, that's great. But I don't see how you can even suggest leaving a dangerous maniac—"

"Consider how much more effective our using the Robert Delany fund and threatening bad publicity would be," he interrupted, "if the CEOs thought this killer was still on the loose and might pay them a visit if they got out of line."

"You can't be serious."

"I'm not suggesting you do anything wrong. Just that you let the idea of him being out there work to our advantage. It would be like having a knife to the throat of the HMO industry—so to speak. And it would work. Remember how

Brama started backing off our patients just before you went to Mexico? Baines fearing that he was about to get his throat slashed probably had a lot more to do with it than you and I screaming at him through the media."

"I know, but—"

"Something both my grandfather and Special Forces in Vietnam taught me was that the enemy of my enemy can be useful in a fight. Think about that before you talk to Riley."

"What do you mean?"

"I'm suggesting that you don't help the detective too much in tracking down this killer. If you do, you'll be working against our best long-term strategy to keep HMOs accountable for a very long time."

"Jesus, Reginald, that's the screwiest thinking I've ever heard you come up with. Your brain must be as fried as mine from lack of sleep." My real reaction was a lot less kind. He was starting to sound as extreme as Jack had been, I thought, but then put what he'd said down to a momentary lapse from all the stress he'd been under the last few weeks. "By morning we'll both be making a lot more sense, and we can each offer our ideas to the police," I added, suddenly feeling embarrassed for the old guy and wanting to afford him some room to back off his loony proposal yet keep his dignity.

He started to protest, then fell silent. "Yes, I suppose you're right," he said quietly after a few seconds, appearing resigned to let the matter drop, but once more he looked disappointed that I hadn't agreed with him. He then drew back his shoulders, pulled himself erect, and reassumed his usual take-charge bearing. "Of *course* it was a silly idea," he said briskly, "born out of fatigue, frustration, and my fear of losing our momentary advantage over managed care. Please forgive me."

"Don't worry about it," I said with a smile. "We all get a little weird when we're short on rest."

"Now you go home and stay in bed until you're better," he

ordered, placing his arm around my shoulder. "Oh, damn!" he suddenly exclaimed. "I forgot. It's budget week!"

I groaned at the sudden reminder that I still had a department to run. In particular, preparing the annual statement of accounts for ER was probably my most tedious task as chief.

"Tell you what," he continued. "Before you leave, if you'll take a minute and transfer the file to my computer, I'll take care of the report for you myself. Then you can convalesce without a thing to worry about," he added, smiling broadly again.

I would have welcomed the offer even if I'd been in the best of health. "Why, thank you, that's most thoughtful—"

"Not at all," he said jovially, seeing me to the door and shaking my hand with the warmth of a perfect host. "Now home with you, to the care of the lovely Janet!"

Fosse had meant well with his warnings, I guess, but the entire meeting left me feeling on edge and strained. I had to admit, however, that if Jack had been wrong, and there was a maniac in the local chapter of the PDL, what Fosse said about me being a possible target made a certain amount of sense. And once I was alone in the parking lot, despite my initial skepticism, the idea had me edgy and imagining things.

Clutching my box of supplies against my chest, I hurried along, jumping at shadows and listening as the wind moaned overhead between the building tops. Down at ground level it gusted in fits and starts, sending the litter scurrying about like marauding rodents.

It had taken a lot more than a minute to locate and transfer my budget files to Fosse's computer, but given the hours of work he'd save me, I didn't mind taking the trouble, despite being so sleepy. What I wished I hadn't done was see the stacks of mail and files on my desk that were waiting to be dealt with.

The dark recesses between the Dumpsters where Riley's men had ambushed me lay ahead. I figured it would take little more than a rat jumping out at my feet to send me screaming through the night again, and I gave the area a wide berth.

Crossing the place where Saswald had been butchered proved no less taxing. I kept looking over my left shoulder, back toward the Dumpsters, expecting to see his killer descending on me, but no one was there. I shivered and quickened my pace, heading for the better-lit doctors' parking area. But surveying the deserted expanse beyond left me remembering the night when Jack's men had come up on me as I'd gotten into my car, and I took an uneasy glance behind me to my right.

He was little more than a moving smudge in the darkness, following my progress from well inside the abandoned lot adjacent to the hospital. If it hadn't have been for the motion of his rain gear billowing in the wind I might never have noticed him. Instinctively I froze, gaping at him, making sure I hadn't conjured up yet another bogeyman, but that pause was enough to start him striding directly toward me like a shrouded angel on black wings, his hooded poncho floating out behind him.

"Jesus Christ!" I yelled, dropping the box, and pivoted, sprinting for my car. After ten steps I could barely breathe. "Help!" I screamed, but at that hour there was no one to hear. I glanced back and saw a long glint from the blade he was carrying as he passed through a pool of light under an overhead sodium lamp. He started to run. On his outfit, distinctive khaki and brown markings of military camouflage stood out in the orange illumination before he passed into the shadows again.

Oh, my God! I thought. Riley had been wrong, and it was Allen after all!

I continued my feeble attempt at speed, fumbling in my pocket for my keys as I ran. I got them out though the vehicle was still a dozen rows away. But I'd covered barely half that distance when my airway clamped itself into a paroxysm of coughing, making it impossible for me to breathe. Stumbling, I made it another ten feet before sinking to my hands and knees, fighting for air and continuing to choke. No sooner did I turn for another look at my attacker than he was on me and yanked my head back by the hair. My neck exposed, he drew his blade up in the air where it remained poised, ready for the killing stroke. My palms instinctively flew up to ward it off, and deep within the recesses of his hood I saw my killer's face.

"You!" I exclaimed, the shock equal to my terror.

Then from the darkness behind him came a booming gunshot, and his features disappeared into an explosion of tissue and blood. What was left of his head snapped forward, spilling its contents onto the pavement in front of me while the rest of his body slumped over on top of mine.

Riley came running up carrying a rifle just as I was getting out from under the still-twitching corpse. "Jesus, Doc, that was close. I was parked in the shadows on the street—too far away for using a pistol—but I had my own bear gun in the trunk of my car. Who is it?"

I was so shaken I couldn't speak, and unsteadily got to my feet. My hands, my clothes, my shoes—everything was already drenched in blood, and the asphalt around us continued to turn red.

Riley tiptoed through the mess and stooped down by the body. The hood of the army poncho was stuck to the back of the head, embedded in the hole where the bullet had gone in. But Riley was able to lift and peel back enough of the front opening to see what remained underneath. The face was gone, turned into a dripping pulp. But the temples and the jaw were there, and so were the thinning white hairline and bristly full beard of Reginald Fosse.

Chapter 24

Why had Fosse done it?

The question began hammering at me even as we stood by his body, listening to the approaching police sirens.

A mobster running a protection racket, Baines had said of the blackmailer. *Let me introduce you to my teacher,* Fosse had said when he'd shown me the faded picture of his grandfather. *Hit the leader hard . . . send a very clear message . . . and you have no more trouble,* the old gangster had once told him.

But as my mind tossed up fragments from the events of the last few weeks, reflexively attempting to provide the pieces that might fit together and give me an answer, I glanced at Riley, thinking to ask, "How did you know to be here?"

He gave a sardonic laugh. "Believe it or not, it was Fosse's insisting that you might be in danger."

"Fosse?"

"Yeah. After I talked with you, he was still on me with that idea of his about a rogue PDL member—making it seem a very credible threat, I might add—except he kept repeating that your providing protection for you should start first thing in the morning. Why not tonight? I thought to myself after he'd hung up. I can't say I was suspicious of him then, but I kept thinking about how this killer had beaten us to the punch with Forbes, and I headed for the airport, just in case."

Three squad cars flashing red and blue came screaming into the lot.

"But as I waited for you to arrive," Riley continued, "I kept

362

mulling over the timing of that murder, and ended up second-guessing why I hadn't made anything of the fact that he'd been the only person outside of my men whom we'd told that Forbes's arrest was imminent. Of course our initial suspicions of Baines being the killer had overridden our thinking that night, but in retrospect, not to have at least entertained some suspicions about Fosse and questioned *him* at that point seemed pretty indefensible. And as I thought some more, I realized that the main reason I'd been so lax toward Fosse was because he'd made it seem as if he was one of us—on my side of the badge, so to speak—by having been so damned helpful—exactly the way he'd seemed today."

The vehicles screeched to a halt around us and a half-dozen car doors flew open, each one disgorging a uniformed officer.

"So rather than be lulled again into missing something by all that *helpfulness* of his, I took a critical look at the man with my cop's instincts turned on full, and that's when I had my first sliver of suspicion about him." Holding his police ID up to his onrushing colleagues, he added, "What if he pushed for a morning start because he didn't want me near you tonight?"

Riley stepped away and quickly briefed the men on what had happened. One of them immediately got on the radio, calling for more cops, and from the comments I overheard, they seemed more concerned about the detective's use of an "unauthorized weapon" to bring down a "suspect" than the fact I'd been about to have my throat cut.

Riley turned back to me. "Once I'd entertained the possibility that he was a threat, what leaped out at me was the extent he'd influenced our thoughts and actions during the investigation. I specifically remembered the way, after Forbes had been killed, Fosse's useful insights on alcoholism and research had nudged you toward a pretty accurate hypothesis about what was going on at the clinic. Had he already known? I wondered. When I put that possibility together with your telling me today that the killer had been blackmailing Baines, I came up with another suspicion. Could Fosse have been priming us to put more pressure on Baines?"

An additional six police cars were entering the lot, lights flashing but without sirens. Behind them came a pair of mobile units from competing TV stations. The officers who'd already arrived had begun erecting a perimeter of yellow tape around where Fosse lay, the large hunting knife still at his side. Riley again broke off talking with me, this time long enough to hand his rifle to one of them. "Tag this for the shooting review, then lock it in the trunk of your car," he ordered curtly. "I'm going to get enough flak without the media getting a picture of me standing over the body with it. 'Cop Bags CEO with Bear Gun' isn't what I want to see in the morning news."

As he took care of business I started to cough, and realized I was shivering. Whether from cold, pneumonia, or a latent reaction to what had just happened, I couldn't tell.

"Jesus, Doc, you need a hot coffee," Riley said, taking me by the elbow when he returned. "I've got a second thermos in my car that I haven't even opened yet. Besides, it's going to be a circus around here."

The steaming, turbid liquid was so strong that it left a grit on my teeth. "Stakeout strength," Riley had called it, but between its warming my insides and the heater working on me from without, in minutes I'd stopped shaking.

As we sat there the detective continued to elaborate about the art of blackmail. "It always involves tormenting the mark with possible exposure to make him or her pay up. So I wondered if Fosse had been laying the groundwork for you to threaten the hell out of Baines with a bang-on accusation about the clinic. If you remember, Fosse also had already set up our meeting with Baines at the Brama building, and it *coincidentally* fell on the morning after Forbes was murdered. It even crossed my mind that maybe he'd been the one who threatened you and Janet over the phone a few days earlier,

creating the pretext he'd need to invite me along when the op-
portune time to pay Baines a visit arrived."

"Oh my God!" I exclaimed, making a connection that had
evaded me until then. "Baines's description of his blackmailer's
voice being 'husky, disguised,' described exactly what the
caller who'd menaced me sounded like. But that would mean
Fosse had it *all* planned ahead, including his killing Forbes."
*A greedy con man on the take . . . a sadist, a murderer, a
blackmailer, an exploiter . . .* Baines's words—everything
he'd mistakenly accused Jack of—now echoed in my head
about Fosse. Yet my instincts rebelled. There had to be more
to the man and what he'd done than that.

"His campaign to terrorize Baines wasn't the only thing, I
figured, which he thought out beforehand," Riley added. "Remember the timely way he pulled out that 'mother hen' book
of his, and used it the next day to establish a link between
Saswald and David Pearson at the clinic? Once again I think
he was setting the stage for me to bring more grief to Baines.
Not that he wasn't capable of also taking full advantage of
opportunities which came to him by chance. When you offered to infiltrate the clinic, he must have jumped to help you,
probably calculating that you'd expose the aversion therapy,
but not the murders, leaving Baines more vulnerable than
ever to blackmail, but Brama itself still in business, at least
enough to continue providing him with a cash flow. Mac-
Gregor launching his campaign a week early probably caught
Fosse off guard as much as it did the rest of us."

Whatever Riley felt or thought about my subterfuge in
going to Mexico, he once more gave no sign of it. Given that I
now owed the man my life, I dreaded his asking why I hadn't
confided in him, and welcomed his apparent willingness to
let the matter be.

"But how did Fosse find out that Saswald had killed David
Pearson in the first place?" I asked.

He flashed me a sly grin over the top of his mug. "Remember the fight his secretary said that he had in his office

with Saswald, the Wednesday prior to the anesthetist being killed?"

"Yeah. Fosse claimed that it had been over the short notice Saswald had given him before quitting."

"Well, if you combine that with what Allen Pearson told us, that's the same day the young Marine said he first approached Fosse, to request his help with getting more information about what had happened to his father. Now here I have to speculate, but Fosse, knowing that Saswald regularly worked at Brama's freestanding clinics, may in all innocence have summoned the anesthetist to ask him if he knew about the addiction center and to request *his* help in finding news about David Pearson. Saswald, freshly returned from the session which had resulted in the death of Pearson, probably freaked. Fosse's secretary said he'd arrived for the meeting already looking stressed—I guess he could have lived with killing patients from other hospitals in distant cities, but having lost one from his own turf, he was probably feeling extremely vulnerable. Who knows, Fosse may have picked up from his reactions that he was hiding something, and bullied the truth out of him. All we know for sure is that when the meeting finished, Saswald had resigned from St. Paul's. Whether at Fosse's insistence or Saswald's, it would make sense from the anesthetist's point of view to keep as far away from the hospital as possible, what with Allen Pearson starting to demand answers."

I downed the remaining swallow of my coffee and chewed on its dregs. "It all sounds pretty convincing."

"It was enough for me to think it could be him. By the time you landed, I'd also decided that Fosse's rogue-member-of-the-PDL story might not only be a crock, but could be his latest attempt to create a scapegoat, this one imaginary, for the murders of Saswald and Forbes. You know that from the beginning the bastard wrote that message, 'Pearson . . . too young,' intending not only to make Baines sweat, but also to ultimately make us suspect Allen Pearson."

I nodded, recalling how Fosse had cleverly led me to that conclusion as well, dropping the photo of David and Allen and casually recapitulating the phrase when he'd said, *Boy, they could be twins, except of course the son is too young.*

"But what really got my heart pounding was when I realized that his touting the PDL notion could also be his seeding an explanation for your murder. Needless to say, I couldn't prove any of it, but when I realized you were heading here, I made sure I found a vantage point from where I could see your parking spot, the entrance to Emergency, and the ground in between."

I shivered, despite the heat in the car, and sat in silence. As Riley refreshed our cups a light rain began to patter on the roof and streak the windshield. "It troubles me why a man like Fosse would resort to murder and blackmail," I finally said, taking a sip of the steaming, dark fluid. It tasted even sludgier than before, but the heat was marvelous. "And perhaps it's my vanity speaking, but I find it particularly galling how he could have brought himself to try and murder me!" I exclaimed loudly, getting over my shock enough to feel the beginning of outrage at his treachery.

Riley heaved one of his huge sighs. "Why people kill is always a grim business, Doc. But in this case, I think we've got a number of reasons. Because once Fosse found out about David Pearson's murder, he must have realized that he had Baines and Brama, along with its billions, at his mercy. Now, he hated what the company stood for anyway, and in my business, money is also always a pretty good motive. As for Saswald and Forbes, he probably loathed them for the part they'd played in Pearson's death . . ."

As he talked I found myself once more rebelling against the detective's version of what had driven Fosse to kill. Drawn in too broad strokes and partly predicated on greed, it struck me as crude and incomplete, the way a police composite often is. And I remained particularly convinced that there had to be a reason *other* than money behind his attempt to take *my* life. So while Riley continued to focus on the man's deceit, I tried to construct a fuller picture of Fosse, hoping for a more accurate explanation by including the times when he'd let the truth of his passion show through. Images floated to my mind: his screaming in outrage over Robert Delany's death; his sending a wastepaper basket sailing over the board members' heads in his fury at their indifference to the tragedy; his public agonizing over Brama attacking and threatening to undo everything he'd stood for throughout his career. I recalled the rage in Fosse's eyes as he'd related to me the "roots" that had forged his purpose and driven him all his life—his parents dying in misery; their deaths plunging him and his siblings into desperate straits; the death of his own wife and unborn child—all, in his mind, the result of arrogance and indifference. I remembered the photo of him with his grandfather, and I could only imagine what lessons in ruthlessness he might have learned from the grim-looking gangster who had helped him survive.

"It was his own fervor that did him in," I interrupted, "and the bitterness that fed it."

"What?" Riley said, his expression curling into puzzlement. "You're not going to give me any of that 'I'm depraved on account of I've been deprived' crap?"

I tried to explain to the increasingly skeptical detective what I thought had twisted Fosse so that he'd been unable to resist a chance to destroy Brama, but my attempt was brought to an abrupt end when a sharp knock on his side of the car interrupted me.

"Sir, the lab people are here and need to know what you want done," said a young policewoman to Riley after he'd rolled down the window.

"Excuse me, Doc," he said, getting out. "Stay here and keep warm. We'll need a statement in a few minutes, then you can head home. And a word of advice: The guy's dead. We don't need to establish a motive because there's not going to be a trial. Neither is he worth dwelling on. As far as I'm concerned, in the end he was after the money and was willing to kill you so as not to get caught."

He was gone before I had a chance to protest that it couldn't be that simple.

Janet met me at the door. Slipping into her arms and enfolding her in mine, I surrendered to the feel of her through her robe, the smell of her hair, the tiny murmurs of relief that came from her throat. For that exquisite moment as we stood clasping each other I was freed from all thoughts of Saswald, Baines, and Brama. Finally she leaned her head back, looked at me with teary eyes, and said, "For the next week you're mine, Brendan's, and Muffy's, while the rest of the world can go to hell."

Except the world intruded despite her orders.

Once she'd settled me in bed and injected me with my next dose of antibiotics, I told her about Fosse.

Her reaction—questioning disbelief, horror, and finally anger at the way he'd deceived us all—left her ashen and silent.

"I was so wrong about the man," she finally said in a faraway voice, "and I was so wrong the other way about poor Jack." For a woman who prided herself on her intuition about people, it was a shattering admission. "It's strange though—how they both could turn so ruthless, be so willing to play God for the same cause, yet be so different that one ended up a murderer, the other a martyr."

We lay in each other's arms the rest of the night, neither of us sleeping very well, and when I did nod off, it was visions of Fosse coming at me out of the darkness that troubled my dreams.

The phone calls from the press started at daybreak, before even Brendan and Muffy were awake.

"Dr. Garnet, do you have any comment about the shooting of your CEO?"

"No."

"Do you condone groups like the PDL?"

"Not exactly, but as Dr. Jack MacGregor once said to me, there's a lot of understandable anger out there."

"What are the lessons to be learned in the Brama fiasco?"

That question harped back to an answer I gave weeks ago. After mulling it over a moment, I decided that the reply still held. "We've got a trillion-dollar health care industry, and the peddlers who market it can make money by giving bad advice without being held accountable. Fix that, and we'll all be a lot further ahead."

Then Janet and I unplugged the phones.

Muffy awoke and happily insisted I walk her. Brendan squealed with delight at seeing me when I got him up, and I reveled in having breakfast with him.

Afterward we all gathered in the living room. Outside, the early morning light waxed, revealing a silver world of ice-covered trees and snow-dusted grass. Immediately Brendan wanted to go and play in it. We got him dressed, and I found his sled in the basement where we'd stored it at the end of last winter. Slipping all the way, I towed him around and around the yard while Muffy pranced and happily ran even bigger circles about our own. Janet watched from a window, hugging herself in a robe and looking somber at first. Then her face softened, and a glorious smile appeared when Brendan gleefully joined Muffy in panting out great white puffs of breath in the frost.

When we came back in, Janet had made fresh coffee and clearly wanted to talk.

"What I don't get is why Fosse chose now to revert to such extreme measures," she started, once we were settled at the kitchen table. "After all, he'd presumably wrestled with those forces from his past for a lifetime without giving in to them."

"Perhaps he felt he was running out of time. Brama was winning, and he was about to retire."

"But why, when he knew he had them dead to rights, didn't

he just go to the police? He could have put them out of business then and there."

As usual, Janet had cut to the bone of the matter.

"Perhaps he wanted to issue suitable punishment himself," I offered. "Certainly the state could never match what he had in mind for Saswald and Forbes."

She shot me a dissatisfied look. "Maybe, but that kind of blood lust alone seems a pretty crude motive to make a man like Fosse embark on such a violent, high-risk path." She paused, frowning as she thought in silence for a few seconds. "However, if what he really intended was to keep the company alive but in his grasp so he could continue to milk it for money . . ." She let her voice trail off into the obvious conclusion that his actions would then have made sense.

I said nothing, beginning to wonder if Riley had been right after all about greed being a major part of Fosse's motives. And I had to admit that the CEO's willingness to kill me rather than risk getting caught was consistent with a guy determined to stay free and spend the cash.

"But I don't see that man doing all he did just for money either," she concluded, casting us both back to square one.

Janet went to work, but the puzzle stayed with me despite Riley's advice to let it drop.

I even tried to put myself in Fosse's shoes at the moment he must have realized he had Brama by the throat.

And that's when I realized what he'd done.

A single phone call confirmed everything.

"I know why Fosse did it," I blurted to Riley when I tracked him down on his cellular.

"Doc, I told you that I don't particularly care, and you should forget about it—"

"Do you want to know where all the money is?"

That got his interest.

"You have to remember, when Fosse first made his decision to blackmail Baines, Jack MacGregor and the PDL weren't anywhere on the scene yet. Not only was he faced with Brama threatening everything he'd worked for, but all the other HMOs were following suit. Just getting rid of Brama wouldn't solve the problem. He'd have to bring them all to heel."

"So where does the money come in?" Riley demanded impatiently.

"That's the point. He figured he could challenge the HMO industry and take more money than he could ever raise, despite his prowess at soliciting endowments. But suddenly he had a ten-billion-dollar-a-year company at his mercy which he could shake down for protection money—indefinitely—to finance his crusade."

"How the hell can you be so sure about all this?"

"Because I just got off the phone with an accountant at St. Paul's."

"So?"

"There are exactly thirteen million dollars in the Robert Delany Fund."

"So why do you think he tried to kill you?" Janet asked softly as we sat side by side on the couch that night. Brendan was in bed, Muffy was asleep at our feet, and I'd just related what I discovered about Fosse and the money.

"It's a mind-set of crooks and soldiers," I answered, having spent most of the day dwelling on the question, "to sacrifice one of their own if he's a threat to the mission. The best I can say for him is that he certainly didn't take the decision lightly. After he found out what I knew at that trumped-up meeting of his, I'm sure he was trying to divert me away from the truth so he wouldn't have to kill me. But once I'd made it pretty clear that I didn't buy his rogue-member-of-the-PDL story and that I wouldn't back off helping Riley find the killer, he had no choice but to get rid of me. Otherwise it was likely that I'd put the pieces together, and he'd no longer be free to carry on with his cause. Of course, I had to die the same way as Saswald and Forbes, in order to substantiate the story that the killer was in the PDL after all—and that this PDL killer blamed me for Jack's death."

"He decided to kill you so he could run the Robert Delany Fund?" Janet cried, her eyes bulging with disbelief.

I smiled at her indignation. "No, it had to be for more than that. I figure it was to keep 'the knife at the throat' threat alive, to be invoked against any CEO who needed a reminder about how to behave. Hell, if he followed his grandfather's rules, he might have intended to dispatch one from time to time so the others would stay in line."

"That's horrific," Janet said with a shiver.

"But effective. And who knows if someone else won't get the same idea as Fosse, if the managed care industry starts resorting to the same old tricks."

That prospect kept us both silent for a while, and I took comfort from feeling Janet's head on my chest.

"Earl," she said quietly after a few minutes. "You sounded good on the radio giving all those interviews."

"Thanks."

A few more minutes went by.

"Have you ever thought of doing what David Pearson did?"

"A radio program?"

"Sure, except you could use it as a forum."

"To do what?"

"To start organizing physicians in this town, while the HMOs are still smarting, and making sure that the doctors stay in control this time, at least around here."

It was something worth thinking about.

LETHAL PRACTICE

by Peter Clement

St. Paul's Hospital. Buffalo, New York.
Scandal rocks the medical community when
someone murders the chief administrator,
plunging a long thin cardiac needle into his
heart with deadly precision.

———◆———

"Clement, a former ER physician, possesses
punchy prose, medical know-how, and a knack for
quirky details, and his hardened depiction of the
realities of hospital administration is disturbing."
—*Publishers Weekly*

Published by Fawcett Books.
Available at your local bookstore.